CUBAN CHARADE

BY

NATIONAL AWARD WINNING AUTHOR

WILLIAM VALENTINE

This novel is a work of fiction. Names, characters, places, and incidents are a product of the author's imagination or are used fictitiously. Any resemblance to actual events, locales, or persons living or dead is coincidental.

Copyright © 2017 William Valentine

Published by Shutterplank Publishing LLC
6800 Gulfport Boulevard, Suite 107
South Pasadena, Florida 33707

Cover Design by Kat Klingerman
Cover photos under RF123 license

Printed in the United States of America

ISBN: 978-0-9894754-8-8 (Print)
ISBN: 978-0-9894754-7-1 (E-Book)

Author's Note :
You might consider tracking the plot with
Google Earth to enhance your reading experience.

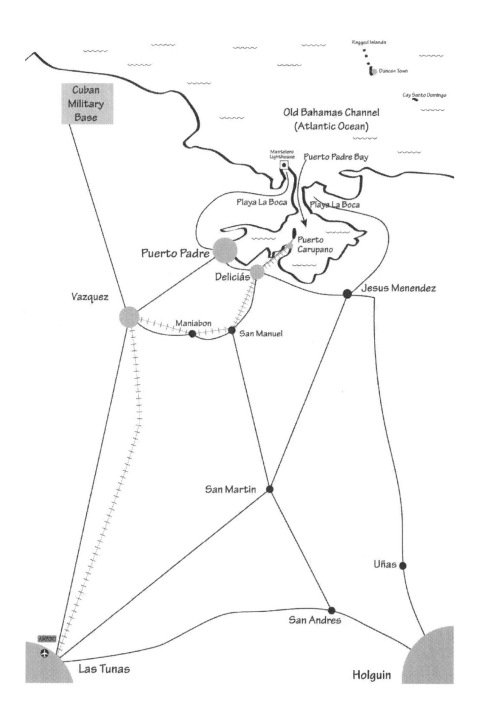

Other Novels — by William Valentine

SALT CREEK JUSTICE ......

Winner-2014-Next Generation Indie Book Awards-1st place-Regional Fiction

Winner-2014-Indie Excellence Book Awards-1st place-Crime Fiction

Indie Book of the Day-March 13th, 2014

COSTA RICAN REPRISE ......

Finalist-2016-Next Generation Indie Book Awards-Action/Adventure

Finalist-2016-Indie Excellence Book Awards-Crime Fiction

CAICOS CONSPIRACY......

Winner-2017-Beverly Hills Book Awards-1st place-Action/Adventure

Winner-2017-Indie Excellence Book Awards-1st place-Crime Fiction

Thank-You

To the talented editors who keep me on track: Andy Arnold, Bob Astley, James Byrne, Dean Karikas, Lee and Page Obenshain, Harvey and Pat Partridge, and G. Louise.

Also to my fishing and hunting buddies (you know who you are), who I have traveled with half-way around the world in small planes and boats. **And** to all my readers and reviewers.

DEDICATION

This novel is dedicated to the unbreakable spirit of the Cuban people.

And of course ...... **Slim!**

Foreword

CUBAN CHARADE takes place after nearly 50 years of Fidel Castro's iron fisted rule. The 1959 Cuban Revolution began with well-meaning socialism. The government's mandate provided housing, food, education, and health care to all the Cuban people. But, economic failures spiraled Castro into Marxist communism when the government was unable to provide its citizens with the basic necessities of life. The Soviet Union stepped in during the early "60's", and propped up Cuba with considerable technical and monetary support. When the Soviets collapsed in 1991 they were forced to completely withdraw.

Every Cuban has the opportunity to be highly educated, but even the most highly schooled professions in medicine, education, law, and commerce are paid only poverty level wages. The people smile and say, "We pretend to work and Castro pretends to pay us." Finally, the Cuban government began to allow capitalist activity to subsidize their failing economy. But they continue to deny their citizens free speech, and basic human rights. Any dissention is met with prison sentences and worse. Another telling fact: In 1959, when the dictator Batista was overthrown, there were five prisons in Cuba ... today there are more than five hundred. This novel gives the reader a glimpse of the harsh reality of Cuban communism. The truth hides behind the pre-1959 facade of racy and hip nightclubs in Old Havana and the Hemingway nostalgia. Once past this masquerade you will find, decaying infrastructure, widespread poverty, and an oppressed and exploited populace. The more than one million Cubans that have defected to the United States and other countries is proof enough that the Cuban people yearn for the basic freedoms and opportunities that have eluded them for more than a century. Their accomplishments and successes in America are legendary.

Read on, as Seth Stone and his crew of "Geezers" take on a sovereign government who has unjustly imprisoned one of their friends. Learn about crafty defectors, high-dollar *Lancheros*, and shady U.S. syndicates who broker Cuban baseball stars to Major League Baseball. See Cuba's cities and countryside through the eyes of her own people and those of everyday Americans. Sit back in your chair and join Seth and his friends in what might be their most dangerous and exciting adventure yet.

CHAPTER ONE

Early fall, 2009 - Pinar del Rio Province, Cuba

THE WALLS of Cinco de Media, Cuba's most notorious prison, were closing in on him and he felt like he was slowly losing his mind. Dave "The Wave" Perozzi was chained to a rock wall in a tiny, windowless dungeon. A narrow, rusting iron door with a small portal separated him from the dark prison corridor. His only sense of time was the intervals between the beatings. Soon he would hear the sound of his captors' footsteps on the corridor's cobblestone floor as they came to beat him again with their fists and a length of heavy rubber hose. They concentrated on his kidneys and upper torso, so as not to bruise his face for his upcoming trial in Havana. Dave was getting close to his breaking point … the guards kept telling him the beatings would stop if he would just sign a confession. But Dave was innocent and surrendering to this tyranny grated against his American values of fair play. Water continually dripped on his head from somewhere above, and he tried not to think about the cockroaches and rats that shared his putrid cell. They scattered and disappeared when the guards turned on the naked light bulb dangling above his head.

Dave still wondered why the Havana Industriales baseball star, Hugo Lugo-Ramirez, had turned him in. Dave had been introduced to him during a neighborhood pig roast at his girlfriend Clarita's house outside of Havana. He shook his hand and exchanged some pleasantries. Dave told Hugo that he had surfed with the Atlanta Brave's José Alvarez back when he was in high school. José's family had come to Tampa during the Mariel boat lift in the "60's". Then he off-handedly told Hugo he could start for any major league team in the United States. Dave just meant it as a compliment. An hour later, the DGI (Dirreción General de Intelligencia), the Cuban secret service, dragged him out of the backyard pig roast in handcuffs — in front of his protesting Cuban girlfriend and parents. Trying to convince a Cuban citizen to defect to the United States *(attempted human trafficking, punishable by up to 15 years in prison)* was the charge. Dave could not fathom how Hugo Lugo had jumped to that conclusion during their brief encounter. He spent two days in a holding cell in Havana's Morro Castle Prison before being transferred to Pinar Del Rio's Cinco de Media Prison in an open truck. Dave wondered now what might become of him — his trial was his only hope. But in the totalitarian state that Cuba had become, he feared his trial might only be a formality. He had a court-appointed lawyer, no United States Embassy, and Clarita's family had no influence. Strains of Warren Zevon's sardonic hit song, *Lawyers, Guns, and Money,* drifted through his mind, but it was no joke to Dave ... the shit **had** hit the fan.

Dave tried to think of happier times to help ease the fear of his next beating. He thought back to his Florida life, growing up in St. Petersburg a couple blocks from Upham Beach and hanging out with the laid back surfing crowd. He skipped school regularly to drive to Cocoa Beach whenever the surf was up ... to ride the big ones. It all came to Dave so easily. He started winning surfing championships at an early age in Florida, then California, and finally Hawaii. Soon he was traveling the world on the pro circuit. Dave was given "The Wave" nickname while riding the big ones in Waimea Bay on the north shore of Oahu. He was in all the surfing magazines and had endorsements with Costa, Rip Curl, Billabong, Hurley and all the top board makers. His fame supplied him with a never-ending bevy of pretty 18-year-old bikini clad girls, *Maui Wowie,* and endless beach parties. He hung out with Hobie Alter, Jimmy Buffett, Charlie Daniels, John Prine, and Gerry Lopez. While surfing the "Big Ones" in Marrawah, Tasmania for the big bucks, Dave was wrenched off his longboard and felt something pop in his lower back. He was thirty-two years old, and two unsuccessful surgeries later Dave the Wave's competitive surfing career was over.

Dave stuck with what he knew and opened the Treasure Island Surf Shop. With the help of his sister, Sonja, and some of his old burnt-out local surfing buddies, he built a solid business that complimented his laid-back lifestyle. For years, you could find Dave at one of the many beach bars up and down the Suncoast, holding court and schmoozing the young beach bunnies. Dave looked like the prototype for surfer Jeff Spicoli (Sean Penn) in the classic 1982 movie *Fast Times at Ridgemont High,* and his life was still one continuous beach party. As his business grew and Dave got older, he started fishing and sailboat racing in the Gulf of Mexico. He loved the competition and always had the latest and fastest boats. He still surfed, but only recreationally. However, he still had an affinity for younger women, and they still liked his blond hair, blue-eyed, tan surfer look.

Dave shook the dripping water off his face and thought back to the party he threw each year for his customers on remote Shell Island at the southern end of Boca Ciega Bay. It was a three-day affair with small boats pulled up on the lee side of the beach, and larger boats anchored out. It featured continuous local bands in a huge tent along with barbecue, roasted pigs, beer, ice, port-a-lets, and overnight camping … all powered by an army of portable gasoline-powered generators. Boats were the only way to get there and the crowds ebbed and flowed day and night. Many people, both young and old had one or more first-time experiences happen on Shell Island during Dave the Wave's annual soiree. The logistics were enormous, but Dave knew how to throw a party. He smiled to himself as he thought about those crazy, happy times.

Dave's thoughts turned back to his first visit to Cuba five years ago. He and a few of his older surfing buddies visited the thousand mile long island, shortly after the Russians pulled out, to check out the surfing and the Cuban women. The U.S./Cuban embargo was in place … you could travel there, but you couldn't spend any money. In other words, you had to be fully hosted. They flew through Nassau in the Bahamas knowing that the Cuban Government would not stamp their passports. Dave figured U.S. Customs would think they were vacationing in Nassau. He could still surf recreationally, but Dave was only a shadow of his former iconic self. A year or two later, George Bush made it illegal for Americans, without special Cuban family member visas, to go at all. By that time, Dave had fallen in love with Clarita, a beautiful young girl from Havana. They met at Cuba's best surfing beach, Cabo de San Antonio, in Pinar Del Rio Province. Dave taught Clarita to surf, then followed her home. She lived with her parents in Jaimanitas Beach, near Marina Hemingway, eight miles from the center of Havana. The family owned a small, neatly kept bungalow in a modest subdivision. Clarita's mother and father were industrious and had converted their free-standing two car garage into three rentable rooms — as allowed by the government at that time. Since the bankrupt Soviet Union abandoned Cuba in the 1990s, the Cuban communists allowed some citizens to run small businesses such as rental rooms(three) and twelve seat restaurants in their homes to help the economy. The revolution was strapped for cash, and could not supply the rank and file with enough food and essential services. The Russians had propped them up in a big way. If the flow of U.S cash, sent each month by their ex-pat relatives in America had stopped — the revolution would have failed.

The communist government owned and controled the entire Cuban economy. Every penny spent went directly to the government. They owned the food stores, appliance stores, gas stations, utilities, the clothing stores, tourist hotels, and all the major restaurants, bars, and nightclubs. Public housing was assigned to families that didn't own a home. Clarita told Dave that each citizen received a free education, subsidized housing, basic medical care, and rationed food. Each Cuban was supplied with a monthly ration of five eggs, four pounds of sugar, five pounds of rice, a half a pound beans, half a bottle of cooking oil, four ounces of coffee, one pound of spaghetti, one kilogram (2.2 lbs.) of powdered milk, a liter of yogurt (35.2 ounces), and cooking gas. Seven to thirteen-year-olds were also given one kilogram of salt every three months, along with one pound of chicken, five additional eggs, and one piece of bread daily. Clarita added that the rations were usually gone seven to ten days into the month. The population was then forced to buy the rest of their foodstuffs and necessities from the government stores and the black market with their meager salaries.

Dave was amazed that the Cuban teachers, professors, and engineers earned only 24 dollars a month for their highly educated work. He was even more shocked that the Cuban doctors made 50 dollars a month, while the Havana police and Cuban soldiers were paid 90 dollars a month and were given superior housing. Most teachers, doctors, and lawyers had second jobs in the tourist industry as bartenders and waiters where they had access to tips because of their knowledge of English. They could earn as much in tips in a couple of nights as they made in a month. English speaking cab drivers who owned their own vintage cabs were the big earners. The average cab charged $25 per hour. Their major expense was paying $650 to the government every month for their taxi medallion. The Havana police shook them down at an average of $20 per day, and they also paid for all their cab's upkeep and gasoline at $4.00 per gallon. The drivers had to gross $40 a day to break even. The airport was 45 minutes outside of Havana, and if they hustled they could average a $100 day during a 12 -14 hour work day. If an average cabbie could keep his cab running 300 days a year he would gross $18,000 - $24,000 and net half of that. A cherry '57 Chevy was worth $50,000 U.S. Most vintage cabs were passed down through their families and had a million miles on them.

Dave recalled a scare he had on his way back from a Cuban visit about a year ago. He should have considered it a premonition. As he cleared the new U.S. Customs office in Nassau, two agents pulled him out of line and escorted him into a small room and closed the door.

They sat him down and the larger uniformed officer said, "Mr. Perozzi, where have you been for the last six days?"

"I've been lying on Cable Beach drinking as many cold ones as possible."

"You've been lying alright, but not on Cable Beach. Let's try again, Mr. Perozzi."

"I want my attorney here before I answer another question."

"Let's cut to the chase — Dave," said the smaller one. "We know you've been traveling through Nassau to Havana. We also know you've been spending quite a bit of money over there. If we catch you coming back again you're going to be arrested and you'll probably do some prison time. Now – get out of here and smarten up."

Dave was shaken by this turn of events. Each time he traveled to see Clarita he brought her several hundred dollars. She spent the money buying air conditioners, refrigerators, TV's, an electric range, a washer and dryer, and two generators to get them through the frequent power outages. Clarita's parents' *casa particular*s were always rented because of the amenities supplied by Dave.

Dave's contacts went deep in Florida, and he had some friends check out the situation. He couldn't figure why Customs had singled him out because he was small potatoes. Why would they follow him to Cuba – or maybe they had a spy network in Havana? The answer proved simpler than that. One of his prominent friends learned that U.S. Customs was buying the Nassau to Cuba flight manifests from the Bahamian Government. Further research revealed that the Mexican Government had refused to sell their Cancun to Havana flight manifests to U.S. Customs. Mexico had always kept strong diplomatic ties with Cuba and had warmly welcomed Fidel Castro during his exile after his first failed coup.

Dave the Wave cooled it for a few months and then carefully slipped into Havana from Cancun. He arrived at U.S. Customs at the Tampa airport ten days later wearing a *Señor* Froggy t-shirt and nobody was the wiser. Dave continued to travel through Cancun to Havana every two or three months.

Because Dave knew everyone in Clarita's neighborhood and spread his largesse around, it became customary for him to buy a pig for a neighborhood party each time he visited. But this last party had changed his whole life. He thought of Clarita and her family ... they had filled a void in his life. All his young girlfriends and surfing and sailing buddies in the states paraded by in his brain ... his dear sister Sonja, his only blood relative, flashed by in his mind. He thought of the fires that burnt down his business twice and the friends that chipped in to help him rebuild. He wished he was anywhere but here. Back on Treasure Island, when things would start to close in on him, he could pull a couple of "Big Bens" out of the cash register and disappear into the beach bar scene for a couple of days. Sonja was always there to watch the shop.

Suddenly, he heard the large iron door clang open at the end of the corridor and the dreaded footsteps got louder and louder on the cobblestones in the passageway. His fond remembrances slipped away and he started to tremble. The next chapter in Dave's nightmare was about to start.

The cell door clanged open and the guards entered his cell. They switched on the overhead light bulb and Dave was temporarily blinded. As he recovered, a large man walked through the door dressed in a casual khaki military uniform. He carried a leather horse crop under his arm.

The man looked Dave up and down and said in broken English, "I am General Ramon Machado … I am the commandant of all the prisons in Cuba. My men here tell me you have been foolish enough to refuse to sign a confession of the charges brought against you by Hugo Lugo. *Señor* Perozzi, must I remind you that there is no American Embassy in Cuba, and your presence here breaks your own American laws. Your people in the states may not miss you for another week or two and there is nothing that documents your arrival here from Cancun. We do not stamp American passports. Accept your guilt … there are witnesses … you tried to entice one of our world class athletes to defect for your own monetary gain. Give me the names of the syndicate investors in Miami."

"But, I am innocent, Sir! I'm being framed for a crime I didn't commit. I know nothing about any syndicate."

"*Silencio*, you Yankee pig! Do not interrupt me. We can beat you until you die and then drop you in the Gulf Stream for the sharks … But, I think I have a better idea. My men will question your girlfriend — and also her mother and father — in much the same way you have been questioned here. All three of them will agree to testify against you … and the guards will, of course, have their way with Clarita and her mother. I understand both of them are quite beautiful."

Dave the Wave hung his head and signed the confession.

***

Hugo Lugo waited at the basketball court in the park near Revolution Square. He knew his phone was bugged and he was being watched. The call this morning was from his friend, Pedro. "Want to play some basketball" was a phrase that meant he had confidential information. They always met in the open air park near Revolution Square. Twenty-year-old Hugo would play third base tonight at *Latinamericano* Stadium in Havana against the Cienfuegos Elefantes. He was sure that after the trial of the Americano he had turned in at a party in Jaimanitas, near Marina Hemingway, he would be reinstated to the national traveling team, and the government would cease surveillance. He felt bad about fingering an innocent man, but it was the only way he could regain the trust of the Cuban Sports Authority. Hugo felt his mission in life was to become one of the greatest players in the history of baseball. He could not fulfill his mission in Cuba, and he knew he was destined to go to America. He told himself the big money was secondary, but deep inside he knew that was not true. This gringo was the second innocent man in a year that he had turned in. Ever since his third attempt to escape while in Dominican Republic two years ago at the Pan American games, he had tried to convince the Sports Authority that he had seen the light and no longer wanted to leave Cuba. Following the Dominican incident, Hugo had been dismissed from the National team and the Havana Industriales. After turning in the visiting Cuban-American electrician from Miami a year ago, he was reinstated to the Havana team. But he continued under 24/7 surveillance. He recognized one of his tenders sitting across the street at a bus stop watching him. When and if the surveillance was discontinued, he would try to defect again. He knew that tens of millions of dollars and fame awaited him in the United States - if he could just get there.

Pedro Sanchez finally walked across the outdoor court and bounced a basketball at him.

"Hola, Hugo. Sorry, I'm late."

"It's okay amigo, I've got almost two hours before I have to be at the ballpark. Let's play *'Caballo'* while we talk," said Hugo as he swished his first shot from the top of the key.

Pedro dribbled to the same spot and put his shot in right on top of Hugo's.

"I heard from Alejandro in Hialeah this morning on the secret phone he gave me through Manolo. He wondered if you're getting any closer."

"Tell him I'll know after the gringo's trial. Don't look ... but right now my 'tail' is sitting on that bus stop bench over there."

"Alejandro says the syndicate has been shopping you around to a few the of the major league teams. He thinks you'll go for 25 million dollars long-term, no problem," as he canned a jumper from the right corner.

"*Jesus Cristo*, I can't comprehend that figure. But, it's just as important that you get your shot with Duke, Indiana, or Kentucky. First, a year of college basketball and then the NBA," said Hugo as he hit the same jumper from the right corner.

"He said the syndicate is going to send a large, fast sportfishing boat to take the two of us out in Pinar Del Rio. He said for us to bring our Cuban I.D. cards. We'll need them at the U.S. border. The phone Alejandro gave me has a GPS — I type in an address or latitude/longitude and it shows me the way on a map. He will phone me the pickup point."

Hugo shot a foul shot with his back to the hoop and made it. Pedro missed and passed the ball back to Hugo.

"**C** for you Hugo, trick shot *pendejo*."

Hugo laughed and lofted a set shot from 25 feet ... and missed.

"Listen, Pedro, I would like to take my girlfriend, Monserrat, when we go through Mexico to the U.S."

"Alejandro prefers you don't, but he didn't say no," said the six-foot nine-inch tall Pedro, as he went airborne and dunked the ball in the basket.

"I'm just glad we don't have to go with the Mexican *Lancheros,* on a 40-foot Cigarette boat with 25 people."

Six-foot tall Hugo could dunk a basketball, but not from the spot where Pedro took off for the basket. The score was soon tied. Pedro hit a long hook shot from the right side of the key, and Hugo bounced his try off the rim.

"Looks like you win this one Pedro, I better start out for the ballfield. I'll let you know if they take the tail off of me. We've got a short road trip to Santiago and Holguin ending after the weekend. Then I have the gringo's trial here in Havana next week."

Pedro said goodbye and strode toward the bus stop, where the tail had disappeared. Hugo watched his friend go and thought about growing up with Pedro. He had been too tall and awkward for soccer and baseball but excelled in basketball and beach volleyball. He made both Olympic teams in Cuba. Pedro had never tried to defect so he made a perfect go-between for the syndicates that were continually contacting Hugo. He convinced Pedro he could make it to the NBA if he played U.S. college ball first. If they made it to the United States — Hugo would ensure that Pedro would prosper.

***

The early morning sun was blinding in the back of the open prison truck as it rumbled towards Havana. Dave the Wave was handcuffed to a bench seat with three other prisoners. He had seen the spectacular natural scenery before on his trips to Cabo de San Antonio beach on the western-most point of Pinar Del Río Province. The countryside reminded him a lot of Costa Rica's western Pacific coast with the odd shaped lava outcroppings on land and in the water. The lush tropical plants, grasses, and trees were interrupted only by large fields of shade tobacco growing under gauze-like cloth canopies. This wrapper tobacco was the backbone of the still lucrative Cuban cigar industry. Large mountains and lush foothills were visible towards the province's interior. The road to Havana was lined with people walking in both directions, and passing trucks hauled all manner of produce and cut sugar cane. Vintage taxis and camel-buses made up the remainder of the traffic. Occasionally, when passing what appeared to be vegetable produce farmland, Dave noticed the absence of tractors tilling the fields. Oxen seemed to be the power of choice, or maybe necessity, to plow the fields. Perhaps the revolution wanted to save precious fuel and fertilize the crops at the same time. The other prisoners ignored him and spoke among themselves so rapidly that Dave could not understand their conversation. He was glad to be out of the Cinco de Media dungeon and away from the painful beatings he had endured. The sun, clean air, and the beautiful scenery were having a therapeutic effect on him.

Later that morning, the truck wound through the outskirts of Havana, past Chinatown, then through the narrow streets of Old Colonial Havana. They passed the Capitol, went by the Floridita Bar, and drove around the statue of José Marti onto the Malecon. There the truck turned right and passed through the tunnel under Havana Harbor and finally pulled into Morro Castle Prison. The last time he went through that tunnel he was a *tourista* on his way to explore the historic fortress. Dave was quickly processed and hustled into a holding cell that held about 40 men.

Dave took up a defensive position in a back corner of the holding cell. He did not want anyone to be able to approach his back. Almost immediately, two middle-aged prisoners of medium build moved over beside him.

"Americano, *señor*?" asked the tall, thinner one.

"Si", answered Dave.

"Where were you shipped in from?"

"Cinco de Media."

"*Carumba*, that is the worst of the worst. You were lucky to get out of there alive. Let me introduce myself; I am Professor Gustave Bolita, late of Havana University mathematics department. *Mi amigo* here is Felipe Monterey, Professor of English at the University of Santiago. We are what Castro calls dissidents. We speak out for Cuban citizens' basic human rights."

"I'm Dave Perozzi, *señors*. Are you here to stand trial like me?"

"We are — several of our colleagues have already been sent to political work camps for 'attitude adjustment'. We have been writing articles and speaking all over Cuba, trying to wake our people up to their totalitarian plight."

"So, there is no free speech or debate?"

"Correct," said Felipe jumping in. "If you express any disagreement, in public or private, with Fidel's policies … you are jailed or worse."

"I have heard there are serious food and medicine shortages, and I understand it is illegal for citizens to leave the country."

"That is all true. Even with urban gardening on every available piece of dirt in the cities, and private truck farming in the countryside by the *campesinos*, we still have massive shortages. The large farm communes cannot grow enough food to feed the country. The inner-tube fishermen, we call *pneumaticos*, have fished out our local waters. You might have noticed there are very few fat people in Cuba. Our medical care system is relegated to the old, crowded, downtown hospitals. The government schedules foreign patients who can pay into the newer modern facilities. Public housing is crumbling. The rapid increase of dissidents and the growth of a huge black market is why there are so many prisons now. Most of the revolutionary population of Cubans are dead or 70 years old, and the remaining population is left to bear the reality of a system that delivers only hardship. Things have gone downhill quickly since the Russians left in 1991. They gave us *mucho* financial aid and built millions of dollars of infrastructure on the island. The Russians wanted a successful model of communism in this hemisphere"

"I'll give you an example," said Gustave. "In 1959 when the Revolution ousted Batista, there were 6.5 million Cubans and five prisons. Today there are 11 million Cubans and 500 prisons. When Fidel became a total dictator, he installed a collective system of revolutionary vigilance. Once established the government knows who lives on every block, what they do, where they go, and who they meet. Each block has a captain who signs people in and out if they travel overnight or longer and keeps files on all the block residents. The police presence on each block interacts with the captain and citizens. They all are obliged to snitch on each other."

"Fucking 'rad', *señors*," said Dave. "Looks like you traded a bad dictator for one that's turned out even worse."

" Amen," said Felipe — "Why are you here, Dave?"

"I'm accused of trying to recruit one of your star baseball players into defecting to the United States. I'm innocent — I just came down here to see a girlfriend and ride a few waves."

"A lot of our ball players have defected for big money over the years. If the government was smart they'd let them go and take a cut. Lord knows the country needs the money," said Gustave. "Unfortunately, trials here are just a formality … your fate has already been decided, as has ours."

"You know," said Felipe. "Communism in Cuba was defeated almost from the beginning. Our classless society had hardly started when the Cuban refugees in Miami started sending money to the relatives they left behind. Those relatives among us became the new wealthy class."

"We'll move our sleeping pads over here with you, Dave, and no one will bother you. Most of us understand that Americans are not our enemies."

CHAPTER TWO

SETH STONE awoke and wondered where the hell he was. The throbbing pain in his right knee gave him his first clue. He pushed the button clipped to his pillow to call the nurse, signaling he was ready for a pain pill. Seth had finally given in to living with the ever-present pain in his arthritic right knee and had it surgically replaced. An old football injury from his days playing defensive back at the University of Virginia had been aggravated over the years and lately reinjured by two unfortunate encounters with his old rival, the late Peter Petcock of Gulfport, Florida. He looked around the private room and his opiate addled brain slowly remembered that he had been transferred from the hospital to the Oceanview Rehabilitation Center. He and his girlfriend, Lori Gudentite, rode over in a medical transport vehicle. She helped check him in and then left for the evening. They promised a 24/7 concierge experience, a seven-day program of intense exercise, and gourmet nutrition to jump start his recovery. It was 6:00 a.m. and Seth pushed the nurse call button. An hour later he was still waiting for his pain pill.

During his short stay in the hospital, Seth was up and walking with a walker the morning after his operation. He continued with the walker, moving up and down the hospital corridors venturing further each of his three days in the Palms of Pasadena's joint ward.

This morning, his first at Oceanside, he un-hooked himself from his CPM (continuous passive motion) machine and discarded his open back surgical gown for a pair of board shorts and a Hurley t-shirt. Seth swung his bandaged right leg off the bed and steadied himself in his walker. He shuffled out the door and headed for the Oceanview nurse's station.

"Excuse me, ma'am, I'm Mr. Stone from room 17. I wondered if my pain pill button is not working?"

The nurse turned around and looked at the desk console and said, "It's working, Sir. The pill cart nurse is in room 14 now and she's working her way up the hall. She'll be with you shortly." With that said, she turned back to her paperwork.

So much for concierge, thought Seth. He took the walker up and down the hall and passed by the huge rehab gym which was starting to fill up with patients and PT techs. He returned to his room just in time for his gourmet breakfast. He ate a cold hard bagel and drank some coffee. The buffet-like eggs and greasy bacon reminded him of those free breakfasts in the chain motels. *So much for gourmet,* thought Seth.

His pain pill came … just as Seth started to hit the ragged edge. An hour later a smiling physical therapy tech named Tara came for Seth with a wheelchair.

"I can walk down with my walker, Tara."

"Ok, see you there in a few minutes."

Seth shuffled into the rehab gym and Tara came over with a clipboard. The gym had at least 40 people meandering about, including the instructors.

"This is your itinerary for today's morning rehab. Just mark it off as you go. I will assist you with the stretching exercises and help get you on and off the machines. Note the time and reps.There will be some lines at some of the machines so I want you to sit while you wait your turn. When you are finished, I will massage your adhesions. I want you to start on the resistance bicycle each day - so sit right here - there are three ahead of you."

Seth sat down, and soon an older man with bloodstained bandages on his left knee and ankle was placed next to him in a wheelchair.

The man was smiling and said, "Hey, you look familiar. Do I know you?"

"I'm Seth Stone. I live here in St. Petersburg."

"Hey, I'm Bobby Perino. My band plays at the Bilmar Hotel on Treasure Island twice a week, and we also play at the Slovakian Club down in Bayboro on Sundays."

"The Slovakian Club is down near my boatyard, Bobby, but I've never heard your band play."

"I play the trumpet and sing … the band is on kind of a hiatus until I get over this knee replacement."

"What happened to your ankle? I mean all the blood."

13

"I fell getting out of bed this morning, trying to find out where my fucking pain pill was. Hey, when you get out of here you'll have to come by the Bilmar and catch a set. I'll buy you a drink."

At that minute, the resistance bike was vacated and the next patient started to mount it. She was a slim, comely octagenarian with perfectly coiffed beauty parlor hair, dressed in a form-fitting silver jumpsuit.

Bobby leaned over to Seth and whispered, "Man, I'd like to get into her Depends®."

It became instantly apparent to Seth that he had to get out of Oceanview as soon as possible. After a two hour PT session that included an hour of waiting and a scouting trip into the far reaches of the nursing section of the facility ... Seth was sure he was not ready to be put in a home.

Once he was back in his room, Seth made phone calls to Lori, to his surgeon Vadim Orlov, and his VIP Doctor, David Hobbit ... He was released to home, given a Percocet prescription, and two-a-day PT home visits with Vadim's personal rehabilitation guru. By the end of the third week, he was off the Percocet and walking a half mile a day with a cane.

**

Three hundred and thirty miles away, Dave the Wave sat in the colonial courthouse building in old Havana. He had showered and was dressed in new clothing, primitive by American standards, clean — though ill-fitting. He sat next to his court-appointed lawyer who had not said a word to him. Like all the other public buildings in Cuba, it was not air conditioned and Dave was perspiring a little. He was not nervous because he knew he would be convicted. The only question was how many years would he serve. On his way in he spotted Clarita and her parents sitting in the gallery. The trials that were adjudicated before his took only a matter of minutes. Most were accompanied by confessions and eyewitnesses. The judges consulted a sentencing book and decided among themselves whether the maximum or a more lenient sentence applied. Gustave explained the night before that there would be no jury as in America. Cuba's legal system had evolved from Spain's and guilt and innocence were decided by five judges. Three judges were Havana Law School educated with the other two being lay people chosen for their intellect and experience.

An hour later, Dave sat at the defendant's table as the prosecutor, a swarthy, sweaty little man with slicked back hair and beady eyes presented the charges against him and read his signed confession. Dave caught the sentencing guidelines - five to fifteen years - but the rest was Greek. Hugo Lugo was called to the stand and delivered his accusations, and then stood up and pointed at Dave when the prosecutor spoke his name. Hugo Lugo made no attempt at eye contact with Dave the Wave and left the courtroom immediately after his testimony. The defense was called but his lawyer rested and threw Dave on the mercy of the court. After a short deliberation by the judges, the bailiff read the verdict: "Guilty as charged — seven years of hard labor". He could hear Clarita wailing and crying behind him. As he turned, he saw her being helped out of the courtroom by her mother and father. Was it romance or finance? Dave guessed he'd probably never know — the whole thing was a bummer.

***

A week after Dave the Wave's trial, Hugo Lugo was reinstated to the Cuban Baseball Federation's world traveling team and received a pay increase to $185 CUC's (Cuba's internal currency tied one for one with the U.S. dollar, but worthless outside of Cuba) per month. He would travel with the all-star team to the Pan-American Championships and start at third base, right after the Cuban League National Championships were decided. Hugo noticed the absence of surveillance a week later. To be sure, he checked out with his Havana block captain for a trip to visit his Uncle Ramon in Santa Clara that was 281 kilometers(.62 of a mile or 174.22 miles) away and a three-hour cab trip from Havana. He took Pedro and his girlfriend, Monserrat, along, signing out and planning to return the following afternoon. Hugo enlisted his cab driver friend, Yassel Fernandez, to drive them. His black, air-conditioned 1957 4-door Chevy Bel-Air had been recently repowered with a Hyundai diesel. Uncle Ramon was pleased to see his famous nephew and threw a large party to show him off. He also provided them comfortable accommodations in his sprawling old ranch house that he maintained as a *campesino* farmer. The trip went well, and no tail was spotted. Hugo, Monserrat, and Pedro were back in Havana to sign in with their block captains late the next day.

Hugo's baseball season was going well — he was third in the league in batting average, first in extra base hits and stolen bases, and way down the list for strikeouts - an important statistic for Cuban hitters. He was golden glove material in the field, one of the Cuban players' major strengths. He met with Pedro several times at the basketball court with still no sign of a tail. He

15

disguised both Pedro and Monserrat and had them follow a couple blocks behind him while he walked around Havana. They never spotted any surveillance.

Monserrat stood naked in front of the window of Hugo's sixth-floor apartment in Miramar. Her lithe form, pendulous breasts, and flowing hair almost took Hugo's breath away. She returned to Hugo's bed and asked: "Have you decided whether to take me to America with you, *mi amor?*"

"The syndicate tells Pedro you would make my escape more complicated. Once I get out and get the contract, I can buy you out of here."

Monserrat slipped back into bed and snuggled with the muscular Hugo under the covers.

"You took me to see your Uncle Ramon. You take me most of the places you go. The block captain might be suspicious when you go to see your mother with only Pedro," said Monserrat as she reached down and felt that Hugo was indeed responding.

"You make a good point," said Hugo smiling. "I'm thinking cowgirl."

"I'll ride you like the posse is right behind us, *caballero!*"

Monserrat started riding, and Hugo slapped her butt cheek and yelled, "*Rapido Chica!*" As Monserrat galloped, Hugo watched her splendid breasts bounce in mid-air.

As the ride reached its crescendo, Hugo gasped, "We're all going to America, baby!!"

Hugo had attempted to defect to America three times previously. The first time when he was 16 years old. He tried to escape on a raft with some high school friends. They were caught five miles offshore. The second time a baseball scout for another Hialeah, Florid, syndicate pegged him as a can't miss MLB prospect, and the syndicate sprung for a regular *Lanchero* defection through Mexico. This consisted of loading 25 Cubans, at $10,000 a head, aboard a stolen 40-foot center console with three high power outboards and three extra drums of gasoline. They boarded in a remote, swampy location. After refueling, they set out across 350 miles of open ocean for Cancun. Once there, they were trucked to the Texas border(under the protection of the northern Mexico drug cartel - *Zeta*) to take advantage of their special refugee status in the United States. Everything went well during Hugo's trip until the weather turned bad and the high seas impeded their progress. They ran out of fuel 50 miles from Cancun and were intercepted by the Mexican Navy, who returned them all to Cuba. Hugo pledged allegiance, admitted his mistake, walked the straight and narrow, and worked his way back up to the traveling team. A regular Cuban would have done jail time, but Cuba doing well internationally in baseball was very important to Fidel. Through those years, Cuba averaged three to four baseball defections a year.

The third time Hugo tried to defect went down a year ago after winning the Pan American Games baseball title in the Dominican Republic. During the post-game celebration at the hotel, Hugo walked out the front door and hailed a cab. No one noticed, and he headed for the American Embassy. As he got out of the cab in front of the Embassy, two Cuban secret service agents, who had been stationed there throughout the games, took him into custody.

Hugo had to make this defection plan work. He was a star now and this new syndicate was willing to spend some serious *dinero (\$)* just to get him to Mexico. Having Pedro make all the arrangements and contacts gave him confidence that the government would be taken by surprise.

***

Seth was walking through the Gisselle Kopsick Palm Tree Arboretum in downtown Saint Petersburg, without the aid of a cane, when his cell phone started ringing.

"Seth, this is Sonja at the Treasure Island Surf Shop. I need to talk to you about Dave."

"Okay, Sonja, what's up?"

"Dave went to Cuba about a month ago to visit his girlfriend, Clarita, and I haven't heard from him. I was starting to worry a little but you know ... 'Dave the Wave time', so I didn't think too much about it. The mail just came and his Cuban girlfriend sent a letter informing me that Dave is in prison for human trafficking with a baseball player. A seven-year sentence, I think. The letter is very difficult to understand. I didn't know who else to call, Seth."

"That's awful, Sonja! I'll come out as soon as I can this afternoon. I have physical therapy at the Orthopaedic Clinic after lunch ... then I'll be out to see you. I'm rehabbing a new knee replacement right now. Make me a copy of the letter. I'll call and pick up our friend José Aguilar at his surf shop in St. Pete Beach on the way. He can translate the letter for us. We'll figure out something."

"I knew you were the one to call. Thank you, Seth."

Seth arrived at the Treasure Island Surf Shop at 3:30 p.m. with José Aguilar in tow. Sonja was normally a tough cookie, but when she saw Seth she lost it and ran crying into his arms.

"I'm sorry Seth, but he's my baby brother, he's all I've got."

"I love him too, Sonja, let's start to figure this thing out."

José read the letter a couple of times and said, " What I get out of the letter is that Dave was at a party at Claritas's house in Havana and met this Cuban baseball star, Hugo Lugo-Ramirez. The baseball player says that Dave propositioned him to defect to play in the United States. Dave said he just complimented him on his talent. An hour later the secret police arrested Dave, and soon after signed a confession. Clarita goes on to say that the penalty for human trafficking, when connected to a Cuban baseball player, is five to 15 years in prison. Dave got seven. She claims he's innocent, so what's the motive?"

"It's not apparent at this time," said Seth. "We're at quite a disadvantage here, with no American embassy, no political ties, and Dave really being there illegally. Our government won't be any help … Joe, do you know any of the Cuban ballplayers who've defected?"

"There's been a lot of them since 1959, probably 60 or 70. I know two of them that retired to Tampa, Juan Montero and "Ricky" Rojas, the famous closer."

"See if you can figure out a motive with them, José. In the meantime, Sonja, I'm going to call a friend of mine in Washington D. C. He may be able to shed some light on this whole situation. But it may take some time."

"You're Dave's only hope, Seth. Why would anyone want to hurt Dave, he doesn't have a mean bone in his body? He loves everybody and everybody loves him. He's just about havin' fun."

"I'm going to give this my best effort, Sonya, that's all I can promise … José, call me as soon as you talk to the Tampa ballplayers."

"I'm on board," said José.

CHAPTER THREE

THE TRUCK headed out to the tobacco fields at first light each morning unless it was raining. When it rained, it traveled towards the city of Pinar Del Rio to a large factory where the prisoners built prefabricated walls, roofs, windows, floors, and doors for schools and hospitals. After his trial, Dave the Wave was assigned to a prison work camp in the town of Santa Maria 20 kilometers southwest of the city of Pinar Del Rio. He shivered every time the truck passed by the walls of Cinco de Media Prison just five and a half kilometers from the center of the province's capital.

Besides convicted felons, the work camp housed a wide range of political dissidents, journalists, religious figures, professors, homosexuals, and discontented young people who did not "understand" the revolution. These people were culled out of the Cuban society by the CDR (Committee for the Defense of the Revolution) and its block captains, and they spent 12 hours a day, seven days a week at hard labor. They received little or no pay depending on their classification, meager rations, and no medical attention. Dave's bunkmate, Modesto, an English and Russian speaking Cuban aviation fuel engineer who had fallen out of favor because of his black market activities, estimated there were at least 200 forced labor camps spread out across Cuba along with another 300 maximum security prisons that were worse. Dave was acclimating himself to the harsh conditions and was determined to survive. Modesto educated him more each night while they ate and then lay in bed trying to fall sleep in the opressive heat. He told Dave that anyone who was a constant problem was tortured until their behavior improved.

Dave worked everday alongside Modesto and was being taught to till, tend, and cut the shade tobacco that was used as wrappers for cigars. Some of the tobacco was used by local factories, but the larger balance was trucked to Havana's cigar factories. The prison work camp was ringed by double 12-foot barbed wire fences with elevated guard houses equipped with searchlights. The sleeping quarters were rows of bunk beds, with screenless windows, housing 40 workers per building. Each building had a two-toilet privy.

After lights out that night, Dave asked Modesto how he had become a jet fuel engineer in Cuba.

"I grew up going to all the good schools in Havana. Each year we had tests and I was always ranked near the top. I went to the best grade schools and the top university high school — most of my classmates are now doctors, lawyers, and engineers. The Russians were very involved in those days and there were many round trip jet passenger flights from Moscow to Havana. International flight rules require that an aviation jet fuel engineer inspect the fuel system before each flight. Cuba had no fuel engineers, so I was one of six graduates picked to go to Russia to be trained. While getting my degree in Russia, I studied Russian and English. There, I met my wife and married her. It gave me more options in Cuba because I held dual citizenship, and they didn't have a stranglehold on me anymore."

"So you moved back here when you graduated?"

"Yes, by then we had our first child and I went to work at the Havana Airport. The pay was only 50 CUC's a month and our housing was poor. My wife, Ruta, complained that the conditions were worse here than in Russia – except the weather was better. I had a lot of free time because the jets only flew every other day. A typical work day was four hours, so I took a part-time job driving tourists around for a Canadian travel agency. My English and Russian fluency earned me large tips."

"How long did that last?"

"Finally, I quit my job at the airport and went full time with the travel agency. The government didn't like it, but I had Russian citizenship so they let it go. Soon I was earning $600 to $800 dollars a month. We bought a house on two lots near Marina Hemingway. I had a wall built around it and built three rental bedrooms."

"*Casa Particulars*?"

"Right, and a swimming pool."

"How did you pull that off with the CDR block captain and everything?"

"I employed every able-bodied man on my block, including the block captain and all three policemen. The units were always rented to Spanish businessmen — they liked the private pool. On holidays I had neighborhood pool parties."

"When did it start to go sour?"

"I guess after awhile I had too much money. I got involved in the fuel black market. Using my fuel contacts, I bought 55-gallon drums of stolen government fuel and had them delivered by a crew I assembled, to remote locations for the Mexican *Lancheros*. They needed to refuel their boats, plus take three or four drums back with them to get their human cargo to Cancun or Isla Mujeres. Each boat transports 25 defectors and grosses $250,000, so they could afford to pay me a generous profit. The CDR and the DGI secret police suspected me but I never touched the fuel since I was the money-man. I finally had enough money stashed to get myself and my family out, which was the plan all along. I wanted to defect to Canada and earn a living as a fuel engineer. The airlines would pay me $150,000 a year there. I sent my family to Russia and was winding things down. I even had an exit date with the same *Lancheros* who I supplied. My government contact who was working with me at the fuel depot got caught and gave me up. They came for me and tortured a confession of sorts out of me and put me here for 15 years. My wife has the bulk of our cash, but I had to give up one of my remaining stashes to stop the beatings. The head of the DGI in Havana confiscated my house and now lives in it."

"Timing is everything, 'Dude'. You're proof of that."

"If I can find a way out of here, my friend, I still have the means to be gone. Tomorrow night I would like to hear more about your meeting with the famous Hugo Lugo, and how you got the name, Dave the Wave. We should sleep now, amigo … tomorrow brings only another difficult day."

"You are right and thank you for being my friend, Modesto Menéndez."

***

Seth drove over to his Treasure Island townhouse and settled into his big chair in the living room. He made some notes and organized the information he would relate to Bobby Thompson. Bobby owned the largest private security and intel company in the United Staes. He had contracts with the CIA, NSA, and the FBI. He also supplied intel and consulting to all of the United State's allies around the world. Bobby played football with Seth at The University of Virginia, and both of them worked for the CIA after graduation. He dialed Bobby's cell phone and Bobby picked up on the fourth ring.

"Well - Howdy, Seth. Is this a social call or do you have yourself in another pickle?"

"Actually, I wanted to tell you my new knee turned out absolutely superb. It's been almost six weeks now, and I feel like I'm 50 years old again. If I were you, I would not wait to fix that nasty left knee you've been dragging around for the last 40 years."

"I hear you, but every morning when I get out of bed, it reminds me of all the fun we had playing football at UVA back in the day," laughed Bobby.

"Right, but I do have an ulterior motive, too. A friend of mine was thrown in jail a couple weeks ago in Cuba. Let me give you all of the information I have up to now. I'm hoping you have some operatives in Cuba."

"More than a few, ol' buddy. We've got agents and double agents — we might even have a couple of triple agents that I don't know about. Sometimes we know what they're going to do before they do. Give me the information and I'll get you what I can. "

Seth spent the next 15 minutes filling Bobby in on Dave the Wave Perozzi.

When he was finished, Seth said, "Get me whatever information you can, so I have something to tell his sister. If you can pinpoint his location, give me all the intel you have for that area. Depending on where they're holding him, maybe I can come up with a plan to spring him."

"You should have stayed in the CIA, Seth. Imagine all of the adventures you would have had by now. Although I have to say, in the last few years you've been making up for it. You certainly kicked some serious butt in the Turks and Caicos a couple of years ago."

Well, I got my butt kicked there, too — until my son, Jeb, flew down and turned it around."

"A famous man once said, *All's well that ends well*. I'll call you as soon as I have something for you. Good to hear about your knee."

"Thanks, Bobby."

Seth ended the call and started downtown to his girlfriend, Lori Gudentite's condo where he spent most of his time these days. First, Seth stopped by Stone's Boatworks on historic Salt Creek in south St. Petersburg. He wanted to pick up a couple of files he kept in his desk chronicling his two trips to Cuba in the late 1990's. As he pulled up to the gate, he noticed the yard was double stacked with boats in various stages of repair. When he exited his Yukon he was greeted by a plethora of shrill sounds emanating from a chorus of air-operated sanders and grinders. It was music to Seth's ears, as it meant there was serious work taking place inside the fence. He made his way through the dusty atmosphere and went upstairs to the offices.

" Good afternoon, gentlemen," said Seth to Jeff and Bob, Stone's office crew. He looked into his son Jeb's office and waved to him since he was on the phone as usual. Jeb had managed the yard for almost ten years now, starting in the boom years then nursing the yard through the great recession. The Boatworks survived and was enjoying the start of another boom period. Seth had been able to mostly retire and pursue his fishing adventures on his 46 foot Hatteras® sportfish, *TAR BABY*, with his old fishing buddies that were affectionately known as the "Geezers". Jeb was married and had a five-year-old son, Cullen Battle Stone. His name carried on a Stone southern tradition of naming the boys after Confederate Generals. Seth's late father was named Robert E. Lee Stone. Seth's brother, Beau, was named after the famous General Pierre Beauregard, the "Hero of Fort Sumter". Seth was named for General Seth Maxwell Barton, a hero at Vicksburg, Mississippi. Seth and Beau's sister, who was married and lived in Atlanta, was named Scarlett. Jeb was named after General James Ewell Brown "Jeb" Stuart.

Brother Beau was a whole nother story. A troubled war hero home from Vietnam, the talented Beau was Seth's partner at the Boatworks. He slowly drifted into alcohol and gambling addictions. At rock bottom, he committed a robbery against the Tampa Mafia to cleanse his debts. Fate forced him to hide out with the spoils of his robbery in Costa Rica after faking his death in a shark tank in Key West. Seth initially saved him from the Mafia in Costa Rica and was the only one who knew he was still alive at that time. Beau beat his addictions, but it took another life threating event two years later to finally put the relentless Tampa Mafia behind him. Seth finally told Jeb the whole story two years earlier and that decision ended up saving Seth's life. When Seth disappeared in the Turks and Caicos in 2007, Jeb called Beau in Costa Rica. Beau flew to Providenciales incognito to help Jeb extricate Seth from certain death. Last year the three of them went fishing in Playa Carillo, Costa Rica, on Beau's Bertram® 31, under the guise of a father and son fishing trip. Seth wished there was a way to bring Beau back into the mainstream, but Beau was encumbered by some heavy baggage. Like his old dad, Robert E. would have said, "Don't do the crime if you can't do the time!" Beau seemed happy living in Costa Rica with his Panamanian girlfriend, Fonda Johnson.

Seth found his files, waved at Jeb who was still on the phone and started back downtown, to Lori's condo. Lori came into his life four years ago during a sailboat regatta. Seth volunteered the *TAR BABY*, as the finish boat for that large St.Petersburg Yacht Club regatta. He and Lori hit it off and they built a lasting relationship from there. Seth was a widower, losing his first wife and the love of his life to a sudden heart attack. Jeb's mother had been a fisherman, sailor, and all-around Florida water person. She really was Seth's best fishing buddy.

Lori was a few years younger than Seth and grew up in St. Petersburg. She returned to St. Pete when her abusive husband in Detroit passed away. Lori had two grown children, Greg, who was married with two children and ran the family business — Gudentite Tool and Die in Detroit, Michigan — and Gladys, a clinical psychologist practicing in Atlanta. After a year's courtship, Seth moved in with Lori at her downtown condo on Beach Drive. They both enjoyed St. Petersburg's vibrant downtown lifestyle. Seth moved *TAR BABY* downtown to the yacht club but kept his townhouse in Treasure Island. He moved out there whenever Lori's family came to visit. Neither Seth nor Lori was interested in marrying again, but they were both happy with the commitment they had forged with each other.

Seth parked his Yukon in the condo's parking garage, but he still kept his BMW® Z-3 Roadster in his garage at his townhouse at the beach and made a point of driving it somewhere with the top down at least once a week. Seth passed by the elevator and slowly climbed the stairs to the 14th floor. He'd been bypassing the elevator for the last week to help regain the strength in his legs. The new knee complained a bit, but each trip up became easier. Lori was waiting for him out on the side balcony. She sipped a chilled glass of Mer Soliel Reserve Chardonnay as she lounged in the sun wearing one of her smaller bikinis.

"Took the stairs again, didn't you, Honey? You're certainly rehabbing that knee quickly."

"I'm not setting any records, but I don't want to go back to that 'home' they put me in when I got out of the hospital," said Seth smiling.

"That place was grim, and I don't blame you for bolting. Are you too tuckered out to give a girl a back rub?"

"Probably not, have you been trying on shoes again?"

"You know they're my weakness. Carole and I went shoe shopping in Tampa at Nordstrom's, Dillard's, and Needless Markup."

"The world series of shoe shopping," laughed Seth. "You must be exhausted."

"Very funny, Big Boy," said Lori sarcastically as she shed her bikini and lay face down on a towel on their King-size bed. "Use some of that Keri-Lotion that's on the nightstand."

Seth started on her back and slowly worked down to her shapely buttocks. He rubbed the back of her legs, then massaged her buttocks some more.

"Concentrate on my back, not my butt, Seth!"

Seth laughed and scratched her back some, then ran his knuckles slowly down both sides of her spine and hips. She moaned softly as he repeated the process. Finally, Seth dropped his board shorts and pulled off his t-shirt. He rolled Lori over, then gently pulled her to the edge of the mattress.

"I can't kneel and put any weight on my new knee, but I think I can operate standing up right here," said Seth huskily.

"What are you waiting for," said Lori as she moved towards him expectantly.

It was over too quickly, being their first encounter in almost six weeks. But they laughed and kissed, and both were glad Seth was back.

After showering and dressing casually, they walked up Beach Drive for dinner at The Birchwood. During dinner, Seth spotted his knee doctor, Vadim Orlov, sitting at the bar with his shapely young girlfriend. He asked their waiter to send a glass of Vadim's favorite wine, Caymus Special Selection Cabernet Sauvignon-2007, along with a Cosmo for his lady, over to them. Doctor Orlov looked across the dining room and Seth gave him a smile and a thumbs up.

Lori and Seth walked home hand in hand, and Seth decided not to mention Dave the Wave's trouble until he knew more about it from Bobby.

***

Hugo Lugo circled the bases in the ninth inning as the crowd went crazy. His left field, full count, home run had driven in the tying and winning runs. This win over the Matanzas Crocodiles put the Havana Industriales into the Cuban National Series where they would play their arch-rival the Santiago Wasps. The whole team waited at home plate to put Hugo on their shoulders to carry him off the field and into the locker room. After celebrating and talking to the press, Hugo hit the showers. While the hot, therapeutic water soothed his tight muscles, he made a momentous decision … he would leave Cuba just before the start of the National Series. The baseball committee would never believe he would consider leaving before the National Series, especially since he was the star of the team. There was no surveillance now, and for sure there wouldn't be any before the Championship. If Hugo had a great series and the Industriales won, they might reinstate surveillance figuring his defection worth had probably doubled. Hugo would tell Pedro later tonight and they'd orchestrate their escape during a visit to Hugo's mother's house in Sandino, west of Havana near Pinar Del Rio. He grew up there before being sent to one of the gifted athlete's high schools in Havana.

The Hialeah investors syndicate's sea captain had picked a spot a few kilometers south of Maria La Gorda's small beach hotel as a night time pick-up point using a 20-foot high-speed RIB(rigid-inflatable boat) to ferry them to the Viking 62 they were sending. During more prosperous times in Cuba, a small boat basin had been blasted out of the rock and jungle at the end of a small sand road off the main road to the hotel. Now it was deserted and surrounded by scrub jungle and a mangrove swamp. Pedro had a hand-held Garmin® GPS with the lat/lon coordinates already transcribed, supplied by his embedded Cuban handler. Hugo remembered the lay of that land from his youth. There was just enough cab and van traffic in and out of the beach hotel that one more car driving in wouldn't be noticed.

Hugo had a secret plan in his mind he would share with no one. He knew if this attempt failed, he would never get out of Cuba. His plan was to give himself one more chance to achieve his imagined destiny, which was to be the greatest third baseman in baseball's history. He asked his cab driver friend, Yassel, to buy him a 9mm pistol on the black market. Cab drivers had the most money to spend in Cuba and were very familiar with the black market. The better vintage cabs were in pristine shape with all of the parts and upgrades, like air-conditioning, being supplied by the black market. Hugo gave him 300 CUCs out of his performance-based baseball rewards money for the gun and explained if the government closed in on them he wanted to shoot his way out. Possession of a firearm in Cuba was strictly against the law and carried heavy jail time. Yassel procured the gun for Hugo and hoped that if anything went wrong it would happen after he dropped them off at the pick-up point. But Hugo's real back-up plan, if he couldn't shoot his way to freedom, was to shoot Yassel or Pedro dead and then claim he had been coerced by them at gunpoint to defect. Sadly, Hugo did not recognize this as psychopathic behavior but only as a possible necessary course of action.

He met Pedro at the basketball court the next morning and they set the date for their escape.

"I've decided to take Monserrat, she thought her absence from a visit to my mother would be conspicuous."

"She may have a point," agreed Pedro.

"We have two days with no practice early in the week before the series starts. So set it all up with the syndicate for a week from this Tuesday … we leave in less than two weeks."

***

Modesto got comfortable after lights out. It had been a long hot day and he felt better after a shower and some *frijoles negro y arroz*.

"So, why are you called Dave the Wave?"

"I was a well-known surfer in Florida in my younger days and competed all over the world on the pro circuit. That's why I came to Cuba almost ten years ago to try the surf out at Cabo de San Antonio. That's where I met Clarita. The surf was OK, but Clarita was spectacular, that's why I kept coming back."

"How did you get sideways with Hugo Lugo?"

" I honestly don't know. I paid him a couple of baseball compliments and was hauled off by the secret police after he left the neighborhood party."

"It is well known that he tried to defect two or three times already. Maybe he is using you to rebuild his credibility. Cuba loses two or three of its brightest stars to defection every year. The Miami syndicates that finance their escapes and brokers them to the American teams must have a network of agents operating here in Cuba?"

"I don't know anything about that, but to put an innocent man in prison for seven years. How can Hugo Lugo live with himself?"

"It takes a dog eat dog mentality to survive in this cesspool that Castro has created for us. I often wondered what it would be like, to live in Miami in "Little Havana". Do you have many friends in Miami?"

"Not really, I know a few guys that used to come up and surf in Cocoa Beach when the surf was up. And I know some good sailboat racers from Miami and Ft. Lauderdale that show up at the big one-design regattas," said Dave. "Other than that I sailed the Columbus Day regatta in Biscayne Bay a couple of times, and I like to stop at Miami Beach Marina on my way back from the Bahamas and party at South Beach. Hey, the rain just started and the wind is blowing … a front must be moving through."

"Yeah, we'll be building more of those prefab room panels if the rain doesn't stop before morning. You know, there are close to one million prisoners in Cuban jails now. That's almost ten percent of our total population. Almost all of them work 10 to 12 hours a day in agriculture, road maintenance, clothing manufacturing, the building trades, and so on. The government gets all that labor for the meager room and board we receive. Do you think it might be some sort of a conspiracy?"

"Sounds fishy to me. Do we ever get a day off?" asked Dave.

"Only Cinco de Mayo and New Year's Day. What is it like in America to work only 40 hours a week and get to go wherever you want and do whatever you want to do, whenever you want to?"

"It's absolutely the best place on the face of this earth, Modesto, believe me!"

CHAPTER FOUR

Seth's cell phone vibrated in his pocket, just after he yelled *pull* at station #8 on the Sarasota black course sporting clays range. He nailed the rabbit as it bounced across the ground in front of him, but missed the quartering midi target by leading it too much. Midis were an optical illusion appearing to be faster because of their smaller size. They tested Seth sorely each time he encountered them. He racked his 20 gauge Beretta O/U in the E-Z-GO® electric cart, sat down, and checked his phone. It was a message from Bobby Thompson. It had been almost a week since Bobby agreed to look into Dave the Wave's situation in Cuba. Bobby's message read; *Have some info on your friend in Cuba — call me when you get someplace you can talk … BT*

Seth texted: *Between 2:00 and 3:00 p.m. OK? SS*

His phone dinged immediately; *K*

Seth returned his phone to his pocket as Freddy "Buckshot" Buckley drove their cart to Station #9. He tried to get his concentration back, Station #9 was a true pair crossing and hard enough even when you were all tuned in.

"Everything okay, Seth?" asked Fred.

"Yeah, just some business that can wait until later."

He checked out the pair as Joe "Longshot" Klugel nailed both targets. Bob "Rabbit" Birky, got both of them, too. Freddy and Seth settled for one apiece. "Shotgun" Sandberg broke his pair, and Jim "Lucky" Montford knocked a couple of chips off both of his. Seth took a deep breath and told himself the news about Dave the Wave would have to wait. Right now, the Sarasota black course was starting to kick his ass. He dug in and got back in the groove. All the SPYC Wingshooter members shot well, but the optical "collusions" created by the use of mini targets, light battues, and midis — slowly took their toll.

They shot the equally difficult red course next and were duly humbled. Mercifully, it was time for lunch and they all trucked off for the Lucky Pelican Restaurant on their way back to St. Petersburg. The banter was light and a good time was had by all. Each week they all got sharper and by fall the doves and quail would be in big trouble.

Seth dropped his load of shooters off at the yacht club and parked his Yukon in the garage. He crossed Bay Shore Drive and walked out on the yacht club docks to *TAR BABY* and sat down in the salon. He grabbed a pen and a notepad and dialed Bobby Thompson's cell phone.

"Hey, Seth … your buddy, Dave the Wave, has gotten himself in quite a pickle. I contacted our agents in Havana and Miami. We have several in both those places and at least two in all of Cuba's 15 provinces. Dave was interrogated at Cinco de Media prison in Pinar Del Rio — they make waterboarding look like a tea party. He signed a confession there admitting that he had contacted and tried to convince Hugo Lugo-Ramirez to defect to the United States. His confession was probably coerced — that's the Cuban m.o. It makes their kangaroo courts work efficiently. He was sentenced to seven years hard labor by a federal court in Havana. There is no political recourse, and Dave was in the country illegally from The United States' perspective. If he keeps his health and works hard they may find a way to keep him longer."

"Where are they holding him?"

"He was assigned to an agricultural labor camp back in Pinar Del Rio Province, in a small town named Santa Maria, 20 kilos south of Pinar Del Rio City. It's a barbed wire, guard tower compound, right out of 'Stalag 17' or 'Cool Hand Luke'. They have armed guards in the tobacco fields with them."

"Any chance of a small clandestine force getting him out at night?"

"Next to impossible — it's too far from the coast, and even a helicopter landing in the tobacco fields during the day would be low percentage. The Cubans still can scramble their Russian Migs to shoot it down. Their ground communication is good because the military and secret police control everything."

"Doesn't sound promising."

"I'll have the Pinar Del Rio agents and my best operative from Havana assess the situation for any possible way out. We call our Havana man '*El Cazador*' — that means 'The Hunter' in Spanish."

"See if it is possible to get some word to Dave that his friends know what his situation is and are working to find a way out for him — he needs to stay patient and positive."

"I'll mention it, but it's all up to our locals on the ground. They may have someone inside the prison system in Pinar Del Rio."

"I'll tell Dave's sister that he's alive and working on a farm and leave it at that for now."

***

Sonja cried when Seth went to see her and told her what he had learned. She was glad that Dave was not injured and was working outdoors instead of rotting in a jail cell. Seth promised to follow any developments in Dave's situation through his sources and keep Sonja in the loop. He counseled Sonja to contact Amnesty International to monitor Dave's situation, ensuring that his case was being tracked by that international watchdog dedicated to prisoner's human rights.

Seth decided at this juncture to do what Dave the Wave would have done himself. He needed a road trip to divert his attention and celebrate life itself. He began to plan a fishing trip to Key West in Dave the Wave's honor. By the time he put a crew together and had *TAR BABY* mechanically checked out, serviced, and provisioned, the holidays would have come and gone. The New Year would bring strong fronts and large schools of Atlantic sailfish to the waters just outside Florida's east coast barrier reef. Charley Blevins had offered his slip in Safe Harbor Marina on Stock Island. His 62 foot Huckins® would be in Seth's boatyard for the month of January getting its bottom painted, hull buffed and waxed, and its Hamilton® jet drives serviced and painted with Stone's special metal anti-foulant system. Charley wasn't scheduled to move *ABOUT TIME* south until a month before spring break.

Seth called Gene Johnson, his retired St. Petersburg police detective friend, and floated some January and February dates in front of him, after filling him in on their friend, Dave the Wave.

"You know I'm all in, Seth. The Keys sound just right after the holidays. Sorry about Dave, though. It sounds like he's hung out to dry in Cuba."

"Yeah, I ran it by Bobby Thompson and he didn't think we could help him in any way. Maybe something will change. Bobby seems to have his finger on the pulse down there."

"Well, count me in. I'll stay the whole time and help you move the boat both ways. How's the knee?"

"I'm just about finished with rehab at the Doctor's clinic. I don't think it could be any better. The pain is gone and I'm feeling younger and walking faster and farther every day. I'll get my 12-week discharge just before we leave for the Keys, which clears me for anything I want to do except running. Dr. Orlov told me, *Don't run unless something big is chasing you.* Probably good advice."

Next, Seth called John Harvey his retired dermatologist and private pilot buddy. John asked about Seth's knee first, then agreed that a fishing trip in the Keys right after the holidays was a great idea. He would fly down as he had a wedding anniversary two days before *TAR BABY* arrived in the Keys. He was equally saddened by the news of their mutual friend Dave's bad luck in Cuba, but pragmatic in his conclusion.

"Those young girls finally got the best of him."

Fred Buckley was Seth's next call. Freddy had nothing on his sailing calendar but the Everglades single and double handed challenge the third Saturday in March. It was an insane 300-mile small boat race from Fort DeSoto in Tampa Bay to Key Largo. There were three checkpoints where each boat were required to check-in; Cape Haze Marina, Chokoloskee Island near Everglades City, and Flamingo Campground — 36 miles before the finish in Key Largo. Fred would be sailing in the single-handed Catamaran class.

"I'll be good for the January, February, and early March fishing, but after the Everglades Challenge in March I have another similar race up in the Carolinas in June. Too bad about Dave the Wave, sounds like a put-up job to me — Is Dino Vino going? I'll probably see him in Key Largo in March?"

"I'm calling him next," said Seth.

Dino Vino was starting his second year in Key Largo after buying a dive center and shop there. Seth waited until 6:00 p.m. to call him.

"Man, I'd like to go, but that's my season. I talked Zoe Fugazi into joining me here. She left Jock on good terms in Providenciales two months ago. He understands we're in love. We're living and working together and I couldn't be happier. I never thought I would meet a woman like her. She likes everything I like, and I'm learning so much about marine biology from her. We're actually going to run three dive trips through Jock's Turtle Divers in the Caicos this spring and summer."

"Sounds like everything's going well for you Dino … if anything changes, you and Zoe are always welcome."

"Stay in touch Seth, and give Lori our best. Worst case we'll drive down one night for dinner, maybe meet in Marathon or Islamorada while you're in Key West in January or February."

Seth started to think about who he should call next. He knew Billy Chandler and Captain Toby Warner would be fishing the Los Suenos Triple Crown billfish tournaments in Costa Rica during January, February, and March. He probably needed to add some new blood to the Geezers.

Scotty Remington came to mind as a possibility. He had retired to St. Petersburg from Long Island, New York ten years ago. After selling his hedge fund, which was based in New York City, he vowed to catch up on the important things in life after 25 fast-paced years on Wall Street ... that excluded everything but work. He had no children and had suffered through an acrimonious divorce. Scotty arrived in Florida ready to make up for lost time. He bought a racing sailboat and immersed himself in the local, then the regional racing scene. There were plenty of talented sailors working at the sail lofts, so he always had a top crew if he bought enough racing sails. When he was comfortable in those circles, he started fishing with charter captains in the Keys and learned to fish inshore and offshore. Scotty had good looks, a constant stream of girlfriends, and 'way in the back ... he had money in the sack'. He was a quick study and became a proficient waterman in a short period of time. Seth invited Scotty on a few overnight trips to the Middle Grounds, 70 miles from Clearwater, and out to the Gulf Stream, which was a hundred miles off St. Petersburg. He did his share of the work on those trips and wasn't looking for the shade. Scotty liked to tip a few beers but didn't drink to excess. He had what Seth characterized as an upbeat personality and could be very entertaining. Scotty also shot clays with the SPYC Wingshooters and hog hunted a few weekends with Seth and the Geezers at Seth's lease in Brooksville. Last summer he fished the Gulf Stream Loop Tournament and stayed offshore for two nights with all the Geezers ... so he wouldn't be a stranger.

Physically, Scotty had boxed and rowed at Harvard, and still skied out west a couple times each winter. He claimed his only mistake educationally was graduating near the top of his class from the Wharton School of Business, which fast-tracked him onto Wall Street — where he almost missed out on the rest of his life. This Key West trip would be a good opportunity to see how Scotty would fit in with the rest of the crew.

Seth thought he would also ask Charley Blevins to come down and fish for at least a few days while his big boat was up on "the hard" in St. Petersburg.

Charley had a floating cottage that was moored in a second slip he owned at Safe Harbor.

After vetting Scotty with Gene, John, and Freddy over the phone, Seth called him and explained the parameters of the trip.

"I'd love to go down there with you guys, Seth. I had a great time this past summer when we went offshore overnight. I'm not scheduled to go skiing until the latter part of March, so the timing's perfect."

"You can ride down to the Keys with Gene and me on *TAR BABY*, or fly down a couple of days later with John Harvey."

"How about I drive my Land Rover® down and we'll have a vehicle to use?"

"Great idea, and thanks for the offer, Scotty."

***

Later that day Seth fielded a call from José Aguilar, "Seth, I heard back from Ricky Rojas in Tampa. He and Juan Montero are on the same page. They both feel that Dave was set up by Hugo Lugo. If a promising ball player gets caught trying to defect, they may turn in some visiting gringo or Miami Cuban exile to regain trust with the government by acting like they have reformed and are living the communist ideology. But, most of them try to escape again."

"All the more reason for us to figure a way to get him out, José."

"If I can help in any way, call me, Seth."

***

Hugo was happy to have his trip sign-out to Sandino over with. He hoped Ernesto, his block captain, had not noticed his nervousness. Ernesto had just wanted to talk baseball, which Hugo was glad to do — after he gave him the particulars of who was traveling with him and the dates of departure and return back to Havana.

"I wish my mother could come to Havana for that part of the series to see me play … but she's too old and frail now. I know a visit from me will cheer her up. At least she'll see it on TV."

"I hope I can get tickets, Hugo, I know the series will be a sellout."

"I brought you two tickets for the opening game. If it goes past four games I'll get you another pair."

34

"God bless you, Hugo. Have a safe trip, and hit one out for me after you get back."

"Okay, I will … see you in three days. Monserrat and I have to get to the bus station and meet Pedro."

Sandino was 240 kilometers away, it would take Yassel three hours or so to get them there in his taxi. There was little conversation. Hugo turned to Monserrat and noticed a tear rolling down her cheek.

"Having second thoughts, Baby?"

"No," answered Monserrat as she brushed away the tear. "I just look at the beauty of our country passing by, and I'm sad there is no future for us here."

They didn't visit Hugo's mother to avoid implicating her later. Pedro brought sandwiches and bottled water along to eat in the car when they got to Sandino's outskirts. When it was dark, Yassel would deliver them to their pickup point, three kilometers past the old Maria La Gorda Beach Hotel on the tranquil Bahia de Comentes. Afterward, Yassel would drive all the way back to Havana and work the Melia Cohiba Hotel late night crowd at the Havana Café, to establish an alibi if needed.

They arrived outside Sandino just before dark. They ate their sandwiches before starting down Rte. 22 to Maria La Gorda, 60 kilometers to the southwest. Pedro sat in the front passenger seat watching the hand-held GPS as it followed the progress of Yassel's taxi down the highway.

Fifty minutes later, Hugo said, "Those lights ahead are the hotel , turn left at their entrance road and follow the sand road."

Yassel followed the sand road along the palm tree lined beach. Soon the palms gave way to native scrub jungle and a couple of kilometers further the taxi's headlights picked up the marina basin and a dilapidated dock. Pedro got out and shined his flashlight around the perimeter of the small deserted basin. He looked back up the road and saw no headlights following. Yassel turned off the taxi's lights. There was only a dim loom from the hotel back towards the northeast. Otherwise, it was pitch black. The friends said their goodbyes to Yassel, thanking him for driving them on this dangerous mission.

" You can change your mind and come with us to America, they're sending a large boat and we will be in Cancun by tomorrow morning."

"How could I leave my beautiful Chevy behind? It has been so good to me and it is worth at least $50,000 U.S. Maybe once you're a big star in America, I'll sell her and buy my way out and join you. But now I should be going. I may need a couple of Havana fares tonight to keep me out of jail if someone noticed a black '57 Chevy in Sandino."

They all hugged, and Yassel went on his way.

"Let's get our backpacks, walk around to the other side of the basin, and hide back in the brush. We have about two hours to wait before the launch comes in," said Pedro.

The trio started around the basin and Hugo patted the pistol in his cargo shorts side pocket just to make sure it was really there. The mosquitos started to bite as the escapees positioned themselves in the mangroves, but that was a small price to pay if their plan worked. Monserrat showed her smarts and didn't complain about the mosquitos. She had signed on for whatever happened.

Pedro said, "When the launch comes in — they will blink a flashlight twice. Then I'll blink mine back three times. The big boat will stay four or five kilometers offshore."

Hugo retrieved a rain jacket from his backpack and put it over his head to shield him from the pesky mosquitoes. Pedro and Monserrat followed suit. A brightly lit cruise ship moved north across the horizon through the Straits of Yucatan headed for the United States. Soon it was out of sight, and the minutes started going by like hours.

"I wish there was a breeze to blow these mosquitoes away," said Pedro.

"It's better with the jackets over our heads," whispered Monserrat.

Suddenly, they could see lights coming towards them down the sandy road. They scrambled back further into the thorny brush under the scrub and mangrove trees. Hugo's heart sunk as a lit-up police jeep arrived in a cloud of dust on the other side of the basin. The Russian jeep had a crossbar with four spotlights on its roof. Two agents in paratrooper pants jumped out with machine guns and flashlights. They shined their lights back and forth across the basin and back into the jungle as the dust settled. Hugo eased his pistol out, not sure at that very moment what he would do, as the trio huddled motionless in the brush. The agents chattered to each other in Spanish.

"*Vamonos, Paco — no hay nadie aqui!*"

The agents jumped back in the jeep and were gone as fast as they had arrived. The trio didn't move or speak for the next ten minutes.

Finally, Hugo exhaled loudly as he put his pistol back in his pocket.

"Somebody at the hotel must have seen the Chevy come this way. I'm glad we were already hiding back in the jungle."

"I thought we were dead and buried," said Pedro.

36

"I wet my pants," exclaimed Monserrat.

The three of them erupted in nervous laughter. Then they moved carefully back to their original hiding spot. About twenty minutes later Hugo said, "Do you hear something, Pedro? Doesn't that sounds like an outboard?"

"Might be, Hugo - it's just about time."

A couple of minutes later they saw two quick flashes of light about a 100 yards from the basin entrance. Pedro quickly clicked his flashlight back. A few moments later a 20-foot gray RIB, powered by a 90-horse four-stroke outboard, slipped quietly into the basin. Pedro ventured out of the mangroves and walked towards the RIB holding up his GPS.

"*Señor* Hugo?" asked the swarthy man holding a AR-15 in the bow of the RIB.

"No, I am Pedro — Hugo is right behind me."

The launch glided up the basins rock wall and the three escapees were helped on board with their backpacks.

"I am Geraldo ... Fernando has the steering wheel. We have been sitting about a 'klick' offshore for about an hour. We saw the police jeep come down the road to check this area out. We were hoping that they had not arrested you."

"They scared the living shit out us, Geraldo, but we were hiding way back in the bushes with the mosquitoes."

"We're going to idle out for about two kilometers so we don't make any loud noise and then we'll throttle-up and run out to the Viking 62. She's about five klicks out —with all her lights off. There's some cold water in the cooler if anybody's thirsty."

Hugo and Monserrat sat on the cooler seat in the stern and watched the lights from the Maria La Gorda Hotel slowly recede in the distance. Hugo thought he'd keep his pistol as long as possible, for whatever eventuality. There were no mosquitoes offshore and when Fernando finally throttled up on plane the wind coming over the bow cooled everyone off. Fernando had the RIB's GPS on dark and came down off plane about a hundred yards from the big boat. As they idled towards her she looked like a ghost ship. The Viking's name, painted in gold on thetransom, was *FAST COMPANY*. Hugo, Monserrat, and Pedro stepped aboard through the vessel's transom tuna door and were hustled inside the cabin. Once the salon door was closed, Geraldo turned on the lights. The windows were blacked out with drawn shades.

"We'll get underway as soon as the RIB is cradled on the bow. The whirring noise you hear is the launch being lifted up on the bow by an electric davit. We are 254 kilometers from Cancun, Mexico and it's just about midnight. Captain Oscar Benitez will pilot the boat all night with the lights off but will have our radar and AIS(auto-identification system) on black screens, at 13 klicks an hour. At 6:00 a.m. we should be about 175 kilometers from Cancun, Oscar will throttle up to 60 kph(37 mph). We should be there by 9:00 a.m."

"How come we're going so slow at night?" asked Pedro.

"If we hit a floating log or a container that fell off a freighter at planing speed — we could sink in a heartbeat."

"How much fuel do we use at 60 kph?" asked Hugo.

"A hundred and fifty-six gallons an hour," answered Geraldo. "Even if we have to divert to another destination we won't run out, she holds 1800 gallons of diesel."

There was a knock on the salon door and Geraldo turned the lights out and opened the salon door … he closed it and turned the lights back on and Fernando and a taller Mexican stood in the salon.

"Meet Nestor. If you need a drink or are hungry, Nestor will get it for you from the galley. For now, let me show you to your quarters."

Geraldo showed Hugo and Monserrat to the port amidship cabin's walk-around queen-size bed, with its own head and shower. Pedro was bunked in the forward stateroom that also had a queen-size bed with a dedicated head and shower.

"Move in and make yourself comfortable. Take a hot shower, there are bathrobes in the closets, and sleep all you want. I'm sure you're tired after all you've been through. Nestor will launder your clothes if you need that. Tell him if you're thirsty — we have Coca-Cola®, beer, rum, and vodka in the fridge. We also have satellite tracking TV, so you can watch a west coast baseball game like the Dodgers or Giants, Hugo. It's still afternoon there. Tell Nestor what you want. Fernando and I are going to ride with Oscar on the flybridge. If you want to come up - use that spiral staircase over there. It's all enclosed and air conditioned up top. By the way, your Hialeah syndicate handler, Alejandro Portillo, will meet you at the dock when we arrive in the morning. I will wake you all in the morning — before we get up and runnng."

"Thank you, Geraldo," said Hugo, chorused with Monserrat and Pedro.

"I'm going to take a shower, and I definitely have a little laundry for Nestor," said Monserrat with a smile.

"I'm in for a shower, something to eat, and a cold Hatuey® while I watch some Major League Baseball. This boat is un-fucking-believable! Nestor — what's for dinner."

"How about some fresh mahi-mahi, rice, and some green beans. You can thank Captain Oscar for the fresh fish, he was a charter boat fishing captain in Venezuela before they fell on hard times with Chavez. We caught two nice ones on the ride over, *Señor* Lugo."

"*Perfecto*, but please call me Hugo."

"I'll have the same as Hugo, Nestor," echoed Pedro as he headed for his shower.

Hugo joined Monserrat in the steaming shower ... a tight fit but perfect for what he had in mind.

Hugo reached around and cupped her breasts in his large hands, "What do you think, *mi amor*?"

"I think we were very lucky and very smart to be one with the mosquitoes. I think we will continue to be lucky from here on out if we don't get too caught up in all this luxury."

"It is easy to get used to ... is it not?" said Hugo, as he cozied up behind her.

"I like the way you make love to me Hugo, you are so unpre**dic**table ..."

"Don't make me laugh, you wonderful slut," said Hugo lifting Monserrat off her feet.

Later, after a delicious dinner and a couple of cold *cervezas*, all three of them started to yawn during the Giants and Astros game. Hugo climbed to the enclosed bridge and thanked Oscar, Fernando, and Geraldo ... before turning in below.

CHAPTER FIVE

DAVE the Wave caught a break when Modesto was promoted to truck driver/laborer and began driving, loading, and unloading a flatbed truck for the largest tobacco farms in the Pinar Del Rio Province. Modesto signed Dave on as his helper. It was still back-breaking work, but when they drove from stop to stop he got a little rest. He also met more Cubans along the way and noticed some of the fields were being picked exclusively by inmates from the women's labor camp. Many of them worked at the grading stations where he regularly loaded and unloaded sheaves of tobacco leaves ready to be dried. The sight of trim, younger women bending over picking the tobacco warmed his heart. Modesto also had more time to work on Dave's Spanish, which made him more aware of what was going on around him. He started thinking in Spanish and that became the first key to speaking the language fluently.

During the third week on the truck route, Modesto came back to the truck from a weigh-in shaking his head and said, "The foreman says the Women's Prison Commandant wants to see me. I hope we haven't broken some rule or regulation. We're ordered to drive to her office at the women's labor camp. Her name is Consuelo Pacheco, and she has a reputation of being a real ball-breaker."

They cleared the guard gate and Modesto parked in front of the prison's main building. Dave slid his hat down over his eyes to catch a quick cat-nap as Modesto disappeared into building.

***

Modesto was shown into the commandant's office. General Machado and Diego Lima, the head of the Havana DGI, were seated on a couch, and Consuelo was seated behind her desk. Nobody was smiling.

"Sit in that chair, Modesto," said Diego Lima, pointing to a chair facing the couch. "What have you found out from David Perozzi?"

"So far, sir, he seems to be totally innocent or he's a great actor."

"Did you know that Hugo Lugo defected a few days ago along with his friend Pedro Sanchez, the basketball star?"

"No sir, we don't hear any news in the prison camps. We eat, sleep, and work."

"Perozzi must be acting. We thought he might be innocent, but Hugo's defection tells us something different," declared General Machado.

"He says he knows almost nobody in Miami and has only been there a few times. He definitely doesn't know Wayne Huzinga, Jeff Loria, or Jorge Mas," said Modesto.

"Maybe we're looking in the wrong place. Maybe the baseball syndicate investors live in Tampa. Think the Yankees and George Steinbrenner. There are 100,000 Cubans in Tampa and just as many Italians. Remember Santo Trafficante? At one time he owned half of Havana. Fidel has always been paranoid about those *Dago Bastardos* getting even with him for taking their hotels and casinos," said Diego.

"We couldn't beat the truth out of him before, and we don't want that kind of confession, anyway. At some point, he'd just tell us what we want to hear to stop the beatings. We need the real names. But, I have an idea," said General Machado. "Dave Perozzi is probably in with the Italian Mafia. Maybe all we have to do to loosen his tongue is ply him with alcohol and women … Consuelo, you could put together a kinky scene here. Modesto speaks perfect English and Perozzi speaks some Spanish. Call it an English class for wayward girls, so they can get a real job when they get out. Lord knows you have enough prostitutes here. Have a dinner once a week, with beer, rum, and food like we eat. Modesto and Perozzi will teach three or four of them English and after more alcohol, the girls will do their thing with both of them. We'll shorten the girls' sentences for their cooperation. Any problem with that, Modesto."

"No, it actually might work. But, I want you to guarantee me again that you'll cut my sentence in half whether I get any information or not."

"Let me assure you that your sentence commutation comes from the highest level. Fidel wants to know who the American baseball syndicate members are. We are losing our best talent year in and year out. When he finds out, our agents in the U.S. will eliminate a couple of the more prominent investors as a 'cease and desist' warning to the others. When we kill their hired agents they just replace them."

"May I interject a thought?" said Consuelo. "I would be willing to take a personal interest in Mr. Perozzi, in a *Mata Hari* sort a way. Also, I could create a Dominatrix role to get me out of the room while the illicit sex was actually taking place. I'll just take one of the girls into my office and we'll play hearts or gin rummy for an hour."

"Okay, it sounds like we have a plan," said General Machado.

"Fidel will appreciate you taking one for the team, Consuelo," said Diego with a smile.

"This plan should bond you and Perozzi even closer, Modesto. Hopefully, he'll slip-up or confide in you," said General Machado.

***

Modesto came out about 30 minutes later still shaking his head, "I've heard rumors about Commandant Consuelo, and now I guess they're true. She asked a lot of questions about both of us, then invited us to dinner at her office tomorrow night. She wants us to work with some of her protégés to improve their English. The rumor I've heard is that she's attracted to athletic, blond-haired, blue-eyed men, but she's also a switch-hitter. Does anyone in this truck fit that description? … Right — only one of us."

"I don't get it, Modesto?"

"You will tomorrow night at 7:00," said Modesto laughing.

"What does she look like?"

"A better than average looking Latino in her 40's, huge zoomers, fairly trim waist, with an authoritarian posture. She carries a riding crop."

"What about the protégés?"

"I'm looking forward to finding out about them. Just remember she'd make a great friend, but a deadly enemy."

"Like her boss … General Machado."

"*Sí*, you're tuned in."

***

When Modesto and Dave returned to their bunkhouse after work the next afternoon, there was a neatly folded stack of clothing on each of their bunks. They showered, shaved, and dressed in their new clothes.

"The khaki pants are a little big, but you can't tell with the Guayabera shirt outside," said Dave.

"I think we look like two gringos from Miami," laughed Modesto.

42

The bunk house guard walked up and handed Modesto an official looking pass, smiled, and walked away.

"Looks like we're going to drive our work truck over to the women's prison camp headquarters," said Modesto while reading their marching orders.

"Like we're sort of trustees," laughed Dave.

"Well, I hope we live up to expectations."

"I can honestly say I'm as horny as a three-peckered Billy-goat."

"She carries a riding crop, Dave."

"Yeah … I don't want to think about that."

Modesto started the truck and headed for the main gate. They passed through three checkpoints manned by smirking guards.

"Do you think they know something that we don't?" asked Dave.

"She carries a riding crop, Dave."

"Well, General George Patton carried one."

"It's not the same, Dave."

They parked and walked to the headquarters door and presented their pass to the guard.

"The last door at the end of the hall, *señors*."

There seemed to be no activity in the building. In fact, it felt deserted. Modesto opened the door at the end of the hall and the pair entered a large room lit by candlelight.

"Come in, Modesto," said a tall woman with long black hair. "Lock the door behind you and bring your friend here (motioning with her riding crop) so I can meet him … and you both can meet my students. We will speak no Spanish while we are in this room, except to explain an English word's meaning. Nobody can leave the room without my permission, except to use the attached bathroom through that door (again pointing with the riding crop). You may address me as Mistress Consuelo."

"Mistress Consuelo, this is Dave Perozzi," said Modesto.

"I have noticed you from a distance, David, and you are even more handsome up close."

"Thank you, Mistress Consuelo. If I may be so bold, I find you quite striking," said Dave with a straight face.

Consuelo motioned towards a large seating area furnished with plush velvet covered furniture.

"These are three of my English students, who share my thirst for the English language, which is probably the most difficult language to master

43

because of the incidence of several meanings for countless words, based wholly on the context the word is being used in. The redhead is Clara, the raven haired one is Camila, and Marta has the curly brown hair. I learned that you studied English in Russia, Modesto, and perfected it as a tour guide for Canadians in Cuba. I have had a special dinner prepared to sharpen our senses. Help yourself to dinner in those chafing dishes, and the beverage of your choice, which you will find behind the bar. Dave, I want you to sit across from me at the end of the dining table."

Dave surveyed the dimly-lit room … behind the couches was a black sheet covering something tall in the far corner and two curtained alcoves furnished with their own couches. After filling his plate, Dave found a Cristal® Cerveza and sat down at the table set for six. Dinner included raw oysters with chopped red chilies, along with an avocado, pomegranate, banana, pine nuts, and arugula salad that looked delicious. They ate olives, honey, and grated walnuts over grilled lobster tails with asparagus and yams for the main course. There were pieces of dark chocolate, strawberries, and figs for desert. They dined and talked about where the girls lived in Cuba, and Dave related tales about the far-flung places where he had competed during his surfing days. He had been around the world more than a few times and recognized this dinner as a first-class, Tom Jones, aphrodisiac feast. They might not have Viagra® in Cuba, but this mix of fruits, vegetables, condiments, seafood, and desserts had staying power written all over it.

Mistress Consuelo maintained almost constant eye contact with Dave, and Modesto was in constant conversation with the young inmates. When dinner was over the girls cleared the table. Consuelo gave Dave a stack of flash cards and said, "Now the English lesson begins."

She handed each girl a test sheet and a pencil saying, "These flash cards contain everyday phrases in English. Dave will hold up the card and repeat the phrase in English. Modesto will repeat the phrase to the girls in Spanish. Then each girl will repeat the phrase in English and write it on her test sheet. Dave and I will grade the tests later in my office."

Dave held up the first flash card and said, "Good afternoon, sir, how may I help you?"

Modesto enunciated in Spanish, "*Buenos tardes, señor, cómo puedo ayudarle?*"

The girls repeated the phrase in English, Dave put the card down, and they wrote it on their test papers in English. And so it went for 30 minutes.

When the flash cards were all viewed, Mistress Consuelo collected the tests and she and Dave retired to her office. Modesto and the three girls were left with Latin music playing in the back ground and an open bar.

Consuelo ushered Dave into her office and locked the door behind her.

"Check the three test papers for mistakes, Dave," said Consuelo as she disappeared into an adjoining bathroom.

She came out several minutes later just as Dave was finishing the last test at her desk.

"Are you finished with the tests?"

"Yes, and the girls did surprisingly well!"

"Good ... now take off your shirt and pants."

Dave complied and Consuelo looked down at him and said, "I knew you'd be ready."

She quickly stepped out of her black slacks and took off her black blouse. Mistress Consuelo stood before him in a black thong, high heels, and a push-up bra, which accentuated her already generous breasts.

"Reach down and grab your ankles, Dave. We're going to play now."

Dave didn't know what to expect, but he complied.

Mistress Consuelo gave Dave a couple of whacks on the behind with her riding crop ... not really hard ... but they stung some.

"Do you like that, Gringo?"

"I'm not sure," lied Dave.

Consuelo whacked him twice again, harder, and said, "What about now, Dave."

"To be honest, Mistress Consuelo, I would much rather just poke you with 'Mr. Woody'."

She laughed, and said, "I have to admit, I've just been kidding you, Dave. I don't get off on dominating men, I like to dominate the young girls. But everybody thinks it's the other way around."

"Whew, that's a relief. Can you imagine how horny I am after being locked-up for over two months in prison?"

"Women like me have the same needs as you, Dave. I think like a man when it comes to sex. When I see a man my first thought is ... *would I fuck him?* If the answer is yes, I either wait for an opportunity or create one."

"So, like most men, you're a sexual predator."

"Right, some of my heroes are Don Juan, Roman Polanski, and, of course, Bill Clinton," said Consuelo with a laugh.

"So you created *English class* out here."

"Yes, out in these remote locations I have to create the situations. I also enjoy bondage with these younger girls, and you'd be surprised at how many of them like it. But I must be careful, so I portray it as an English class. It gives our get together a purpose, but everything else aside, the girls **do** learn to speak English. When they're finished serving their sentences they can find employment at hotel front desks, travel agencies, or waiting tables if they speak English. The access to tourist dollars will put them in a wealthy class of waiters, bartenders, tour guides and taxi drivers on our poor island ... like Modesto was."

"You are an unusual woman, Mistress Consuelo. Hard on the outside, but soft on the inside."

"How else could a woman rise as high as I have in a communist party dominated by men and the Castro brothers? I can't show any weakness ... well enough talk Dave, stand-up and show me what you've got, but don't kiss me."

Dave was glad he'd had a couple of beers with dinner. He didn't want to explode like a schoolboy having his first experience. He joined Consuelo on the couch and put the "wood" to her. She basically took charge and Dave did what he was told.

When it was over, Consuelo sat up on the couch and said, "You're everything I thought you'd be Dave, you're interesting and a good lover. There will be a next time."

"Thank you, Mistress Consuelo."

"We can go out now, and I'll choose a girl to bring back here for a bondage session. You and Modesto can take whichever of the other two you like into those curtained alcoves. Like the bible says, *Eat, drink, and be merry, for tomorrow we die.*"

"You've got that right, *Hermana.*"

"No Spanish, Dave."

"Sorry."

Mistress Consuelo chose Marta and went back to her office.

I guess she'll tie her to a chair, or whatever bondage practitioners do, thought Dave?

Dave gave Modesto first pick, and he chose Camila. The two *amigos* drank more *cerveza*, ate more oysters, and then took their *chicas* into the alcoves.

After a torrid session with Clara, the redhead with the pale white skin, Dave asked, "What's the black sheet in that corner covering up?"

"Oh, that's a big parrot cage with two old parrots in it. If the cover's off they squawk so loud you can't hear yourself think," said Clara.

Dave exhaled lightly and was glad that there would be no more surprises in store.

Finally, Consuelo and Marta appeared and proclaimed the party was over. They all got dressed and left. Everyone kissed each other goodbye except Consuelo ... *I guess everybody has their own fetishes*, thought Dave?

Modesto rumbled through the last checkpoint just as Dave finished telling him about his private encounter with Consuelo. He stopped and parked the flatbed outside their bunkhouse.

"Quite an English class, hey - Dave?"

"Fucking 'rad' ... Consuelo really played me before she came clean. I was sure she was going to whip me black and blue. Also, I thought there was a rack or a whipping post under that black sheet. But, it turned out to be a great night."

"You couldn't tell anybody about this, no one would believe you ... we better sleep fast, it's going to be a long day tomorrow," said Modesto yawning.

***

Seth walked out of Doctor Vadim Orlov's office feeling like a new man. His 12-week check-up was perfect. His knee's range of motion was back to normal, his latest physical therapy time and distance test scores topped the charts, and his x-rays were excellent. Vadim told him that he should wear a knee pad, but he could kneel and squeeze around in *TAR BABY'S* engine room. Seth was worried that his offshore boating days might be over if he couldn't make emergency repairs out at sea if necessary. The 225 mile trip to Key West would be his first test. Anticipating a late January departure, he and Gene started loading fishing equipment on board and provisioning the non-perishables. The engines and generator were serviced and their impellers and v-belts were replaced.

Thanksgiving had come and gone, now Christmas was just around the corner. Seth and Lori spent Thanksgiving with Jeb and his family. Now they would both fly to Detroit on Christmas Eve and spend three days with Lori's son Greg and his family, along with her Gladys who flew up from Atlanta. After Christmas, Seth and Lori would rent a four-wheel drive Jeep and drive up to Torch Lake to celebrate the New Year with a group of her summer friends. Seth thought he must be in love to brave the sometimes below zero temperatures in that winter wonderland. He had to admit that the fires in the fireplace were cozy, and the wine warmed the cockles of his heart. The romantic environment sometimes led to some excellent lovemaking in front of the crackling fire. The daily snow-mobiling and warp-speed ice-boating was exhilarating, but a week in that climate made him glad he was just visiting and lived in balmy Florida. He fully understood why the snowbirds flocked to Saint Petersburg.

Seth realized that his trip planning would interfere with Valentine's Day, which was on a Sunday that year. So after the holidays, he had a logistics meeting with Freddy, Gene, John, and Scotty in the first-floor tackle room at his townhouse. He brought the subject up and suggested they all fly their significant others down for that weekend. Seth's friend, the Monroe County Sheriff, Billy Ray Stodgins, had a friend who would rent his five bedroom house on Sunset Key to them for the weekend. Everyone thought the idea would earn huge points and make re-entry at the end of the month much smoother. Sunset Key was the former Tank Island across the main channel from the Key West Aquarium, the cruise ship docks, and the Westin Hotel. It had been tropically planted and fully developed, was exclusive, expensive, beautiful, and private. It had two full-service pools, a spa, a beach, and two outstanding restaurants and bars. If you weren't staying there you could only make a lunch or dinner reservation and come over on a private 10-minute ferry ride that ran on the half-hour. Sightseeing was prohibited and no private or charter boats could land or moor at their docks. The small island's northwest sunset view was across the Northwest Channel and the uninhabited Barracouta Keys. It was the antithesis of rollicking, wild-ass Key West. They would take Lori, Fred's wife, Penelope, John's wife, Stacy, Gene's wife, Helen, and whoever Scotty's current girlfriend was at the time, over to Key West one night for a dinner at Louie's Backyard or Marquesas. On another night they'd take in a Mallory Square sunset and a Duval Street crawl … and maybe a late morning brunch at Blue Heaven some other day. The rest of the time they'd dine on Sunset Key, lounge at the pools and spoil the girls with umbrella drinks and spa treatments. The sunset cocktail hour would be on the rental house's magnificent back porch, with the exception of a Key West Harbor sunset cocktail cruise on Valentine's Day aboard *TAR BABY*. None of the girls had ever been on Sunset Key for more than lunch. Seth was planning on leaving for Key West at first light Wednesday, January 28th — weather permitting.

***

The knock on the cabin door at 6:15 a.m. woke Hugo and Monserrat from a deep sleep.

"We're going to pick up and run fast in about 40 minutes. The seas are two to three feet right now, but they might get bigger if the wind picks up after sunrise," said Geraldo through the stateroom door.

Hugo Lugo swung out of bed and hurried to the head. Monserrat heard the head flush and Hugo brushing his teeth. He was out in a moment, and she followed suit. When she walked back in the stateroom, Hugo had the nightstand light on and motioned her to his side where he kissed her deeply.

"Good morning, *Cariño*, it looks like Mexico before lunch," said Hugo.

"*Gracias Miel*, I'm so glad I'm here with you. I feel so *libre* for the the first time in my life! Not only will we be free to speak our minds, but also free to do what we want, when we want. There are common-sense rules in America, but the government has to follow them too. It will take some time getting used to that."

"I can't wait to actually get there, *mi amor*," said Hugo as he turned and pulled his cargo shorts on.

Pedro, Hugo, and Monserrat sat in the salon sipping steaming coffee, eating fresh cut pineapple, and munching toasted English muffins slathered with *mantequilla*, as they watched the sun rise behind *FAST COMPANY*. Nestor refilled their coffee cups as the sun rose higher and the visibility increased. Finally, Oscar moved the throttles up to cruise and the 62 foot Viking jumped up on plane and rode through the morning chop like it was on rails.

The three escapees looked at each other, smiled, and just shook their heads.

"Pinch me!" said Pedro.

At 9:30 a.m. Hugo could see the island of Isla Mujeres through the flybridge windshield. Its shape had been on the radar for 15 minutes, and on the GPS chart for over an hour.

Geraldo explained, "We will run past the north end of Isla Mujeres and then west to IGY's La Amada Marina about 13 klicks away. The marina, condos, and resort are 5 or 6 klicks from downtown Cancun. We have been here for a month, so no customs personnel will check us. You'll stay out of sight until after dark, and then we'll move you to a condo that Alejandro rented for you. He will explain it all to you when we get there."

The vast skyline of the tall beach hotels on the sugar-sand barrier island and the low-rise city behind on the mainland created an illusion of a much larger city. Soon they cleared the breakwater at the IGY marina, and Hugo was amazed that better than half the yachts in the marina were longer and bigger than *FAST COMPANY*.

Oscar maneuvered into their slip and the mates had the Viking secured and the power converted in a matter of minutes. A tall, distinguished, Latin gentleman appeared on the dock and was helped aboard by Geraldo. He entered the yacht's salon and strode towards Hugo, extending his right hand. "Ah, Hugo ... I am Alejandro. I trust your voyage has been pleasant so far?"

"More like a dream, Alejandro, *gracias*."

Alejandro turned and said, "You must be Pedro, and you, Monserrat — it is a pleasure to meet both of you. Without you, Pedro, I'm not sure we would be this far."

"Nice to meet you, Alejandro."

"Before we get too far into this, Hugo, I need for you to sign some papers that put into writing what we verbally agreed on in Cuba ... through our Havana agent, Manolo. The Hialeah syndicate will get half of your signing bonus, whatever it is, and 15% of your long-term contract, payable annually. They will have three or four Spanish-speaking agents for you to chose from, who will help you negotiate your contract and organize two structured workouts for the major league scouts. Most agents charge four to six percent of your gross salary and endorsements. The syndicate will pay for the yacht charter, your Cuban handler, Manolo, and the four brave *Lancheros* who got you this far. Another part of their organization will take you to Laredo, Texas, as soon as the syndicate transfers half the funds which total $400,000 for your escape from Cuba. Any questions so far?"

"I'm not complaining, but that's quite a figure!" said Hugo.

"There's a simple explanation. I'm sure you remember your unsuccessful escape attempt from Cuba with the small boat *Lancheros*. You were put on a high-speed 40-foot center console, with three outboards, and 24 other defectors. You were packed in that open boat like a sardine, along with two or three 55 gallon drums of gasoline for refueling in route. Your first syndicate paid the *Lancheros* $10,000 to deliver you to Cancun. Then you would have been squeezed into a panel truck with ten or twelve other defectors and shipped to

Laredo 1690 miles away, under the protection of the Mexican Los Zetas drug cartel, who also get a cut."

"I'm getting the picture, besides being escorted and traveling in comfort this time, there are many payoffs," said Hugo.

"I knew you would understand. In your case, the three of you will be riding to Laredo, a 30-hour trip, in a Prevost motorhome straight through the 1690 miles with a few safe pit stops. You will be supplied with visas issued in Ecuador, in the unlikely event we are stopped. The Zetas representative and the other driver will be armed. When you set a dry-foot in Texas, an immigration lawyer will be waiting for us. Two days later all four of us will fly to Miami, but only after the *Lanchero* organization has been paid in full."

"I know Cubans have a favored immigration status with the United States., said Hugo.

"Yes, ever since 1959 when President Eisenhower gave Cuban defectors unlimited access to the U.S. and lifted any quotas. In 1966 Lyndon Johnson decreed that through the Cuban Adjustment Act, that Cuban refugees could immigrate for family and employment reasons and be immediately accepted, and given all available benefits, green card status, and a path to citizenship in a year and a day. It has remained unchanged except for the inception of "wet-foot/dry- foot" in 1996. Cuban defectors who came by water and were intercepted were sent back. Those who made it to shore could stay. Thwarting communism at America's back door in every way possible was the reasoning, but we couldn't particpate in the actual defection."

"How long will we be in the condo here?" asked Pedro.

"Probably two days. Lounge around … watch TV. Swim — your condo has a private splash pool. Order your meals from the La Amada Hotel room service. But, please do not leave the condo. I will check in on you. If you need anything, you will have my cell phone number. Geraldo and I will move you to your condo when it's dark."

"We'll behave, Alejandro," smiled Hugo Lugo.

"I know you will. Now let's get these papers signed and get things moving. I'll have completed copies for you when we reach Laredo."

CHAPTER SIX

THE TOBACCO harvest and drying season was coming to an end. The cured leaves hung inside the barns waiting to be delivered to the cigar factories.

"What will we be doing next, Modesto?" asked Dave as they bumped up the road to the city of Pinar Del Rio to deliver a truckload of cured tobacco to the Francisco Donatien Cigar Factory where they make Romeo y Julietas and Trinidad Fundadores, one of Cuba's great thin cigars.

"If it's like last year we will help plant next year's tobacco crop, make more of the pre-fab school and hospital components, and deliver a couple loads of tobacco around the province each week. We might even get transferred if the weather gets rainy early and we have to help get the sugar cane out of the fields, a few hundred miles from here."

"Well, I'm looking forward to our English class tonight, Dude ... I like the food and the company. But, maybe not in that order."

"Hey, I'm glad that Consuelo has the hots for Dave the Wave," said Modesto.

"She pretty much thinks like us, except for the bondage ... but I still like the young girls best, they're like cotton candy to me," said Dave.

They pulled up to the receiving dock and unloaded the sleeves of wrapper tobacco, stacking it by hand on pallets. Dave walked through the cigar rolling department to visit the *baños*. With only 60 rollers it was one of Cuba's smaller plants. Legend had it that Cuban cigars were rolled on the thighs of beautiful young women, but Dave hadn't seen anything like that in the Pinar Del Rio cigar factories yet. The youngest roller, in the Romeo y Julietas section, was pushing sixty — it wasn't a pretty sight.

Modesto and Dave drove back towards the prison camp. Once out of the city they stopped intermittently to pick-up and discharge walkers along the highway.

"How come I never see advertising billboards anywhere we travel — except about the revolution?"

"The Castros decided that was the way it would be since the government owns almost all the businesses — it's just the same old revolutionary slogans, their pictures, and Che's. There are not many people in Cuba that remember the revolution — it was 51 years ago. Most of them are dead. The young people don't know what it was like back then. They just know they can't do what they want to or be what they want to be. Can you believe being a heart specialist living in a system where a cab driver earns 20 times more than a doctor? But, they better be one with the revolution or they'll end up like us or worse."

"With all the farmland, sugar cane industry, fine tobacco, free education, health care, and beautiful beaches you'd think everyone would be doing fine here. There should be plenty to eat and the country should be prosperous," said Dave.

"Cuba has all those things, and initially the free health care and education was a big improvement. The guaranteed housing and government food rations erased hunger and homelessness. The Soviets lavished financial aid and infrastructure on us in the 70's and 80's. But, when they left in the 90's it was obvious they had propped us up. Castro seized all the sugar mills and cane fields and nationalized the sugar industry in the 60's. Every year after that, production dropped. The large corporations like Hershey Chocolate and U.S. Sugar were forced out. The Russians bought all our sugar and paid far above market for it to cover our losses. In the meantime, Brazil's private corporations mechanized their sugar planting and harvesting and took over the world market. Instead of mechanizing our sugar and food farming, Cuba moved backwards using oxen and horses in the fields. The majority of Cuba's private farmland was confiscated and turned into communes. The communes are worked by displaced Cubans from all walks of life. Food production has diminished as the real farming families, who were forced off their land, either defected or pursued other careers fueled by free education," said Modesto.

"Sounds like the blind leading the blind."

"The theory sounded good, but you're looking at and hearing the reality. To keep the revolution intact Fidel became a totalitarian dictator. No criticism was tolerated and the prison population increased exponentially each year. Newspapers and TV became government institutions, the internet was outlawed, and the military was strengthened to discourage any uprising. The general population has become lethargic, hustling only for what they need to add to the government dole to survive. Finally, Fidel had to fall back on his only real achievements to sustain the revolution, since the country's economy didn't produce enough money for him to supply even the most basic necessities to Cuba's growing population."

"What achievements, Modesto?"

"Education and medical research."

"I don't understand. Those were done for the people."

"This is the grim reality, I saw it while I was in Russia, and now I see it here. The economy needed a shot in the arm. Cuba's modern heart, lung, and cancer hospitals were opened to paying customers from foreign countries. Now, our citizens wait in line at the old inner city hospitals. Castro started leasing our doctors and dentists to other countries that had no medical schools. The Cuban doctors rental cost in Uganda, Venezuela, or Yemen, averages $75,000 per year, and that money is paid directly to the Cuban government, plus the doctor's room, board, and travel expenses. Cuba pays the leased doctors $900 per year — and it's paid to their families who have to remain in Cuba. The government keeps the balance to help fund the communist regime. Last year there were 40,000 leased doctors. Do the math — that's three billion dollars from the doctors. Add all the leased supporting nurses and technicians, and it's another three billion. Cuba's second highest export is leasing teachers and engineers at 3.2 billion, third — sugar at 410 million, fourth — cigars at 257 million , and fifth — metals at 130 million. Tourism brings in 2.5 billion and the money sent here from relatives in America adds 2.2 billion."

"The medical personnel and educators scheme smells like slave labor, doesn't it?" said Dave.

"If anybody said that out loud, they'd end up like us. One thing to their credit, however, is our government does supply doctors to some really poor countries like Haiti and Bangladesh at no charge."

"So where does Cuba go from here?"

"Nowhere, as long as the Castros are alive. When they're gone we'll go the way of all Marxist communist societies … we'll slowly move towards capitalism and become socialists, maybe like the Europeans. The masses here have no guns, no money, and little or no equity in anything. There is a saying among the Cuban people that sums our situation up; *we pretend to work and Castro pretends to pay us.* The people are dependent on the government for their very existence. Once they earn some equity in a small service business, restaurant, hotel, bakery, or *bodega* as those things are allowed by the government to keep harmony and improve the economy, Cuba's reality will also slowly improve. One day we might get to vote for democracy … it's happened elsewhere. I don't know, Dave … I'm just a raggedy-assed old fuel engineer, not a philosopher."

"You make a lot of sense, *Compadre*. The Cuban people are resourceful and hardworking if they see a future. The success of the refugee Cubans in America is legendary."

"Amen," said Modesto as he stopped at the guard gate and smiled. "Time to park the truck and get showered and shaved, Dave the Wave."

***

TAR BABY planed under the Skyway Bridge at 24 knots (1.15 x greater than a mph. or 27.6 mph.) as the sun came up in the east casting different shades of pastel pink and blue across the calm waters of Tampa Bay. The Skyway's super structure reflected the warm early morning sunlight off the bright yellow cables that held the span above the bay's lapping water. It was a magnificent sight to start the day. Seth was glad to have his knee replacement behind him and was looking forward to fishing the Keys once again.

"If it stays this calm all the way down we could make Key West in eight hours," said Gene.

"By the time we get to Fort Myers Beach, the afternoon westerly sea breeze will start. Then it will pick up to 15 knots in Florida Bay and kick our ass."

"Like it always does," laughed Gene.

"I'm going to push it, and try to get to Safe Harbor before dark."

"I'm looking forward to a hogfish sandwich at the Hogfish Bar and Grille tonight," said Gene

"We have a lot of memories at Safe Harbor Marina, and what a cast of characters," said Seth, laughing.

"You've got that right. Joe O'Donnell and his tree house … Do you remember his tattooed girlfriend and, Hugh Spinney, the seaweed magnate? Good people!"

"Joe usually has two girls with him. How about all the Mel Fisher graduates there. There must be five or six of them that were part of the *ATOCHA* mother-lode crew. They all still wear the real gold coins around their necks and have the ruby dive rings. There's still a couple of treasure hunters' boats tied up in the marina. But, Charley Blevins told me Stock Island is going uptown," said Seth.

"Yeah, the Stock Island Marina Village mega-yacht marina is finished. And over by Robbie's boatyard is the new marine trades' complex. I heard they're building condos and townhouses as fast as they can junk the single and doublewide trailers."

"We should drive up to Bobby Mongelli's barbecue joint on Geiger Key to remind us of the old Key West. Plus, I hear the barbecue is still good, even though he's becoming a restaurant impresario."

"Well, it will be fun seeing the changes since we really haven't spent any time there in the last two or three years with all the down-island fishing we've been doing," added Gene.

Seth steered southwest from the bridge leaving Egmont and Passage Keys to starboard, then he angled west out the unmarked channel off the north tip of Anna Maria Island. It was easier to navigate when the wind was blowing and there were breaking waves on the shoals on both sides of *TAR BABY*. He ran out about a mile, turned south – southeast, and headed for Key West. Seth set his autopilot with Key West's waypoint and turned the helm over to Gene.

"I'm gonna' hit the head and get rid of this morning's coffee, want anything?"

"I'm happy right here. Why don't you take a nap and spell me in a couple of hours?"

Seth returned to the flybridge and stretched out on the flybridge settee, forward of the helm. He thought about his friend, Dave the Wave, and wished there was something he could do to help him. He pictured Dave cutting tobacco all day in the hot Cuban sun. Even if he escaped on his own, how does a blond, blue-eyed, white boy hide out in Cuba? Right, he doesn't. Seth fell asleep feeling helpless.

***

The Prevost Marathon H3-45 Bel-Air motor home rolled west across route 180 towards Veracruz 800 miles away. They left Cancun at 6:00 in the morning. Veracruz was the half way point on their trip to Laredo, Texas, 1690 miles from Cancun. They were somewhere west of Nuevo Progreso, eight hours out of Cancun. Hugo watched the scrub jungle whiz past as he sat back in one of the Prevost's two leather recliners. Pedro was relaxing in the other recliner as they both watched the Cincinnati Reds play the St. Louis Cardinals in a day game on the bus's 32-inch satellite TV. Monserrat was curled up on the 78 inch sleeper sofa, where Pedro would sleep that night, looking through a Cosmopolitan magazine. Hugo and Monserrat would occupy the aft cabin king size bed tonight, which also had its own head and a 50-inch flat screen TV. Alejandro napped in the middle cabin on a bunk bed. The motor home's large walk-in shower was located in that cabin. The Los Zeta representative, Javier, was driving and the relief driver, Miguel, snoozed in the shotgun seat, with an AR-15 on the floor next to him.

"This bus is almost as nice as the Viking *barco*, Pedro."

"*Sí*, Hugo, they are taking good care of us. There is *cerveza* and *Coca-Light* in the *refrigerador*. I wish we could stop and stretch our legs."

"Yeah. But Alejandro says it's dangerous to stop … it attracts attention. So far Mexico is not beautiful like Cuba, *sí*?"

"We will drive through the mountains when we pass Mexico City sometime tomorrow. Maybe it will get better."

This model Prevost was a double-slide, so when driving the center aisle was narrow, like in a school bus. If they pulled over and stopped, which was not the plan, they could slide the salon and master suite out about 36". Alejandro only planned to stop for diesel fuel once, outside Mexico City, given a 230 gallon fuel tank and 6-7 miles per gallon usage.

Hugo still had the 9mm automatic in his cargo pocket, but he knew he would have to ditch it when they crossed the border. At that moment, Joey Votto, the Red's first baseman hit a towering home run with two men on base.

"Did you see that ball … he hit that sucker up in the upper deck. I think he'll be the National League MVP this year. He always hits over .300 and drives in over 100 runs. I think I can hit 35 to 40 home runs or better with the number of games they play. I can't imagine what Votto's next contract will cost the Reds when his present contract is up."

"If you were the third baseman on that team, they would win the World Series," said Pedro.

"I can't wait to get there, man. And in the off-season, I want to watch you play basketball."

"How are we going to do that?"

"After I'm set — I'll get my agent to get your Olympic and Pan-American game films. Then we'll put you in one of those summer basketball camps for graduating high school seniors. The films will go to Kentucky, Duke, USC,

North Carolina, and Indiana. Then it's up to you. You play a year or two then turn pro."

"If that doesn't work, I can always try the Pro Beach Volleyball circuit."

"Think basketball, Pedro, just basketball."

Monserrat made them all sandwiches for lunch from the well-stocked galley. They napped and watched TV and watched the Mexican landscape roll by. At dusk, they crossed the Rio Coatzacoalcos River that flowed into the Gulf of Mexico and rumbled through the seaside city of the same name. The topography started to get hilly as it got dark and they climbed closer to Mexico City. The Prevost passed through Mexico City at 10:30 p.m., stopping for fuel on the north side, at Hidalgo, before continuing into the mountains all night. The service station was spacious with many pumps, and all but deserted at that hour. Hugo and the whole crew stretched their legs and then settled back in for the night drive. At dawn, they were descending towards Saltillo and Monterey. Alejandro made fresh coffee and Monserrat toasted some English muffins for the troops. By lunchtime, they passed through Monterey and had three hours left to Laredo. They would arrive in Laredo between 3:00 and 4:00 that afternoon. Alejandro made several calls on his Iridium sat-phone, then placed it back on the dinette table.

"Hugo. I have alerted our immigration lawyer to meet us at the border at the Gateway to the Americas Bridge. We are going to walk across because there is less traffic. North of the Port of Entry at the Laredo Juarez-Lincoln International Bridge, 15,000 cars, trucks, and buses enter Laredo through 15 lanes from Mexico every day. The Gateway Bridge, where we're headed, handles non-commercial traffic: 11,000 pedestrians and only 2300 vehicles per day enter there. I have a U.S. passport — all you three need is your Cuban I.D.'s. On the Mexican side, show only the Ecuadorian visas I gave you. As soon as you step foot on United States soil, show your Cuban I.D.'s and you will have asylum. We have hotel rooms for you and we'll go to dinner once the entry paperwork is finished."

"How long will we be held in Customs?" asked Hugo.

"Our lawyer thinks he can get us through in about two hours — if you just walked in it would take eight to twelve hours."

The ride to Laredo went quickly. Hugo, Monserrat, and Pedro were nervous, excited, relieved, and expectant — all at once. Nuevo Laredo, the Mexican half of the city split in two by the Rio Grande, had the look of a typical Mexican City — it was dusty and a bit worn, but the brightly painted colonial architecture made it all look quaint. The Prevost pulled up to the Mexican Customs bridge entrance and stopped. Javier opened the door and stood up. Hugo and his crew said their thank-yous and goodbyes to Javier and Miguel. Alejandro got off first, already talking to the lawyer on his sat-phone, while pulling his small roll-around suitcase. Hugo's crew had their backpacks slung over their shoulders. The motorhome pulled away and the four of them shuffled into the line of pedestrians headed for the bridge.

"When we get to the U.S. side, look for a Hispanic man in a dark blue suit and red tie, carrying a briefcase and holding up a HUGO LUGO sign," said Alejandro to six-foot nine inch Pedro.

They were processed and stamped through in about 20 minutes, using forms already filled out by Alejandro. Next, they headed for the bridge's crowded walkway across the Rio Grande. To their left, three long lines of cars and pick-up trucks crept towards eight toll booths on the other side of the river. As they reached the middle of the bridge, Hugo threw something small over the railing just before the sign that read **The United States of America Border.**

"What was that, Hugo?" asked Alejandro.

"Just a bad dream, Alejandro, nothing that matters now. We made it amigos!"

Hugo grabbed Monserrat — kissed her, and hugged Pedro. Five minutes later Pedro spotted the lawyer standing by a door in the customs building, next to the line leading to the crowded pedestrian entrance.

As they gathered around him he said, "I am your lawyer, Joaquin Martinez. Your syndicate in Miami has arranged for expedited processing. This is our government escort, Manuel Fonseca. He will guide us through the process."

"Follow me, and feel free to speak English or Spanish — Laredo welcomes you. Laredo's population is approximately 250,000, and our citizens are 95% Hispanic."

They showed their Cuban I.D.'s at the first station and were escorted to a different part of the facility. This was the smallest of Laredo's four federal customs facilities, and the Cubans could not get over the enormity of its size and scope.

Manuel said, "There are almost 90,000 people processed through customs in Laredo every day, and that doesn't count trains, planes, buses, and trucks. There are 34 more points of entry on our southern border — the numbers are staggering."

Joaquin and Alejandro helped the Cuban trio fill out the necessary forms and in an hour they were finished and had their photos taken. While they waited for their visas, Joaquin explained what rights Cuban immigrants had in the United States.

"Your visas and work permits are good for a year," explained Joaquin. "A year from now you will be granted permanent residency and be given a green card. From today on, you are eligible for welfare, food stamps, government loans, and Medicaid if you need them. There are numerous Cuban charities here in Laredo to assist Cuban immigrants with travel costs, lodging, and food. There are also agencies that will help you find employment in America. I doubt you three will need that help, but it's there if you need it."

"God bless America," said Pedro with tears in his eyes. "The generosity is overwhelming."

"Wow," said Hugo, as Monserrat shook her head in disbelief. "They told us in Cuba that the *Yanquis* were all stingy, heartless, capitalist bastards."

Finally, the visas arrived and they were ready to go.

"Thank you, Joaquin and Manuel!" said Alejandro. "Now let's get a cab and head for the Posado Hotel and some dinner."

CHAPTER SEVEN

SETH ran *TAR BABY* down the Northwest Channel towards Key West. The sun was quartered behind him as it headed toward the western horizon. He turned around, extended his right arm, and placed his flat palm between the horizon and the blazing red sun. Seth could fit about eight fingers in that projected space. At 15 minutes a finger, he had about two hours of daylight left. He could see the two-story houses on Sunset Key, and downtown Key West in the sun-lit background. The sun colored a white cruise ship pink as it graced a dock just south of Mallory Square.

"We made fair time, considering Florida Bay bounced us around most of this afternoon," said Gene.

"We've got plenty of daylight left, and we should be docking at Safe Harbor in twenty minutes or so."

"Not that the daylight matters very much to you, Seth. I remember when the Russian Mafia was after our asses here a few years ago, after the drug bust with Sheriff Billy Ray. We all left in two boats and a small plane in the middle of the night. I still can't believe you ran this boat up to Newfound Harbor inside the reef and anchored out there all night by yourself."

"As my old dad, Robert E. would have said, 'God helps those who help themselves'."

"Man, the war the Russians had with the Tampa Mafia shortly after that pretty much wiped out both sides," exclaimed Gene.

"We were fortunate to get out of that whole mess with no casualties."

Seth cut the corner around Fort Zachary Taylor and headed inside the reef for the Stock Island Channel. He passed Louie's Backyard, the Casa Marina Hotel, the White Street-Compass Rose Pier, Key West International Airport, and Cow Key. He slowed down and made a wide turn into the Stock Island Channel across from Oceanside Marina's narrow channel cut.

Charley's Safe Harbor slip beckoned, Seth backed in, and Gene tied them up inside of ten minutes. Seth shut down the engines, came down off the flybridge, and plugged into shore power, while Gene readjusted *TAR BABY* with a couple of spring lines.

Seth recognized Scotty's Land Rover, which was pulled into a parking place right behind the slip. He walked over and read a note Scotty had left under the windshield wiper.

Having a cold one at the Hogfish bar. Call my cell - 727- 439- 6768 - if you need my help.

Gene was already hosing off the boat's foredeck. Seth ducked into the cabin, transferred to shore power, and shut down the generator. He called Lori to let her know he had made it all right. The call went to her voicemail and he left a *"We're here safely — I love you"* message.

"Scotty's at the bar. We'll join him when you're finished hosing down the boat. We'll have a couple of beers while we wait for the decks to dry. Man, this place brings back some memories," said Seth surveying the large, funky marina.

"Yeah, Deputy Pearce and Peter Petcock. I'm glad that crazy bastard Peter is dead," said Gene.

"You and me both! Maybe we can take Deputy Pearce, "Big Dog" Arnold, and Chief Billy Ray out fishing again," said Seth.

"They're great guys … they make me proud to be a lawman," said Gene.

As they started off the dock, Hugh Spinney came out of his large houseboat in the next slip and said hello.

"Hey, Seth and Gene, how long are you down for?"

"About a month," answered Seth, "Maybe we can talk you into going fishing with us? At least once."

"All depends on the seaweed, this time of year the sailfish bite when the winds are howling … It's the same time we clean the most seaweed off the beaches."

"Well, let us know, you can jump on anytime. We're going up front for a beer, can you join us?"

"My dinner's ready here, but I'll take a raincheck."

Seth and Gene eased into the crowded restaurant and spotted Scotty talking to two sunburned young ladies at the bar.

"Hey Scotty," said Seth as he approached.

"Seth and Gene, meet Judy and Alexis, they're renting Charley's floating cottage this week. They're veterinary assistants from Detroit. Pull up a couple of stools," said Scotty.

Seth ordered two beers as Gene scooted over a couple of barstools.

"Y'all got quite a sunburn there," said Gene smiling.

"It's worse than you think, they drove up to Geiger Key and went skinny dipping off the deserted beach at the end of Old Boca Chica Road," said Scotty.

"There's no other place you can get an all-over tan around Key West," said Judy, a tall good-looking blonde.

"Looks like y'all ought to take a day off tomorrow," laughed Seth.

"Dr. Remington here, told us he invented a special cream while he was practicing — that would keep us from peeling," gushed Alexis, a pretty, petite brunette with a pixie haircut that matched her smile.

"Dr. Remington?" said Gene looking suspiciously at Scotty.

"Imagine our luck to run into a retired plastic surgeon on Stock Island? Have you ever seen his card? Board Certified even," said Judy pulling out his card from her beach carry-all.

"I didn't know you still carried business cards, Dr. Scotty," said Seth with a smile.

"They help me get a better table in the up-scale restaurants, among other things," quipped Scotty.

"I thought you were a Gynecologist, Scotty," said Gene trying not to laugh.

"That was *before* I was a Plastic Surgeon," said Scotty with straight face.

"Anyhow, girls, we have a retired Dermatologist flying in tomorrow, maybe he can give you two a second opinion," said Seth still smiling.

"What do you want to do for dinner, guys?" asked Scotty.

"Let's just have a hogfish sandwich here, and turn in early … we've been on the water since dawn."

"You made good time," said Scotty.

"Looks like you've been making pretty good time yourself," said Seth grinning. "Do you ladies want to join us?"

"Not tonight, thank you. Dr. Remington is going to mix up some of his burn lotion for us and we have a Publix chicken ready to heat up. We need to get in the air-conditioning to try and cool down," said Alexis.

"I'll walk back with the girls," said Scotty. "I'll put my duffel on board, mix up the magic potion for the girls, and be back in 30 minutes."

"Take your time … Gene and I are going to have another cold one. Nice to meet you, ladies."

As Scotty herded the girls down the dock, Gene turned to Seth and said, "Looks like Scotty is going to liven things up, he definitely has an off-beat sense of humor. He and Dino Vino would make quite a pair."

"You got that right, I wonder what he's going to mix up in his magic sunburn potion."

"We'll know in a half an hour."

"Bartender, how about two more *cervezas*?"

"Comin' right up, gentlemen."

"Looks like the weather should change here in a few days," said Seth.

"Yeah, I checked MyRadar© on my cell phone once we got a signal coming in this afternoon. A strong front is moving through the Midwest with lots of snow, then a little rain for us and some wind."

"That should translate into a couple of days of great sailfishing right outside the reef. I'll check PassageWeather© on my laptop to pinpoint the optimum wind and wave conditions. We'll have the boat and the tackle all tuned in by then. John Harvey should be at the airport FBO about 11:00 a.m. tomorrow — he'll call for a ride after he lands."

Seth and Gene nursed their beers until a smirking Scotty showed back up.

"So, how did it go, "Doc"?

"About like I thought it would. When they went in the cottage, I told them to crank up the A/C, take a cold shower, and wrap themselves in beach towels. And … I'd be back with my magic ointment in 15 minutes."

"What did you mix up?" asked Gene.

"Well, I was going to use mayonnaise, but I found a six-pack of vanilla yogurt in the fridge."

"You used my yogurt!" said Gene.

"Not all of it …don't worry, I'll replace it. Anyhow, I found a gallon of white apple vinegar under the galley sink and some baking soda in the fridge. So I mixed it all together in one of those plastic containers we use for left-overs. A very soothing mixture I must say. I know the baking soda prevents reefer odor, but what's the white vinegar onboard for, Seth?"

"I use it to flush out the engine and generator heat exchangers. I close the seacocks, then pour it in the raw water strainers, turn the engines over a couple of times, and let it sit awhile. There's three more gallons stashed in the engine room."

"I only used a cup, and a hand full of the baking soda. I also found a bottle of salt pills in the first aid kit, and had the girls take two each so they wouldn't be dehydrated."

"Did they like the lotion?" asked Gene.

"Well, they dropped their towels and asked me to rub it on. The yogurt was cold from the fridge, so I know it felt good. They both have nice bodies, and Alexis wanted a boob-job consultation … Judy doesn't need any help. With that degree of sunburn, neither one of them will be ready for any real touching for a couple of days. Anyway … it's all fun."

"Good luck," said Gene.

"I don't think there's any luck involved," laughed Seth.

"Let's get a table, I'm hungry and I want to talk about fishing … that's why I'm here," said Scotty.

***

Last night's *English class* was history, but Dave the Wave savored the memory as he wielded his hammer on the pre-fab school wall panel crew. After another wonderful dinner, and the obligatory flash card session, Consuelo was more arduous and inventive. She chose Clara for her office bondage session, and Dave was paired with Marta and a new girl named Luciana. He had little control during that ménage a trois. Modesto had a second encounter with Camila.

He and Modesto were slated for a tobacco pick-up and delivery route tomorrow, but things were slowing down in Pinar Del Rio. A third of the camp's barracks were empty because of worker transfers to various provinces that were harvesting sugar cane.

They were up and ready to go at dawn the next morning.

"I'm really stoked about going to the next English class, Modesto."

"The last English class was a wild one, and it sure helps to break-up the monotony. Maybe I'll get double-teamed next week," smiled Modesto.

"Just that one big dinner every week, along with the five or six beers, and I've stopped losing weight," remarked Dave.

"Yeah, and I like our driving job better than harvesting the tobacco in the hot fields all day. We could have it way worse."

"What's our schedule today?"

"We're going to San Luis, to pick up a big load of wrapper leaves at Robaina Plantation to deliver to Havana. We also have pickups at two small tobacco farms in Vinales. They'll send a guard with us since we're headed to Havana."

They set out for the Robaina Plantation with Julio riding shotgun, as the rising sun promised another balmy day. After loading better than half the truck at that vast plantation, he and Modesto fastened a tarp over the cured leaves of valuable wrapper tobacco. They had two stops in Vinales, both at 100 acre size farms where the owners helped them load. The first farm was manned by the whole Carneros family, who helped them load the leaves from their drying barn. The second farm was Casa de Vequero, where farmer Simon Tarcoles joined in on the loading. Simon gave Modesto, Dave, and Julio each a freshly rolled cigar for the trip to Havana. Both families were prosperous *Campesinos*, talented farmers whose production exceeded their government quotas. They were allowed to sell the overage at market prices. Their production and others like them kept the Cuban cigar industry growing to meet the world's demand for the best cigars on the planet. With the truck filled to capacity, Modesto started the two hour drive to the cigar factories, but they couldn't talk freely because of Julio. Modesto continued east towards Havana in light traffic, with a smattering of the ever-present foot traffic moving slowly in both directions. Dave grooved on the beautiful foliage and the majestic mountains to the south. After an hour of farmland going by, the Havana suburbs started springing up. Soon they were winding their way through Miramar with its stately embassies and large homes owned by wealthy foreigners. They passed the Castro's four square mile estate that was walled, barb-wired, and not visible from the road. The military guarded and patrolled that entire area.

The bulk of the cigar factories were in central downtown Havana. Their first delivery was to the Partagas cigar factory located on Calle Industria at Centro. Dave had been there before but was always impressed by the five-story, multi-level structure that resembled a colonial mansion. It was a stunning piece of Caribbean architecture. Modesto drove around to the loading dock and backed in.

"I don't know about you two, but I'm headed for the *baños,*" said Dave.

"We'll be right behind you as soon as we sign all these manifests and receipts," said Julio.

Dave walked across the bustling cigar rolling floor, where 90 female rollers had their skirts pulled up and tucked under their crotches as they rolled the wrapper leaves, tightly to the cigar's core, on their inner thighs. *Only five more days until English class,* thought Dave, as he walked quickly into the *Hombre's baños* to take a leak.

As he concentrated on the job at hand, a man approached him from behind and whispered, "Do not turn around. I am going to slip a note into your right pants pocket. Do not read it until you are all alone — then destroy it. You are not forgotten."

With that, he was gone.

Dave finished his leak, buttoned up, and was washing his hands when Modesto and Julio walked through the door.

"Start unloading the Partaga order, Dave. I'll be back to help you in a few minutes," said Modesto.

As Dave walked back through the plant he suppressed his urge to read the note. He would be patient. After all this time it was his first ray of hope since the trial in Havana. He would wait until he was back at the barracks and read it in the privy, tear it up in small pieces, then flush it down the seat-less toilet. Dave pulled back the tarp and started to unload Partaga's sheaves of leaves.

Once Partaga's order was unloaded, they headed through the city streets to 14th Avenue and the H. Upmann factory, also in the Chinatown section of Centro, to drop off wrapper leaves there. Upmann was producing the popular Romeo y Julietas brand at the moment and also the perennial Montecristo. According to Modesto, the government switched production of its 100 cigar brands between the different factories as demand increased and decreased in an effort to keep them uniformly busy. H. Upmann's, like many of the Cuban cigar companies, had changed hands many times since the industry took off in the 1840's. All of that came to an end after the coup in 1959 when the government nationalized the industry.

The next stop was the immense La Corona Cigar factory at Mayo y Linea Streets, next to the baseball stadium. The factory was Cuba's largest and employed 675 people, and produced as many as 30,000 cigars per day. They left that day's largest order there.

Modesto detoured the truck over to 25th Avenue and a peso snack stand. They used a government voucher that was issued to Julio, to purchase a lunch for each of them. After a hasty meal of hot beans, rice, and coconut water costing 10 pesos, they started their way back towards Miramar and their last stop before heading back to Pinar Del Rio. Modesto headed for 146th Avenue and the famous El Laquita Cohiba factory west of Miramar, which also looked like a mansion at first glance. Cohiba rolled a number of diversified brands and is the most beautiful cigar factory in Havana. The dazzling white, two story, facility produces one of Fidel's favorite cigars, the Lancero, developed by his favorite bodyguard, *Chicho*. Lanceros are the Cohibas that he gives to visiting foreign dignitaries. That delivery emptied the truck of its last bundles of leaves.

Modesto started back to Pinar Del Rio and the three travelers lit up the cigars they were given that morning. Soon the smoke billowing out of the truck's cab reminded Dave of a Cheech and Chong movie. They passed many taxis as they drove out of the city and suburbs. Some taxis and vans were new imports, but the majority were still the United States' cars and station wagons of the 1950's, repowered and repainted. They were a testimony to the quality manufacturing and engineering prowess of Detroit's "Big Three". As they cleared the suburbs and traveled west along the highway, Modesto stopped to offer pedestrians a ride, a Cuban expression of solidarity since the revolution. They arrived back at the labor camp in Santa Maria 15 minutes before dinner and joined the other prisoners. Another 12 hour work day had come to an end.

After dinner, Modesto headed for the shower. Dave said he had to visit the *baños* first. He palmed a pack of matches he'd purloined during an English class and headed for the outhouse. Once ensconced, he struck a match and pulled the note from his pocket and read; **Dave, greetings from El Cazador - We have agents watching you – be vigilant – don't lose hope – we're working with Seth.**

Dave tore the note in little pieces and flushed it away, hid the matches, and joined Modesto in the shower.

"What are you grinning about, Dave?" asked Modesto as he dried off.

"Was I grinning? ... I guess it has to be the excellent cigar I smoked on the trip back from Havana. Best I ever had!"

Half way back to the barracks Modesto said, "Shit, I forgot my truck log notebook in the shower house. See you back at the barracks."

Modesto had forgotten the log on purpose. He retrieved it and stopped by the *baños* on his way out. He checked around both bowls, and in the second one retrieved two torn pieces of paper stuck under the back rim. On the first piece, written in block letters was *AGENTS WATC*. The second piece contained the letters *DAVE* and *CAZAD* over *HOPE* ... it was obvious to Modesto that Dave had been passed a note in one of the cigar factories. It probably took place in the Partaga factory, which was the only time Modesto wasn't with him for the whole Havana trip. Maybe Dave **was** a Mafia agent.

Modesto would pass these scraps of paper to Consuelo at the next English class and chat Dave up about Tampa when it was appropriate.

**

Hugo Lugo wiped the sleep from his eyes and noticed the room was filled with daylight. Monserrat was not in bed but was gazing out the window intently.

"What is so interesting outside, *mi amor*?"

"I am looking at freedom. I am looking at our new country."

Hugo got out of bed and snuggled up behind her and said, "As the saying goes, 'today is the first day of the rest of our lives'."

"I am so excited, I almost held my breath the whole way here from Havana. I can't believe we made it."

The snuggling aroused Hugo, so he pulled up her sheer nightgown and pulled her close.

"Our first union in the *Estados Unidos*," gushed Monserrat as Hugo gently lifted her off the floor.

"Maybe we can fly United to Miami later this afternoon," laughed Hugo as he picked up the pace.

"Let's finish in the shower, *Cariño*, they have a hair dryer in the *baño* and I want to wash my hair."

They uncoupled and retired to the shower for more fun and games in the luxurious hot water and bubbly shampoo.

"Hurry up and finish your hair," said Hugo over the din of the hairdryer, "We're scheduled to meet Alejandro and Pedro in the hotel coffee shop at 9:00."

"I'll be ready, *Papi chulo*."

They all gathered around a four-top in the coffee shop and Alejandro filled them in on their upcoming flight to Miami.

"We're flying first class and a limo will be waiting for us at the airport. We have rented a two bedroom condo in Miami Beach for you and Monserrat. It's month to month so you can move whenever you need to — once you have a contract. The syndicate will front you $6,500 a month until you sign a contract and you need to take Pedro's living expenses out of that. Shopping for clothes in Miami will be fun for all of you. You will also need telephones. We've set Pedro up in a one bedroom apartment in Hialeah until he sorts out his basketball and volleyball options. We have also set-up gym memberships and you can also run on the near-by beach. Once you receive your half of the signing bonus, you're on your own, but you will have an agent to guide you. We will start to interview them tomorrow at their offices."

"It all sounds great, Alejandro, and I look forward to meeting the agents. Do any of the agents have other Cuban players for clients?"

"*Sí*, they all have at least one Cuban player as a client."

"I'm looking forward to seeing Miami, and playing baseball again!"

CHAPTER EIGHT

John Harvey and Fred Buckley arrived at the Key West Airport about six hours before a strong cold front started through. When John was finished tying his Piper Lance down, Seth and Gene drove them back to Safe Harbor.

"Hey guys, I rented two rooms for you in Joe O'Donnell's four-room floating motel that's moored across the basin."

"Great, I'm famished," said John. "I've been looking forward to lunch at the Hogfish."

They pulled in, got settled, then met Scotty, at a big table under an even bigger umbrella dockside, at the Hogfish Bar and Grille.

"Flight down a little bumpy, Fred?" asked Scotty.

"Nothing we couldn't handle, but the front pulling all that wind into it from the south made for a stiff headwind. Once it comes through, NOAA predicts 15 to 25 knots of wind tomorrow and a bunch of rain."

"I think we'll sit out tomorrow and fish the next two days. We can rig ballyhoo, and get live goggle-eyes at the Key West Bait Shop in the Bight," said Seth. "There should be a bunch of sails tailin' down sea by then."

"Hey, Dr. John … here comes Dr. Remington's two sunburn patients," said Gene. "He promised you would give them a second opinion on their all-over sunburn."

"Dr. Remington?" said John quizzically.

"Show him your business card, Scotty," said Gene. "Just play along for grins."

John looked at Scotty's card, shook his head and laughed, "I always knew you were a pervert."

"We're just havin' some fun, and these girls are not what you'd call prudes."

As the girls approached, Scotty stood up and greeted them with, "How are we feeling today girls?"

"A lot better, thanks to you Dr. Scotty. We took the Tylenol® P.M. you suggested and your ointment worked great," offered Judy with a smile.

"We could use another application of your magic ointment, Doc. It really did the trick," added Alexis.

"Freddy and Dr. John … meet Judy and Alexis, two nudists from the Motor City," said Scotty.

The girls giggled and Alexis said with a wry smile, "Maybe you can help Dr. Scotty lotion us up tonight, Dr. John?"

"It appears that Dr. Scotty has everything under control, but I'll take a look if you have a relapse."

"Can we join you and buy a round? I mean what are friends and neighbors for?" asked Judy.

"Not necessary, but sure … get them a couple of chairs, Scotty," said Seth. The afternoon lunch party began and stretched into a dinner of hogfish, black beans and rice, and many more beers. By then it was pitch black and raining with thunder and lightning as the front stormed through. They raced back to the boat and cottage, went their separate ways, and turned in for the night.

Seth awoke early the next morning feeling groggy along with a definite headache. He took two Tylenol and brewed a pot of strong coffee. Seth took his jumbo Tervis® cup up on the flybridge and enjoyed the sunrise coming up over Boca Chica Key. He was glad the polycarbonate wind screens were in place as the wind was gusting to 25 knots. Seth thought about Dave the Wave and switched his iPad from local weather to Google Earth. He zeroed in on the little town of Santa Maria near the bigger cities of Pinar Del Rio and San Juan y Martinez. There had to be some way to get him out of that prison camp. He followed the sparse roads in the area down to the coastal town of Punta de Cartas. Near the point, he found the San Juan River and a swamp on the southeast side of the town of 3,800 people. Only one road led back to San Juan y Martinez about 16 kilometers away. Seth looked up information about each town, San Juan y Martinez, a town of 45,000 residents, was touted as the "Mecca of Tobacco". The best tobacco in the world was grown at Hoya de Monterrey and Plantation Robaina. Google Earth showed the San Juan River entering the Bahia de Cortes Bay about three kilometers from Punta de Cartas in a swampy area, not accessible from the town. The river and large swamp continued about eight kilometers north with access through a tall mangrove thicket to the paved highway, just short of a government housing project for agricultural workers. The river went underground a kilometer or two north of there then resurfaced on the other side of the road. Seth's mind started into overdrive at that point. He pictured a military-grade high speed inflatable boat, large enough to carry two motor bikes and six men that could get them up that road towards Dave's location. His concentration was broken for a moment when Scotty emerged from Charley's yellow cottage in the next slip. Scotty moved silently across the seawall and stepped down on *TAR BABY'S* transom gunwale and slipped inside. Seth had to chuckle to himself. He could only imagine the scene with Scotty and the two lobster-red women ... actually, he couldn't imagine it. His mind immediately returned to Dave the Wave. He quickly picked up his satellite phone and dialed Bobby Thompson.

.... "Hey, you're calling early. I'm just crossing the Potomac River on my way in, Seth."

"Sorry I called so early, but I've been thinking about Dave the Wave. I'm down in Key West fishing with Gene, John, Freddy, and another friend for the next three or four weeks."

"Wish I was with you. But, funny you should call, I got word yesterday from *El Cazador*. He slipped Dave a note in the Partagas cigar factory men's room while they were making a tobacco delivery in Havana. Remember you asked me to somehow assure him we were trying to figure a way out for him?"

"Yeah, that's super, Bobby! How did he look?"

"*El Cazador* has his agents watching him. They said Dave was on the thin side ... probably has dropped 25 lbs and lost his beer belly. He was taken out of the fields and given a job delivering cigar wrapper tobacco with a Cuban trustee prisoner who drives the truck. They let the two of them drive alone in the local area, but when they deliver to the Havana factories an armed guard goes along."

"Maybe that can work into an idea I cooked up while looking at that area on Google Earth earlier. I think I could put some men ashore half-way up the San Juan River near Punta de Carta with two motor bikes or small motorcycles. The river runs through a mangrove swamp, and it flows along the side of a paved road, so the mangroves would hide a large inflatable boat. It puts us less than 20 kilometers from Santa Maria. I thought we might grab him out of a tobacco field, but this truck thing sounds more promising."

"It will be much easier now that he's picking up and delivering tobacco," said Bobby. "Let me get some idea of his schedule — if there is one. I'll call you back later today or tomorrow."

Seth went below for more coffee, but he clipped his sat-phone to his belt. He walked into the salon and there was Scotty toasting a bagel.

"Sleep tight, Scotty?"

"Well, you could say that, Cappy. I was waylaid by two 'redskins' last night. When we all ran back here in the pouring rain, they pulled me into the cottage. I admit … I didn't put up much of a fight, and I don't remember all of it. But, we took off our soaking wet clothes and threw them in the dryer. Then there we were — stark naked. The A/C made us cold, so we jumped in the queen-size bed together and got warm, like **really** warm. The two of them are still asleep and they both snore. That's something I can easily overlook as they both have outstanding attitudes."

"So they took advantage of you?" inquired Seth sarcastically.

"Exactly, I couldn't have put that better myself," laughed Scotty.

Gene came out of his cabin, got some coffee, and said, "The wind sure is honking."

"It'll blow the stink off ya," said Scotty.

"Yeah, we'll pull the drags on the reels, rig some ballyhoo, and put a dredge or two together today, and make sure the kites and balloons are all in good shape. Scotty and I will drive down to Key West Bight and get some live goggle-eyes this morning. Tomorrow the wind prediction is 20 knots, knockin' down to 15 in the afternoon. We'll need some fuel before we go out, too."

At that moment John and Freddy arrived and started cooking up some breakfast.

"The floating motel did some rockin' and rollin' last night … thought I was out at sea for a while," laughed John.

Soon the boys were busy in the cockpit. Scotty and Seth checked out the baitwell pump, then drove down to the Bight for the goggle-eyes.

After a light lunch, the boat was proclaimed ready and the crew kicked back with the day's first cold one.

"Lookin' forward to the fishing tomorrow," said Freddy. "We haven't fished the Keys with Seth since 2004."

"We're set up to troll or use live bait, we'll just see what they want," said Gene.

Seth's sat-phone started ringing up in the flybridge and he answered immediately, "Yeah, Bobby, let me get down in the cabin where I left my iPad."

Seth came down the ladder and disappeared into the salon and the air-conditioning.

"Hey, Bobby, go ahead - I've got Google Earth on Punta de Carta now."

"Good, *El Cazador* says his agent, Cesar, in Pinar Del Rio, determined they pick-up and deliver on Tuesdays and Thursdays. He knows when they come out through the guard gate if they're going to Havana because a guard will be in the cab with them. Cesar called him last week when Dave went to Havana and he knew which cigar factories they were supplying from previous surveillance. The farmers keep the tobacco in curing barns on the farms and deliver it only when it's needed. The cash poor government owns the cigar factories and has to pay these farmers. They go to several small farms and two large tobacco plantations in San Juan y Martinez for pickups before going to Havana later in the week. Cesar reported that they work at a pre-fab school plant that's behind barbed wire the other days. The tobacco has all been harvested now. There are very few roads — so their path is predictable."

"What about the trustee truck driver, will he be a problem?" asked Seth.

"*El Cazador* went to school with him, he is a renegade jet fuel engineer, named Modesto Menéndez, who made too much money in the black market and got caught bribing a high ranking communist party member. He would probably like to defect — his Russian wife left Cuba just before his arrest and is in Russia with their two kids."

"I'll continue to follow the routes on Google and figure what equipment we will need, like two motorcycles, a big inflatable with a 60 HP four-stroke outboard, and I already have a high powered silenced rifle to shoot out the delivery truck's tires. I'll figure it out, there's a lot of logistics involved. We'd need extra fuel for sure. I see us coming in from Mexico with the big boat ... Punta de Carta is too far from the Caymans. Then we have to go back to Key West from there — going back to Mexico is not an option. I might have to get a larger boat. I'll try to sort it out in the next week or so in-between fishing. If you get any more news, call me."

"Alright, call me any time. I can have my Cuban agents contact you by sat-phone if and when you decide to make your move, so you know when Dave is actually on the road," said Bobby.

"Realistically, I can't make a move for at least a month, so maybe the Pinar Del Rio and Havana agents can continue to compile Dave and Modesto's delivery movements and we'll have a more accurate schedule. It seems like the monthly Cuban cigar exports are important to their national economy."

"You're right about that, I'll keep them on the job, Seth."

"Thanks, Bobby."

Seth climbed back in the flybridge and studied Google Earth some more. He found a far-flung string of uninhabited keys named Cayos de San Felipe about 20 kilometers (12 miles) south of Punta de Cartas. He zoomed in on several that appeared to have good anchorages on their north side. He would run it by Freddy, who had cruised his 68 foot Irwin ketch through the Gulf of Batabano a couple of years ago on his way to Panama.

"Seth — Freddy, John, and I are going to Wet Willies up on Duval to hear some blues music and have another beer. Wanna' come along? Gene's taking a nap down below," said Scotty shouting up to the flybridge.

"Thanks, but call us around dinner time … Gene and I will taxi down and meet you, maybe at Meson De Pepe's or wherever you want."

"Okay, we'll make it an early night."

Scotty and the crew drove off in the Land Rover and Seth got busy on the internet. After comparing the speed, weight, and off-road capabilities, Seth settled on a Honda® 150cc Ruckus motor scooter with a GY6 power swap and stretch seat options, all in black. The souped-up model would do 60 miles an hour and accelerate like a motorcycle, and off the road it really shined. All that in a 216 pound package that would handle a 340 pound payload for $1700.00 msrp. Seth would negotiate a discount at Keys Motorsports for a "two-fer". Next, he combed the internet for a suitable inflatable boat. He found what he was looking for at Zodiac® Inflatable Boats; he chose their heavy duty Mil/Pro 530, 17.5 foot long x 7 foot beam, black, with a roll-up aluminum floor with stringers and keel, 1.2mm thick dual-coated Hypalon fabric, 22" tubes, and six separate air chambers. The 530 could handle 3792 lbs. and carry up to 12 people, and was standard equipment for the U.S. Special Forces. Seth already had a small electric Campbell-Hausfeld® compressor aboard to inflate it. It came in a 350 lb., 60x30x15 inch storable package. The best deal Seth could find was from Defender Marine at $28,500.00, with free shipping. Suzuki® Key West on Stock Island had a low-hour 2008, 60hp four-stroke outboard (weight 230 lbs.), for $5600 with a tiller handle and ignition switch.

To make long voyages to remote locations where there are no or few fueling locations along the way, precise planning is necessary. There's no Sea-Tow® out there. Seth dug in and did the math on *TAR BABY'S* fuel usage and figured he'd need two 55 gallon plastic drums of fuel for insurance. Key West to Cancun is 400 miles. *TAR BABY* holds 650 gallons of fuel in her main tanks, but she has an auxiliary tank in the centerline bilge to hold 150 gallons more(former F/G holding tank/replaced with a 40 gallon plastic tank and a Lectrasan® sanitary system) that can be transfer pumped. Add that to the 110 gallons in barrels and the total is 910 gallons. The Hatteras 46 Convertible cruises at 21 knots/burning a total of 32 gallons of diesel per hour including the generator. That's 17 hours and 544 gallons, giving *TAR BABY* a 30% cushion on the way over – Seth made a mental note that 10% is really unusable because of the pick-up height inside the tanks.

Once in Cancun, Seth would fill the fuel tanks and run 200 miles to the San Felipe Cays, using about 260 gallons. When the rescue mission was over, he'd run 320 miles back to Key West using close to 425 gallons, for a total of 685 gallons with a safety factor of 25%. If the voyage was slowed down by high winds, currents, or bad weather they could slow down to 8 knots and 9 gallons of usage per hour. In 10 hours they'd travel 90 miles and use 90 gallons, rather than traveling 240 miles and burning 320 gallons. Instead of traveling ¾ of a mile per gallon, they'd travel at 1 mile per gallon, thus saving 25%. If they did the whole trip from Cancun/San Felipe/Key West at 8 knots they'd use 520 gallons rather than 685 gallons. All the figuring and planning was necessary for successful voyaging, but it was starting to bore Seth and he was getting a headache. Mercifully, Gene climbed onto the flybridge with two cold ones.

"What are you trying to figure out, Seth?"

"Oh, I came up with an idea to try and get Dave the Wave out of prison in Cuba. Bobby's agents have been keeping an eye on him."

Seth spent the next half-hour filling Gene in on his plan and bouncing different scenarios off the old detective. As they were weighing the pros and cons, Seth's cell phone rang.

"Yeah, Freddy, we'll meet you at The Whistle Bar and then go over to Bagatelle for dinner. See you in 20 minutes or so."

"They've been pub crawling?" asked Gene.

"For most of the afternoon, I'll call us a cab."

Seth called a taxi and soon he and Gene were on their way to lower Duval Street.

"I think your plan has a lot of merit, the weakest part is when we're anchored out at those offshore cays waiting for Bobby's agents to call."

"I need to talk to Freddy about how isolated it is there and whether there's any enforcement."

"How do you plan on moving and storing the two motor scooters — and installing that 230 lb. engine on the Zodiac?"

"*TAR BABY* still has a built-in gin pole from the old days when we weighed the marlin at tournaments. I still have the stainless steel davit and the block and tackle that fits on top under the fly bridge cowling. It will lift 1500 lbs."

"I forgot about that … The other thing is stopping the delivery truck."

"I thought I might just pull up alongside them while riding the scooter. Dave will recognize me and have Modesto stop. If not, I'll just shoot out the tires."

"Maybe Bobby can have an agent slip him another note when we're anchored offshore. Then Dave could let this Modesto fellow in on the plan if he wants too," offered Gene.

"That could work. I'm planning on taking him with us if he wants to come, or we'll just tie him up and leave him in the truck if he doesn't. That way they won't think he was in on it … did you say when **we're** anchored out?"

"Yeah, I did. Do you want me to come?" asked Gene.

"Of course I do, you've been a major part on every other caper we've been on."

"Shitfire! Here we go again."

"This one is a little different, it's the first big government we've taken on, and I've got to front this one financially," said Seth.

"They can't be tougher than the Mafia, but we don't know that yet."

"I do have a contingency plan to pay for this operation."

"How?" asked Gene.

"Well, the Cuban baseball player that framed Dave, Hugo Lugo — will defect to the States sometime soon, and that's what this is all about. He will sign a huge contract for 25 or 30 million dollars, who knows these days. It's a kid's game for 'Christ's-sake'. I'm going to give him and his agent an itemized bill for our expenses and make him cough up like $1,000,000 for Dave the Wave. If he pays we don't go away mad … we just go away," said Seth.

"What if he blows you off?"

"I'll front a civil suit for Dave that will ruin Lugo's reputation and poison his endorsements and we'll win a judgement. I'll get that high profile lawyer Barry Schwartz from Tampa to go after him. I realize life was no bed of roses for him in Cuba having all that talent and not being free to reach his potential. But he owes a debt to Dave for the dishonest and self-serving act he committed. If he takes care of it, no one else needs to know. If he doesn't, well …we'll **make** him pay. I hope he and his agent are smarter than that."

The cab finally stopped in front of the Bull and Whistle, and Seth and Gene exited the cab. They filed up the stairs and found their crew holding down a table in the corner.

"Hey, Seth, the band is T.C. Carr from Tampa Bay. Man, he can really play that blues harmonica!"

"Yeah, I catch him out at Ka'Tiki on Sunset Beach, and down at the Hideaway Café on Central Avenue when he's in town. He **can** play that harp."

"Let's listen to the rest of this set and then eat dinner," said Freddy. "Six a.m. is gonna roll around before you know it."

***

TAR BABY left her slip and glided past the lit-up Keys Energy Service plant on Stock Island Channel at 7:00 a.m. They were the first boat at the Oceanside Marina fuel dock and filled up. The first rays of light shone in a morning sky that was dominated by high, wispy, frozen clouds. The wind was brisk as they cast off, even in the protected channel. Seth had the windscreens down, and the crew had their foul weather gear handy in anticipation of some ocean spray. The boat idled into Hawk Channel and Seth pushed the throttles up to 15 knots. The northerly wind blew streaks and foam from aft of the transom. They headed for the barrier reef less than five miles away from Stock Island. There were breaking waves along most of the reef. Seth found the choppy Stock Island Channel opening, leaving Western Sambo reef to port, and powered through. The crew set *TAR BABY* up to troll and she quartered down the swells that increased in size as they worked south away from the reef. Two short skirted ballyhoo baited flat lines ran next to bridge controlled teasers, and two naked ballyhoo swam off the long riggers — all secured to #7 circle hooks. Ten minutes later, Freddy got the first bite on the left flat after a sail came up behind the teaser. Seth wound the teaser in from the bridge and Freddy positioned his bait in front of the lit-up sail. When the sailfish picked up the bait Fred lifted his rod and free spooled, allowing his line to fall gently on the water with no pressure for five or six seconds, as the fish slowly swam away. Then he pushed the drag lever up to strike and pointed the rod tip at the fish while reeling smoothly. A few seconds later the reel screamed and the hooked sailfish rocketed out of the water. Seth kept trolling in a large circle as Freddy's fish took lots of line. Within two minutes John and Gene were dropping back and hooking two more sails from that pack. They settled down and Seth maneuvered the boat as they reeled the sails in one at a time. This pattern was repeated in different degrees as Seth moved *TAR BABY* first closer, then further away from the reef. The boys caught 12 sailfish and lost six in the first two hours. All of them were soaking wet, wind-burned, but happy.

As the sun rose higher, Seth called down to the cockpit, "I'm going to make one more loop out here, and then we'll move just inside the reef and put out live bait in 35 feet of water for a while."

Seth's proposal met with approval as the crew slid around the cockpit in the rough seas. He knew they were getting tired. Halfway through the loop, John landed a sail. A few minutes later, Scotty got a bite and dropped back. He counted to four and pushed the drag lever to strike, but nobody was home. Scotty reeled in and there on the end of the hook was the dreaded *sancocho*. Only the head of the ballyhoo remained. He hung his head and said, "I guess I used too much thumb pressure." Scotty looked down at his blistered thumb, shook his head, and made his way to the first-aid kit for a Band-Aid®.

The crew pulled in the lines and secured the outriggers and Seth motored back through the cut and then turned east along Western Sambo. The seas flattened out and were more tolerable, but still choppy, and the "Geezers" had time for a quick sandwich. The reef knocked down most of the Atlantic's impressive swell. After lunch, the crew used the same light trolling rods and reels filled with 20 lb. mono and tipped with a 6 foot long, 50 lb. test fluorocarbon leader. The #7 circle hook was attached to a dental floss knotted loop that was needled through the top of the goggle-eye's back just in front of the dorsal fin. The circle hook point was crisscrossed through both loops. This allowed the bait to swim naturally compared to piercing the bait's flesh with the hook. Freddy and Scotty cast out two goggles.

John climbed to the bridge as Seth started to slow troll the live baits using the outriggers. Gene was ready to pitch one out of the baitwell if John or Seth spotted a sailfish closer-by. Seth slowly worked the bait schools near the edge of the reef.

"Gene," shouted John — "there are two sails 20 yards to starboard."

Gene grabbed his rod and cast a goggle-eye off the starboard side, 10 feet from the sails. His rod went off almost immediately, his drop back was short, and he hooked up.

"The other fish sounded!" shouted John.

Freddy's rod suddenly doubled over and started to scream, and the sailfish took over 100 yards of line in a matter of seconds. Sailfish were considered the fastest fish that swims and were capable of speeds over 60 miles per hour. It's no wonder that lightweight sailfish reels were filled with 300 or more yards of monofilament line. Seth let the boys fight the fish from a dead boat, only turning when the fish swam forward of the beam. Soon three more sailfish had been released.

"Let's put a couple goggle-eyes out about 75 feet under balloons and we'll see if we can pick up a wahoo for dinner, Gene," shouted Seth from above.

After setting up the live baits, the boys missed the first two bites, while Seth bumped further east along the reef in about 30 feet of water.

Twenty minutes later they had a 35 lb. wahoo in the box and were headed for Safe Harbor. Once all the gear was stowed, they all came up on the bridge with a cold beer.

"Seth, what a day!" said John. "I'm wet, I'm cold, I can't feel my fingers, and I have a raging case of itchy-ass, but right now — I wouldn't want to be anywhere else in the world. Thank God … for you and the Geezers."

The rest of the crew slapped Seth and each other on their backs, and yelled, "Hear-Hear!"

Scotty went below and was back in a flash with another cold 6-pack as Gene said, "Sixteen sailfish, and a nice wahoo — and, we only missed nine or ten fish all day — a great start."

"The bite was good today, for sure. Usually, you get rewarded for coming out when it's blowing 20 knots, but you're going to get beat up. Today it was a young man's game, and the Geezers hung in there. Tomorrow probably won't be as good, but it will be more comfortable," said Seth.

"Do we have enough flags to put up?" asked Scotty.

"Yeah, but just put one sailfish and a wahoo up, we'd just have to take them all down in the morning. I have 30 of those little red release flags — we'll put them up if we decide to enter one of the tournaments and do well."

The boys docked the boat and hosed it off while thinking about a hot shower, dry clothes, a grilled wahoo dinner, and a couple of stiff drinks or a large glass of red wine.

CHAPTER NINE

THE PLANE flew in over Miami Beach, and Hugo saw the rows of waterfront high-rises and the sprawling metropolis that was Greater Miami from his first class window seat. Monserrat had done well, once she got over her fear of flying for the first time. She gazed out the window with Hugo and was awestruck. Pedro sat with Alejandro across the aisle looking intently out the window on his side. The plane landed and taxied to its gate. Alejandro led his charges off the plane and they headed for the baggage claim. As they came down the escalator into the baggage area, Pedro spotted a limo driver in uniform waiting with a small sign that read HUGO LUGO.

"Looks like you've arrived, amigo!" exclaimed Pedro.

Hugo smiled at Alejandro and said, "Nice touch *Señor,* gracias."

"Welcome to Miami, Hugo Lugo," smiled Alejandro, as Monserrat threw her arms around Hugo's neck and kissed him.

The driver collected the luggage on a cart and escorted the entourage out to the waiting limousine. After a lunch at Monty's in Coconut Grove, the limo drove them to Hialeah where they dropped Pedro off at his newly furnished apartment. His unit was fully equipped and the complex's interior courtyard had a swimming pool.

Alejandro handed Pedro a box and said, "This is a Samsung® phone I bought for you. It's programmed for free long distance in the U.S. and has my number, Hugo and Monserrat's number, and your apartment manager's number, in contacts. I have the same phones in the limo for Hugo and Monserrat, also pre-programmed. They will handle most of the apps you might want, including Wi-Fi and email. When Hugo signs his contract you can buy your iPhones and accessories, meanwhile, this should work for now. Tomorrow morning at 9:00, I have a lawyer and guidance counselor coming here to set up contacts with the universities you're interested in. I have DVD's of four of your better games in the Olympics and Pan-American games to send to any interested coaches. The lawyer will make the contacts much like a parent or high school coach would. The guidance counselor will assist you with any transcripts and testing. Your proficiency in English will help you immensely."

"Thank you, Alejandro. And Hugo … none of this would be possible without you, *mi amigo*," said Pedro.

"I'll call you when we get settled with our new address. You can taxi over and see our condo, and we'll get some dinner later," said Hugo.

"Here's $300, Pedro. I'm going to set up a bank checking account and credit card for Hugo tomorrow morning, right after I introduce you to your advisers. You will have to work out your own financial deal with Hugo, but the apartment's paid for until he signs a contract."

"Maybe you can help me find a part-time job until I get in school, Alejandro?"

"Now there's a refreshing concept — let's see how it goes."

Fifteen minutes later the limo turned off US 1 north onto Broad Causeway and drove over the water towards Bal Harbor. Monserrat's eyes were popping out of her head just checking out the real estate.

"Your condo is about two blocks south on Bay Harbor Island right on the canal. There's a Publix supermarket about six blocks east in Surfside, a Starbucks coffee shop five blocks away, and all the Bal Harbor shops like Michael Kors, Gucci, Tory Burch, and Neiman Marcus further up. There are numerous restaurants within easy walking distance on A1A — from pizza to seafood to filet mignon. Most of them deliver."

The Water Club third floor condo was old but well maintained and had a large canal-side pool with a sundeck out over the water. The living room opened out through a sliding glass door to a deck furnished with a round table and four chairs.

"Call me if you need me. I had your refrigerator and pantry stocked with some essentials; *cerveza*, *Coca-Light*, water, coffee, milk, butter, eggs, bacon, bread, cold cuts, cheese, a couple tomatoes, and lettuce. Also, potato chips, pretzels, mayo, mustard, and catsup — plus Italian dressing, hot dogs, buns, and a half gallon of vanilla *gelato*. After we go to the bank tomorrow and take Monserrat to Publix, I'll help you interview a couple of agents. Later, I'll take both of you to the gym I set-up for you — it's on A1A."

"Sounds good, I need to work out, but really … I was in top shape when we left."

"The sooner you get an agent and have the scouts' watch you hit and field, the quicker you get the contract you deserve. It's good for everyone. Here's $500 in cash until we go to the bank tomorrow."

"Thanks, and thanks for helping out Pedro. If it wasn't for him … I'd still be sitting in Cuba," said Hugo.

"If you're happy, Hugo, I'm happy — read your phone instructions and have a good night. *Mañana, mi amigo.*"

The next morning Hugo and Montserrat ran two miles on North Miami Beach.

"This reminds me of Cuba a little," said Monserrat as they jogged along the water's edge.

"*Sí,* most of the buildings are old, but well cared for, and this is the same ocean. We're only 200 miles from Havana. Let's run back to the condo and take a swim. Alejandro will be coming over soon."

"So far almost everybody here speaks Spanish."

"I noticed, but speak English. The big bucks for us are in English. Someday I will be on TV saying, 'I am Hugo Lugo and I drive a *Chef-rrolay. Merde*! I'll never learn to say that word without an accent."

"Hey, you're doing fine, Hugo. All Tony Perez ever learned to say was, '*Biesabol has bean bery, bery, gude to mi*'."

Alejandro arrived at 10:30 and whisked Hugo to the local SunTrust Bank, after dropping Monserrat off at the Bal Harbor Shoppes, with $200 and her new phone, to check out the shopping.

"She won't get in too much trouble with only $200 in **those** stores," said Alejandro with a wink as he and Hugo headed for the bank.

When the banking was finished they called Monserrat and met her at the Starbucks a half of block away.

"Your credit card should come in the mail in two days and your checks in about five. You have ten temporary checks and an ATM number. How was the shopping, Monserrat?"

"The clothes and the shoes are unbelievable, but so are the prices. I bought a new bikini and some nice underwear."

"There are more reasonable stores like Macy's and Dillard's in Miami. Let's get some lunch now. We have to meet the first agent, Alex Esteban, at his office at 1:30."

After a lunch at Flanagan's Grill, and a Publix drive-by, they dropped Monserrat at the condo and headed for Alex Esteban's office in Miami Shores.

His plush offices were filled with memorabilia and photographs of baseball legends and his own clients.

After greeting and salutations, the athletic looking Alex went right to work.

"Hugo, I'm not the cheapest and not the most expensive agent in baseball. I'll work for you for 5%. That will include your signing bonus, contract, and any endorsements we can set up for you. Your command of English will help you with your fans and sponsors. Do you have any questions?"

"Do you represent any Cuban players now?"

"Yes, outfielder Alexander Perez, who's playing in Japan right now, but he will soon get a contract in the U.S. Also, Danny Arroyo who pitches for the Kansas City Royals, Escobar Yunel, a shortstop for the Toronto Blue Jays, and José Inglesias, another shortstop who plays for the Boston Red Sox."

"I played next to Escobar on the Industriales in Havana. He defected while playing in Canada along with Noel Argolis from the 2008 Cuban National Junior team."

"I represent Noel too. He had shoulder surgery last year and hopefully will be playing with the Royals this season. Here is Escobar's phone number, call him and ask about me."

"What is the largest contract you ever negotiated?"

"I won't go into names or exact amounts, but I have three clients now who have multi-year packages of over 50 million dollars, and that doesn't count endorsements."

"What do you think you can get for me?"

"Well, a good fielding third baseman that hits for a high average and has power is valuable. Think Mike Schmidt, George Brett, Chipper Jones, and Wade Boggs. The best third baseman right now is Evan Longoria at the Tampa Bay Rays. I'd bet that his next contract will be worth 100 million dollars for ten years. I think I can get you a 3-4 million signing bonus and a minimum of 25 million for a five year deal. Your stats, base stealing ability, and clutch hitting with the Industriales is well known to the scouts. If you keep your nose clean, play well, do some charity gigs, and talk to the reporters, I can get you several more million in endorsements within a couple of years."

"I need some batting practice."

"Your syndicate indicated to me that you are in top shape since you just finished your Cuban season leading your team to the Cuban championship. I have arranged with a high school coach friend of mine for you to work out at Miami Edison High School's baseball complex. The Miami Marlins batting practice pitcher will help us out. I can schedule a work out at Marlins Park in a week or so for the scouts, and then schedule another one at Dodgers Stadium in Los Angeles. After that, the bidding will begin. One other thing to remember, Hugo. I have assembled a staff here to pay your bills, invest your money, give you advice on cars, buy your insurance, and help you buy and sell homes and boats. We'll even put you on an allowance to insure you have the money to retire. And … an independent CPA firm audits everything we do for you."

"What made you become a baseball agent, Alex?" asked Alejandro.

"I played baseball from the third grade all the way through college. I was drafted by the Yankees, but I chose Harvard Law School instead. Could I have made it? Probably not … but I'll never know. This is as close as I can get to the game I love."

"Thanks for your candor, Alex. I have another appointment set up for Hugo in an hour with Roland Alvarez."

"It was a pleasure meeting you, Hugo, and thank you, Alejandro, for the opportunity. Roland Alvarez is a good agent. If you decide to work with me, Hugo, I'm ready to shift into high gear."

They all shook hands and Alejandro and Hugo were on their way to Coral Gables to interview Roland.

"I liked him, Alejandro, and I could tell he loved baseball. I'll call Escobar when we're through with Mr. Alvarez."

"He is passionate about it and he has a good reputation."

"The way he's set up, I could concentrate on baseball and leave the details to him, and I like the CPA review."

They were ushered right into Roland's office by a pretty young secretary who had a radiant smile and a figure that wouldn't quit.

Roland was a little older than Alex and sported a comfortable paunch and a neatly trimmed mustache. He seemed laid back and had his diplomas hung on the wall, University of Florida, and Stetson Law School in St. Petersburg.

"It's a pleasure to meet you, Hugo. I've been going over your latest statistics from Cuba. You had quite a season!"

"Thank you, Mr. Alvarez, I'm anxious to give the major leagues a try."

"Your command of English is excellent, Hugo. It will be an asset. Please call me Roland."

"One thing that Cuba does have is excellent schools. I worked hard at English looking forward to this day."

"Let's get to business, my fee is 4% of your signing bonus and contract. I have fee-based services for investments, personal secretary services for bill paying, hotels, and tickets. I will personally negotiate any major purchases you make if you want me to. I'll also set up an east coast and west coast hitting and fielding exhibition at two major league fields for the scouts and general managers. Then we will review offers from the interested clubs."

"What do you think I'm worth?"

"If you have good workouts in front of the scouts, maybe 20 million over five years and at least 2 million for signing, maybe more . You should be in top shape having just finished your Cuban season."

"I just need some hitting and fielding practice over the next week or so. Another question, do you have any Cuban clients?"

"Yes, Yuniesky Castillo with Kansas City, and Juan Cuesta, the pitcher, with Philadelphia. I would be happy to make you my third."

"I'm going to make my mind up quickly. Can I have Yuniesky and Juan's telephone numbers?"

"I'll call them, get their permission, and forward them to Alejandro."

"Okay, Roland, thank you very much," said Hugo standing up and extending his right hand.

Hugo was quiet on the ride back to the condo.

"You're thinking it over — what do you think at this point, Hugo?"

"They were both good, but I'll make my mind up after calling Escobar, Yuniesky, and Juan. Alex has more services and a set fee, and Roland never mentioned endorsements. Also, Alex has workouts already planned for me here."

"Call the players, then get back to me," said Alejandro as he stopped in front of the condo and let Hugo out. "If you want to interview another agent we can arrange that too."

Monserrat was sunbathing by the pool, so Hugo went up to the condo and called Escobar. He was on the phone for almost 45 minutes catching up with Escobar and filling him in on his defection.

"So, you like Alex, and you wouldn't change agents?"

"*Si*, Hugo, he treats me like his own son."

"Well, I liked him too. I'm glad to hear you live in Ft. Lauderdale in the winter. I wondered how cold it got up there in Toronto."

"Too cold for my wife and me. I met her in Florida. She was born here but her family came from Columbia. I'll call you back when she gets home and I can check our calendar. We'll come down and go out to dinner with you and Monserrat. Tell her, *Hola*."

Hugo got ahold of Yuniesky in Kansas City and got a good report on Roland, but a lukewarm report about his personal secretary and investment services. Juan didn't answer and Hugo didn't bother to leave a message. His mind was made up. He would call Alejandro and tell him his agent would be Alex.

***

Dave the Wave leaned back in a dining room chair and drained his second *cerveza* of the night. Dinner was over and a lively conversation concerning the suitability of women participating in military combat operations was in progress. Since he was the only non-Cuban at the table he thought discretion would be the better part of valor — so he kept his mouth shut. He also reminded himself he was there for the sex, so why make enemies. Modesto was dead set against co-ed combat, conceding only female equality with weapons - until they had to go hand to hand. The speed and strength argument was a good one, but Consuelo cited the success the Israeli army has had with its mixed brigades. Modesto countered with the fact that a woman's physical weakness compared to a larger man could put other soldiers in that platoon in danger.

"What do you think, Dave?" asked Consuelo.

"Well, .. Ahh … I.." hemmed and hawed Dave, while trying to think of something to change the subject. "I think there are more important things to consider in an English class such as this."

"Such as what?" asked Consuelo.

"Well, consider this … why is the human male the only mammal or primate on this earth that doesn't have a penile bone? All the others do — monkeys, apes, bears, horses, dogs, whales, and rhinoceros, etc. So we should be discussing … ***How does the penis get hard when there ain't no bone?***"

The three young girls all looked at each other and started giggling. Consuelo and Modesto cracked up laughing and she said, "Are you making this up, Dave?"

"No, Mistress Consuelo, let's retire to your office and look it up on your computer."

"Okay, we will," said Consuelo. "Modesto, you can handle the flash cards and tests tonight. We'll correct the test papers later. Dave and I will be back shortly."

Consuelo started the computer in her office and hit her Google icon. Dave typed in *penile bone* and 12 articles popped up. The first one was titled – *'The Human Penis Is A Puzzler, No Bones About It!'* They both read through it and Dave was right on.

"You couldn't have picked a better question to change the subject, you sly fox. Let's do some research right here," said Consuelo as she cleared the top of her desk with a swoop of her arm and stepped out of her slacks.

Dave undressed while Consuelo locked the office door and stripped off the rest of her clothes. Her unfettered breasts swung invitingly as she sat on the edge of her desk and pulled him towards her. Dave scrambled up, and she gasped as their bodies met. The two beers at dinner gave Dave some staying power as she moved beneath him. When they finished … they both were soaking wet with perspiration.

"It's amazing what a change of scenery can do for the old libido," said Dave grinning.

"I'll have a fond memory every time I sit down at my desk," smiled Consuelo, as she ran her fingers through his long blond hair.

"Go back and check on the English class and send Luciana back here," said Consuelo.

"Capital idea," said Dave thinking about the nubile girls waiting for him in the lounge. Another beer, a couple of oysters, 20 minutes rest, and he'd be ready for another tryst. Variety was the spice of life.

Later, when Consuelo and Luciano returned from their "bondage" session, she asked Dave to go to her office and grade that night's tests.

After Dave left to grade the tests, Modesto asked Consuelo to step back into one of the alcoves. The prostitutes were busy eating what was left on the buffet table and quaffing the remaining *cervezas*.

Modesto handed her the note scraps and told her where he found them. "I've been questioning him whenever there's an opportunity, and he seems to be innocent. He doesn't have ties or friends in Tampa. But somebody slipped him a note on our latest Havana trip … maybe the DGI can figure something out from these pieces I retrieved?"

CHAPTER TEN

TAR BABY plowed through the large Atlantic swells again, the morning after their first Key West outing. The wind had subsided to 15 knots and was clocking to the northeast. Seth trolled right outside the reef working east past Western and Eastern Sambo towards Pelican Shoal. They missed two long-rigger bites while zig-zagging up to windward. He finally turned the boat on top of a swell, surfed down into the trough, and headed downwind. Seth throttled back some and continued to head west. John hooked a sail on the right flat line after Seth wound the teaser away from the lit-up fish. Shortly after that fish was released, Gene pitched a bait at a sailfish tailing down a swell next to the boat and got a hookup and a release.

When the sun rose higher in the sky, Seth yelled down to the crew to pull the spread in and get two kites ready. He turned *TAR BABY* into the wind and the crew deployed two Aftco® kites, one through the left rigger and the other through the right rigger. Gene, then Scotty, clipped their lines with a circle-hooked live goggle-eye attached at the business end, through the kite's Blacks® release clip — as Freddy and John let the kites out from the short kite rods located on the rocket launcher. Gene and Scotty held the live bait rods ready to let more line out to keep the goggle-eyes splashing on the water's surface when the puffy wind lifted the kites. Seth kept the bow pointed into the wind by bumping the transmission in and out of gear at idle speed. Once everything was set up right and the kites were 150 feet or so from the transom, the "outriggers" in the sky worked their magic. As the wind puffed, the baits splashed in and out of the water. They were hooked just behind their dorsal fins. The splashing and commotion on the top of the water sounded like a dinner bell to the voracious sailfish. It didn't take long before both rigs were hooked up. Freddy and John reeled in the kites, and Seth maneuvered the boat to release the doubleheader. The drop-back off the kite clip was usually long enough to affect a hook-up. If the bite didn't release the line out of the clip — the angler dropped the line back for a 5 count.

The crew switched positions and caught 12 more sailfish out of 17 bites using the kites, and also put a couple of wahoo in the fish box before Seth called it a day.

"Sixteen sails and two nice wahoo, not a bad day for a bunch of old Geezers," crowed John as the crew rinsed the gear and put it away.

"And — we're not wet and cold like we were yesterday. I think the wind is down to 12 knots now," added Gene.

"It's only 1:00 o'clock, why don't we just hose the boat off and have a late lunch ashore?" asked Seth. "Everybody get a brewski."

They all gave him a thumbs up, so he throttled up and was back at the dock in 20 minutes. On the way in Seth called Lori.

"Hey Seth, I wondered when you were going to call me. I did get your phone message and then your text. But I like to hear your voice. Have you been fishing? It's been windy up here."

"Sixteen sails and two nice wahoo, today. The wind laid down to 12 knots this afternoon."

"Ooh, good numbers. Are you having fun?"

"We all are, but I miss you a lot. Is everything all right?"

"Everything is fine. But, I miss you too, and I can't wait to see you on Valentine's Day. Call me after you go fishing next time, Love."

After hosing down the boat, they drove over to Stock Island's Hurricane Hole Marina where the Waterfront Bar and Seafood Grill is located. The Waterfront had great burgers and terrific mahi tacos. After lunch, Seth sipped a cold Rolling Rock® beer brewed in Latrobe, Pennsylvania.

"I haven't had a "Stone" since I left The University of Virginia," said Seth to Freddy. "I bet Bobby Thompson drinks Rolling Rock down in D.C. I've been talking to him about Dave the Wave."

"So, have you figured out how to get Dave out of Cuba?"

"I told Gene, before you got here, that Bobby has some agents in Cuba. They've been watching Dave, and they say he's all right. But, he's being held in a heavily guarded prison work camp a couple hours west of Havana in tobacco country. Somehow they got a note to Dave telling him that we're trying to figure a way out for him."

"You said he got seven years for some trumped up charge, didn't you?" asked John.

"Right, one of their star baseball players, in Havana, framed him — claimed he tried to talk him into defecting."

"Bobby says the ballplayer has tried to defect three times before but was caught each time. Fingering Dave was a way to get the commies to trust him again. He's apparently a helluva ballplayer and would make millions if he ever got to the U.S."

"Tell them about Dave's delivery job, Seth," said Gene.

"Bobby's head agent in Havana told him that they transferred Dave out of the fields. He'd been harvesting tobacco 12 hours a day. He's working on a truck now, loading and unloading tobacco all over that Province with a trustee driver. They only have a guard with them when they drive to Havana once or twice a week. I scoured the area on Google Earth. There are only a few roads in that area of tobacco farms, but one leads down to a little bay town that has a river that runs through a mangrove swamp alongside the road. A small boat could run up the river a couple of miles and only be 12 miles from their local pickup route. If we had a couple of motor scooters on the boat, we could intercept the delivery truck. Bobby's agents would give us the truck's location by sat-phone."

"How would we handle the trustee?"

"Bobby's Havana agent knows him from the elite elementary and high schools, and he is sure he would defect. His Russian wife and Cuban-born kids are back in Russia. If he doesn't want to go for some reason, I don't think he'd try and stop us, we'd just tie him up and leave him with the truck ... Freddy, when you sailed your Irwin 68 through the Gulf of Batabano a couple of years ago, did you stop at the San Felipe Cays near Punta de Cartas?"

"Yes, we anchored there for a couple of nights."

"Was the anchorage good?"

"It was OK," said Fred. "The mainland and mountains protect the little bay there called *Bahia de Cortes*, but a current sets your beam to the wind. You need two anchors like you do in the Bahamas ... you have to kedge one to keep your bow into the wind."

"Was there any enforcement or customs out there?"

"Not really, you don't have to check in anywhere, but they have a ranger station there. A ranger in a small outboard came by just to say hello. There's three or four of them at the ranger station — they switch out every two weeks like our Coast Guard guys on Loggerhead Key in the Dry Tortugas. They're about twelve miles from Punta de Cartas. He told us they were just there to protect the birds and wildlife, like iguanas. The local people coming over from the mainland were wiping everything out for food. They were very friendly, we gave him a bottle of rum we bought in Cienfuegos for three dollars."

"I've got the fuel usage all figured out. We'd have to go from here to Cancun, then San Felipe, and straight back to Key West from San Felipe. We'll need an inflatable Zodiac®, with a 60 HP outboard. I can have Defender Marine ship one here to Safe Harbor. Key West Suzuki has the four-stroke in stock. We can store the deflated Zodiac package on the foredeck in front of the life raft. The outboard can be stowed behind two 55 gallon plastic fuel drums against the cockpit cabin bulkhead. I also located two Honda Ruckus scooters at Keys Motorsports. They have big off-road tires, so we can go overland in case we run into roadblocks," said Seth.

"Where would you stow the scooters? They have to weigh a couple of hundred pounds apiece," said Freddy.

"One aft in the cockpit in front of the fighting chair. We'd have to stow the chair footrest in front of the flybridge steering console. The second one goes in the salon. I'd unscrew the dining table from the base and lash the scooter to it. We could still use the salon couch with a little difficulty. If it gets really rough or we feel crowded on the run home — we can always jettison the two scooters."

"If we have good weather we might want to tow the Zodiac with the scooters in it, and put the drum diesel in the tanks as soon as possible. Then cut the drum tops off and jettison them," said Scotty.

"All good ideas," said Freddy. "How are we going to move all of this heavy stuff around and put the engine on the Zodiac?"

"*TAR BABY* has a gin pole," said Gene. "Seth still has the old block and tackle and stainless crane stowed under the flybridge cowling."

"How are we going to pay for all the equipment and fuel, split it up?" asked John.

"No, I'm going to front all the equipment and fuel," said Seth. "Everybody that goes will keep an expense report like we did when we recovered Charley Blevins' *ABOUT TIME*. We'll chip in and keep track of the incidentals. If Hugo Lugo defects and gets a contract in the U.S., I'll make him an offer he can't refuse and we'll all recoup our expenses and get paid for our time ... plus we'll get Dave the Wave some financial compensation. Hopefully without a lot of wasted time and legal fees. Anybody interested besides Gene?"

"Well, I'm getting too old to back out now," said John. "And … I spent quite a few years' sailboat racing and drinkin' beer with Dave the Wave. Count me in."

"I've spent the last couple of years sailing my big boat around the Caribbean and sailing in survival single-handed marathon races, but I've never approached the adrenalin rush I got jammin' the rotating draw-bridge on Providenciales and watching that Suburban explode right above me," said Freddy. "Count me in too, Seth."

All eyes turned to their new crew member, Scotty.

"Gentlemen, I don't know Dave as well as you do, but I've sailed against him, hoisted a few brews with him, admired his taste in women, and envied his laid-back lifestyle. If the same thing happened to me, I'd hope the Geezers would come after me too. I'm honored to be asked, and I humbly accept."

The four original Geezers thumped Scotty on the back and welcomed him aboard. When everyone calmed down Seth said, "It will take at least two-to-three weeks to assemble and test our equipment, and remember, we have the girls coming down to Sunset Key for our Valentine's Day weekend. If the weather cooperates, Dave's extraction should take seven to ten days beginning to end. I'm going to ask Charley Blevins when he comes down to fish with us next week if he'll shadow us in case we have a breakdown or need another boat for any reason. I wish we could get Dino Vino, Captain Toby, or Billy Chandler to crew with him, but they all have fishing tournament and diving commitments through the spring. I think Jeb will ride with Charley if I ask him. Let's think about who might fit in."

"Do you want to go fishing tomorrow, Seth?" asked John.

"Sure … do you?"

"Well, all of a sudden it doesn't seem as important. The wind's about gone until the next front comes through. Why don't we get the Honda scooters, order the Zodiac, and buy the Suzuki outboard before it's gone? We need to get traveling covers for the scooters, and outboard. Let's test the scooters on some tough terrain — Sheriff Billy Ray probably has a place we can ride them off the road. Then we'll fish the next front … by then we should have the Zodiac to assemble, inflate, and test run. How long is it?"

"Seventeen and a half feet long, with 22 inch diameter tubes," said Seth.

"Wow, a big one! We can practice installing the outboard with the gin pole and practice moving the other heavy stuff around *TAR BABY'S* cockpit. And … there's nothing wrong with drinkin' a little beer and kickin' back either," said John.

"It all sounds good to me, guys. Let's go back to the boat and get started," said Fred.

Seth fired up his computer, ordered the Zodiac from Defender, and got two-day free shipping. Then Scotty and John drove Seth to Keys Motorsports where he bought the two black Honda Ruckus motor scooters, along with two helmets and two storage covers.

"How long to install the GP6 performance packages and extended seats?" asked Seth.

"Comeback in two hours and you can drive them home," said the salesman.

"What about license plates?" inquired John.

"I do that right here too. Sign these forms and give me $50 for both, and I'll have the registrations ready and the plates on the scooters when you get back."

Scotty drove back to Key West Suzuki on Stock Island and Seth bought the 60 HP four-stroke outboard. It took all three of them to lift it into the back of Scotty's Land Rover. When they got it back to Safe Harbor, Seth walked over to Joe O'Donnell's warehouse along the south docks and knocked on his door.

"Well, Seth Stone — it's been awhile." They shook hands and Joe said, "C'mon in."

"I see you're still living in a Costa Rican rain forest," laughed Seth — referring to the huge Banyan tree that occupied the inside of Joe's living space in the two story warehouse.

"Yeah, I'd sure like to live down there near Lake Arenal, but this is the next best thing. What brings you back to Safe Harbor, Seth?"

"I'm over in one of Charley's slips with some of the Geezers. His boat's going in the yard for a couple of weeks. We came down to sailfish, but I have a little business to take care of in Cuba in a few weeks and I need your help."

"Hmmn, business in Cuba," said Joe with a smile. "How can I help?"

"I need a space to store a seventeen and a half foot Zodiac, a 60 HP outboard, and two 150cc motor scooters until we leave after Valentine's Day."

"I have some space that just opened up in unit #2, just this side of the restaurant. An A/C outfit that needed more room moved out. You can use it for free if you don't mind some dust. My guys are going to clean it up to get it ready to rent."

"No problem, I'll get a couple of tarps at Home Depot to throw over our stuff. Want to go fishin'?"

"Thanks, but no. The new Mega Yacht Marina and commercial village is keeping me busy, and I'm still helping Robbie spruce up his boatyard over there. Image is important to these high-dollar yachtsmen. But, I will accept any wahoo or tuna you might steer my way. I still remember the fish fry you put on last time you were here."

"I remember both of the women you brought … it would have been tough to make a choice."

"I couldn't make my mind up either," laughed Joe as he opened a key keeper behind a cluttered desk. "Here's a key to that unit."

"Thanks for the favor. I'll drop some wahoo off later — we caught two nice ones today," said Seth as he left.

Scotty drove Seth and Freddy back to Keys Motorsports and they picked up the motor scooters. After a quick checkout with the salesman, they took off up Southard Avenue and headed for Safe Harbor.

At the first stoplight, Freddy said, "This puppy has some pep, and I like the wide tires."

"I think they might run better than 50 miles an hour with two big guys on them, and still get more than 100 miles per gallon. I want to stop at Home Depot and buy two tarps. "

"OK, I can't wait to try these off the road."

The Geezers put the scooters and Suzuki outboard in Joe's warehouse and covered them with one of the tarps.

That night they grilled wahoo and enjoyed the balmy weather. Safe Harbor Marina's quaint picnic and grilling area was a good place to be. Seth and the whole crew had learned to clean their wahoo and mahi on the boat. If they cleaned them at the marina's fish cleaning station they were overwhelmed with "zip-lock" fisherman (ie. marina residents and regular bar patrons who sidle up to kibitz and admire your catch. However, somewhere during the conversation they will ask for a filet, and produce a zip-lock bag from their back pocket). Scotty invited the two veterinary assistants, who were by this time quite tan and on their last night of vacation, to dinner. They wanted to crawl Duval their last night but couldn't get any takers besides Scotty. The Geezers had a night cap, but Scotty felt duty-bound to show the girls a good time and went off downtown.

The next morning Seth took a steaming mug of coffee up into the flybridge. He dialed Billy Ray's cellphone and got through immediately.

"Why Seth, how are you?"

"I feel great, Billy, I had my bad knee replaced about three months ago, and I feel 50 years old again. I've got *TAR BABY* docked over in Safe Harbor and we've been sailfishing."

"I hear it's been good."

"So far that's true. Charley Blevins is coming in to fish with us just before the next cold front. I'm hoping you'll come fish with us too."

"You won't have to twist my arm. I can use a little R&R before the spring-breakers start driving us crazy."

"We're going to stay until after Valentine's Day, and then we have a little expedition to help a friend in Cuba — that's on the QT."

"I understand … you always seem to have something going on under the radar."

"I guess it seems that way, but I just don't like to see my friends get the short end of the stick when they don't deserve it. I'll fill you in later. I'll firm up a fishing date after I see the long term weather forecast. We'll probably go in three or four days — like the second day after the next front comes through."

"Sounds good to me. I'm looking forward to seeing you and the boys."

"I have a question for you. We need to practice some off-road riding on a couple of Honda Ruckus motor scooters that I just bought. We'll need them in Cuba."

"The county has an off-road course set up behind Mount Trashmore, and we also use the Air Force's facility over on Boca Chica. I can get you on both."

"How about today."

"No problem. I can have Big Dog meet you later. He has some time on his hands right now."

"Nothing serious, I hope."

"He had to kill a perp during a SWAT team arrest, so he's on administrative leave for two months. It should only be a formality, but the perp was connected. He kidnapped his estranged his wife and child and held them at gunpoint. We knew he had a long record of substance abuse and mental problems. After a four hour standoff, Big Dog heard him cock his revolver. So he was forced to make a move … Big Dog shot him just as the perp raised his gun to shoot the wife. The perp's parents are in denial, after being vilified by the press for bailing him out … time after time. They hired a big-time, mouthy lawyer out of Miami."

"Typical bull-shit, huh?"

"Right! Call me around lunchtime. I'll set you up at both places."

***

Hugo hit another ball over the left field fence at Miami Edison's practice field. His agent, Alex, sat behind the screen at home plate recording each hit.

"That's enough hitting for one day," shouted Alex. "Let's field some ground balls."

Hugo retrieved his new glove and trotted out to third base. Edison High School's star pitcher Luis Gonzmart wiped his brow with his forearm and said, "I'm glad I don't have to face you in a real game, Hugo."

"Hey, your slider was tough to hit and when your fastball hopped you made me hit it on the ground. Keep working on that curve ball and you'll be tough for anybody to hit."

The Edison High coach, Barry Hemphill, walked out of the dugout towards home plate with another canvas bag of balls and a bat.

"Luis, get your first baseman's mitt and field Hugo's throws at first. I'm going to hit some grounders to test his range."

He signaled to the two young outfielders he had shagging Hugo's power strokes to come in closer to third base.

Barry turned to Alex behind the screen.

"These boys are having the time of their lives practicing with a player like Hugo, Alex. Thanks."

"No, **thank you** for making this happen, I hope we can do this a couple more times before his scout's workout at the Marlin's Stadium next week."

"No problem Alex — it's offseason and it's a great experience for these boys."

"I want you to bring them along to shag, but I'm going to use Jack Russell, the Marlin's batting practice pitcher, for that workout. He still has a formidable fastball."

"Yeah, he has a good one!" said Barry.

Hugo gobbled up the first grounder and threw a clothes-line strike to Luis. Barry mixed it up and tested Hugo's considerable range.

"You've got a winner here, Alex," said Barry, a little out of breath after 15 minutes of hitting grounders. "He's going to get a big contract."

Hugo took a breather, then ran some wind sprints with the high school boys. Then he ran around the bases four times with Barry's stop watch on him, and the workout was over.

"He runs the bases as well as he hits and fields ... his best time around the bases was 14 seconds flat. He'll steal a lot of bases, and turn an outfield single into a double - if the outfielder loafs at all. He's a natural," said Barry to a grinning Alex.

"How about another practice ... day after tomorrow?"

"Same time — you got it."

"I'll e-mail out his practice stats to all the head scouts tonight. I already sent his Cuban season statistics to all the clubs yesterday. He had a 67% slugging average today, and half of them were homers. Wait until they see his time running the bases. I bet we'll have nearly all 30 teams represented at the workout next week."

CHAPTER ELEVEN

SCOTTY woke up with a start and realized he was lying naked in the queen-size bed all by himself. He rubbed his eyes and tried to ignore the tequila generated headache that was fogging his memory. Finally, he looked around the floating cottage's small bedroom and focused on a note that was taped on the mirror above the dresser. Scotty slowly rolled out of bed and snatched the note off the mirror. *Dearest Dr. Remington, We had to catch an early flight back to Detroit and didn't have the heart to wake you. Thank you for getting us through our sunburn episode, and for you and your friends' hospitality. We had a wonderful time with you, especially last night after the Duval crawl. Look in the mirror and you'll see what we mean. If you ever get to Detroit, here are our phone numbers 313-433-5552-Judy and 313-443-4327-Alexis. P.S. We knew you weren't really a Doctor, but we didn't care – you're really quite a guy!*

He stood in front of the mirror and recoiled at what he saw. The girls had circled his nipples with bright red lipstick and just below that they had lettered NUMERO UNO across his lower abdomen. He took it as "just desserts," laughed, and headed for the shower to scrub it off. Scotty didn't remember much about last night after several tequila shots at the Hogs Breath, Sloppy Joes, and the Garden of Eden. But it appeared that everyone had a great time. The steaming water in the shower brought him back to reality and he looked forward to a hot, black cup of coffee and a ride on the souped-up Honda motor scooters that Seth had bought the day before.

"Hey, Scotty," said Seth as he walked up the steps into *TAR BABY'S* salon. "We thought you might have been kidnapped again by the Motor City girls."

"That's exactly what happened. Then they cut out of here early this morning to catch a flight back to Detroit … leaving me passed out to face a 'Tequila Sunrise' alone."

"Well," laughed Gene. "You got a lot of mileage out of them, and vice-versa."

"Yeah, they left me a note telling me they knew I wasn't a doctor — but they didn't care."

"Those two just wanted to have fun," said Seth. "Speaking of fun, Billy Ray called and we're setup over at the Mount Trashmore off-road vehicle course. Why don't you and I drive the scooters over? Gene, can you get Freddy and John and meet us there."

"Let's do it, but I need a cup of coffee and an English muffin first," said Scotty as he tossed Gene the Land Rover keys.

Later, Freddy and John returned from their first lap around Mount Trashmore's two-mile course and were elated at how the Hondas handled the terrain.

"Plenty of power and the wide tires gives them traction and stability," said John.

"Let's mix up the drivers, then try two men on each bike. That's the way we'll exit Pinar Del Rio Province. We'll run the scooters down the road or across the farmland to return to the Zodiac," said Seth.

After another hour it became apparent the Honda could exceed 50 mph on the straightaways with two riders.

"These scooters have really exceeded my expectations," said Seth. "Billy Ray has us cleared to use the Air Force's course on Boca Chica after 2:00 p.m. today — they were having some kind of training exercise there this morning. He says Boca Chica course is rougher in some spots and has some long, paved straightaways. Let's get some lunch over at Bobby Mongelli's Barbecue joint on Geiger Key. We have to drive right by it to get to the base's off-road course behind the runways."

The pulled pork was terrific at Bobby's and they all had iced tea instead of a beer. As they ate, Bobby came out of the kitchen with his manager, Sarah. He immediately recognized the Geezers from the Hogfish Bar.

"Hey, you guys are good for business, thanks for coming over."

"We've liked the barbeque here for years, Bobby," said Seth. "But we really like what you've done at the Hogfish since you bought it. Your new menu and the guest chefs are great. I even think the hogfish sandwich is better … if that's possible."

"After I bought it, I found out that everything was being cooked on a George Foreman electric grill or it was deep fried. I updated the kitchen equipment, the chef stepped up, and I was able to expand the menu. Joe O'Donnell helped me get six slips next to the restaurant and that increased my traffic. Business is good, and we haven't lost our Stock Island regulars or our Old Key West flavor."

After lunch, they drove down to the Boca Chica Base rear gate and arrived at the off-road training course. Freddy and Seth took the first turn around the five mile course. They came roaring back six minutes later neck and neck.

"You guys averaged almost 50 mph."

"Man," said Freddy, wiping some mud off his face. "It has bigger moguls, a couple of banked turns, and some shallow water hazards, as you can see."

"This course is better practice for what I am anticipating in Cuba," said Seth.

Everyone took a couple of turns before calling it a day. Seth and Scotty drove the Hondas back to Safe Harbor and hosed them off behind TAR BABY. They dried them off before putting them under cover in Joe's warehouse.

"Look what's in here," said Seth as he wheeled the scooter in. "Two big cartons ... it's the Zodiac I ordered from Defender — Joe must have had somebody put them in here with a forklift."

"How are we going to move the boat around? Didn't you say it weighs 325 pounds with the aluminum floor in it?"

"Six men can move it without the engine on it, but I've got two, four wheel V-cradle skate dollies shipping in from Amazon Prime®. They'll help us move it around on the dock. I also ordered a combo outboard cart/dolly from West Marine that will handle the 230 lb. Suzuki. We'll store the engine on it in the cockpit and then easily move it under the gin pole to install it on the boat in the water. We should be able to pick the cart up tomorrow."

"Are we going to carry the inflated Zodiac onto the foredeck?"

"Yes, I'm sure that five of us can slide it up and over the welded bow rail once the engine is removed. We can also tow the Zodiac with the engine on it at planing speeds because the aluminum floor has a keel structure that bolts underneath it. I have a 70-foot tow rope and bridle for it. But, if we have bad weather we'll turn it over, bottom side up, and lash her down on the foredeck."

Seth gathered up the rest of the crew, took his portable compressor, some tools, and a 12-pack of cold ones to the warehouse. There they assembled and inflated the Zodiac. Once it was together it looked awesome. It would easily carry six men and the two motor scooters. When they got the dollies and outboard cart they would put the package together in the water. The boys hit the showers and after another round of beers on TAR BABY drove to the Conch Republic Restaurant down in the Bight for a casual dinner.

***

Modesto pulled into their usual parking spot at the Santa Maria labor camp, and he and Dave headed for the showers. It had been a hot and humid day on the road picking up wrapper leaves that would be delivered to the

Havana cigar factories tomorrow. But tonight was English class, that wonderful respite from their monotonous days and nights of living in captivity.

Dave wondered how close to a mental breakdown he would be if it wasn't for the kinky Mistress Consuelo and her comely consorts. Maybe there would be a fresh face and body tonight to pique his imagination. Dave looked forward to the delicious food and a chance to drink a few *cervezas* and get a little buzz going.

Modesto found their exit pass under his pillow. They pulled their party clothes from their foot-lockers and were gone before the general population returned from the mess hall. A half hour later they were enjoying their oysters, lobster bisque, and a nice rare cut of beef tenderloin. The young girls were engaged in a debate about romance and finance. They were divided two against two. There was a new girl, named Rona. Clara was gone, having served her sentence. Rona and Marta were on the more practical side of the issue and felt there needed to be some balance. Even in a communist society, it seemed to matter. Camila and Luciana, who were taking the idealism side of the argument, would only marry for love. But they assumed an ideal society would take care of all of their needs. They all admitted the Cuban government only provided 50% of the material necessities; the rest came from hard work, connections, or illegal activity. Nothing was solved, but a lot of English was spoken. Mistress Consuelo was strangely preoccupied and after dinner, as her consorts worked with the flash cards, she moved close and whispered in Dave's ear, "I have something important to tell you, but I must talk to you alone. Finish up here as soon as possible, and we'll go to my office were we can talk privately."

Dave nodded and rushed through the flash cards. He and Consuelo took the written tests to her office, as Modesto put a new Julio Inglesias CD on the stereo and mixed drinks for the girls.

Dave followed Consuelo down the dark hall and into her office.

"I received word this week from General Machado that I will be transferred in a couple of weeks to Las Tunas Province to run the women's prisons there. I can get you transferred to a men's labor camp in Las Tunas to help with the sugar cane harvest. I know you have noticed men being transferred out of your Santa Maria work camp to the sugar cane areas. Until now, I made sure you weren't transferred. My question is, would you like to have Modesto transferred to Las Tunas with you?"

"Of course I would, we have become very good friends."

"I like him too, but not like I like you. I have arranged for you to work on the railroad train that runs from Las Tunas to Vazquez through Delciás to Puerto Carupano and back each day. You and Modesto would supervise the loading of the cut sugar cane at numerous locations on the way to the Delciás Sugar Mill."

"Sounds good to me. Will we have an English class in Las Tunas?"

"Absolutely, I'm taking Marta and Rona with me. There will be new girls in Las Tunas. You will leave in two weeks with Modesto."

"I'm ready when you are."

"Now take me on top of my desk like you did before," said Consuelo, as she started to undress. "But this time I want you to *bésame mucho!*"

"No Spanish, **Mistress** Consuelo — that's **your** rule," said Dave laughing.

"Climb up here, surfer boy, and I'll show you what I mean!"

Consuelo kissed Dave lustfully and cupped her hands on his lean buttocks. Dave responded to her passion and it felt like he was with a different woman … she finished quickly with a shudder — but kept the pace until Dave was spent.

Dave kissed her again and said, "Was it me or the desk, Consuelo?"

"I don't know, *Cariño,* but it was very good."

"Maybe you should move the desk to Las Tunas too?" laughed Dave.

They dressed quickly, joined the others, and Consuelo chose Camila. She whispered to Dave on the way out, "Why don't you tell Modesto about the transfer? I'm sure he'd like to hear it from you."

"I will."

Dave filled Modesto in on their impending move, which pleasantly surprised him. Then Dave suggested that Modesto engage Marta and Luciana, as they popped open two more beers. When Modesto was situated, Dave headed for the open alcove with Rona for some more Cuban horizontal cha-cha.

***

Scotty drove Seth down to West Marine on Caroline Street, near the Bight, to pick up the outboard engine cart. The rest of the crew was busy moving the Zodiac along the dock on the newly acquired skate dollies. The fully inflated and assembled Zodiac was positioned on the dock behind the Hatteras 46 when the Land Rover pulled back in.

"Scotty, why don't you and John go with Freddy and put the outboard on the cart?" said Seth as they unloaded the cart from the SUV's rear hatch. When the outboard was wheeled up, the boys removed the dollies under the Zodiac and slid it across the dock and dropped it down in the water.

"Heavy, but manageable," said Gene.

"The manufacturer designed it to be dragged over rocks — the fabric is three millimeters thick and double coated with Hypalon," said Seth.

The crew took the Suzuki off the cart and handed the cart down into the cockpit. All five of them wrestled the 230 lb. outboard into the cockpit and back onto the cart. Seth installed the crane and the block and tackle on top of the gin pole. Gene wheeled the bulky engine under the block and tackle.

"John, move the Zodiac over to the starboard side of the cockpit with the bow facing aft — then secure it fore and aft to the gunwale," said Seth.

Gene clipped the block and tackle hook to two slings that were fitted to the engine and lifted the engine clear of the cart, then up higher to clear the cockpit coaming. Scotty pushed the engine out over the Zodiac's stern. The crane rotated to the desired spot and Gene let the engine down on the plywood transom as John guided the bracket into place. He tightened the two clamps with a wrench until they were "good'n'tight".

"There's a gear bag forward with a foot-pump and patch kit, white and red/green flashlights, survival knives, whistles, flares, and a first-aid kit," said Seth.

Scotty and Gene handed down two 12 gallon Scepter® low profile gas tanks. John hooked the engine's battery cables to the Optima® Bluetop 34M 12 volt battery, then hooked the starboard fuel tank to the engine and squeezed the priming ball a few times. He turned the ignition key on the tiller and the engine started immediately.

"Nice," said Scotty. "Started on the first turn."

"There's 880 cranking amps in that battery. Everybody get your foul weather jacket, climb aboard, and let's see what this air-bag will do," said Seth as he boarded the sleek black Zodiac.

Freddy laughed, threw a life jacket bag aboard, and they were ready to rumble.

John idled out of the marina and shifted in and out of gear to familiarize himself with the engine. Once they passed the power plant, John put the boat up on plane. They sped past the Oceanside Marina Channel, and when they entered Hawk Channel John increased the speed again.

Seth had his handheld GPS with him and said, "We're running at 25 mph. Turn downwind, John, and pick up the pace some more."

"That's ¾ throttle, Seth," said John when he had twisted it up.

"We're running 35 mph with a load of about 1500 lbs. That's not even half the payload. When we add the two scooters at 200 lbs. each, it might cut our speed five miles an hour. Turn upwind and see what we can do ... there's about 10 knots of wind right now."

John decelerated, turned, and slowly worked up to full throttle. The boat started to bounce a little in the one foot chop.

"Forty-five mph," said Seth holding on to his hat. "Take her down to about 40 and take some small turns."

The Zodiac turned smoothly at 40 mph, and Seth motioned for John to head back to the marina.

Seth said to Gene and Freddy, "I think she'd do close to 40 mph in this calm sea, fully loaded. If the waves were bigger we'd have to slow down, but so would anything chasing us ... except maybe a Cigarette type racing boat."

"How much fuel will she use at cruising speed?" asked Gene.

"I figure five or six gallons an hour at 25 miles per hour, to be safe. She's not as heavy as a 17-foot flats boat when she's all loaded up."

They tied the Zodiac to Charley's dinghy dock at the floating cottage's back door.

"Hey, Charley's here," said Seth. "That's the jeep he keeps at the airport. He must have flown in while we were sea-trialing the Zodiac. I bet we'll find him at the Hogfish Bar."

"He probably flew in to beat the cold front here," said John.

"Let's leave the Zodiac in, I'd like to try it in some rough water," said Seth. "Even though Cortes Bay, in Cuba, is protected, think about how Tampa Bay kicks up in a blow."

"I'll go with you," said Freddy.

"We'll try it. We won't go fishing until the day after anyhow ...when it starts to knock down. Then the third day I want to take Billy Ray and his boys out fishing."

"That's a plan," said Gene. "Let's go find Charley."

They found Charley nursing a cold one at the Hogfish bar with Joe O'Donnell.

"Hey, Charley when did you get in?" said John.

"About an hour ago. I wanted to be on the ground well before the front comes through later tonight. There was a little headwind at first, but the flight only took an hour and forty-five minutes."

"Still have the Cessna 182?" asked Gene.

"Yeah, a nice, easy airplane - averaged 155 mph."

"Right, you get up in the 200 mph class like a Malibu or Bonanza — and the maintenance goes off the page," said John.

All the Geezers shook hands with Joe, and Scotty was introduced to him by Seth.

"Thanks for the wahoo, Seth," said Joe. "It was great — I grilled it rare with a little lime juice on it. I think I like it better than tuna."

"I agree."

"Are you going out tomorrow, the sails should be biting."

"No, we'll probably go out the day after next. Now, it's too rough, wet, and cold for us old guys. We'll wait a day for it to calm down a little, then maybe we'll get lucky again."

"I hope so. I saw your sexy black Zodiac in the warehouse. Are you guys going to overthrow a foreign government or something this go around?"

"Nothing that serious, Joe," laughed Seth. "We'll call it a little clandestine recovery mission."

"Well, good luck fishing. I've got to meet an electrician over at the mega-yacht docks ... we have a low voltage problem on one of the docks. See you later."

"Like my dad, Ol' Robert E. used to say, Joe, 'It's like a whore with a bloody nose ... If it ain't one thing, it's another'."

Seth sat down next to Charley while the boys ordered a round of cold beers, and filled him in on the Dave the Wave situation.

"I'm hoping that you will act as a backup boat during this operation. I'll get you a couple of crew members, like maybe my son Jeb, "Jingles" Jones, Doug Clorey, Norm Hogan, or Kevan Flinch."

"When exactly are you planning on doing it?" asked Charley.

"Right after Valentine's Day," answered Seth.

"I should be out of your yard by then, and my girls don't have Spring Break until right after Easter. I'll do it as long as I'm in Nassau, docked at Atlantis, by the first week in April."

"I don't see a problem and, remember, I'm banking on making expenses from Hugo Lugo if he defects."

"I'd do it anyhow. I raced against Dave for a lot of years and drank a lot of beer with him. Surfed with him a bit in the early days too. I consider him a friend, and I don't want to see you and our Geezer buddies stranded somewhere off the coast of Cuba."

"That's great, Charley — when you move *ABOUT TIME* down here after you're finished at the Boatworks, I'll move the Hatteras over on the wall."

"Can I get a ride in that inflatable tomorrow? I'm looking for a bigger tender."

"Freddy and I are taking it out in the morning to run it in some rough water."

"I'll come along. What does it weigh? My davit will pick up 1000 pounds."

"The dry weight with the Suzuki DF-60 HP four-stroke is less than 600 pounds."

***

Hugo Lugo started his workout at the Miami Marlins Stadium with a brief introduction of himself at home plate. Alex thought Hugo's command of English should be showcased. The scouts and general managers in attendance would understand he would not have any communication problems.

"Good afternoon, I'm Hugo Lugo-Ramirez and thank you all for coming to check-out my baseball skills. It has been my dream to play baseball in the United States major leagues. I will hit first, then field and throw, and finally, I will run the bases. Please see my agent, Alex Esteban, who is now standing and waving his business cards over his head, in the box behind home plate. You may take videos of this workout for your own use only. You all should have a copy of my biography and my Cuban League and tournament statistics. I am sure you remember the great Marlins pitcher, Jack Russell. He will pitch to me today. So let the games begin," said Hugo with a smile.

Hugo grounded the first two pitches up the middle. On the third pitch, he settled down and started to hit with power. In between homers and balls hit off the walls, he sprayed line drive hits up both power alleys. The uniformed Miami Edison outfielders scurried around fielding balls that hit the walls, line drives on their first and second hops, and the occasional fly ball at the base of the wall. Alex had arranged for snacks and refreshments in the stands, and the scouts applauded after each towering home run.

When the hitting exhibition was over, Hugo toweled off in the dugout and took a five minute breather.

Alex slipped down into the dugout and said, "Your hitting couldn't have been much better! I think the scouts are starting to salivate right about now. There are representatives from 27 teams here."

"Maybe, we won't need to go to California, Alex?"

"Oh, No, Hugo. We're going to be patient and let these guys bid you up. Go ahead and do the fielding now. The high school kids have moved the pitcher's screen."

"Jack Russell still has some heat on his fastball. It helped me get a few high ones over the fence. He threw me two sliders just to show me what he really had."

"He was the real deal. Go get 'em Hugo!"

Barry Hemphill hit grounders and a few line drives, and Luis manned first base. Hugo was on his game and showed great range and a strong, accurate throwing arm.

Then Alex walked up to the plate with the microphone and announced, "Okay, gentlemen, get your stop watches out. Hugo is going to circle the bases for you."

He dug a starting pistol from his pocket as the stadium's sound system played the theme from *Rocky*. Hugo picked up a bat and stood in the batter's box. Alex fired the starting pistol, Hugo threw the bat away and took off running. Fourteen seconds later he crossed home plate.

Hugo waved to the small crowd, and they gave him a hand. He shook hands with Coach Hemphill and all the Miami Edison High School players before disappearing into the dugout.

Alex turned the microphone and announced, "Thanks to all of you for coming. I look forward to hearing from those of you who are interested in signing Hugo to a contract. We do have another workout scheduled for early next week in Los Angeles to accommodate some scouts and executives who could not make this one. Again, thank you for coming."

Alex walked down through the dugout and into the Marlins locker room, just as Hugo came out of the shower.

"Lay low through the weekend. I mean go to your gym, and run on the beach, but no night clubs or any situations that could lead to bad publicity. Monday we leave for Los Angeles. I figure we'll have some offers by then, but if you have a good workout there, it'll jack everything up."

"Is Jack Russell pitching to me in Los Angeles?"

"No, we're going to use Dexter Simpson, a San Francisco AAA pitcher from the Sacramento River Cats. It's better if you hit against two different pitchers. Dexter lives in L.A. in the off-season, and he has good speed on his fastball, but it doesn't move much. I made a deal with the San Fernando High coach, Jack Guzman, whose players won the L.A. City championship last year, to bring his outfielders and first baseman. The coach will hit you ground balls."

"Thanks for all your help, Alex."

"I'm just doing my job. I want the maximum I can get for you. It makes my paycheck bigger too."

"I realize that, but I feel you have my best interests at heart."

"I do ... Now — low profile and keep your nose clean. If the sportswriters from the newspapers want to interview you, be polite — just give them my card and I'll talk to them. Here's a handful of cards. You're good under pressure, Hugo, that didn't go unnoticed."

CHAPTER TWELVE

DAVE the WAVE looked out the half open door of the slow moving boxcar. He and Modesto sat on their small footlockers with their backs against the wall and watched the countryside go by. There was straw on the floor if they wanted to sleep, and a guard was stationed in each boxcar. They peed out the half open door and the guard rationed the drinking water from a five gallon plastic pail. The distance from Pinar Del Rio to Las Tunas was 825 kilometers or 512 miles. There were 32 men in each boxcar, and Modesto figured the government transferred over 300 prisoners on this train to cut sugar cane in Las Tunas. When they stopped in Havana, they were allowed to use the *baños* and were given some rice and beans. The next stop, according to Modesto, would probably be Santa Clara.

Their spirits were not downtrodden, unlike their compatriots who had not taken this trip before. The old hands slept and talked among themselves, and the first timers fretted about moving to unknown surroundings and labors. Dave and Modesto were optimistic about their sugar cane train roles as labor gang foremen and hopeful that Consuelo's English class would not change much. No matter where you went it mattered more who you knew - than what you knew. Dave hoped that whoever had been watching him in Santa Maria and Havana would clue Seth in on his 500 mile change of location.

Modesto asked Dave, "I often wondered what Tampa and Ybor City are like? I am told there are many Cubans living there."

"Most of them came to work in the cigar industry 50 or 75 years before the 1959 Cuban Revolution. Now, the cigar business has shrunk from 150 factories to only a few factories that are still making cigars. Arturo Fuentes,

Tabanero, and J.C. Newman are still there, but Hav-A-Tampa just moved their factory to Puerto Rico. The 100,000 Cubans that live in Tampa have assimilated into all walks of the American way of life."

"What became of the factories?"

"Most were torn down for new construction, but the 20 or so that are left have restaurants, offices and large disco bars in them. I'm getting to old to go to them ... most of the discos don't open until 11:00 o'clock at night."

"What about the Italians in Tampa? I read once that they took over the Tampa Cuban's illegal *Bolita* lotto, and turned it into their own numbers racket. Do you know any of those Mafia characters?"

"No, my father moved our family to St. Pete Beach from Tampa in the early "50's" to escape that Italian/Mafia stigma. He was not a fan of the Trafficantes."

The train stopped in Santa Clara. They were given more beans and rice and access to a *baño*. Modesto noticed some trucks had pulled up and were loading more prisoners into freight cars farther back in the train.

Dave said, "It appears we're in the middle of a major pork shift to the other end of the island."

"Yes," said Modesto. "Maybe they've had a lot of rain and are having trouble getting the cane out."

"Don't they burn it to get rid of the outside leaves and tops?"

"They do, but you can't burn it if it's wet."

"Looks like they're loading up the train again, Modesto. When do you think we'll get to Las Tunas?"

"Probably late tomorrow morning, after a stop in Camagüey around dawn. We'll be in the lowlands, but you'll see beautiful mountains off to the south."

They were led back to their boxcar and loaded up as night fell.

"Who's your favorite baseball team, Dave?" asked Modesto as the train started out of Santa Clara.

"Man, you're full of questions, lately."

"What else have we got to do?" asked Modesto.

"Well, I used to like the Cardinals, but now I'm a Devil Rays fan. How about you?"

"I've always been a Yankee fan, did you ever meet Steinbrenner?"

"No, can't say I have. But he's larger than life in Tampa. I'm going to get some sleep ... see you in Camagüey in the morning," said Dave.

111

As the large diesel locomotive started the train forward Dave mounded up some straw for a pillow and almost immediately fell asleep.

***

The northwest wind blew a steady 22 knots as Seth fiddled with his GPS map up in the flybridge. He had the clear windscreens zippered down, and the boat rocked a little on her beam in the gusts pulling her lines taut in the slip. The sun had been above the eastern horizon for only an hour.

"Seth," called Gene from the cockpit below. "Let me hand these coffees up to you ... I've got the Key West paper too."

Seth grabbed the coffees and Gene climbed up and plopped down into the Murray Brothers passenger chair.

"It was crowded at Tom Thumb's. We're not the only guys that are waiting until tomorrow to fish."

"You get tired of getting beat up — we did it for years when we were working and only had the weekends. But ... like ol' Robert E. used to say, 'A bad day fishing is better than a good day working'."

"The *Key West Citizen* says it will be 15 knots from the north-northeast tomorrow," said Gene.

"We can handle that. I called Billy Ray while you were gone and he, Big Dog, and Deputy Pearce will be fishing with us the day after tomorrow. It should only be blowin' 10 to 15 knots by then."

"That's what the paper says. Is Scotty still sleeping?" asked Gene.

"Probably. I haven't seen him, Freddy, or John. Just after you left, Charley Blevins came out of his cottage, waved to me, and took off in his Jeep. He hollered he'd be back to ride in the Zodiac in an hour. I'm plotting waypoints for our Dave the Wave extraction in Pinar Del Rio. The Key West to Cancun leg was already in the GPS. So, I put in the route from Cancun to Cayos de San Felipe. Then I just plotted from there into our regular return route north through the Yucatan Straits and then northeast to Key West."

The crew slowly filtered into *TAR BABY'S* galley for coffee, and Charley returned with his Jeep.

"What's going on, Charley?" asked Seth. "You look perturbed."

"They informed me at the airport FBO that I couldn't park my Jeep there for free anymore. Now it's free parking for one week, then $5.00 a day. I've been just throwing a cover over it for the last five years and leaving it in a back corner of the lot."

"What are you going to do?" said Gene.

"Well, Joe will be finished building his eight-story elevator parking garage that looks like a lighthouse in a couple of months. It's going up right in the middle of the Stock Island Marine Village. He's selling those spaces to the mega-yacht guys. He'll still give me the pre-construction price of $35,000 and throw in free valet to and from the airport. He sold 50% of them before he poured the foundation. I'll buy a new Jeep and won't have to leave it out in the weather and storm surges."

"It'll probably turn out to be a good investment," said Scotty.

"That's what I thought. I bought on the eighth floor. It's opposite from a condo. The second floor is the most expensive because you can just drive it down the ramp."

"Yeah, and the first floor's the office and a wash rack, right?" asked Freddy.

"Right," answered Charley.

"They'll be some super expensive exotic cars in that garage," said John.

"And ... Joe gets a lit-up Florida landmark for his marina village," laughed Seth. "He's always got all the angles figured."

"Charley ... Seth and I are going to suit up and test the Zodiac in the rough seas for an hour or so. Does anybody else want to go?" asked Freddy.

"John and I are going to take Scotty up to Robbie's in Islamorada to feed the giant tarpon, see Hemingway's *PILAR* replica at World Wide Sports, and then have lunch at the Islamorada Fish Company. Do you need anything in Marathon?" asked Gene.

"Can't think of anything," said Seth.

"We'll be back in time to rig a cooler full of ballyhoo before dinner," said John.

Underway in the Zodiac, all three mariners were glad they had their foul weather gear on and a fleece underneath. At 10 mph the boat bobbed over the waves and threw spray in their faces. The seas were rough enough at three to four feet inside the reef in Hawk Channel.

"Try a little more speed, Fred," said Seth looking at his handheld GPS. At 15 mph the boat moved through the waves smartly.

"Wind her up a little more, Fred," said Seth. At 18 mph the Zodiac started to pound a bit, and everybody got wet. Fifteen miles an hour was determined ideal for comfort versus speed, and Fred turned the boat down wind and sped up to 25 mph. He quickly throttled back to 20 to prevent the boat from surfing down the wave too fast into the trough. At 20 mph it was just right.

"Go through the reef opening and let's try the five to six footers, Fred," said Seth.

Freddy took the Zodiac through the opening at 10 mph, continued south for a couple hundred yards, and turned back into the wind. After some experimenting, eight mph was as fast as they could handle. When they got back through the reef Fred turned the Zodiac over to Charley.

"Get up under the lee shore a bit, Charley, then give her some throttle. We had her up over 40 mph yesterday. In fact, run down the shoreline and take us around to the Bight … we'll eat lunch at Dante's and listen to the blues band. After lunch, we'll buy three dozen live goggle-eyes at the Key West Bait Store, in the Bight, and go home the back way past Dredger's Island."

Charley eased under the island's lee shore and put the 17.5 foot Zodiac through its paces in the calmer water.

"She really handles nice for a roll-up floor," said Charley.

"There's a bolt-on aluminum keel structure under the floor and a deep-vee built into the fabric. I think it handles more like an RIB," said Seth.

They docked at the Conch Resort Marina and sat under the thatched roof at Dante's open-air bar listening to Dickey Betts, Butch Trucks, and his nephew Derek perform Floyd Miles's *Back to Daytona*. The Fort Myers ferry crowd was beginning to shuffle into the pool area, and would not be looking forward to making the Sunday 5:00 p.m. trip into the brisk north wind. Even the 155 foot three-tiered power catamaran would have to slow down to run into the six foot seas in Florida Bay. Aboard, the trip would be miserable for those afflicted by *mal de mer*. Most of them were already toasted after a hedonistic weekend on Duval Street. Many of the women had shed their tops and some of the inebriated couples played grab-ass in the pool as though they were invisible.

As Seth's party finished their lunch, Dickey and Derek were playing dueling guitars at the end one of Dickey's Allman Brothers Band hits, *Ramblin' Man*, which he wrote in 1973. They ordered another cold one, not wanting to leave until the set was over.

"I never thought I'd see those guy's again," said Charley, as they walked over to the bait store.

"Yeah, me neither. Dickey kept their sound alive after Duane died," added Seth. "I heard Gregg was getting a liver transplant in L.A."

"It's too bad Gregg and Dickey broke up the band ... I guess the Trucks' didn't take sides."

They left the Conch Resort Marina with three dozen goggle-eyes in two new five-gallon pails, purchased at Key West Bait. The lids had a few holes drilled in them for ventilation. Fred secured the pails next to the fuel tanks.

Seth took the helm and steered out of the Bight, following the channel northeast around Fleming Key, then back southeast to Dredgers Key. From there he steered south to the Overseas Highway A1A Causeway Bridge from Stock Island to Key West, passing the Hyatt to the west and the Key West Golf Course to the east. Once under the causeway, Seth followed the mangrove shoreline down to Cow Key. He swung east under Cow Key then motored north up the Stock Island Channel.

"That's a nice ride, Seth. I've never come around this way," said Fred.

"You can't get anything much higher than the Zodiac under the A1A Bridge. Let's get these goggle-eyes into *TAR BABY'S* baitwell as quickly as possible."

"I like this Zodiac, Seth," said Charley. "It would make a great tender. Do you think they make a steering console for this model?"

"I don't think so, but Zodiac makes an RIB this size that has one."

When the bait was secure in the baitwell they went their separate ways with visions of a little nap before dinner.

***

The Monday flight to Los Angeles had been exhausting. Hugo had not learned to sleep on an airplane yet. Alex insisted that Monserrat accompany Hugo to lend support. The plan was to rest Monday and have a light workout Tuesday. The exhibition workout would be on Wednesday at Dodger Stadium — after Hugo was over any jet lag.

The L.A. scene was even more overwhelming than Miami. The Tuesday morning workout went well, but Alex wanted Hugo to get the feel of Dodger Stadium. Hugo met Dexter Simpson at Dodger Stadium and hit about 30 pitches ... the ball seemed to carry out to left field longer, and he hit a few balls in the stands without straining. The San Fernando High School coach and players, who would work with him the next day, were there and he shook hands with all of them. He fielded some grounders and liked playing in the low humidity that prevailed in California. Hugo hardly broke a sweat.

After a late lunch with Monserrat, they spent the afternoon sightseeing — finally returning to the Fairmont Hotel in Santa Monica Beach on Wilshire Boulevard at mid-afternoon. Alex reserved Hugo and Monserrat a bungalow that opened onto the Fairmont's busy swimming pool area. Monserrat wanted to sunbathe and swim. But, Hugo had something else on his mind. They compromised, and Hugo called the concierge from their room to reserve two poolside chaises for 4:00 p.m.

Monserrat slipped off her Alfani® wedge sandals, shed her new Chico® capris pants, Tribal® flowing silk blouse, and Victoria's Secret® lace underwear— and started for the king-size bed.

"Not there, *mi amor*, let's try the leather couch in the living room."

"That sounds like more fun, Hugo! We've never tried it on a couch so elegant."

Hugo kicked off his Nike® Airs, dropped his Givenchy® jeans, and shrugged out of his Calvin Klein® t-shirt.

As he pulled off his Saxx®-ball park briefs he said, "I love you and America more each day."

"I feel the same way, Hugo."

She sat demurely on the couch as Hugo stood over her. After some inventive fore-play, Hugo pulled her up and kissed her passionately.

"It's couch time, *Cariño.*"

Soon he was in a frenzy as she pushed back against him.

"*Aqui viene!*" exclaimed Hugo. He smacked her butt with his free hand ... and collapsed on the couch next to her.

"Are you all right, Hugo?" asked Monserrat.

"Never been better, *mi amor*, **you** just get better and better."

Twenty minutes later they were basking in the sun on their chaises by the pool. Monserrat sipped a Mojito, and Hugo drank a *Coca Light* with a lime wedge.

"We'll swim when we get hot and later we'll shower and dress. Tonight we'll walk out on the Santa Monica Pier and have a light dinner. I need a good night's sleep ... tomorrow is all about the big bucks."

***

The pit stop in Camagüey lasted just long enough for a *baño* call and a regulation cup of beans and rice. Dave had a second ration of water in the boxcar. As the train got up to speed, the sun peaked over the horizon and started to light up the endless acres of sugar cane fields that flashed by. The monotony was only broken when they went by a burned or harvested field. Several times the occupants of the boxcar coughed and choked on the smoke from the upwind fields that were burning before the cutting crews swept through them. Dave remembered a smoky trip across Lake Okeechobee and the waterway canal and wondered how "Big Sugar" got away with the same air and water pollution in Florida. The clacking sound of the boxcar's wheels and the gentle motion of the train finally put Dave to sleep again.

"Wake up, Dave," said Modesto, shaking his shoulder. "We're coming into Las Tunas."

Las Tunas reminded Dave of the city of Pinar Del Rio - only it was larger. They disembarked at the train station and were loaded onto open trucks along with their guards. Each prisoner and his footlocker was logged off the train and logged onto a truck. The boxcar guard, whose name was Pepe, had a suitcase and told Modesto that he was transferred here for the sugar cane season. More prisoners needed more guards - made sense. They drove north for about 20 minutes into a small suburb called San Juan, just past the large Las Tunas Airport, and stopped at a large fenced and barb wired stockade next to a railroad track. They were driven inside and passed by prefabricated barracks identical to the ones they slept in back in Santa Maria. The camp was set up almost exactly the same as the one they had just left.

The truck stopped abruptly and they jumped off the rear with their small footlockers. They were assembled in two lines in front of their barracks and as their names were called, they were checked in again. A sergeant read a list of standard rules and explained they would be integrated in the morning with different cane cutting crews depending on need. They would be trucked out and would board the Las Tunas to Puerto Carupano sugar cane train each morning after breakfast and delivered back before dinner. Pepe gave each prisoner a bunk number in Barracks 36 and dismissed them all until dinner.

Pepe approached Modesto inside as they unpacked and said, "I had instructions to bunk you and David Perozzi together and was told that you will be picked up and delivered every Thursday night at 6:30 to the women's work camp up the road to teach an English class. I wish I knew English better so I could get a tourist hospitality job."

"I know what you mean, Pepe, that's where the big bucks are," said Modesto.

"Also, when we board the train with the harvesters tomorrow, you will board further up the train into the office car near the locomotive. There you'll meet Mateo Santiago, who supervises the loading and unloading of the sugar cane. It is my understanding you will assist him."

"Thank you, Pepe," said Modesto. After Pepe had gone Modesto turned to Dave and whispered, "As you Gringos like to say, it looks like Mistress C. has 'greased the skids' for us."

Dave the Wave smiled and replied, "Fuckin' A!"

***

Charley Blevins reacted quickly to the bite on the left long rigger when the sailfish popped his line out of the clip. Charley put the reel into free spool and counted to six as his line fell off his raised rod tip gently onto the water. At six he lowered his rod tip to horizontal and pushed his drag lever halfway up to strike and felt the fish come tight. The sailfish rocketed skyward and the fight was on with the #7 circle hook set securely in the corner of its mouth. Seth circled the boat down sea as John and Scotty dropped back to where Charley's bite had been. Both rigs got bites, but after the drop backs only Scotty hooked up. A double-header was enough in these rough seas, and within 10 minutes both fish were released. High fives and congrats were exchanged as the crew got the spread back out quickly. After a few more sailfish releases and a couple of *sancochos* in between, John pulled the hook on a big 50 lb. wahoo after a 15 minute battle. Seth decided to move *TAR BABY* back through the reef into calmer water and use live bait. The boys ate an early lunch of pre-made sandwiches, including a freshly cut up pineapple that Charley brought along.

"I don't think this front is as strong as the one last week," said Gene, as he handed up a sandwich to Seth.

"I think you're right, let's get set up to kite fish. I think the wind is blowing 12 knots now, maybe 15 in the gusts."

Soon they were set up with Seth bumping *TAR BABY'S* bow into the wind, with two kites deploying goggle-eyes splashing just at the edge of the reef. The action was almost non-stop and the boys opted to call it a day after catching at least 2 sailfish apiece.

"Great day, guys!" hollered down Seth. "My count up here is 18 sails, plus a couple of nice wahoo. How many goggle-eyes are left in the baitwell?"

"I count 14, Seth," said Fred.

118

"Those live goggle-eyes almost ought to be outlawed. They certainly have a high hook-up ratio," said Gene.

"That might be enough live bait for tomorrow. Maybe we'll Sabiki some bait down at the day marker near Fort Zachary in the morning. Remember, we have Billy Ray and the deputies coming tomorrow," said Seth.

"No problem. The way the wind is laying down we can probably use more dead bait tomorrow," said John.

Charley came up on the bridge and said, "Thanks for asking me, Seth. I had a great time."

"Hey, you were 3 for 3 today, and those long rigger dead ballyhoo bites are the hardest."

"Yeah, you've got to be patient and really make sure they bite it. If they're just playing with it and you drop back they'll never find it."

"You've got to miss a few to figure that out," chuckled Seth.

"You got that right," laughed Charley. "Listen, I can't go tomorrow. I have to check out some new seaweed removal machinery with Hugh Spinney up in Miami. It's time for some newer, more efficient equipment down here."

"Yeah, I know you're a big part of that venture. When do you go back to St. Pete?"

"Day after tomorrow. We'll keep in touch on the Dave the Wave project."

"I'll call you and run the crew list by you before we sign any of them on."

"I know you'll get the right guys, and I'm glad to finally be on the inside of one of your adventures."

"Welcome aboard, Charley."

"Hey, I'm not leaving the Jeep at the airport, since I'm coming back by boat. So I'm leaving it right here. Feel free to use it. The keys are under the floor mat. Hugh will take me to the airport."

Seth called Lori and told her about the sailfish they had caught that day and Charley Blevin's excellent three for three on the left long rigger.

"We're thinking about running over to Nassau and south to fish for marlin for a few days when Charley brings his Huckins down."

"Getting tired of sailfish, Seth?"

"Something like that, and I just feel lucky."

"Do it while you can, Seth."

"I love you, Lori!"

CHAPTER THIRTEEN

PEPE and his charges jumped from the truck and scrambled up on a cane car near the end of the long train. The truck continued towards the diesel/electric locomotive that powered the train. The empty cane cars looked like a skeleton of a boxcar, with just the frame remaining. The roof was gone and four steel I-beams were welded cross-ways across the deck. Dave and Modesto were dropped off right behind the locomotive at the only passenger car on the train.

"You must be the new *hombres* from Pinar," said a middle-aged, swarthy, black-haired man with sparkling green eyes, and a droopy mustache — as Modesto and Dave entered the passenger car. "I am Mateo Santiago."

"I'm Modesto and this is Dave. We are at your service, sir."

"You'll just stick with me today until you learn the ropes. We have several stops to deliver harvesters and pick up the raw sugar cane from trucks and carts. Some of the stops have cranes to help load, others have to be loaded all by hand. We have two labor crews of 12 men each. You will run both crews once I train you. With 24 men, we get everything loaded quickly. When we get to the Antonio Guiteras Mill in Delicías our crews will assist the mill crew in attaching chains around the cane before an overhead crane unloads it car by car. We want to work ahead to conserve time, and the plant has several sets of chains. Then the mill crew loads 100 kilo bags of refined sugar with forklifts. The train will deliver that sugar out to Puerto Carupano, six kilometers away on Puerto Padre Bay, for export shipping. From there the train runs back to Las Tunas, picking up the harvesters along the way."

"Sounds like we're in for an interesting day," said Modesto.

"Here are two green hard hats which designate you as supervisors, two pairs of gloves if you have to jump in and help, and two pairs of safety glasses," said Mateo as the train started to move. "Follow me at each stop."

Dave and Modesto took seats in the rear of the passenger car and watched the sugar cane field's klick by. The little town of Velasco Triente was the first stop, and the crews unloaded and secured six trucks of cane and off-loaded 50 harvesters. The next stop was Vasquez about 20 kilometers down the track. It was a larger town and had a crane-assisted loading facility. As each truck was unloaded, it was filled with harvesters. The trucks drove off in different directions. A hundred cane cutters, along with their guards, departed the train there. Fifteen kilometers to the east at Maniabon, another hundred men were transported into the fields emptying the train of harvesters, as the train crews hand loaded three more cane cars from the trucks. More cane came aboard in San Manuel, as the train turned back north and headed for Delíciás, making another stop at a small railhead where the crews hand loaded the last three empty cars.

A half an hour later, the train arrived at the huge Delíciás sugar mill. Dave was taken aback by its enormous size and scale. There were multiple tracks and switches leading into the mill's large buildings. The adjacent tracks were littered with rusting cane cars, and the hulks of ancient steam locomotives from Cuba's golden age of sugar production. It appeared that only two rendering boilers were in operation in a plant that once operated six. Smoke and steam belched from the tall stacks that loomed over two of the old buildings. The train had a green light to enter the easternmost mill. It pulled slowly through the mill and stopped next to the cane unloading bunker. An overhead crane dropped a dangling chain harness on top of the stacked sugar cane stalks, and the train's labor crew pushed and pulled the slack chains under the cane that rested on the cars' I-beams. The crew secured the chains with their attached hooks. The crane lifted the load of cane out of the open-topped cage and dropped it into a bunker where the chain was removed and mill workers hand-loaded the cane onto conveyor belts that fed the boilers. Mateo's crew wrestled identical chain harnesses on the remaining cane so they could be hooked to the crane quickly. Amazingly enough, the entire train was unloaded in less than an hour.

"I thought we were in for a huge cluster-fuck with the chain and everything, but it worked quite well," said Dave to Mateo.

"There's a new Brazilian-designed sugar mill in Holguin where they unhitch the car on both ends and chain the car to a steel pad and hydraulically tip the car 120 degrees to unload it. It only takes two men to do it. But with the hitching and un-hitching, this old method is much faster, plus labor is cheap in Cuba."

The train left the boiler building and stopped in front of a warehouse where forklifts loaded pallets of 100 kilos (220 lbs.) bags of refined sugar on the empty cane cars. The train left the mill and eased through the town of Delíciás, which looked like any typical Cuban mill town except for its location on the beautiful tropical shores of Puerto Padre Bay. They picked up speed as they wound out of town and crossed the narrow man-made isthmus that led to Puerto Carupano six kilometers to the northeast.

"What a beautiful bay," commented Modesto. "My family brought me to a beach near here when I was just a child."

"There is a resort beach called *Playa La Boca* at the entrance of the Bay. It's right on the Atlantic Ocean," said Mateo.

"So this is a natural deep water harbor?" asked Dave.

"One of many in Cuba, but none is as well protected," said Mateo.

The views out either side of the train were stunning and Dave could see the small colonial city of Puerto Padre across the placid bay out of the left-side window. Two large freighters, one with a Venezuela hailing port, the other from North Korea, were docked at the wharfs on the west side of the port. The refined sugar skids were unloaded by the port's stevedores manning diesel forklifts. The train turned around in a mostly rusted out tank farm at the end of the isthmus and headed south for Las Tunas. The train stopped and picked up the waiting cane harvesters they had dropped off that morning, and when they finally pulled into San Juan, night fell.

***

"That's right, Hugo, 32 million dollars!"

"I just wanted you to say it again, Boss. I can't believe it."

"I'm not the boss, Hugo, you are."

"But you're the greatest, Alex. Yesterday we were at 20 million."

"That was before I got them bidding against each other. You can play for the San Diego Padres for 30 million or the Chicago Cubs for 32. The signing bonus is 3 million - either club."

"It's a no brainer, Alex … Chicago — snow, ice, shootings, air pollution, crooked politicians. San Diego — no snow, the ocean, the sun, no humidity. It's San Diego."

"Two million less."

"The incentives are better in San Diego, maybe I can make more in San Diego?"

"You're the boss, Hugo, and I think you're making the right decision. You had two great workouts and you ran the bases under 14 seconds in Los Angeles. Everybody wants speed and power. I'll call the San Diego GM, and we'll fly back out there and sign. Then we'll go condo shopping."

"Maybe a house?"

"Well, why not keep it simple to start? First, half your signing bonus goes to the Hialeah syndicate. Second, you owe them 15% of your salary and any bonuses from the club for the next five years, and my fee is 5% on top of everything. So you net $1,350, 000 on your bonus less 35% to the U.S. Government, so really you net $877, 500. That will almost buy a decent condo in San Diego. Your yearly salary is six million, you net $4,800,000, after me and the syndicate, less 35% U.S. income tax, 13.3% California State Tax, add in Social Security, Medicare, and Obamacare investments taxes of approximately 10% and you net about 2 million, or 10 million over 5 years. I want you to have at least 5 million in an investment account for your retirement or if you get hurt. Five million dollars invested in municipal revenue bonds would give you around $250,000 of tax free income a year for life. So you're on an allowance of $80,000 a month."

"You're the doctor, Alex. I mean I'm used to making like $200 a month! But, I want to buy a car for myself, Pedro and Monserrat. Why don't you put me on a $40,000 a month allowance and invest the rest in real estate? You know, like offices or apartments? Something I can drive by and stop and touch. I also need to give Pedro two or three thousand a month until he goes pro. He came over this morning and told me that his lawyer had him sign a letter of intent with North Carolina at a place called Chapel Hill. 'A full ride' – he called it, but he will need the car, insurance, and spending money."

"That's good news too! You're smart to save as much money as you can. Sports careers can be as short as an Achilles tendon or a rotator cuff."

"Pedro will call you when he goes pro. I told him all about you. Wait until he hears about 30 million."

"Get your bag packed, we'll probably fly out to San Diego tomorrow."

"Can I take Monserrat?"

"Of course, you're the boss," said Alex.

Hugo hung up and looked up at Monserrat who had been massaging his neck during the entire conversation.

"I had a tough time concentrating on what Alex was saying while you were doing that the whole time. But, don't get me wrong, I'm not complaining, and don't stop."

"I'm looking forward to going to San Diego with you. He certainly had a lot to tell you."

"Yes he did and it was all good," said Hugo

"Let's celebrate the 30 million dollar contract and Pedro's full ride at that Ruth Chris Steakhouse Alex keeps telling us about," said Monserrat, as she gently squeezed his bulging neck muscles.

"Okay, I'll call Pedro, and make a reservation. You start packing so we'll be ready to go at a moment's notice."

"Bueno! Bueno! Bueno!" squealed Monserrat as she headed for the bedroom.

***

Andy, Big Dog, Arnold, was hooked up to a big wahoo that had almost spooled him on its initial run. The fish bit a splashing goggle-eye under a kite outside the reef. The wind was down to 8-10 knots and they'd already caught five sailfish. Seth turned the boat and was idling towards the fish as Big Dog carefully reeled in the 20 lb. line. If Seth moved towards the big fish too fast he would create a huge loop in the line and Big Dog would have to loosen the drag to prevent the line from breaking. He backed off the drag a couple of lbs. anyway just to be safe. They worked in tandem and got all but 200 feet back. The wahoo struggled against the drag, stopping periodically to shake his head. The see-saw battle went on for 30 minutes, and Big Dog got the fish close enough for Seth to get a look from the flybridge.

"Looks, at least like 80 or 90 pounds, maybe twice the size of the 50-pounder in the fish box - don't horse him - we're not in a hurry," yelled Seth.

Big Dog played the waiting game with the big fish, he'd gain a few feet, and then the big fish would take it back. All at once, the rod bent almost in two, and Big Dog was dragged across the transom and thrown against the port gunwale. As he struggled to recover, the pressure was suddenly released and Big Dog stumbled backward landing in a heap on the cockpit sole. He jumped right up saying, "I think the line broke?"

"I don't think so, Andy," said Seth. "I saw a large dark shape come up behind the wahoo and there was a big swirl just before your rod bent. Reel in your line. I think a big shark got him."

Big Dog reeled the line in and brought in the largest wahoo head that anybody aboard had ever seen.

"Take a picture of the head. That wahoo was easily over 100 lbs.!" called down Seth. "Let's get the kites back up and some baits out."

Ten minutes later they were fishing again, but the boys were still buzzing about the wahoo and the big shark.

Seth took a little time between fish to bounce his Cuba plan off of Billy Ray.

"The way you've planned it should give you a high percentage of success. You have the element of surprise, and you'll probably get away without anyone knowing you've even been there — especially if your friend's partner cooperates," said Billy.

"That's the way I'd like it to go. Bobby Thompson says his head agent down there knows Dave's partner and thinks he would want to defect. He's married to a Russian and he sent her and their children to Russia. He was involved in black market fuel and his timing was bad. He was arrested two weeks before he was planning to defect and join them. Do you think Big Dog might want to go along? He'd just ride with Charley Blevins in the back-up boat. It's the Huckins 62 from the drug-bust, that we refurbed at the Boatworks."

"I know he'd want to go, but he needs to keep his nose clean. But I think Deputy Pearce might want to go. He retired six months ago and just does special event parking control and that sort of thing now. He's a good man and he's a 'Conch'— grew up on shrimp boats."

"I could pay him $50 a day, the whole thing shouldn't take but 10 days max."

"The Huckins 62 … he'll probably go just for the fun. I'll ask him."

With that said, Deputy Pearce hooked up a nice sailfish, and Scotty had another within 10 seconds of that bite. The afternoon went by fast as they steadily caught fish. They called it a day with another wahoo. Seth's tally was 14 sails and two wahoo out of 22 bites. The live bait really helped the hook-up ratio. They ran in and drank a couple of cold ones while the boat was scrubbed and the tackle was rinsed and put away. Billy Ray took a picture of Big Dog with his giant wahoo head. John cleaned the two smaller wahoo and gave each lawman enough for two dinners. Seth delivered some to Joe O'Donnell, Hugh Spinney, and Bobby Mongelli. That's how to make fast friends in Florida. The boys decided to take a lay day and Seth grilled the remaining wahoo rare. That night's galley crew added green beans with Everglades Seasoning®, tossed salad with blue cheese and bacon dressing, and cheese hash-browned potatoes. Seth and Scotty shared a bottle of Klinker Brick Zinfandel, from Lodi, California, while the rest of the crew concentrated on a bottle of Mount Gay dark rum and Coca Cola.

Seth and Gene turned in early. Scotty, Freddy, and John headed for Casa Marina's Ocean Bar.

The next morning, Seth sat up in the flybridge with a cup of coffee and watched the sun climb over Stock Island. Gene was back at the Tom Thumb getting some bagels and a newspaper. Later today they would go to Publix on Roosevelt and restock the galley and the boat's *cerveza*. Seth didn't hear Scotty come in last night, but his Land Rover made it back okay. Seth saw it parked behind *TAR BABY*. Gene arrived and Seth handed down his empty cup.

"Please toast me up a bagel, will you, Gene? Just holler and you can hand it all up to me."

Gene was back in 10 minutes, driving Charley's Jeep. He handed everything up, then climbed up and sat in the passenger chair.

"I put a few more things on the grocery list. We need cream cheese and more coffee cream. Can you think of anything else, Seth?"

"No, I can hear the jets taking off at Boca Chica, they must be scrambling or flying an exercise."

"Probably — the long term weather forecast shows a cold front coming through just before the girls get here for Valentine's Day. Maybe we can get a couple of days of fishing in before they arrive."

"I hope so because we'll be on the way to Cuba after that, weather permitting."

"What kind of firepower do we have aboard?"

"Same weapons we had in the Turks and Caicos: my Remington hog rifle, two tactical shotguns, four Glock 9mm's, two Smith and Wesson .38's, Tasers, two Ruger .380 ACP pocket guns, and that lightweight mesh body armor that Billy Ray gave me. I did add an AR-15. I have one at Lori's condo downtown, and the one that's on the boat now I normally keep at the townhouse in Treasure Island."

"I'm glad Charley's going. He can carry extra fuel and provisions and he provides us with a huge safety factor."

"Right."

Gene relaxed and started to read his newspaper.

"Not much on the *Citizen's* front page today; just stimulus packages from the government and bailouts to the guys who caused the mortgage problem. They did let a few of them fail. Now my money market pays me fucking .03%. When I retired in 2002 it paid 4.6%."

"Yeah - just when I don't have a mortgage anymore — I can get one for 2.5%," laughed Seth.

"Well, maybe this change thing will help race relations. Did you ever think we'd have a black president?"

"Not in my lifetime, but I'm all for it if he brings us together," said Seth. "I still believe in what Martin Luther King said when we were still kids."

"What was that, Seth?"

"'Don't judge people by the color of their skin, but by the content of their character'."

"Amen! …… Hey, here's something on the sport's page. What was the Cuban baseball player's name that framed Dave the Wave?"

"Hugo Lugo."

"Here, I'll read it to you — *Hugo Lugo-Ramirez recently defected from Cuba, signed a five-year no-cut contract with the San Diego Padres yesterday for 30 million dollars, plus a 3 million dollar signing bonus. The Cuban star third baseman, who crossed the border in Laredo, Texas, recently, and his agent, Alex Esteban, from Miami, arranged an east coast and west coast workout for MLB scouts, coaches, and general managers. Hugo Lugo accepted 2 million dollars less to go to San Diego, rather than going to Chicago to play with the Cubs. His reputation as a slick fielder, power hitter, and base stealer for the Havana Industriales preceded his defection. Hugo Lugo circled the bases in L.A.'s Dodger Stadium last week in 13.97 seconds. The San Diego Padres new Vice President of Baseball Operations, Josh Byrnes, is hoping Hugo's acquisition will help put them into first place in the NL West this coming season.*"

"I **knew** he'd defect," said Seth. "When we get Dave out of Cuba … Hugo Lugo will pay. Alex Esteban will be the first guy I look up. I bet Bobby can get me copies of Dave's trial transcript."

"I'm glad Dave knows we haven't forgotten him."

"Please keep that newspaper article for me, Gene. I want to look up Alex Esteban on the computer. Let's get our list and go to Publix. We'll leave a note for Scotty and the guys."

Gene and Seth were in the Publix Deli section when Seth's phone rang.

"Yeah, Bobby, good to hear from you."

"I'll get right to it, Seth. Dave the Wave has been transferred 500 miles away from Pinar Del Rio to the northeast coast. *El Cazador* called me and said Dave was transferred by train with a few thousand other prisoners around Cuba to work the sugar cane harvest in Las Tunas Province. He says none of this is unusual. It happens every year. He may be transferred back this coming spring when they start to plant tobacco in Pinar Del Rio. Meanwhile, his delivery truck partner, Modesto, was transferred with him, along with 350 men from the Santa Maria prison camp. My agents in Havana tracked the train there, and we have our agent in Las Tunas watching them at the San Juan prison camp near the Las Tunas Airport. He reports they are in Barracks 36. Modesto and Dave have been assigned to a sugar cane train. They reportedly stayed on the train and rode in the supervisor's passenger coach. They did not get put on any of the trucks that took the other prisoners out to the cane farms to cut the burnt cane. I have instructed *El Cazador* to send two more agents to Las Tunas to help out. The local agent has an informer in the work camp."

"What is the train's route?"

"It runs from Las Tunas City to the Puerto Padre/Deliciás area on the Atlantic coast and then out to Puerto Carupano, a sugar, molasses, and fuel oil port, on a round-trip each day. The train picks up harvested cane along the way and delivers it to the sugar mill in Deliciás. They also deliver labor to the farms where they stop. Then they pick up the labor and the extra guards on the return trip and take them back to the prison camp."

"Call me back when you get a solid schedule from your agents. In the meantime, I'll look for a way to get him out of there."

"Listen, I've got another thread going from some information I got from the Pinar Del Rio agents. Dave and Modesto started driving to the women's work camp every Thursday night at 6:30 and back about 10:30. They had papers to check out and back in. All we could find out was they were teaching an English class sponsored by the commandant of the women's prisons in that province. She just was transferred to Las Tunas Province. We don't know if there is any connection between her transfer and Dave's."

"Well, education seems to be the big thing in Cuba."

"I'll get as much information as I can and brief you again this afternoon."

"Thanks, Bobby ... Oh, the Cuban ballplayer Hugo Lugo that framed Dave defected ... Gene just read in the *Key West Citizen* that he signed with the San Diego Padres for 30 million dollars."

"Wow!"

"Yeah, when we get Dave out I'm going to make him pay Dave $1,000,000 and bill him for all our expenses — so send me a bill."

"Believe me, Seth, you don't want a bill from me ... and you won't get one. What I will send you is an email outlining all this new information."

"Thanks, right now I'm standing in the middle of Publix holding a package of bratwurst. One other thing, can you get me a transcript of Dave's Havana trial — I'll need it later."

When Seth got back to the boat from Publix he printed Bobby's email and went right to work on his computer. He clicked up Google Earth and rode the rails from Pinar Del Rio to Las Tunas on the other Cuban coast that faced the Bahamas. Seth found the prison camp and the train track in San Juan near the Las Tunas Airport. He followed the railroad tracks north to Vazquez then east through Maniabon and San Manuel, then back north to Deliciás Sugar Mill. They finally dead-ended out at Puerto Carupano. He noticed that an old railroad spur ran west 10 kilometers from Deliciás to the old colonial city of Puerto Padre.

Seth liked what he saw. Puerto Carupano was a natural deep water port several miles inland from the Atlantic Ocean located in the middle of a large bay. It sat on the end of a narrow isthmus, partially man-made, a few miles from Puerto Padre and Deliciás. The isthmus divided most of the bay in half. Freighters coming in from the Atlantic reached the port through a fairly narrow channel that split a small beach resort in two. The well-marked channel was, however, wide enough for freighters coming and going to pass. He zoomed in on the Playa la Boca beach cottages and hotels on both sides at the mouth. A Google picture yielded a small car ferry that delivered people and cars across the channel. There appeared to be plenty of small boat traffic coming and going – one more boat, day or night, would not draw attention. The shortest road around to either side of the beach from Puerto Padre was 25 kilometers. The small beach town quickly gave way on both sides of the channel to uninhabited scrub jungle and mangroves all the way to the port. There were also some small uninhabited islands on the east side of the port. Seth zoomed in on the ship approach and found what looked like a lighthouse on the west side. He checked his paper charts and found; *Punta Mastelero Light, 49 feet tall, white light every eight seconds, west side of Bahia de Puerto Padre entrance.*

Puerto Carupano itself was small, and could only handle three to four freighters at a time. There were some warehouses and sugar loading equipment near the wharves, which were all on the west side. The north end of the narrow isthmus had several rusted oil tanks and most of them appeared unusable. The isthmus necked down towards the mainland to a three mile man-made stretch that was only wide enough for a two-lane road and one railroad track — then the road and track continued through two miles or so of mangrove swamps and some scattered farmland. The sugar mill in Delicias was enormous. Seth counted 20 large three or four story metal buildings, plus eight or nine railway switch tracks that ran through some of the buildings. A single track ran out of the Delicias Sugar Mill north to Puerto Carupano where a turnaround wound through a rusting tank farm at the far north end.

Seth's mind was definitely on overload. He had two or three escape scenarios running through his brain simultaneously, but he needed more information from Bobby Thompson. He zoomed in on the old city of Puerto Padre. It was built out like a wagon wheel with boulevards as spokes meeting at the center hub — the smaller streets overlaid them in a grid. The Google pictures of the city revealed beautiful colonial architecture and charm, and it looked like a great place to visit. Delicias was populated by small houses and stores that had grown up around the sprawling mill as they were needed. Seth zoomed out and surveyed the big picture, looking for the best route there from Key West and for a jumping off point near Puerto Padre. The shortest way would be south past the Cay Sal Bank, swinging around the southern tip of Andros, then southeast around the southern tip of Long Island and back tracking to Clarence Town for fuel. That would be close to 500 miles … stretching his fuel consumption to the limit. The safer route would be to run over to Nassau and fill up the fuel tanks, then travel down to Clarence Town and refuel again at Flying Fish Marina. Long Island was the nearest fuel stop 140 miles north of Puerto Padre.

Looking closer to Cuba, the Ragged Islands caught his eye. He had flown there to bonefish with John Harvey a few years back. They were a tiny group of islands and cays belonging to the Bahamas, west of the Acklin Islands. Duncan Town, where maybe 50 people lived, was 80 miles from Clarence Town and had a grass airstrip. More importantly, Duncan Town was only 60 miles from Puerto Padre. Seth knew he couldn't get fuel there, but he wouldn't need any. There were only a few decent anchorages, again he only needed room for his and Charley's boat. Seth didn't plan to go closer to Cuba with *TAR BABY* than international waters allowed, which meant they had to stay 12 miles offshore. There was a lot of freighter and tanker traffic in that area because of the "Old Bahama Channel". That channel was the shortest way to the U.S. and the north-flowing Gulf Stream from the Windward Passage, between Haiti and the east end of Cuba. Seth could track all that traffic on his "receive only" AIS, while not looking conspicuous on Cuban radar or showing up on any other vessel's AIS screen.

Even at night, the Zodiac could easily make the 12 mile trip into Puerto Padre Bay. They could hide in the mangroves during the day if it fit a timetable. Meanwhile *TAR BABY*, along with their back-up boat, *ABOUT TIME,* would be idling back and forth among the freighter traffic while communicating with the rescue operation by sat-phone. He was almost certain that Charley would have no problem if this whole plan jelled, as it was just a short hop back up to Nassau for college spring break at Atlantis.

Now, he needed more information from Bobby to try and formulate a workable plan on land.

CHAPTER FOURTEEN

Hugo Lugo was on a whirlwind tour of San Diego, accompanied by Monserrat, Alex Esteban, and Josh Byrnes, that was into its second day. They explored Coronado Island, ate lunch at the old Coronado Hotel, and toured the Padres ballpark, Petco Park, which was located on the waterfront. Later they drove through La Jolla and enjoyed waterfront dining at Duke's overlooking La Jolla Cove. Tomorrow they were scheduled to fly to Phoenix to tour the Padres' 145 acre spring training complex in nearby Peoria, Arizona. Hugo would be reporting there for rookie spring training during the middle part of February.

Alex, Hugo, and Monserrat would fly back to Miami from Phoenix, two days hence, for a meeting with Alejandro to transfer a million and a half dollars to the Hialeah syndicate.

As their limo headed back to the Omni Hotel, which overlooked Petco Park, Alex said, "After we transfer the syndicate their signing bonus money, I will set up an automatic fifteen percent bank check to be generated payable to the syndicate from each Padres salary and bonus check deposited into your bank account. I'll issue a $40,000 deposit to your personal account each month and invest the other $40,000 in real estate, as we discussed. The balance will be invested in tax free bonds and growth stocks in your retirement account. "

"Sounds like a good plan, Alex. How lucky I am to have friends like Pedro, Monserrat, and you. We will wait a week or so for the real estate lady we picked to have several condos ready for us to look at before we fly back out to San Diego. I'm sure we'll find something before the regular season starts."

"My head is spinning, Hugo — everything is happening so fast," said Monserrat.

"I will be there for both of you … every step of the way," said Alex with a smile.

"I'm tired," said Hugo. "What time is our flight tomorrow morning?"

"Eleven o'clock," said Alex.

Once in their room, however, Hugo announced he had other plans.

"I thought you said you were tired," said Monserrat shedding her dress and under-garments.

"I was tired of talking business, but I'm never tired of making love to you *mi cariño.*"

"Then let's go out on the dark balcony and enjoy the cool night air. We can play indoors … any time."

Once on the private balcony, Monserrat looked down at the Padres' partially lit up Petco Park Stadium. She grabbed the railing and arched her back as Hugo approached her. They both looked down at Hugo's new workplace as he tested the railing's mettle.

"Way better out here, *mi amor,*" cooed Monserrat.

"I feel like I'm on top of my game," laughed Hugo, enjoying his own joke.

When their moment was over, they kissed, and slipped into bed exhausted … still not yet fully realizing the enormity and inconceivability of their journey.

***

The sat-phone rang at 4:30 in the afternoon, and Seth answered on the second ring up in the flybridge.

"Hey, Seth, I've been working on Dave the Wave all day for you. I even passed off some newly intercepted information pinpointing the location of an upcoming North Korean bomb test to my assistant. I mean, that crazy bastard shot two missiles into the Sea of Japan on the Fourth of July. Our agents think they'll set off their first successful underground nuclear bomb test by this time next year."

"Shitfire! It's always something somewhere."

"Yeah, and this new Obama guy in the White House is kind of a pansy. He wants to limit how we interrogate, and who we can surveil. That puts our agents at a disadvantage and leaves our citizens possibly in peril."

"I hate to hear that! I hope that his inexperience and naivety doesn't put us behind the eight ball," said Seth.

"So the train schedule went almost exactly the same today … more agents, more info. They will probably keep the same schedule seven days a week. We will be watching for any changes. There is no rest for the weary in Cuba. Three armed guards stay with the train, one in the diesel locomotive, and the other two with the loading crews. Dave and Modesto are each supervising a crew and the train supervisor jumps in wherever he's needed. The other guards go along with the labor crews that are dropped off at the different sugar cane fields along the route. When the train has unloaded all its raw sugar cane in Deliciás, it is reloaded with sacks of refined sugar and the train delivers them to Puerto Carupano where they're unloaded by their stevedores using forklifts. When they're not working, Dave and Modesto ride in the passenger car with the supervisor and a statistician. The train runs the 36 miles back to Las Tunas empty at about 50 mph, making three stops to pick up the labor crews and their guards. Between Deliciás and the port, they run 35 mph. They leave at dawn and get back at sunset around 6:00 p.m."

"I've got a plan formulating in my head, Bobby. We still need the motor scooters and the Zodiac to get him out. We'll stage at the Ragged Islands 60 miles off of Puerto Padre. Our closest fuel stop is at Clarence Town only 80 miles back north. Then we'll travel southeast from Duncan Town to within 12 miles of Playa la Boca, towing the Zodiac with the scooters in it. Four men will run the Zodiac in under the cover of darkness. The Mastelero lighthouse and a handheld GPS will guide them into Playa la Boca Inlet and they'll have their navigation lights on until they reach the bay. They'll slip into Puerto Padre Bay with the navigation lights off and hide in the mangroves on the east side of the bay along the isthmus just south of the man-made part. There's a small sand path from the port road and railroad tracks back through the mangroves to the water at that spot. About 3:00 p.m. the next day we'll send the motor scooters to the Deliciás mill to follow the train back up towards Puerto Carupano."

"I'm following this on my real time satellite feed and so far I'm with you."

"I need your help, on few points," said Seth. "We need your agents to slip Dave a note, on the morning of the rescue. Maybe mention the black scooters. I picture a small C-4 cell phone bomb on the rear coupling of the passenger car controlled by the scooter personnel. Up the line further, I look to the two men left in the Zodiac to remove a section of track, about a mile or two from where the cane cars will be uncoupled by the explosion, to de-rail and stop the locomotive. After they remove the track section they'll return the Zodiac under the mangroves at the end of the sandy path. If the locomotive stops before it is derailed, the result will be the same. The supervisor and locomotive guard will want to run back to the cane cars. Dave and Modesto will step over to the road and our motor scooters will race in to scoop them up. The drivers will be armed in case any guards interfere. I think the element of surprise will take care of any resistance. If there's no hot pursuit, they will load the scooters back in the Zodiac and head for Playa La Boca at 20 mph, slowing down to 10 mph through the two mile narrows leading to the Atlantic. They should be moving through Playa la Boca at about dark. From that point, they'll increase to a top speed governed by the sea conditions. I would expect to see them an hour or so after dark out in international waters."

"Sounds like a good plan. Will you tow the inflatable Zodiac back to Duncan Town?"

"It all depends on the sea conditions. *ABOUT TIME* has a 1000 lb. electric davit and can put the boat, motor, and scooters on the aft part of her flybridge. But, initially, we want to tow the Zodiac as fast as we can north and put some miles between us and Cuba. I have a 70-foot polypropylene towing line and harness for that purpose. If the scooters have to be jettisoned at any point in the operation, that's okay too."

"What's the inflatable's payload?"

"About 3800 lbs. I figure with the outboard motor, fuel, gear, two scooters, and six men — we're loading only about 2000 lbs. on the way out. Once we have everyone back aboard the big boats, the Zodiac also becomes expendable. But I have a trump card if things turn sour."

"What?"

"We'll be in international waters, and Guantanamo is right around the corner. I'll call the U.S. Coast Guard if need be. I don't think the Cuban Navy wants to mess with them."

"I think you're right, but I have a suggestion or two — first, there is a large Cuban military base on the west side of Puerto Padre. It is there because of our military presence in Guantanamo. We need a diversion. My agents can set a big bomb off in the public *baños* in the City of Las Tunas' Vicente Garcia Revolution Park. We'll explode it in the middle of the night so we won't hurt anyone. The army will send a division to put down any resulting unrest and the secret police will investigate. Their focus will be there. My agents can plant the small C-4 bomb on the train car coupling the same night. I will call you with the bomb's phone number the next day."

"I'll rent a few more sat-phones before I leave here," said Seth.

"My agents will keep monitoring the situation and I'll keep you posted if anything changes."

"Thanks for everything, Bobby. We have the girls coming in for Valentine's Day this Thursday, then we'll be ready to leave sometime early next week for the Ragged Islands. Charley's boat is finished and will be launched at the Boatworks tomorrow."

Seth headed down the ladder into the cockpit to brief the crew who were gathered and were cracking their first cold one of the day. After the briefing, they all seemed eager to go.

"Let's practice on the scooters and Zodiac some more," said Freddy.

"I agree, let's load up all the gear in the Zodiac and try it fully loaded so we know what to expect. The front should be here tomorrow night. We'll make everything ready for a day of practice. Then we can sailfish the day before the girls come in," said John.

"I think we should run the Boca Chica track with two men on each scooter even though we'll only run maybe a kilometer or two on them with two people in Cuba," added Scotty.

"All good ideas," said Seth. "As my ol' Dad Robert E. would have said, 'Plan your work, then work your plan', or was it, 'Practice makes perfect'? He had so many, I can't remember all of them anymore."

***

The week was racing by for Dave. The train work was agreeing with him and he was happier using his head again instead of his back. He actually fit a little nap in on the passenger car during the return trip today. Modesto felt the same way. Tonight was the first Las Tunas English class. Dave had to admit that he was already getting horny as he thought about the possibilities. He was actually looking forward to seeing Consuelo, although it was the younger girls he really craved.

"I'm thinking there will be a couple new girls tonight," said Dave as he watched the Cuban countryside race by at 50 mph.

"I guess we'll know shortly after we get back today. We only have enough time for a quick shower before we're picked up. I hope the food is as good as it was in Pinar Del Rio," said Modesto.

"It's nice to have something to look forward to each week."

A truck with a guard came by Barracks 36 as Dave and Modesto toweled off in the cold shower. They dressed hurriedly and jumped in the back of the truck. Fifteen minutes later they cleared through a checkpoint at the women's barbed-wire surrounded compound and were dropped off at the commandant's office. The guard took them halfway down a long hall and pointed to a door at the end saying, "Through that door … but knock first, *señors*."

Modesto knocked on the door and Marta opened the door with a big smile on her face. She hugged and kissed Dave and Modesto then closed and locked the door behind them.

"Good to see you both, we've missed you."

Consuelo walked out of the open door of a small room off the large dining room and lounge, with her riding crop tucked under her arm. Rona and a new girl followed.

"Welcome, gentlemen. You know Rona and this is Darly. Darly, this is David and Modesto. They were part of our *English class* in Pinar Del Rio. Make Darly feel at home boys."

Rona kissed and hugged Dave and Modesto, and they both kissed Darly on both cheeks.

"This lounge reminds me of the one in Pinar Del Rio, Mistress Consuelo," said Dave.

"These buildings are all prefabbed at the prisons — all the provincial schools, hospitals, barracks, and government offices are the same. Help yourself to a *cerveza*, and there's more shrimp and oysters on the buffet."

Soon they were at the dinner table eating the same "Tom Jones" menu, and chattering in English.

Dave was trying to size up Darly, but Consuelo was sitting right across from him making sizzling eye contact. When dinner was over he wondered if he would get his chance tonight. But he also knew the drill. After the flash card session, Consuelo grabbed the test papers and his hand and they disappeared through a small ante-room door and into her office.

"I have missed you, Dave, three weeks became a long time. But that is over now."

"I missed you too, Consuelo, though, I was not sure you missed me. You were so formal at dinner."

"You are the first man in a long time that I have developed feelings for. I would like to keep that private, just between us. I have a position to maintain."

"Of course, I understand. Did you bring this desk from Pinar? I see you've already cleared the top of it," laughed Dave.

"Don't be silly, they are all the same — like the pre-fab buildings."

She pulled Dave close and kissed him hard while groping his Johnson with her free hand.

"Now, take off your clothes and let's start on the desk," said Consuelo, huskily, as she started to undress.

"How about, *un poco la mamada antes de?*" asked Dave, pushing his luck a bit as he stepped out of his pants.

"You want me to blow your whistle?" said Consuelo sternly.

Dave nodded nervously and gave her his best smile.

She looked at him quizzically, then responded admirably.

When they ended up on top of the desk, Dave felt like he had unleashed a tsunami. *I know she's fallen for me. But, I hope I'm not creating a permanent resident status when my sentence is up*, thought Dave. *Right now, I can handle it. She's still got her bondage girls, and I have access to the young ones.*

When Consuelo was spent, they kissed like teenagers for a while, then joined the other group. Consuelo chose Rona for her bondage routine and Dave got his crack at Darly. After some innocent foreplay, they moved back into an alcove. Dave pulled the curtain across, and Darly bent over the couch. From that vantage point, he admired her spectacular body, which reminded him of a long-past encounter with a Brazilian beach volleyball player. Her hair was streaked with blond and she didn't look a day over 18. Dave was stoked and was further amazed at the astonishing curve that Darly could get in her back.

Modesto looked at his watch. He purposely finished with Marta early. Consuelo slipped him a note when they first came in that read: *Baño at 10:00*. He excused himself and walked to the bathroom and opened the door. Consuelo was already there, entering from a second door that led to her office.

"The DGI thinks the note to Dave came from a shadowy dissident known as *El Cazador*. He is believed to be the brains behind an underground movement here in Cuba that is much like the radical 'Weathermen' in the U.S. during the "60's". They blow up Federal buildings and cause chaos as a form of protest. They might get some funding from the CIA. But we're not sure. Do you have anything new?"

"No, I've questioned him about his Tampa contacts, and he doesn't seem to have any. The only big time people he knows are entertainment types like Jimmy Buffett, Charley Daniels, and famous surfers. I think he's the congenial beach boy that he seems to be."

"I am starting to see him in that same light myself. But, General Machado and Diego are puzzled by this *El Cazador* connection and are moving more land, sea, and air security assets into the Las Tunas/Puerto Padre area. The security level here is now 'Code Blue'. Meanwhile, we're counting on you to keep digging."

Modesto and Consuelo shook hands and exited the *baño*, stage right and stage left.

Later that night, Dave replayed the evening in his mind as he lay in his bunk. He hoped he was making too much out of Consuelo's professed "feelings" for him and hadn't set a trap for himself.

***

The week in Miami flew by for Hugo and Monserrat. Pedro went off to North Carolina for the fourth academic quarter so he could practice with the basketball team. Hugo bought him a brand new Honda Pilot and gave him a $1500 per month allowance. Pedro's full ride would take care of tuition, books, meals, and a room in the athletic dorm. Hugo worked out and relaxed at the pool with Monserrat. They flew down to Key West for two nights and stayed at the Hyatt on Front Street, dined at Meson de Pepe's, and checked out Mallory Square. They had dinner the second night at Latitudes on Sunset Key and did Duval Street later that night. Hugo allowed himself a couple Budweiser beers and they marveled at the crowds.

"I'm not used to being around all these *maricones*," said Hugo. "Back home they put them all in prison."

"First, you must get used to this being your home," lectured Monserrat. "Second, your new country is very tolerant of deviant behavior and diversity."

"Alex has told me the same thing, and I will not express my true feelings. He says if I do it will hurt my endorsements."

"Alex is a wise man."

"In two days we'll be back in San Diego to look for a condo. Alex says the real estate lady has five or six units to show us."

"Am I going to spring training with you in Phoenix?"

"I don't think so, the rookies have to live in a dorm during spring training and we have a curfew. We all ride the bus to and from the spring games. All the games are right around Phoenix, but you can't stay with me. I'll fly you over every week for a couple of days. Next year we'll rent a condo."

"Good, but it'll be bad during the regular season, too."

"It's the profession I chose, and I think we both should be happy. The money is good, and we get to vacation during the whole off-season."

"You are right, Hugo, I missed you when you had road trips in Cuba, too. Maybe that is why we have so much sex when we are together?"

"That is probably the reason," said Hugo. "I get all pent up when I'm on the road."

Hugo smiled to himself and thought, *I love her dearly and she is the best, but the baseball groupies on the road are a lot of fun. I wonder if she would be tolerant of that kind of diversity.*

"Speaking of pent up, let's go back to the hotel and give that king-size bed a workout. We have to catch a plane to Miami in the morning, repack some clean clothes, and then head out to San Diego at 7:00 p.m."

"It would be nice to find a condo and be able to furnish it before you head to spring training. We need driver's licenses, too," said Monserrat as they threaded their way off crowded Duval Street onto Front.

"I thought that would keep you busy, between trips to Phoenix, while I'm at spring training. We'll buy cars in San Diego. Alex said to buy them there so we would have a relationship with the dealer."

"Well, yeah … I'm planning on hiring a decorator to help me with the condo."

"That sounds like a plan, *mi cariño,*" said Hugo, smiling as he opened the door to their room.

Late the next night, Monserrat's ears popped, waking her, as the American Airlines A-320 descended into the San Diego Airport's landing pattern. She looked over at Hugo who was sound asleep in his first class window seat. He was wearing his new Bose® Soundlink headphones and a Paris Hilton skin-flick flickered on his new iPad.

This boy is insatiable, thought Monserrat as she leaned over and switched the screen off with her index finger. They'd made love at the Hyatt in Key West, then again at their Miami condo after re-packing for this trip … "One for the road" as Hugo put it. *I don't always want sex when Hugo does*, thought Monserrat, *but I've never turned him down. I've loved him faithfully and he's taken me out of the hellhole Cuba's become to a new, bright future. I wish he would marry me, so we could have some children, but I have taken the birth control pills the government gave me in Havana, where each new child born is another dollar drain on the Revolution. Now in Miami, I get free birth control from Obamacare, a welfare check from U.S. Government each month, and food stamps since we're not married and I have no job. If Hugo doesn't marry me soon … I may just have to quit taking them.* The internet was banned in Cuba, but Monserrat was no dummy. She had figured out how to use Hugo's iPad while he was jogging every day, and she Googled up U.S. paternity and child support regulations on the internet. In one way or another, she was going to get her piece of the pie.

Monserrat woke Hugo with a poke to the ribs as the plane made its final descent into San Diego.

They stayed in the same Omni Hotel, different day, and different room.

"The real estate agent just called from the lobby, Hugo. Are you ready to go?"

"I'm changing my shirt. I must have gotten a little of my dinner on the front of it on the plane. I'll be right there."

Eileen Estevez, dressed and lacquered to the nines, whisked them away in her black four door BMW 7 Series into the hills surrounding San Diego Bay. The empty condos quickly became a jumble of identical bedrooms, living rooms, studies, guest rooms, bathroom suites and Jacuzzi tubs, his and her closets, and parking garages … all with views of San Diego Bay. After lunch, Monserrat settled on a two bedroom, three-story townhouse, with a media room, a small office, large living room, dining room, an eat in granite kitchen, with a huge covered porch - all overlooking La Jolla Cove. The unit had a two-car garage, with a laundry/exercise room/bathroom behind the garage, and an elevator. They could jog on the beach, swim in a communal pool right outside their exercise room, and walk to trendy restaurants and shopping — all this for only $990,000. Hugo put Eileen on the phone with Alex and he told her, in light of the continuing recession, to offer $895,000 cash. She said, "*no way*," but she would submit it. The seller accepted the offer, the money was wired, and the closing took place three days later.

Eileen matched Monserrat with a decorator friend of hers, and the whirl-wind began. The first purchases were a king-size bed and sheets, a leather couch, a 60" TV, and a kitchen table and chairs. They still ate out or had food delivered. Hugo's first Padres' check arrived at Alex's office and $40,000 was wired to his new bank account in San Diego. Monserrat started to wear out Hugo's Visa card, and Alex put her on a $25,000 per month decorating budget not to exceed $100,000 total. Alex spoke with the decorator, and she got the picture. Hugo's personal business manager in Alex's office oversaw the project and approved the payments. Just before reporting to spring practice, Hugo bought Monserrat a black BMW X3, and that same day they both passed the State of California's driver's test. Later that afternoon, he bought both himself and Monserrat an iPhone 4. The next day, Hugo drove away from the Penske

Mercedes-Benz® dealership on Kearny-Mesa Road, near the Miramar landfill, in an S-class white 4-door sedan.

Later that week, Hugo kissed Monserrat good-bye, drove 356 miles on U.S. Route 8 to Phoenix, Arizona in four and a half hours and reported for spring practice. Monserrat was scheduled to fly in for a visit in two weeks for the first spring training game. She decided to quit taking birth control the day she got her driver's license, iPhone, and car.

CHAPTER FIFTEEN

SCOTTY took a wave in the face, but he shook it off and throttled the outboard up higher. The scooters were in their storage bags and lashed in the Zodiac amidships. Freddy and Seth stationed themselves forward, John sat aft, and Scotty manned the helm. The extra speed put them up on top of the waves, and the boat's weight helped move them through the chop. The whole rig loaded, including the boat, fuel, Suzuki engine, four men, two scooters and safety gear was close to 2000 lbs. The wind howled at 20 knots and the seas outside the reef were a good four feet. Their speed was fair, about 10 to 12 knots, and with the stern plugs removed, the Zodiac self-bailed nicely. In conditions worse than this they probably would have to postpone their mission. But, off the wind and down-sea, they surfed along at 15 to 18 knots. Once inside the barrier reef, the boat was capable of over 20 knots, cutting through the water smartly. Back at the dock in Safe Harbor, they rinsed everything off, including themselves, with fresh water.

After practicing unloading the Honda's, Gene and John ran the scooters up to Boca Chica Key. Scotty, Freddy, and Seth followed in the Land Rover. John and Freddy drove the course first and as they pulled away from the start/finish line, Scotty started the stopwatch on his Omega® Seamaster. Gene and Seth started 30 seconds later. Several minutes later, John and Fred came over the last mogul and roared by Scotty, who recorded seven minutes and 30 seconds on his stop watch. Gene and Seth limped in two minutes later, wet and muddy.

"Are you guys all right?" asked Scotty.

"Yeah — we just lost it and slid through a large mud puddle," laughed Gene.

"Let's see," said Scotty figuring in his head. "Fred and John averaged just under 40 mph."

"It would take a freakin' hedge fund guy to figure that in his head," said Seth while wiping mud off of his face.

"Just thinking about dividing that is giving me a headache," laughed John.

"Seriously, we only lost 10 miles per hour adding another man," said Seth. "Let's practice another hour and call it a day. Scotty and John can run down to the Bight and get a couple dozen goggle-eyes. Gene and I will rig some frozen ballyhoo for tomorrow's fishing on the Hatteras."

After Seth finished rigging the ballyhoo, he called Billy Ray Stodgins.

"Hey Billy, Seth here. Could you put me in touch with Deputy Pearce? I want to see if he'll ride with Charley Blevins on the Huckins."

"He already told me wants to go and he'll pay his own way. He likes you guys and he could probably use some adventure."

"That's great, give me his cell phone number, if you will, and I'll fill him on the dates — we leave the middle of next week. When this operation is over and I get Hugo Lugo to pay up … he'll get at least $100 a day. We'll have all the food and drinks covered."

"Did you say, Hugo Lugo? … He's the ballplayer that turned in your friend in Cuba, right?"

"Yeah," said Seth.

"I just read about him in the *Key West Citizen*. I know his agent Alex Esteban. He just got him a huge contract."

"Gene and I read the same article. So you know Alex?"

"Yes, I got a couple of his players out of a scrape down here a couple of years ago. They drank too much and trashed a hotel room. Alex took care of all the damages and smoothed the whole thing over with the hotel. We just charged them with disturbing the peace. Neither the players nor Key West needed the bad publicity. Alex is a stand-up guy."

"If I get my friend out of Cuba, will you introduce me to Alex?"

"Sure, I'm sure he'll get his client to do the right thing."

"Thanks, Billy … and thanks again for setting us up in the Sunset House. The girls will be down here in a couple of days."

"Glad to do it, have fun."

The fighter jets were starting to come back into Boca Chica Air Force Base from their afternoon mission and were using the west to east approach. They flew, one after another, right over *TAR BABY* with their flaps down, their jet engines making a deafening roar as they landed one-by-one. When the last one landed, Seth got on his sat-phone and called Doug Clorey.

143

"Hey, Doug, where are you, man?"

"Down at Useppa Island — what's up?"

Seth explained Dave the Wave's plight and filled him in on the onboard personnel.

"We had an operation planned to get him out of Pinar Del Rio, but Dave was suddenly transferred during the sugar cane harvest to Las Tunas Province at the east end of Cuba — so we couldn't pull it off there."

"Now our plan is to leave for the Ragged Islands in the lower Bahamas early next week. That will be our jump off point for Cuba. Duncan Town is only 60 miles from Puerto Padre in northern Las Tunas Province. Charley Blevins is bringing his Huckins 62 down to back us up. Do you want to ride along and help him bring *ABOUT TIME* down?"

"What's the whole time frame?"

"We were originally down here just to catch sailfish when we got word that we might be able to get Dave out of Cuba. We have our significant others flying down this weekend for Valentine's Day on Sunday and we don't want to cancel that for obvious reasons, so we want to start down island Wednesday. Charley's leaving St. Pete on Monday and he'll be here in Safe Harbor on Tuesday. Our little flotilla should be anchored near Duncan Town by early Friday. John Harvey has his plane here in Key West, so I was planning on him flying down to Duncan Town, in case we need to fly anybody out of there fast. You can fish back to Florida with me, motor up to Nassau with Charley and fly home, or fly directly back to St. Pete with John. We'll only be in Duncan Town and the Puerto Padre area for three or four days, but you could dive the Ragged Islands' pristine reefs for at least one or two of those days."

"That's hard to pass up, Seth. There aren't many people that have ever done that and I've wanted to go along on one of your adventures for some time. Dave's a friend of mine too. He taught me how to surf when I was just a kid. He gave me my first surfboard."

"We could really use your diving and boat handling experience on Charley's boat. I signed on a retired deputy sheriff from Key West yesterday. He's a 'Conch', named Bill Pearce, who we met down here a couple years ago when we recovered Charley Blevin's Huckins. I know you'll like him. *TAR BABY* and *ABOUT TIME* will stay in international waters the whole time. There's not much chance of things getting too dicey out there since the U.S. Coast Guard is right around the corner in Guantanamo."

"Count me in — I can make it work in one of those time frames."

144

"Do me a favor, Doug, and call Norm Hogan to see if he can come — we could use one more experienced waterman. Having a retired DEA agent along might help. He's worked a lot of under-cover operations in Florida, Central America, and the Caribbean, during his career. I know Norm has run big boats and can fly airplanes ... and I'm sure he'll be cool under pressure. He always asks me to remember him for crew when I see him at our fishing club meetings. Same deal for Norm, fish back or fly back. Charley's cellphone is 727-439-2121"

"I'll track him down and call you right back ... and thanks for asking me, Seth."

Charley was Seth's next call. He filled Charley in on Deputy Pearce and Doug Clorey.

"I'm hoping Norm Hogan can crew for you, too. Doug is trying to line him up right now. You'll be getting a call from Norm or me."

Seth hoped both of them could manage to come. They would fill out both crews perfectly. During the operation, Gene would run the Hatteras with Norm, and Deputy Pearce and Doug would crew for Charley on the Huckins. John, Freddy, and Scotty would front the assault with Seth. Something in the back of Seth's mind told him he needed more insurance when they stopped the train near Puerto Carupano. He wasn't sure what to add to the plan he and Bobby made, but the thought still nagged him.

Just as Scotty and John came back from Key West Bight and were putting the goggle-eyes in the baitwell, Seth's phone rang.

"That's great, Norm, glad you can make it. Did Doug give you Charley's number?"

"Yes, he did. Can I bring anything?"

"No, we'll take care of all the food and drinks, and we have plenty of weapons on board if they're needed."

"I have a couple of short barreled Beretta® SCP AR 70/90's that can shoot rifle grenades with a GL barrel adapter. I can bring a couple of cases of grenades and 1000 rounds of ammo, they're leftovers from my Columbian war on drugs days."

"Bring them, Norm. Charley has a hidden gun closet we built for him when his boat was refurbished after it was stolen. The Berettas will give us more firepower if we need it. Give Charley a call, he's expecting to hear from you, and we'll see you Tuesday."

"Thanks for asking me ... I can use a little action."

Seth headed for the shower and then joined the rest of the crew at the bar in The Hogfish Grille.

"Winds are knocking down, Seth."

"Yeah, Freddy, but I still think we'll have a good day fishing off the reef tomorrow."

They had a couple of cold ones and sat at a table with their hogfish dinners. The crew was tired after the Zodiac and scooter practice. The wind, sea, moguls, and mud had taken their toll. Seth filled them in on the new crew additions and their reactions were all positive.

"I remember when Doug Clorey first got in the fishing club," said John Harvey. "His first trip with us was to the Panama Canal, where we fished in Lake Gatun for peacock bass. The club organized a tournament that had 18 professionally guided flats boats with two anglers per boat. Doug hooked himself in the back of his head, on his first cast, with a big treble hook Bomber® lure. He was bleeding so bad the guide ran in and took him back into Panama City to a hospital emergency room. He got a bunch of stiches in his head and was bandaged up like a mummy. Doug came back to the lodge in a taxi just in time for lunch and the trophy presentations. We gave him the trophy for landing the biggest fish. He laughed at himself and really handled the situation well … that's when I knew I was really going to like him."

"Yeah, he's a good fisherman and handles a boat well, too," said Gene.

"Norm has loads of war stories from his undercover days. He's a case in point that fact is stranger than fiction," said Seth.

"He can fly my plane … if I can't," said John.

"Amen, brother," said Scotty.

"Let's be on deck at 7:30 a.m., gents. We'll troll until the sun gets up a bit, and then we'll put the goggle-eyes under the kites," said Seth yawning. "I'm ready to turn in."

***

Hugo finally started to break a sweat on his second round of wind sprints. The low humidity in Phoenix made the morning heat quite comfortable for someone used to 95 degree temperatures at 89% humidity. He was easily the fastest man on the Padres team and maybe the fastest man in baseball right now. His recent fielding and batting practice rounded him back into top form and he looked forward to his first spring series game against the Los Angeles

Dodgers tomorrow. Hugo's command of English had already made him popular with the Padres veterans and the spring training sports writers. Alex coached him during daily phone calls on how to handle the press and made sure he smiled like a politician while he spoke. Yesterday after practice, he made a dinner date for tonight with a persistent groupie, named Naomi, who had a gorgeous body. If things worked out he would have her rent a motel room in Phoenix for a tryst. All he had to worry about was making the 10:00 p.m. bed check back in Peoria. The Padres' two All-Stars, first baseman, Adrian Gonzalez, and pitcher, Heath Bell, stayed in private condos and had no curfew when on the road. Adrian confided in Hugo that his agent had negotiated that perk in his last contract. Hugo filed that information away in his brain for five years from now. He ran his last wind sprint and didn't let up until he crossed the finish line.

"Your fastest time of the day, Hugo," chortled Jake Rupert, the third base coach. "I can't wait to see you steal some bases in a game. You're gonna drive the pitchers and catchers crazy!" — "OK guys, that's it for today," shouted Jake to all the players. "Time to hit the showers — be in the locker room tomorrow at 10:00 a.m. sharp for the Dodgers game."

Hugo met Naomi in a CVS pharmacy parking lot and took her to Phoenix to watch an early showing of *Moneyball*, starring Brad Pitt, a movie about major league baseball that Adrian Gonzalez told him about. Hugo bought two Coca-Colas and a huge bucket of popcorn and they settled down in two seats in the nearly deserted theater. The movie was interesting and he put his arm around Naomi. They started to make out a little. She let Hugo feel her generous breasts when they kissed, but she pushed his hand away whenever he moved it under her skirt. Hugo's patience was wearing thin and he considered trying a "popcorn surprise" to establish the ground rules. But Naomi surrendered to his next advance and also returned the favor. She spent the remainder of the movie tracing the outline of Hugo's denim covered red-necked friend.

After an early dinner at La Santisima Gourmet Tacos, they retired to a motel in nearby Glendale. After her slow start, Naomi proved to be a practiced and ardent companion ... teaching even Hugo a few new tricks. He dropped her off at the CVS with promises of a repeat performance and easily made his curfew. As he drifted off to sleep, Hugo wondered if it would always be this simple after he became famous.

***

"Left rigger, left rigger!" yelled Seth as he saw a dark shape come up behind the naked ballyhoo.

John was ready when the line snapped out of the rigger clip, but he didn't feel a bite. His reel was in free-spool, and he held the line motionless with his thumb.

"He's back!" yelled Seth.

John felt a tug, took his thumb off the reel, and let it free-spool for four seconds, then he pushed the drag lever up to strike and pointed the rod tip at the fish. The sailfish came tight and started grey-hounding and jumping. Seth put the Hatteras into a turn and circled back towards John's bite. The right long and the shotgun went off, so Fred and Scotty were hooked up too. That left Gene to clear the flat lines and long teasers. Seth maneuvered the boat favoring first one fish and then another as they jumped and ran. Finally, he settled on John's as the most tired and backed down on him as Fred and Scotty played over and under across the transom. John's fish changed directions and headed right for the boat. He reeled furiously but when the line came in the fish was gone.

"He was probably just bill-wrapped John," yelled Seth as he started after Fred's sailfish.

"Your lines are crossed," yelled Seth at Fred and Scotty. "Put your rod tips together and have Gene sort it out."

Fred went under and around twice, but it was too late. They lost both fish to broken lines. Fred's fish jumped a few more times on its way out of town, and Scotty's just disappeared as they reeled in the remaining line.

"What a cluster-fuck that was," muttered Scotty as he stuck his rod-butt in the rocket launcher.

"Hey boys, we're going to have some bad luck along with the good," said Seth. "We still caught eight sailfish this morning. Let's shake it off, re-rig those rods, then we'll move next to the reef and kite fish with the goggle-eyes. There's no telling what we might catch."

The boys sucked it up and set the kites out through the long riggers after snapping their 20 lb. line into the kite's Blacks clip. The goggle-eyes were circle-hooked right in front of their dorsal fin. Seth steered the boat into the north-east wind and bumped it in and out of gear to hold it there. Within minutes they had a smokin' wahoo on. Soon, the sailfish started nailing the live, splashing goggle-eyes and double-headers became the rule. By 2:00 p.m. everyone was ready to pack it in.

"Let's call it a day, guys. We've caught 15 sails and a nice wahoo. And we made a nice recovery from our mid-day slump. We need to give the boat a good scrub, and I have to pick up the key for the Sunset House from Billy Ray. I have a list for Publix and the liquor store that Gene and John can get going on, while Fred and Scotty scrub the boat. We'll move the groceries over to the house's dock late this afternoon on *TAR BABY*, along with Fred and John's stuff. The Hatteras will stay there for the weekend. I'm going to have Scotty drop Gene at Enterprise later to rent a car. We'll need an extra car while the girls are here.

Seth eased the Hatteras up to the Sunset House's dock and Freddy jumped off to tie her up, while John lassoed the tie poles off the northwest side of the dock.

"We couldn't tie up here if there weren't tie poles," said Seth. "There is some wake here from boats running in the Northwest Channel. Scotty and Gene will come over later on the ferry after they park the cars in the Westin's garage downtown."

Seth dialed up Lori and she answered on the third ring.

"Hey, Seth, I just finished packing."

"Well, I can't wait to see you tomorrow. We have a great weekend planned. We're just moving into the house now, and stocking it with groceries and drinks. I know you're going to love it."

"I'll love seeing you more."

"Me, too! How are you getting to the airport?"

"Stacy will pick me up, along with Penelope Buckley. Helen Johnson is picking up Scotty's girlfriend, Pam, in Seminole. Parking's free at St. Pete/Clearwater International."

***

The girls got off the Piper Aztec and headed for the Key West Terminal. They all brought way too much luggage, but the sturdy Aztec got it there.

"Good flight, girls?" asked Seth as he gave Lori a hug and a kiss. They all answered "yes" as they walked out to the parking lot.

"It's just Scotty and me here because of the luggage. Y'all will have your own reunions down at the ferry dock. The boys are waiting for us there."

Seth and Scotty caravanned down Roosevelt to downtown and parked the cars in the Westin garage. They wheeled the luggage to the ferry stop and were greeted by John, Gene, and Fred. By the time everybody got kissed and hugged, the ferry pulled in.

"The ferry runs every 30 minutes from 6:30 a.m. to 12:00 midnight. After that, you call the number on the sign," said Seth. "We have two six-seater golf carts waiting for us at the ferry dock, and the resort's porters will deliver the luggage to the Sunset House. But first, we're going to have welcome drinks and lunch at Latitudes on the covered veranda … then we'll go up to the house."

The girls twittered and smiled and Penelope said, "I like this first class treatment, gentlemen … I hope we're as tan as y'all when we leave Monday."

Everyone was smiling and laughing as they pulled up to the covered ferry dock. Margaritas, Mojitos and an iced tub of Heineken® beer awaited them on the veranda. Lunch was superb, and the girls enjoyed the style and the service provided by Latitudes. The view overlooking the Northwest Channel and the quiet ambiance was a welcome respite from the hustle and bustle of downtown Key West.

"We drew for rooms in the house yesterday, so let's go up to the house and get settled. The resort's waterfall pool has bar service, so let's meet there after we get moved in," said John.

The couples filed, one by one, into the pool area which was within easy walking distance of the house. The tropical foliage and seating areas lent themselves to conversation and relaxation.

"The house is beautiful, Seth. All the rooms are really nice," said Helen.

"I see that *TAR BABY* is at the dock," said Stacy.

"We're going to have a harbor cruise on Valentine's Day at sunset," said Lori. "It should be fun with all the schooners and cruise boats out there."

"What's happening tonight?" asked Pam.

"We're going to toast the sunset from our own porch. Then we have dinner reservations at Marquesas on Fleming Street, with a nightcap planned back on our porch," said Fred.

The next morning Penelope and Lori walked around the island twice. Pam swam laps in the pool, while Helen and Stacy chatted on the porch. The boys straggled out with their coffee in hand and watched the commercial traffic sail in and out of Northwest Channel. When everyone was assembled they rode the ferry, walked up Whitehead Street, and cut over to Blue Heaven on Thomas Street for brunch. The private courtyard, which once hosted Hemingway's boxing matches, was filled with strutting roosters, pecking chickens, lounging cats, and visiting diners. Their large group was seated in the indoor "Tree House". After brunch, they walked down Duval Street, giving the girls ample time to explore the different shops along the way. There was no need for lunch, so the couples made their way back to Sunset Key where the girls were treated to an afternoon of spa treatments. Seth and the Geezers headed for the larger, more crowded Sunset Pool for some conversation, rest, and a cold one. Their significant others joined them for a swim late in the afternoon. After their swim, Seth and Lori walked back to their room.

"Let's get reacquainted, Seth," said Lori locking their bedroom door. "I've missed you in the middle of the night and especially in the mornings. It's been almost three weeks since we've been together."

"I know. In our case absence makes the heart grow fonder, but we were both too tired to do it justice last night."

"Come over here now and let me show you how relaxed and well rested I feel right now," said Lori as she shrugged out of her swimsuit.

"We're lucky our bed doesn't squeak," laughed Seth as he tested the bed.

"Enough talk," she whispered as Seth rose to the occasion. "I can't wait another moment."

Three weeks apart was a long time for these lovers and they both responded ardently. They kissed as they basked in the afterglow.

"I think we should try that again tomorrow, my love."

"I agree," smiled Lori. "And, I'm glad our bed doesn't squeak."

That evening they took in the sights on Mallory Square, watching the mimes, the famous "Cat Man" show, during which he actually herds cats. The sword swallowers, the high wire juggler, the human statues, the Bagpiper, the magicians, the unicycle juggling comedian, and all sorts of musicians were there. Lori had her picture taken, for $10, with a pair of pirates. One was a dwarf, the other a giant, both had parrots on their shoulders. Everyone tipped the Cat Man, and Seth thought the Bluegrass banjo picker deserved a $5 tip. Key West is truly where the weird turn pro. They ended up at the Westin's 245 Bistro and toasted the sunset with a round of Mojitos.

"We have a late reservation at Louie's Backyard," said Gene. "Let's grab a couple of cabs and ride up to Casa Marina and have another drink overlooking their pools and the Atlantic — then we'll walk over to Louie's 15 minutes before our reservations."

The outside bar at Casa Marina Hotel was balmy, and the ocean had calmed down and was almost as still as a lake. A round of "traveler" Mojitos were ordered. The girls were taken with the hotel's beautiful, park-like grounds and unmatched views. Seth wondered how many of the other couples had also made love in the Sunset House that afternoon. All the girls had rosy cheeks and looked relaxed … his money was on Cupid. The lilting breeze rustled the scores of queen palm trees covering the property as they strolled through the lush grounds on their way to Louie's. They were seated immediately and enjoyed a five-star dinner overlooking the now placid Atlantic.

Seth told the table, "Years ago, the first Hemingway marlin tournaments were headquartered here at Louie's when it was just a beach bar. Later, before new owners took it upscale, a now famous song writer/singer lived upstairs over the garage next door and played here for tips. His name is Jimmy Buffett."

"It was really Margaritaville in those days," laughed John.

"What's in store for us tomorrow, boys?" asked Helen.

"We thought we'd take kind of a road trip," explained Scotty. "But, we're going to do it on *TAR BABY*. We'll cruise up to Little Palm Island close to Newfound Harbor. It's only accessible by seaplane or boat. It's an exclusive resort and we wanted y'all to see the Keys from the water. We have lunch reservations."

"Tomorrow night, we've planned cocktails and dinner at our Sunset House," added Freddy. "I'm grilling filet mignon steaks, and you'll sample each man's specialty when we're cooking on the boat. Seth does the vegetables and picks the wine, Gene handles the potatoes, John makes the salad, and Scotty is the dessert guru. You're in for a treat … Oh! — and we clean it all up, too."

"Hear – Hear!!" cheered the women in unison.

"Then we're going on a Duval crawl and do a little dancin'," said Seth.

"What about Valentine's Day?" asked Pam.

"We'll all be sleeping late from the Duval crawl, and then have a lazy day doing whatever we want. We're joining the sunset cruisers and tall ships in the harbor channel on *TAR BABY* for cocktails, and we have a romantic dinner planned at Latitudes in a private area for our last night."

"You boys sure know how to treat a lady," said Stacy.

CHAPTER SIXTEEN

DAVE the Wave's crew of laborers chained the last batch of raw sugar cane together on the railroad car and hooked it to the overhead crane. They scrambled to the ground as the crane operator lifted it off and dumped it in the hopper. Dave's two lead men jumped in and unfastened the chain harness and the crane pulled the harness free. The prison labor crew's work was done for another day. The laborers all jumped on the last car, along with their armed guard, as the train slowly pulled out of the Deliciás boiler room and headed for the finished sugar warehouse 200 meters ahead. There, two diesel forklifts stacked 220 lb. sacks of sugar onto pallets before loading them on the train's flat-bed cars further forward near the locomotive. The next stop was Puerto Carupano, 20 minutes further by rail.

The 39 mile trip back to Las Tunas was uneventful. The train picked up the labor crews along the way and arrived at the prison camp just as the sun dipped below the horizon. Modesto smiled at Dave as they exited the train's passenger car ... tonight was English class night.

Dave stood under the cold shower and reflected on how lucky he'd been all his life. He hadn't done much in school but just get by. If the surf was up he'd skip school in a heartbeat. He dropped out in his senior year to join the pro surfing tour and never looked back. Dave used his natural athletic ability to become a surfing star. Training hard or having a surfing coach like many of his peers was not an issue. He was just good at it. Dave partied hard and didn't worry about much. When his spine let him down, he took his fame back to St. Petersburg and invested what money he had in a surf shop. He was a natural salesman and instinctively knew what products and innovations the surfing crowd was going to want. His shop sold a ton of surfboards. When Dave became bored working in the store day after day he was lucky again. His no-nonsense, very pleasant sister ran it for him and hired some of Dave's old surfing buddies to help. Dave the Wave worked when he wanted, went to the surf market shows, did the buying, and was the shop's icon. The shop did well, while Dave traveled, sailed, fished, and pub-crawled. Then one night, the shop burned down while he partied hearty down in St. Pete Beach. Dave lost his shop and his apartment upstairs. He had just paid for his Christmas inventory and it was all due to ship in the next two weeks. His cash flow was a bit on the weak side, and his everyday stock, including all of the surfboards, was gone. The building was covered by insurance, but the inventory was not.

Dave got the insurance company to quickly raze and haul away what was left of his frame building. He rented a huge tent from the rental company that supplied three of them every summer for his customer appreciation party on Shell Island. They erected it over the only thing that was left, a concrete slab. He moved onto his sailboat, which was docked two blocks away.

Dave, Sonja, and his shop staff spent two full days recreating his customer list with help from Visa, MasterCard, Discover and SunTrust bank. Dave sent personal letters to every customer offering a unique deal: For a $250 donation to the Treasure Island Surf Shop Rebuilding Fund, he extended each donor a lifetime 20% discount on everything bought at the store. It was a masterstroke — $40,000 was collected in the first 10 days. Dave called all his surfboard, board shorts, flip-flop, and bikini suppliers, and they rushed their shipments to him. He had always paid his suppliers on time and this is when it really paid off … *Fast pay makes fast friends*. As the inventory poured in, Dave had Smith Fence put a six-foot chain link fence around the tent and he installed an air-conditioned 10' x !2' Wally Watt building for an office. He or an employee slept there each night. Dave put up a new Treasure Island Surf Shop sign on the fence, along with a fire-sale banner, and had his highest grossing Christmas season ever. After Christmas the shop and his apartment were re-built and his life-style was restored.

Dave had to smile … here he was in his sixth month of incarceration in one of the most brutal and repressive prison systems in the world, and once a week he's invited to a gourmet cocktail/dinner party, followed by sex with an attractive older woman, who's 20 years younger than him. After that, he has a couple of hours of free *cerveza* and his choice of two or three 18 to 25-year old Cuban beauties. You couldn't touch a night like that in Vegas, Dubai, or Bangkok for $2000. *I'd rather be lucky than good*, laughed Dave to himself.

"What the hell are you grinning about," asked Modesto as he turned on the shower next to Dave.

"You wouldn't believe me if I told you all the unbelievable things that have happened to me."

"I'm kind of into that myself … and it ain't over yet," laughed Modesto.

As Modesto and Dave walked into the headquarters lounge that night, Consuelo pointed her riding crop at a tall, attractive, raven haired, Afro-Cuban who sat on the couch next to Rona.

"Dave and Modesto, meet Chantelle. She's a new inmate from Cienfuegos, who wants to learn better English."

They both went over and kissed her on both cheeks. She reciprocated as they welcomed her to their group. Soon they were all chatting about the rain, humidity, and the weather that was warmer than the previous winter. The girls drank an excellent Prado Rey 2008, Tres Barricas, an oak-fermented Verdejo white Spanish wine, while Modesto and Dave drank Hatuey Cervezas. Dinner was the same featuring excellent lobster, but tonight there was also fresh grilled head-on red snapper.

After dinner and the regular classwork, Consuelo took Dave into her office but chose an old corduroy couch for their tryst when they finished grading the tests. She was affectionate and kissed him repeatedly during a relatively calm session of lovemaking. She finally climaxed while she was on top, surprising Dave a bit.

"I wish I could figure out how to do this twice a week with you, Dave, but it might blow my cover."

"You'd get awfully good at English," laughed Dave.

"The revolution doesn't have a sense of humor."

They joined the girls and Consuelo chose Darly for her bondage session. Dave sat in an alcove with Chantelle and began to get acquainted with her while working on another Hatuey. Modesto slipped quietly into the other alcove with Rona and Marta.

Dave asked Chantelle, "So you like sex and bondage?"

She answered, "Yes, both."

"Which do you like better?" asked Dave.

"It's hard for me to say, but it's not about better. If you sat me in that dining room chair backwards, and tied my ankles to the back legs, with my arms and wrists tied over the back and gave me a pretty good whipping … I'd climax during regular sex, afterward."

"Do you ever get off without the bondage routine."

Chantelle shook her head and said, "Hardly ever."

"Bummer … Maybe we could try a little spanking first?"

"I'm up for almost anything, Dave," said Chantelle with a smile.

It was a weird scene, but English class was over too soon for Dave that Thursday.

**

Monserrat arrived at the Peoria, Arizona stadium an hour before game time. Alex flew out from Miami, waited for her at the airport, and then checked Monserrat into her hotel. They had a pair of comped box seats right behind home plate.

Later at the stadium, Alex said, "I'm getting good reports on Hugo's performance during training camp."

"He's been calling me almost every night. He went to see *Moneyball* last night and liked it, said Monserrat."

"How are you doing?"

"I'm keeping busy with the decorator, furnishing the condo and all. San Diego is a great place to explore and I have a car. I'm used to him being gone on road trips. It was like this in Cuba, but I miss him during the season."

"Hey, there he is … it's his turn for batting practice."

Hugo hit a couple of line drives, then a long fly ball left, before hitting the next three pitches over the wall in left field. He put his hand up and trotted back to the dugout.

"He looks sharp, Monserrat. Do you want something to eat or drink? I'm going to get a Diet Coke."

"Coca-Light for me, too, and a small popcorn, thank-you."

The game started and Hugo threw the Dodger third batter out at first after back-handing a grounder that hopped over third base. The first Padres batter walked and the second batter was hit by a pitch. The Dodger rookie pitching prospect, Garret Gould, was having a bad case of nerves in his first major league appearance. The pitching coach trotted out to the mound and tried to calm him down. The umpire shouted, "Play ball!" and the pitching coach trotted back to the dugout as Hugo Lugo stepped into the batter's box. Hugo took the first two pitches for balls, then hit a line drive to right-center on Garret's third pitch. A run scored and the other runner went to third. Hugo stopped at first as the ball was thrown in to second base.

Hugo took a generous lead off first base and Garret threw over to the first basemen. He bounced back on the bag just ahead of the throw. Garret toed the rubber, took his stretch, checked Hugo's lead, and coiled to throw. As soon as Garret's left leg started up Hugo took off for second base. The catcher's throw sailed into centerfield, the third base runner trotted home. Hugo sprang up and headed for third base. He beat the throw by two feet. The fans were on their feet cheering.

Monserrat and Alex leaped up and started hugging each other.

"They love him, they love him already!" yelled Alex. "What an exciting ball player — he makes things happen."

"He played like that all the time in Cuba," said Monserrat above the cheering. "They couldn't throw him out."

"He's just what the Padres needed," exclaimed Alex. "If he hits one out today my phone will ring off the hook with endorsement offers."

The Padres led 4-0 in the bottom of the sixth when Hugo came to the plate for the third time and faced California league prospect, Chris Withrow, with a runner on first. Chris got him out on a ground ball back in the third inning and was pitching him low and away. With a 3-2 count, he threw Hugo a high hard one and Hugo put it halfway up the grandstand in the left field seats. He got a standing ovation as he circled the bases.

"We couldn't have hoped for a better start, Monserrat," said Alex excitedly. "I can't wait to see the *San Diego Tribune's* sports page tomorrow. My phone **will** ring off the hook."

After the 6-0 Padres win, they waited for Hugo outside the locker room. He finally appeared and swept Monserrat up in his arms and shook Alex's hand.

"Great start, Hugo — two for four, a home run, three runs batted in, one run scored, two stolen bases, and a great backhand fielding play at third. You'll be the focus of the sports writers in tomorrow's paper along with the San Diego pitching."

"It was good to be playing again, and the training paid off, Alex. Thanks for coming."

"I'm going to leave you two lovebirds alone for the evening and have dinner with Josh Byrnes. I fly back to Miami in the morning. I'll get some phone calls from local businesses in San Diego tomorrow wanting you to endorse their car wash or restaurant. They won't be able to afford you halfway through the season. That's the way it always starts. Just keep smiling and play your best every day."

"There were two reporters talking to me in the locker room before I came out."

"A great beginning, Hugo. I'll be back on opening day in San Diego. We'll be talking on the phone. Bye, Monserrat."

Hugo drove Monserrat to the Glendale Hampton Inn. They made passionate love, then went out to dinner. Monserrat filled him in on the condo furnishing during dinner.

"I'm glad you're staying for two more days, I have missed you very much," said Hugo. "We go over to Merryvale and Scottsdale the end of next week to play the Brewers and the Giants. The following week you can come back for the Chicago Cubs and the Indians — back to back right here."

After dinner, it was back to the Hampton. Hugo left almost immediately to make his 10:00 curfew.

On the way out he said, "I love you, *Cariño*, and I wish I could wake up next to you tomorrow morning."

"We'll be together in San Diego in April. I will come to you here, whenever you want me. Hit a home run again tomorrow, and I will do something very special for you."

"You're the best, Monserrat."

Hugo hit a homer in each of his first three games, he stole two more bases and was hitting over .500. The sportswriters were predicting big things for Hugo and the Padres. Each night, back at her hotel it was more *Choo Choo La La*. When she finally caught her plane back to San Diego she was worn out.

***

Back in the tropics, the Duval crawl was a big hit. The group started drinking and dancing at Sloppy Joes. They progressed to Rick's and the boys got braver. They took them upstairs to the Bull and Whistle's third floor - clothing optional, Garden of Eden. The band was tight and by that time the girls thought it was a hoot — but nobody in their group shed any clothes. Wet Willie's was next, followed by some dancing at the gay Club Aqua, where they also watched a drag show. They finished up at the Green Parrot before stumbling back to the Sunset Key ferry.

The next morning started slow and then tapered right off into nap time. But the troops rallied for the sunset cruise. Motoring alongside the 75 and 80 foot schooners with their full accoutrement of sails up is an exciting experience. Add to that, the large power and sail catamarans and a 71 foot rebuilt World War II PT boat powered by three Packard engines totaling 4055 HP. There was plenty of action, great cocktails, and a wonderful sunset. They departed *TAR BABY* back at the Sunset House's dock and boarded the six-seat golf carts for the short trip to Latitudes.

A candlelight dinner in a private grotto awaited them, where they chatted and laughed while reliving their favorite experiences during their whirlwind weekend. There was a long string of toasts after dinner, mostly humorous, thanking Seth and the other Geezers for the beautiful weekend. The Geezers reciprocated with toasts to the women for being such good sports. When they finally retired for the evening, the Sunset House became a cacophony of squeaking beds.

"Apparently our bed is the only one in this house that doesn't squeak," laughed Lori as she and Seth enjoyed their last night together in Sunset House.

"At this point, Lori, I don't think they give a damn!"

The next morning was classic — "Parting was such sweet sorrow", and they all pledged to get the group together in St. Pete when the boys returned from the Bahamas. Scotty didn't want to leave his Land Rover in Key West, so Pam and Penelope drove it back to St. Petersburg after dropping the other girls off at the Key West International Airport.

"Quite a weekend, Seth. I know Helen really enjoyed it," said Gene as he helped John load the Suzuki outboard into the cockpit with the gin pole.

"Stacy had a blast, she couldn't believe Key West could be that much fun," added John.

"Lori thought it was a great mix of people, and nobody was a party pooper," smiled Seth. "She really enjoyed Penelope and Pam, too. They both have good senses of humor."

"That's the first time I can remember five woman laughing at Scotty's five-cent joke," snickered Gene.

"I must have missed that one," said Freddy as he and Scotty helped wheel the inflated Zodiac next to the dock.

"Tell it again, Scotty," laughed John. "It's not real long."

"A grandfather took his six-year old grandson to the zoo in the morning and then for lunch and some ice cream before taking him home. He ordered lunch and the grandson started playing with the salt and pepper shakers while they waited to be served. He gave the youngster three nickels from his pocket and said, 'Play with these buffaloes and leave the shakers alone.' The grandfather's cellphone dinged and when he looked up from the text, his grandson was choking and the nickels were gone. He grabbed the child and slapped him on the back and the boy coughed up two of the nickels. He pounded on the child's back to no avail and his grandson continued choking and started to turn blue. The grandfather panicked and yelled for help.

A well-dressed, attractive woman wearing a blue business suit calmly folded her newspaper, stood up and walked across the restaurant. When she reached the boy she carefully pulled down his shorts and took hold of his tiny testicles. She squeezed them gently, then more firmly. The boy stopped breathing and the woman calmly twisted them and gave them a yank. The little boy sprang back to life, convulsed rather violently, and coughed up the last nickel - which she deftly caught with her free hand. She released the boy's testicles and handed the nickel to his grandfather as she returned silently to her table.

The grandfather pulled up his grandson's shorts and saw that he was okay. He rushed over to the woman's table and started thanking her, saying, 'Thank you, I've never seen anyone do that before. Are you a doctor?'

'No,' replied the woman, 'I'm a divorce attorney'."

When Freddy finally stopped laughing he said. "I don't know why I'm laughing, it's the absolute truth."

"You got that right, Freddy," said Scotty with a sardonic smile.

Frivolity aside, the crew had the Hatteras almost totally packed and provisioned when *ABOUT TIME* idled into Safe Harbor Marina later that afternoon. Charley chose to tie up to the wall across the basin from *TAR BABY*.

They all had dinner at the Hog Fish Grille and retired afterward to Charley's salon on the Huckins for a team meeting. Everybody knew each other from St. Petersburg, except Deputy Pearce. Seth, John, Fred, and Gene knew Bill from the drug bust and recovery of *ABOUT TIME* at Safe Harbor about six years before. Scotty, Charley Blevins, Doug Clorey, and retired DEA agent Norm Hogan were all introduced to him and the meeting was started.

"Sounds like the Huckins 62 had a nice ride down. It's not lobster season so you didn't have to dodge lobster trap buoys all the way across Florida Bay," said Seth. "Tomorrow will be a lay day. We'll get both boats fueled up, change any filters or v-belts that need it, and Charley and I will coordinate our waypoints all the way down to Ragged Island. Deputy Pearce will move aboard the Huckins. John and Fred will fill the last two bunks on *TAR BABY*. We'll keep some fishing gear outside in plain sight on the Hatteras since that is always our cover story. Tuesday morning we'll run about five hours at 18 knots to Key

Largo and anchor for the night behind Rodriguez Key. It looks like the fronts are slowing down, and the next one won't be coming through here until later in the week. We'll leave at first light Wednesday, run across the Gulf Stream, then across the top of Andros Island, and through the Northwest Channel past Chub Cay to Nassau."

"How long is that leg?" asked Scotty.

"One hundred and ninety miles. If we still have fair winds we can run at 20 knots and make it to Nassau Harbor in about eight hours. Charley made two reservations at Hurricane Hole Marina on Paradise Island — it's getting a little dicey to stay on the Nassau side, with all the crime and big city bullshit. We'll take on fuel when we arrive there. If the weather forecast holds we'll be gone the next morning to Flying Fish Marina in Clarence Town, on the south end of Long Island. That leg is 225 miles and we'll run at 24 knots — we should make it in eight to nine hours. If the weather kicks up we'll take two days and stop at Davis Harbor on south Eleuthera, or anchor further along at Conception Island overnight. Any questions so far?"

"Do you think it would be wise to limit our boat-to-boat conversations to our sat-phones?" asked Charley.

"Right, I rented four sat-phones from Satellite Communications in Naples, so we would have secure communication on the ground in Cuba and in the islands. With my sat-phone and Charley's we have six."

"Are we going to carry the two 55 gallon diesel drums aboard *TAR BABY*?" asked Freddy.

"No, they're going to be strapped on *ABOUT TIME's* swim platform along with a drum of gasoline for the outboards. That will allow us to store the uninflated Zodiac on the foredeck and the Suzuki outboard in the cockpit along with one scooter — frees up our salon space. Charley will store the other scooter alongside his dinghy on his bridge afterdeck. His davit will make short work of that."

"Sounds like you've got everything all balanced out. Are we going to practice at all with the grenade-launchers that Norm brought?" asked John.

"I brought along two cases of grenades," interjected Norm.

"Wow, fucking grenades!" said Doug Clorey. "I **knew** this was going to be fun."

"I think we'll have plenty of time somewhere in the middle of our run between Clarence Town and the Ragged Islands. Once we get around the south end of Long Island and head for Duncan Town, I'd be surprised if we see another boat during that 80 mile stretch. Why don't you pick up a few blow-up beach toys for targets tomorrow, Scotty?"

"What kind of firepower do we have besides the grenade-launchers, Seth?" asked Deputy Pearce.

"I'll show you the secret gun locker tomorrow, Bill. Charley has one too. I have several 9mm pistols and .38 revolvers, and an AR-15 Bushmaster. I also have a Remington®700 hog rifle with a night scope, laser sights, and a silencer/suppressor — along with two Remington 870 tactical 12 gauge magnum shotguns with lights. We also have the body armor and Tasers® that Billy Ray gave me after the drug bust. Tell him what you have, Charley."

"Basically, three Glock®9mm semi-automatic pistols, two Bushmaster rifles, and two tactical shotguns. Just like Seth's, there's a false back in the master stateroom hanging locker. It's held in place with Velcro all around. Remove the clothes and foul weather gear and pull the false wall out with the two bronze hang-up hooks. There's a gun and pistol rack and watertight ammo boxes behind."

"Okay, guys let's get a good night's sleep and make everything ship-shape tomorrow. Familiarize yourself with the sat-phones, especially the internal contacts list. When you call out — dial it just like a cellphone. Just remember it costs $1.50 per minute," counseled Seth.

The next morning Seth talked to Bobby Thompson from the flybridge.

"Right, we're going to leave tomorrow. If the weather stays fair, I figure we'll be anchored in the Ragged Islands Friday or Saturday. It will take a half-day to set up the Zodiac and scooters, then we'll go in that night. We have plenty of support with Charley's boat backing us. We also acquired a couple grenade launchers. *ABOUT TIME* even has a 12-foot RIB if we need to send reinforcements in from 12 miles out," said Seth.

"Call me when you get to the Duncan Town area. I will set up the diversion explosion in Las Tunas the night you go in. Our other agents will attach the cellphone bomb under the train car coupling on the other side of town and alert Dave. I will call you with the cellphone number that will detonate it. If you have a problem out in international waters call our Coast Guard and me in that order. I can call the Guantanamo Coast Guard Commander, Heywood Jablome, on his cell phone and get things moving fast," said Bobby. "Old 'Woodie' has been a friend of mine for years."

"Do you have your satellite feed on?"

"Yes, I'm looking at Las Tunas right now."

"Scroll over to Deliciás and Puerto Carupano and zoom in on the railroad tracks going out to the port … see where the tracks turn to the east and run about two miles or so then turn back north and run over the man-made causeway to the port complex?"

"Yeah, I'm on it."

"That's where the track is going to be removed — the locomotive and passenger car will either stop or be derailed. The sugar cane cars will be left a mile or two behind after we detonate the C-4 cellphone charge. We could use a man there, back in the mangroves, on the other side of the tracks and road, to cover us if the guards from the cane cars react quickly."

"I really can't chance that, Seth. Politically it would be an act of war. If that man was traced back to us it could cause international repercussions. Our agents are all Cubans and their cover is that they will only admit to being dissidents. As long as you're in Cuba you are on your own. Once you're 12 miles offshore, that's a different story. Why don't you have your brother Beau, come in to do that?"

"Wha-what … Beau … you know?"

"Of course I do. He surfaced on my radar when he was shopping for his new identity in Costa Rica. It didn't take me long to put it all together. I've used him as a sub-contractor in Columbia, Ecuador, Venezuela, and Nicaragua. He has the assassin skillset, carries a Canadian passport, speaks fluent Spanish, and looks Spanish with the black beard. He's perfect for us."

"Why didn't you tell me, Bobby?" asked Seth.

"I just did."

"I get it … first and foremost you're a spook."

"And a good one, too. Look, I made a deal with Beau. He didn't break any U.S. laws robbing the Mafia and the guys he eliminated were all criminals. No law enforcement agency knows any of that shit went down. Actually, you were an accessory after the fact yourself. But, Beau can resurface in the states if he wants. He has five CIA departmental outstanding service commendations in his file. Beau can write off the Key West shark tank story as a ploy to get him into deep cover. Ricardo Cabeza was killed by his greedy cousins, who have disappeared. I can get his U.S. passport reinstated tomorrow. But, right now he seems to be happy in Costa Rica."

"Would it be possible for you to hide an AK-47 rifle in that area, with a few banana clips filled with rubber bullets, along with a couple of Micro Ace smoke grenades?"

163

"I can do that, and I'll add a 9mm Glock, and a clip of real AK-47 ammo in case things get really rough. I'll have *El Cazador* bury them on the edge of the mangroves and I'll text you the exact GPS coordinates."

"How can we get Beau in and out of there? My crew can't know it's him."

"I'll call *El Cazador* and see what logistics are available and I'll call you back," offered Bobby.

"I'm hoping we'll have enough time to load the scooters in the Zodiac. I don't want to leave any evidence behind."

"You can come back and work for me anytime, my friend. Good luck — if it's not cloudy I'm going to watch the whole thing from the satellite."

CHAPTER SEVENTEEN

HUGO LUGO stepped back into the batter's box with a 3 & 2 count. He knocked the dirt out of his spikes with the end of his bat, dug his clean spikes into the dirt and adjusted his jock strap with his left hand. He took a couple of warm-up swings and settled into his stance while moving the top of his bat in a tiny circle. The pitcher checked the runner at first, paused, then thrust his left leg towards the plate and delivered an off speed curve ball. Hugo was patient and waited for the spinning missile. It hung for just a moment as it curved towards the plate, and Hugo uncoiled his powerful body and struck the ball flush. The ball leaped off his bat and disappeared over the left field wall of Peoria's Stadium. It was a walk off, bottom of the ninth inning, homer beating the San Francisco Giants. Hugo was leading the Cactus League in batting average, homers, and stolen bases. Wilson® was making overtures as well as Reach®, Louisville Slugger®, and Spaulding®. Nike® and Adidas® were angling with Alex to have Hugo endorse a new shoe to celebrate baseball's next exciting base stealer. Alex was in no hurry — as Hugo excelled in each game his value kept increasing.

Monserrat was in the stands again, arriving that day for the Giants game and staying for tomorrow's Colorado Rockies game. She sat at the game with some of the other players' wives and girlfriends. She met them at a team party after an afternoon game during her trip to Peoria the week before. She found they all had a lot in common and the talk about travel, loneliness, boredom, and raising children with nannies comforted her. She had already heard some stories about the ever-present groupies that chased their men. Monserrat thought Hugo was so incredibly horny whenever she visited that he couldn't be playing around. The condo decorating and furnishing was a slow and laborious process, but she enjoyed learning from the decorator and it kept her busy. She was glad she had worked hard on her English, just as Hugo had, to help them follow his baseball dream. Now they were starting to live it, and it was far beyond anything she could have dreamed of. Just being able to go to a supermarket and find almost anything you wanted was an incredible experience after the rationing and empty shelves at the *bodegas* in Cuba. Suddenly they had been transported into the top one percent of American society earnings-wise. Monserrat marveled that even the poorest classes in America had far more than their Cuban counterparts that chose to work.

It was just about three weeks since she had stopped taking her birth control. She would wait to take the over the counter urine test until she missed her first period, which was due in a few days. If she didn't get pregnant for a while, she would have to feign illness during the first few days of her period to keep Hugo from knowing.

***

The Geezers were up early and shared the chores associated with an open ocean voyage. The advantage was they were all experienced sailors.

Bobby Thompson was right, thought Seth. *Beau had all the skills that were needed for this job. In fact, he was over qualified. Beau had been an Airborne Ranger sniper and covert operator in Vietnam. He was embedded behind enemy lines and was responsible for the deaths of many important Viet Cong politicians, generals, and high-ranking officers. Some he killed from a mile away, and others were killed with a knife or his bare hands. What made him perfect now was that Beau had a Canadian passport and was a permanent resident in Costa Rica. His new identity, which he had purchased with a small part of the $3,000,000 he had purloined from the Tampa Mafia, listed him as Robert B. Cornett, from Toronto, Ontario, Canada. He could fly in and out of Cuba and travel its interior as Cuba's number one source of tourists.*

The call back from Bobby had come in less than an hour. Seth jotted the info down and marveled at the efficiency of Bobby's networking.

Seth took his sat-phone and walked to the southwest corner of Safe Harbor Marina, where nobody could overhear his phone call. He stood behind a Bertram owned by Steven Johns, a seafood broker from St. Petersburg, and dialed Beau.

"Hey Bro', what gives?" answered Beau.

"Can you talk?"

"Yeah, I'm on my way to Puntarenas to check on my Bertram. I'm having the bottom painted and the cutlass bearings changed out."

"I'm down in the Keys at Safe Harbor standing behind Steven John's Bertram 46."

"Definitely bigger than mine."

Seth launched into a condensed version of Dave the Wave's Cuban saga, and within 10 minutes Beau understood the situation.

"I thought we agreed after the Provo thing a couple of years ago that you were going to fish more and turn in your commando badge."

"I did come down here to fish and it's been good. But, I had Bobby Thompson watching Dave in Cuba and they took him out of prison and put him in a work camp. Now they've made him a labor gang foreman on the sugar cane railroad. It looks like we can get him out," related Seth.

"Well, you know … Dave the Wave and I go way back. We ran up and down that beach road together in Pinellas County for decades. What do you want me to do?"

"Well, first I have to tell you that I was very surprised this morning when Bobby told me you have been doing some jobs for him," said Seth.

"I probably should have told you, but he said it was on a 'need to know' basis. He also told me you worked with him at the CIA for a while."

"I'm still trying to forget about that. But, I'm guilty as charged. Anyhow, I may need some cover fire and smoke after we get Dave off the train. Bobby can't chance getting one of his agents caught because of world politics. He told me we were on our own for the heavy lifting until we get back out into international waters. But, he will bury an AK-47 and some banana magazines of rubber bullets, a 9mm Glock, and a couple of Micro Ace smoke bombs at the spot I want – there's mangroves to hide a boat in and a back way out to the bay."

"Rubber bullets! Are you crazy?" questioned Beau.

"Hey, we don't want to kill anybody, we just want to slow them down. I checked out the rubber bullets — they'll break bones and ribs, put out your eye, and pretty much take the fight out of you."

"So, how do I get in and out of Puerto Padre? I don't want to come out of the closet, so I can't have any contact with your crew."

"Bobby just called me with the info. His chief agent, *El Cazador*, has it arranged. I need you to be in place by Friday, so you can do a day of scouting. We'll be coming in for Dave Saturday or Sunday, weather permitting. When you get back to Tambor today you can look at all this on Google Earth. Can you pull over and take some notes?"

"Yeah, I'm just approaching Puntarenas now …… Okay, I just pulled into a Super Mercado parking lot. Let me get a pen and some paper — Okay, shoot."

"You'll fly into Havana Thursday morning on Copa flight 1123, and fly that afternoon to Las Tunas on Cubana flight 124, it's an hour and forty minute flight. Reserve a car at Budget at the Las Tunas airport (VTU) and drive 53 kilometers to Puerto Padre. From there drive out to Playa La Boca which is located at the inlet from the Atlantic into Puerto Padre Bay. There's only one road to the west side of the inlet and its 25 kilometers from Puerto Padre. *El Cazador* made reservations for you, using your Canadian identification, at the Socucho Hotel, telephone (+53 31 16543), overlooking the inlet. There's a ferry if you have to get to the other side for some reason, and it can transport several cars. There's another road back to the mainland on that side too. Your cover story is the excellent tarpon, snook, and permit fishing on the flats of the bay. Light tackle fisherman travel there to catch world records. So, take your fly rod and spinning gear."

"Sounds like fun," laughed Beau, as he wrote down flight numbers and other information

"It's a wide inlet, like a quarter of a mile wide, with a big bay behind it. Freighters pass through to load and unload at Puerto Carupano on a skinny peninsula that was built out into the bay near the Deliciás Sugar Mill. Your contact is Jorge Mendoza at *Pescar Robalo,* telephone (+53 31 51575), a couple blocks south of the hotel. There will be a flats boat reserved for you with no guide required. Print out your own charts from Google Earth and Google Maps. The weapons will be buried at latitude 21° 12' 36" N 76° 33' 1" W. A pile of fresh dog turds will be on top of the freshly turned sand to help you find it. Bring your own hand-held GPS. Any questions?"

"Thanks, Bro', I got it all — just follow my nose, eh'."

"Do you have a sat-phone?" asked Seth, laughing.

"Yeah, Bobby gave me one a few years back."

"Make sure your SIM card's valid. Pack it along with your fishing gear, but don't declare it. The Cuban government is paranoid about sat-phones … and don't use it in front of anyone. They probably won't search your luggage, but if they take it, email me or Bobby from your iPad at Budget Rental or the hotel, and Bobby will get another one to you post-haste. We're going to coordinate this whole operation on sat-phones, but the other Geezers will think I'm talking to one of Bobby's Cuban agents."

"I'll get the airline tickets and car booked *pronto*, and let's check in with each other along the way."

"Bobby told me he had established a path for your re-entry into the U.S. as a citizen, with the CIA commendations and everything. He said he could get your passport reinstated."

"You know, Seth … right now I'm just happy being Robert B. Cornett, originally from Toronto, now retired in Costa Rica. What would I do in St. Pete? You're retired, and Jeb's got the Boatworks under control. I've beat my alcohol and gambling addictions, and I live next to maybe the best fishing grounds in the world. I have plenty of money and could live well just off my rental houses. I have a superb little sportfishing boat. The Costa Rican people are great, and there's enough ex-pats around to keep it interesting. Bobby feeds me a little action now and then and I've seen my brother and my nephew a time or two a year since the Turks and Caicos kidnapping. I hope Fonda Johnson will come live with me full time when her mother passes away. I'd gladly give up the local *chicas*, expat widows, and divorcees for her."

"Hey, Beau, no pressure. I'm just glad we're all alive and things are going well for you. We're leaving for Key Largo tomorrow and I'll text this itinerary to you so you can check your notes. Also, I'll call you when I get to Nassau. Thanks for signing on."

"You'd do it for me if I asked."

***

One day was like the next between Thursdays, although the train work was harder and more complicated when it was windy and raining. The prisoners toiled seven days a week as the government tried to maximize their sugar cane harvest. As Dave dressed for work before dawn he felt something in his right work boot as he slipped it on. He took it off and stuck his hand in the boot and felt a piece of paper. He looked around in the dark, saw no one near, and heard Modesto still snoring. He stuck the paper in his pocket, put the boot back on, and laced it up.

Dave shook Modesto awake saying, "We just have time to grab some *arroz y frijoles* before the train pulls out."

They made the train with time to spare and washed down their rice and beans with some coffee that was brewing in the passenger car. The locomotive guard came through the forward door with two empty cups on a tray.

"Any *leche* this morning for the engineer's coffee?"

"There's a bottle of milk in the cooler next to my desk," said Rosita the statistician.

Mateo sat in the back of the car chatting with Modesto and Dave.

"The weather is getting better. It's not supposed to rain for the next week," said Mateo.

"That means we'll be handling more cane each day as the fields dry out and the equipment doesn't get stuck in the mud," said Modesto.

"The volume shouldn't matter. The dry cane is way easier to handle," added Dave.

"A good week will put our numbers back in line and get the party bureaucrats in Las Tunas off my back," smiled Mateo. "Like the rain is my fault."

"I've got to use the *baño*," said Dave. "This coffee is just running right through me this morning."

He walked forward, entered the restroom across from Rosita's desk and closed the door behind him. He fumbled with the button fly on his work pants and got a stream going, then reached in his pocket with his other hand and pulled out the note. When his stream subsided he unfolded the note: *Be Alert. Be on the train every day. +Modesto. Leave no Stone unturned. Soon.*

Dave tore the note into pieces and flushed it. He took a deep breath, buttoned up his pants and tried to look calm as he exited the *baño*. He almost bumped into Modesto who was standing right outside.

"Oh, man, sorry!" said Dave, getting red-faced.

"I guess I have the same coffee problem," laughed Modesto as he entered the restroom quickly.

After breathing a sigh of relief Dave sat back down across from Mateo as the train lumbered down the track. He was glad he had time to flush the pieces of the note down the toilet and retrieved some bottled water to help the coffee story fly.

He ran the note's wording through his mind. *Seth Stone was coming for him. They were going to get him off this train. Modesto could come. It would happen soon ... How should he broach this opportunity to Modesto?*

Dave knew Seth Stone was his friend, and he knew Seth was capable and resourceful. There were enough rumors flying around St. Petersburg to know that Seth and his fishing crew were actively involved in a major drug bust along with the Sheriff's department in Key West. It went down the same time they recovered Charley Blevin's stolen Huckins. He'd heard first-hand accounts of automatic weapon fire with perps and deputies getting shot — when a couple of the Geezers had too much to drink. Seth and his crew were also involved when Peter Petcock was killed in the Turks and Caicos after he escaped from federal prison two years ago. There wasn't much information in the *St. Petersburg Times*, just an official press release from the federal warden at Coleman Federal Prison stating that Peter had been apprehended and his body was being shipped back to Florida for interment. A rumor circulated that Seth had killed Peter in self-defense with his bare hands. To think he had a friend like Seth, who could arrange to get him out of Cuba, blew Dave away.

Their train day went well and Dave rehearsed in his mind how he would approach Modesto. He was relatively sure Modesto would join him, but not knowing the exact details might make him back off. Nonetheless, Modesto had more than 13 years left on his sentence. Dave would pick his spot, but he needed to tell him soon since he didn't know which day the escape plan might materialize.

***

Modesto became suspicious when he noticed Dave dressing in the dark early that morning. He continued to make a snoring noise and watched Dave take a piece of paper out of his boot and stuff it in his pocket. Later, when they first got on the cane train Dave rushed to the *baño* in the office car. Modesto moved close to the door when Dave took longer than usual. When he finally exited, Modesto was standing right there. Dave's face was red, and he appeared to be stressed. Modesto entered and closed the *baño* door behind him. He quickly checked the toilet for any paper scraps. There were none, and he flushed the toilet for affect.

During the cane unloading in the Deliciás sugar mill, Modesto feigned a shoulder sprain. Back at the prison camp, he told Dave he was headed to the infirmary for some aspirin before showering. He bypassed the infirmary and went to the main office and requested to see the commandant. The commandant had been briefed on Modesto's status and put him on the phone with Consuelo. Modesto briefed her on the situation and suggested that the train's office car holding tank should be carefully examined that night for pieces of a new note that might have been flushed.

171

***

The plan called for John Harvey to fly his Piper Lance to Nassau on Wednesday, then down to Clarence Town on Thursday. Doug Clorey took his place on *TAR BABY's* crew. The boat trip to Key Largo was uneventful. Hawk Channel had a light chop and both boats made good time. Both vessels went in past "Crash Corner" and fueled up at Key Largo Harbor Marina, then motored out and dropped anchor behind Rodriguez Key. Charley launched his dinghy and both crews had an early dinner aboard *TAR BABY*. The camaraderie made the time pass quickly and the newer members' conversations were full of anticipation. Now that they were officially Geezers, the newbies were regaled by Gene and Freddy with tales from past adventures. Doug, Norm, Scotty, and Bill Pearce couldn't believe the resourcefulness of John Harvey when Gene described him slipping down a fence line in the Five Cays Dominican neighborhood, on Providenciales, to set a Chevy Suburban on fire for a diversion. The stories flew about Dino Vino's karate destruction of two Russian Mafia hit men in Key West, and the hilarious tale Freddy told about Dino getting humped by a gay dolphin at Hawk's Cay Resort. Deputy Pearce related being shot by Peter Petcock while he tried to escape during the Key West drug bust and how his body armor saved his life. After some prodding by Gene, Seth told the chilling story of his final encounter with Peter Petcock in the Tiki Hut Restaurant men's room in the Turk's and Caicos. You could have heard a pin drop. Charley's dinghy departed early and the crews turned in with the expectation of pulling anchor at first light.

The two-boat flotilla motored out easterly the next morning, past Carysfort Reef Light, anticipating the rising sun along with the promise of a good weather forecast. The Gulf Stream was some 18 miles away. As soon as the sun rose above the horizon they throttled up to 20 knots. Within an hour, Seth could see the Gulf Stream ahead. It was a deeper blue and had a light chop across it. There was even the illusion that it was six to eight inches higher than the water they were planing through now. The Stream flowed north at approximately 3.5 knots, so Seth and Charley had fudged their courses a few degrees to the south to compensate for the northerly drift. Their course would take them around the top of Andros Island north of the Joulter Cays, then southeast to New Providence Island and the city of Nassau. Two hours later they saw the light blue, almost white, loom of the Bahama Bank and left the dark blue water of the Gulf Stream behind. Two more hours went by on the same course and they entered the deep blue tongue of the ocean. Seth changed course to 135° and turned the helm over to Gene.

"I'm going to go below and ask Scotty and Doug to make lunch. I'll have Freddy get three 50 lb. rigs ready to go, two with Moldcraft® wide range lures. We'll rig the other pole with a red and black skirted silver bullet and a #5 hook like they use in Bermuda. I'll have him throw the mirrored teaser in the whitewater, too. Let's slow down and troll at 12 knots during lunch to give everybody a change of pace."

"We might as well troll a little, we're only about 80 miles from Nassau according to the Garmin chart plotter, and it's just a little after 11:00," said Gene with a smile. "The Tongue of the Ocean ... Wow! The bottom just went from 60 feet deep to 4000 feet, and it's still getting deeper! We could hook a marlin or a wahoo right here."

Seth radioed Charley and gave him the plan.

"It's been a nice ride, Seth. Deputy Pearce and Norm have been switching off at the helm and they're plotting the course on a paper chart. So far they're the best crew I've ever had. I'll get lunch started and have Bill get some rods out. But, I don't have outriggers like you."

"We're not going to use them. Make sure you put out a bullet-nose for a wahoo. Grilled wahoo on your fantail would be a better option than going to dinner at the Poop Deck in Nassau."

Seth went below and got things started. When lunch was ready, the boat was slowed down, and he went forward with his sat-phone.

"Hey, Bobby, everything is good with Beau. He should be flying to Cuba tomorrow."

"Good. One of *El Cazador's* men got a message to Dave the Wave. No details, just: *Be on the train every day. Be alert.* I also had them write, +*Modesto, Leave no Stone unturned* ... so he knows it's you and Modesto can go."

"Clever."

"The train is not really guarded at night — it sits on a side spur outside the camp's fence. The tower guards shine a search light out on it every five minutes. The C-4 charge is half the size of the little Samsung snap phone that will ignite it. Our agent will attach it under the coupling. A super-magnet will hold it there."

"Alright, we're about 80 miles from Nassau, slowing down to eat lunch. You were right about Beau, he's happy being Robert B. Cornett."

"But, he still likes the danger and adventure now and then."

173

"I do, too."

"I think we all do ... keep me posted."

Seth texted Beau's cellphone, which would work until he arrived in Havana, with an update. Then he would contact everyone via his sat-phone.

Seth stepped down into the fishing cockpit saying, "Where's my sandwich, Fred?"

"It's in the fridge in a plastic bag. Is everything okay?"

"Yeah — just checking in with Bobby, thanks."

Seth went back up in the flybridge with his sandwich and looked down into the crowded cockpit. There was a scooter lashed under the flybridge ladder. The Suzuki outboard on its four wheel cart was lashed in front of the bait freezer. The tackle drawers were accessible, but the outboard had to be moved to get in the freezer. It was fortunate that Charley agreed to come, as the other scooter and two fuel drums would have clobbered the remaining space. He sat down in the passenger seat, ate his sandwich, and drank a cold one.

Gene slowly zig-zagged the *TAR BABY* towards Nassau as the crew leisurely finished their lunch. All of a sudden the left-side reel started to scream.

"Blue Marlin," yelled Gene.

Scotty was the nearest to it and he silenced the clicker and took the rod to the fighting chair. Doug hooked him into the bucket harness after Scotty stuck the rod's butt in the gimbal. Fred reeled in the center rig first to get it out of Scotty's way, as Doug started to reel in the right-side rod. Fred pulled in the mirrored teaser, and Gene turned the boat and started after the fish.

"Did you see the bite, Gene?" asked Seth as the big marlin started to greyhound.

"Yeah, he really piled on it. The fish looked so big he has to be a blue."

The marlin jumped and danced, but soon Scotty had most of the line back from the fish's initial run. Gene turned the boat down sea forcing the big fish to swim up sea.

"Ease off your drag a little, Scotty, and reel up the catenary in the line," yelled Seth.

The fish surged from left to right as Gene turned the boat more down sea and throttled up a bit. The line ripped out of the water as Scotty reeled as fast as he could. In a matter of seconds, the big bow in the line was gone. The fish made two more sideways jumps and settled down.

"Ease your drag back up, Scotty. I'm going to back down hard and see if we can get a quick release. If he goes down we'll be here another half-hour."

174

Gene backed towards the fish hard and fast. Seawater smacked the transom and cascaded over Scotty in the chair as he reeled furiously. Hatteras installs generous cockpit scuppers, so the water never got beyond ankle deep.

"I see the double line, keep cranking!" yelled Doug.

The Bimini twist went through the rod tip and Doug soon had the leader in his hand. Gene stopped backing and Freddy grabbed the green and black wide range lure that had worked its way up the leader. He cut the leader below the lure with his Sportsman release knife. The magnificent fish turned slowly, looked at the boat with his huge left eye, and then disappeared into the depths with a flick of his powerful tail.

The crew responded with whoops, hollers, and high-fives as they pounded Scotty on the back.

"What a fish!" said Seth. "And what a masterful job of handling the boat, Gene."

"Learned it watching you, Buddy."

"Well, you made it look easy and I know it's not."

Seth radioed Charley to tell him they were going to resume the run to Nassau.

"Hey, Seth — looks like you had a big one on. We could see him jumping from over here."

"Probably 600 lbs. — we were lucky and got a quick release on him."

"While you were showing off we caught a double header wahoo. Both are about 45 lbs. Norm reeled one in on the bullet-nosed lure and Bill Pearce caught his on a purple and black Bobby Brown."

"Fantastic, we're going to pick up and run now … dinner is at your house tonight, Charley."

CHAPTER EIGHTEEN

THURSDAY was another sunny day in Las Tunas, and the workday was busy for Dave and Modesto. The cane cars were filled to capacity and the offloading took them long into the late afternoon. Darkness had fallen before the train arrived back at the prison camp. Dave and Modesto took a quick shower, dressed, and started walking towards the gate where Consuelo's driver was waiting.

"You've been preoccupied all day," said Modesto as they neared the dirt road that would take them to the main gate. "Is something wrong?"

"No, actually something good is about to happen, but I need to know where you stand."

"What do you mean?"

"I got word yesterday that a friend of mine from Florida is going to help me escape from Cuba in the next few days. I found a note in my boot yesterday and this is the first time I've had a chance to talk to you about it. My friend has had someone watching me as far back as Pinar Del Rio. A man slipped me a note in the *baños* of the Partagas Cigar Factory in Havana back then. The note told me my friend had people watching me and was trying to figure a way to free me."

"Why are you telling this to me now?" asked Modesto, stopping on the road.

"He said you could go, too."

"What did the man in Havana look like?"

"I don't know, I was taking a leak and he told me not to turn around. He slipped the note in my back pocket. By the time I turned around he was gone."

"So, you don't know when, or how?"

"No, but I do know this man is resourceful, and always keeps his word. The last note read: *Be alert. Be on the train every day, +Modesto. Leave no Stone unturned. Soon.*"

"If he knows my name, he must be for real."

"Seth Stone is for real … Do you want to go?"

Modesto thought for a long moment and said, "I need to tell you something, and I hope you will understand. I have not been totally truthful during our time together."

"What do you mean, Modesto? I thought we have become good friends."

"We have, but the government made us bunkmates for a reason. They offered to cut my sentence in half if I would find out who you knew in the Miami baseball syndicates. Fidel is desperate to stop the flow of Cuba's best talent to Major League Baseball in America."

"Well, fuck me!"

"Look, you have every right to hate me, but we **have** become good friends. I've reported back to General Machado and to the head of the DGI that you don't have any questionable ties in Miami or Tampa."

"Oh, that explains all the questions, lately."

"I had to ask those questions. But, as I've gotten to know you, I think you're a talented, likeable guy, who loves people and wouldn't hurt a fly … the only reason they haven't called off this whole thing off is the notes."

"You already knew about the two notes?"

"Sort of. The first one I figured you got at the Partagas factory in Havana. You acted a little strange the rest of that day. When you headed for the *baños* that night, I figured something was up. Two of the torn up pieces of paper stuck to the bowl. The DGI figured out it was from *El Cazador*, but nothing else could be deciphered. You lucked out on the message you flushed in the train yesterday."

"How did you know about that one?"

"I woke up when you found that note in your boot. I feigned snoring and watched you stuff it in your pants pocket. I called Consuelo when we got back to the prison camp and told her to search the train office car's holding tank."

"My fucking head is spinning! So … you didn't hurt your shoulder and you called Consuelo from the infirmary?"

"Our prison camp's commandant has been in on it from the start. I went to his office, and he put me on the phone with Consuelo."

"So, the English class is just a sham?"

"Yes, General Machado cooked it up to soften you up with sex and alcohol."

"Well, I can't hate him for that," laughed Dave.

"Look, it all started out as a scam, but you and I have become good friends, and now 'Mistress' Consuelo is madly in love with you. Some *Mata Hari* she turned out to be!"

"What about the bondage scene with the prostitutes?"

"They just play hearts or gin rummy in her office."

"Really! But ... now they know that something's going to happen, concerning me, very soon!"

"It's not that bad. I was handed this note when I got off the train tonight. Here ... read it," said Modesto pulling the note from his pocket.

Dave took the note written in Spanish and translated it in his head: *DGI found all the paper scraps in the holding tank, all were intelligible. Black beans and rice diet dyed the paper brown. Stay vigilant, we heightened the Province's security level to 'Code Yellow'.*

"Well, Modesto what's it going to be? Are you going to turn me in, or do you want to come along? Zero years is better than six."

"First, I will not turn you in! Second, you have the better deal and I think it's worth the risk. But I won't go unless you believe that you are my friend."

"I believe you, and I fully understand the position that they put you in. You could have gained points by making up shit like the ballplayer did."

The two friends shook hands and embraced. Modesto grinned and started walking towards the waiting truck, saying, "C'mon Dave, let's not miss what could be our last Thursday night in Cuba, *Arriba, Arriba - mi amigo!*"

***

The two-boat flotilla arrived at Nassau from the west and entered the channel between Nassau and Paradise Island flying their yellow quarantine flags. Charley took the lead and Seth fell in behind as they idled past the cruise ship docks and headed for the bridges. Seth could see the bright pinkish Atlantis towers splashed by the afternoon sun, off to port. They cruised under the two bridges and stopped outside of the Hurricane Hole Marina on the Paradise Island side. Charley switched from channel 16 to 68 and asked to fuel before proceeding to *ABOUT TIME's* assigned slip. Seth followed suit and

178

soon they were both, fueled, tied up, and plugged in. Being already fueled would guarantee them an early start in the morning.

The captains met with the Customs officers and obtained their Bahamas cruising and fishing permits. The crews hosed their boats down, took showers, and then filed, by ones and twos, over to the Parrot Bar, a picturesque spot on the marina property overlooking the harbor and bridges. John came in by taxi from the airport and found them at the bar. Finally, all nine of them sat around a round table, each drinking a cold one. Scotty was in the middle of reliving his 600 lb. marlin battle.

"Biggest one I've caught so far," said Scotty. "What's the biggest you ever caught, Seth?"

"Like you, Scotty, it was one of my first — I think the fourth to be exact. It was a 650 lb. blue marlin I hooked on the La Guairá Bank in Venezuela. But I caught it on 30 lb. tackle. It took five and a half hours. After that, I was the one who was hooked."

"Why were you fishing 30 lb. there?" asked Freddy.

"There's quite a variety of fish on that big bank. Blue marlin, sailfish, white marlin along the edges, yellow fin tuna, big mahi-mahi, and swordfish at night. The bank is about 14 miles long by 4 miles wide and is 400 feet deep, but it's surrounded by 1500 foot deep water. There have been more grand slams caught there than any place that I know of. We fished live bonitos on three 80 lb. rigs, and closer to the boat dead ballyhoo on the 30 lb. for sailfish and white marlin. My big marlin passed up the live bonitos and inhaled the ballyhoo. The only reason we could catch the marlin was that it could only go down 400 feet. Otherwise, it would have spooled us. We were fortunate the captain, Oscar Benitez, was an excellent boat handler. To make matters even more difficult, the afternoon sea breeze kicks the seas up to four to five feet. So it was rougher than hell."

"I was on that boat that day in 1998, along with Billy Chandler and Seth, and even with the five hour fight we still had a grand slam that day, and another the next day," added John.

"I wanted to go back, but the next year there was a mudslide off the mountains above the northern-central coastal towns that put 20 feet of mud in La Guairá, killing 25,000 people, and destroying all the boats. It took three years to clean that up and by then the deteriorating political situation made it too dangerous for us to go back to Venezuela," said Seth.

"Let's go back to the Huckins and have some dinner, guys," said Charley as the stories wound down. "Bill and Doug have a salad made, and I'm ready to grill the wahoo, with a little help from Seth. I know you like it rare. There's plenty of cold beers in the fantail cooler, so help yourselves."

Charley added a couple of loaves of sliced Cuban bread and the crew chowed down. They all turned in early in anticipation of a long day tomorrow.

Seth texted Lori from his cabin after dinner, then turned out the light; *Great trip from Key Largo to Nassau, fished for about an hour just past Chub Cay. Charley caught two wahoo for dinner, and we released a BIG marlin. Off to a good start, going down island tomorrow — we'll try to make Long Island. Love you and miss you. Seth …. p.s. Valentine's Day was sure fun!*

Thursday's dawn broke over Nassau to clear skies and a light northerly breeze. The two-boat flotilla eased out of Hurricane Hole. They headed east, leaving Rose Island to port until they cleared the harbor. Once clear, they steered an east-southeast course across the Bahamas Bank and headed for the Exuma's Ships Channel Cay and South Eleuthera beyond. With the light northerly wind quartering behind them, they both ran at 24 knots. About an hour into the run, John Harvey buzzed low over them, rocking his wings, at 165 miles per hour. He was on his way to Deadman's Key Airport nine miles north of Flying Fish Marina near Clarence Town on Long Island. The boats ran over the crystal clear, coral head rich, shallow bank for about an hour and a half until they finally passed Ships Channel Cay and entered the deep water again.

They adjusted their course just a bit easterly and headed towards the very bottom of South Eleuthera. A three hour run took them past Davis Harbor and Little San Salvador. Seth kept the same course, and they continued to make good time in the moderate seas. They could see Cat Island to port with its high, rocky cliffs as they headed down that 50 -mile long island towards Hawk's Nest Marina and Devil's Point. All this deep water, called Exuma Valley, was prime fishing grounds. Years ago near Davis Harbor, Seth caught a marlin only a hundred yards from shore, off Bamboo Point, while fishing with Capt. Toby Warner, one of the original Geezers.

When they passed Hawk's Nest they would be about three hours from the Flying Fish Marina at Clarence Town. Seth would leave uninhabited Conception Island to port. As he passed Cape Santa Maria at the north end of Long Island, he wondered how things were going on Rum Cay, ten miles to the east. The recession in America and the high diesel prices had been hard on the Bahamian businesses that counted on the American sport fishing boats to come this far to fish each season. Rum Cay Marina was managed by their Bahamian friend Benny Martin. If the rescue went as planned in Cuba, Seth would try to stop by and see Benny on the way back.

Seth adjusted his course and followed Long Island's 80 mile long east coast 55 miles down to Clarence Town. If everything held together, they'd be tied up at Flying Fish Marina soon, making the entire passage from Nassau in a little over eight hours. If Seth had not been on a mission to save Dave the Wave he would have chugged down there at 8 knots and saved hundreds of gallons of fuel. Prices for diesel were fluctuating in the five to six dollar per gallon range at the marina pumps. But Seth was confident that Hugo Lugo would be paying for that fuel, among other things, especially since he got the big time - no cut contract.

The fishing in this part of the middle Bahamas was also outstanding. San Salvador was especially popular because either way the wind blew there was an end of the 13 mile long island in the lee. Gene and Seth traded off the helm every two hours and the rest of the crew took turns as lookouts and relief on the bridge. Likewise, Charley, Norm, and Deputy Pearce had a similar rotation schedule over on *ABOUT TIME*. The time went fast and soon they saw Clarence Town's white Moorish church towers standing tall on the hills surrounding the harbor. John Harvey was waiting for them as they pulled up to the dock and backed in. There were only a few boats tied up there, but they were sixty to seventy footers. John and the marina owner, Mario, tied the stern lines, while Doug and Freddy handled the bow pilings. Gene handed the 50-amp shore power cord to Mario, as John walked over to the next slip to help ABOUT TIME who was backing in.

"Thanks for coming in guys, we appreciate the business."

"Both boats will need fuel, Mario. We ran all the way down here from Nassau."

"We've got plenty of fuel, and the pump hose will reach both these slips. Business has been slow, and I hope it picks up this spring. You're plugged in now. Come on up to the office when you're ready for fuel," said Mario as he walked over to help tie up *ABOUT TIME*.

John got onboard when Charley was tied up and said, "How was it, Seth?"

"Uneventful, just a long ride — what have you been doing since you buzzed us this morning?"

"I rented a car at the airport, drove to Dean's Blue Hole, and snorkeled all around it for a couple of hours."

"I always wanted to do that. Do you still carry a tank and everything in your plane?"

"Yeah, but I didn't use the tank because I didn't have a buddy to dive with."

"What's it like?"

"It's the deepest Blue Hole in the world at 660 feet. At the surface, it's about 300 feet in diameter and it opens up into a cove with a beautiful white sand beach. The beach is more like a sandbar because part of the limestone cliff fell in the sinkhole. Looking down from the cliffs that are left above, it's breathtaking."

"Maybe I'll get to dive it the next time," said Seth

The crews took over and got both boats hosed off and fueled. Seth took that opportunity to text Bobby, Beau, and Lori an update of the flotilla's progress. When the boats were shipshape, he called a team meeting aboard Charley's boat.

"Gentlemen, the rest of the afternoon is yours. Rest, or go up to Rowdy Boys pool bar for a swim and a cold Kalik®. Maybe some of you can talk John into driving you a few miles up the road to see Dean's Blue Hole. I'm going up the hill to Rowdy Boys Bar and Grille for a cracked conch dinner tonight, and you all are welcome to join me. Let me know how many, so I can make a reservation. We leave tomorrow morning at 8:00, and we're about 80 miles from the Ragged Islands and Duncan Town. John will fly the Lance down mid-morning. That will put us all there around noon, including a stop to test Norm's grenade launchers, so we can read the reefs and channels with the sun overhead. Did you get the targets, Scotty?"

"Yes, I did," said Scotty with a smile.

"Is the anchorage there shallow?" asked Doug.

"No, it averages 8 to 20 feet, but there are lots of coral heads and unmarked reefs on the way in. We need to read the water until we get our bearings."

"I understand the few boats that travel there are sailboats that draw five to six feet. My Huckins draws less than three and I believe your Hatteras draws just over four feet," added Charley.

"When we get there and are anchored we'll have a lot of work to do. We have to set up the inflatable Zodiac and motor. Then load the scooters, tools, and weapons aboard. Next, we'll assign duties and coordinate our plan of attack. We also need to plan in advance for contingencies and test our communications system. I am hoping to start the mission Saturday night."

"When will you make that decision, Seth?" asked John.

"I need to coordinate with Bobby and his Cuban agents before noon that day. Then he can create the diversion and backup that we need. We'll go over it in detail. Charley has satellite Wi-Fi so we can review and zoom in on the Puerto Padre area with Google Earth to supplement the charts that I've already made. So, relax while you can."

Everybody signed up for dinner and John headed for the Blue Hole with a carload of Geezers, including Bill, Doug, Seth, and Charley. Scotty and Freddy headed for the pool at Rowdy Boys. Gene and Norm took a three mile walk around Clarence Town.

The cracked conch at Rowdy Boys was the best in the Bahamas. The crew sat at a long table at the end of the dining room which featured a life size picture of an attractive brown and white female goat that was hung over a set of French doors. Rowdy brother Bernard Knowles oversees the family's hotel and restaurant. Seth asked Bernard one evening when he was bartending, about the significance of the goat portrait.

Bernard smiled and replied, "Maribelle was one of our family pets when we were growin' up. If you know anything about goats ... she was a 'good' goat."

The bar and grille and small hotel is a sideline for the large, hospitable, family that owns and operates a heavy equipment construction business in the Bahamas. But they do it right. Bert and Chloe Knowles, and their "Rowdy Boys" help make Clarence Town a great place to visit.

"How was the Blue Hole, Seth?" asked Gene.

"It was everything John said it would be," said Doug.

"I was down this way a lot in my early commercial fishing days and I didn't even know it existed," said Bill Pearce. "We never had much time for sightseeing on the shrimp boats. We'd trawl all night and anchor near dawn and cull the catch. Then we'd eat a big lunch and try and get a few hours sleep before it got dark again."

"Why do shrimpers trawl at night?" wondered Scotty out loud.

"There isn't anything that swims in the ocean that doesn't like to eat shrimp," explained Bill. "They hide down in the seagrass during the daylight hours and come out at night to feed."

Seth settled the check and the crew walked down the hill back to Flying Fish Marina. Tomorrow started the real reason they were down here. John was ready to fly his plane to Duncan Town tomorrow morning and Charley would launch his tender to bring him out from the beach at the south end of the Duncan Town runway after the two-boat flotilla was anchored.

***

This Thursday night progressed like all the others, and Dave and Modesto did their best not to act preoccupied. As usual, Consuelo snatched Dave away from the group immediately after the girls finished their tests. She ushered him into her office and sat on a large, beautiful leather couch that graced the same space that had once held the old, ratty corduroy couch.

"This couch is new to the room, and the old corduroy one is gone," said Dave. "Where did you get it?"

"It was confiscated from a dissident's house in Las Tunas. I thought it would add to our possibilities, and make us more comfortable on Thursdays."

"So, you're tired of your desktop?" said Dave with a smile.

"I didn't say that. I just said — possibilities and comfortable."

Dave sat down on the couch next to her. He took her in his arms and said, "*Bésame.*"

She kissed him fervently. Dave *French* kissed her and Consuelo responded in kind ... adding a little *Spanish* suction.

"That reminds me, *Cariño... la mamada, por favor.*"

She looked at Dave incredulously and said while slowly shaking her head, "I never thought I would do this for any man ... you are the only one."

"*Lamerlo,*" whispered Dave softly.

Consuelo complied as Dave massaged the nape of her neck.

Soon, they became intimate with almost every square inch of the comfortable new couch as they stretched their imaginations almost to their breaking points. Exhausted, they rested for a few minutes before joining the young girls and Modesto. Consuelo, resplendent in her black mistress outfit and boots took Chantelle on what might be his and Modesto's last Thursday night in Cuba. Dave chose Darly and Marta for maybe his last hurrah, and Modesto smiled knowingly in Dave's direction, as he escorted Rona to the other alcove.

CUBAN CHARADE

***

Monserrat first noticed the blood in her underwear in the Neiman Marcus ladies room. She had only been back in San Diego a couple of days from her last trip to Arizona. She was prepared with some 'just in case' Tampax® in her purse. She was at once depressed and elated. There had been second thoughts and recriminations in her own mind. Did she really want to trap Hugo with a baby? If he didn't marry her, their child would never really know a father's love. If he married her and felt she had trapped him, their life would eventually turn into a living hell. She took stock of her blessings. Hugo had indicated for a long time that he loved her. She was in America and living in a luxury condo. She had her own new car. Hugo and his manager gave her a generous allowance. She would get a green card and a path to citizenship. She spoke almost perfect English and could thank Hugo for that. Monserrat could get a job because of the English. She decided to start taking her pills again that day. It would be two weeks until she returned to Arizona for a long weekend of baseball and Hugo. She would be safe again by then.

***

Seth checked PassageWeather on his sat-phone as *TAR BABY* passed the Little Harbor anchorage where six sailboats were on the hook, waiting for the next front to take them south. It was apparent that the last northerly front had stalled up in the Florida Straits. That was good news for their two-boat flotilla and Dave the Wave. They'd gotten an early start out of Clarence Town and would be rounding Long Island's southernmost point in about 45 minutes.

Beau texted Seth last night about 11:00 p.m. Seth retrieved the message this morning: *Flights went okay for Cuba, but nobody's in a hurry here. Checked into the Socucho Hotel, found Jorge, set-up with a flats boat. Even got a cast net. Will scout the port and bay mañana on Saturday. Beautiful area, wide inlet with big lit up bell buoys, like Egmont Channel, as far out as I can see. A light flashes every eight seconds from a lighthouse about two miles out of town on the western side of the inlet. The cities are proud, the beach towns quaint - all are run down. I'll report on Puerto Carupano tomorrow.*

Seth turned the corner with Charley nearly abreast. They adjusted their courses to south–southwest and continued at 20 knots. Seth forwarded Beau's text to Bobby and settled in with a fresh cup of coffee courtesy of Gene, who just climbed up in the flybridge.

185

"Before we cast off this morning, I downloaded the weekend edition of *USA TODAY* from Flying Fish's Wi-Fi to my new iPad. It's full of all the regular political bullshit, but here's an interesting article from the sports section," said Gene. "I'll read it to you." — *The Phoenix, Arizona, major league baseball spring training league is growing again. The Cincinnati Reds joined this year after, forsaking Florida for a new stadium and warmer weather. Both Ohio teams, Cleveland and Cincinnati, share Goodyear Stadium in suburban Avondale. San Diego shares Peoria sports complex with the Seattle Mariners, while nearby Scottsdale's Stadium hosts the Giants and just down the road the town of Salt River houses the home state Diamondbacks and the Colorado Rockies. The Dodgers share Camelback Ranch's facility in nearby Glendale with the White Sox, as the Oakland A's go it alone at Hohokam in Mesa, two blocks from the Cub's Sloan Field. To no one's 'Surprise', the Kansas City Royals and Texas Rangers camp right there a few miles north of Peoria. The Brewers play right in the middle at Maryvale in Phoenix, while the Angels reside in Tempe.*

The Phoenix Chamber of Commerce announced that the 15 Cactus League teams pump 300 million dollars a year into Phoenix's economy during the two months of spring training each year. The stadiums' use is maximized by sharing and the teams' travel costs are minimized. The Cactus League favorite to finish first this year is the San Diego Padres, already a good team that has been powered up by their rookie third baseman, former Cuban star, Hugo Lugo. He is leading the Cactus League in batting with a .397 average, stolen bases at 10, and is third in home runs with 6. Hugo adds a new dimension to the Padres."

"Sounds like our boy is going to have the *dinero* to pay for his sins. If he maintains his present level of play he'll be swimming in money by mid-season just from endorsements," said Seth.

Seth glanced at the Garmin chart plotter, then looked off the stern. Long Island was no longer visible. There were no other boats to be seen, even on the 24-mile radar. He called Charley on his sat-phone to keep their conversation secure.

"Charley, time to shut her down and have some target practice."

"Roger that. Let's make some ground rules and shoot off both boats while we're moving. It will be more combat realistic," said Charley.

"Have Norm demonstrate loading and shooting a grenade off your fantail at idle speed. Then we'll both speed up and I'll set the targets out. I was trained to shoot rifle grenades in the Army, so I'll do the 'show and tell' over here. Bill Pearce probably was trained to use them, too. Each boat has one Beretta AR70/90-GL and a case of grenade shells. There's 100 grenades in each case, so everyone can fire a couple off and we won't miss them. The ones I shot in

186

Vietnam had about a 1000 foot range. You have to learn to shoot them like a rainbow," said Seth.

Charley and Seth slowed down to a dead idle and the weapons were brought up into *TAR BABY'S* fishing cockpit and onto *ABOUT TIME'S* fantail. Norm took their Beretta and showed it to Doug, Charley and Deputy Pearce.

Gene steered while Seth went down into the cockpit and showed his crew the weapon. "As you all can see, the grenade launcher attachment fits under the rifle's forearm. It has its own trigger, pistol-grip, and safety. To load a grenade, push the attachment's forearm forward like a pump shotgun, load a shell in this round chamber, and pull it back until it locks, — flip off the safety on the pistol-grip, figure the trajectory to the target, and pull the trigger. At the same time, this rifle is still a semi-automatic rifle holding 30, 5.56 NATO cartridges."

Seth called over to Norm to shoot one off, which he did very smoothly. The grenade shell left the launcher with a sharp report, but when it hit the water, 600 feet away, it made a loud explosion with a large puff of white smoke. Seth demonstrated the launcher for his crew, then turned the weapon over to Fred and returned to the flybridge.

"Climb down so you can shoot the launcher a couple of times, Gene. I'm going to take one Beretta in the Zodiac, and leave the other on *TAR BABY* during the operation. Also, will you get the 110 volt compressor out of the lazarette, and help Scotty blow up the targets?"

Seth called Charley and said, "We're going to inflate Scotty's targets. We'll alternate running and firing from a hundred to two hundred yards and see how we do. Keep an eye on the radar and if we see a boat coming we'll shut our test down."

Seth could hear the compressor running and the crew in the cockpit laughing. He got out of the helm chair and looked over the railing and couldn't believe his eyes. There were two blonde, three-orifice, life size-technicolor blow-up dolls laying in the cockpit. Gene and Scotty were busy blowing up a brunette that looked a lot like Sasha Grey. There appeared to be a redhead still in a box.

"What the fuck, Scotty!" laughed Seth. "You didn't get those at West Marine?"

"No, I got them down at the Fairvilla adult store next to the Pirate's Museum on Front Street," said Scotty. "I remembered they were on sale when

I went there for some toys to keep the Detroit girls occupied — since I was outnumbered all of the time. They were only $18.99 apiece ... anything this big at West Marine was over $25.00."

"Well — throw them overboard, it's time for target practice," said Seth, shaking his head in disbelief.

Scotty deployed both blondes a hundred yards apart as Seth and Charley moved their boats away from the targets. *ABOUT TIME* went first, running at 20 knots. Deputy Pearce showed what training can do and he narrowly missed at 100 yds. Seth took the same track and Scotty overshot the 100 yard blonde by 50 yds.

"Too much elevation, Scotty," called down Seth.

Norm took the next shot at 100 yards and missed by only 15 feet which was close enough to deflate that blonde. Both boats cheered his effort. Freddy, who also had Army training, took a shot at the 200 yard blonde and missed by only 50 feet, but the blonde survived. Deputy Pearce nailed the 200 yard blonde spot on and she was vaporized. Doug took a 200 yard shot at the brunette and was 25 yards short. Gene took a shot at 200 yards and had a near miss, then relieved Seth at the helm so he could take a turn. Seth overshot her by about 25 feet. Scotty sunk Sasha at 200 yards. Just as Freddy was loading a grenade in the Beretta to shoot at the red head, Seth's sat-phone started ringing — it was Charley.

"Seth, there's a large boat entering our quadrant. We better call it off."

"Okay guys — put all the hardware away — there's a boat bearing down on us. It's getting close to time to go anyway."

Freddy unloaded the Beretta and said, "What about the red head, Seth?"

"We'll just leave her, we're definitely not putting her in the cabin. The prevailing wind will put her up on one of the Raggeds' or Cuba. Some beachcomber is in for a big surprise!"

CHAPTER NINETEEN

THE RAGGED ISLANDS soon came into view. Seth and Charley slowed down as they approached Hog Cay cut, which was 10 to 20 feet deep but full of reefs and coral heads. Hog Cay is just north of Ragged Island, where Duncan Town is located. Charley only drew two and a half feet with his Hamilton jet drives, so he volunteered to lead the way into Southside Bay. From a GPS waypoint outside the reef in 36 feet of water, Charley steered south/southwest. The charts and cruising guides suggested leaving Black Rock Point on Hog Cay and the very visible black rock in the water to starboard. The rock was indeed black and was ringed with a dark brown reef. The depth was 21 feet as he passed the black rock and he steered 10 more degrees to the west leaving the submerged, but visible, inner reef to port. The channel between was a deep, vivid blue. The inner reef displayed a montage of brown shades, and its hard, unforgiving surface lurked just inches below the surface. Once the reef was on his stern, Charley worked south around Gun Point until he was safely in the back bay, which was a paler pastel blue signifying 10 to 12 feet. Seth noticed two sailboats anchored well off of Gun Point. Closer to shore the color slowly faded to white which indicated shallow water over sand. Seth followed Charley down the west side of the island for a couple of miles to Southside Bay which was at the end of the airstrip and within walking distance of Duncan Town. The "Boat Harbor" anchorage averaged eight feet at low tide and afforded good protection from the prevailing south-easterly wind. Two sailboats were anchored out to the west in deeper water. There was a small white sand beach right in front of them to land their dinghies.

Seth could have set a more southerly course from the southern tip of Long Island and motored down past Little Ragged Island and its southern cays and then circled back north into Boat Harbor. But now the flotilla had two ways in and out if needed. The course from Boat Harbor to Puerto Padre, Cuba, was a straight shot 225° for 60 miles. The only impediment was tiny Cayo Santo Domingo (Bahamas), and it would be left well to port. The Cay, which was 35 miles from Cuba, and had a flashing red light at its highest elevation of 40 feet.

Eight square mile Ragged Island also had a red flasher on its highest point of 110 feet.

Once anchored, Seth started the crew assembling and inflating the 17.5 - foot Zodiac. Charley deployed his dinghy and brought Bill and Norm over to help out. Seth scoped the shoreline from the flybridge with his binoculars and saw John Harvey standing under some palm trees near the little beach.

"Charley, would you motor in to pick up John in you dinghy. He's standing in that clump of palm trees just above the little white beach."

"Sure. This is certainly a beautiful spot and the water clarity is off the charts. The limestone cliffs and stretches of white sand are a beautiful contrast to the different shades of blue. It was easy to read the water on the way in."

"You did a nice job, Charley. But, you've only seen the pretty leeward side close up. When we get the chance, we'll walk over to the windward side — every piece of garbage in the Atlantic from Portugal, Africa, and South America washes up here or on Cuba."

"I guess you're right. It's like the seaweed removal business in Key West, but worse, because there's no place to dump it."

"Right, they try to burn what they can."

Charley went in to pick up John, and Seth busied himself by installing the crane top and hooking up the block and tackle to the gin pole. Charley was back with John in 10 minutes.

"Hey, John," called Seth over the racket from the little portable 110 volt air compressor. "How was the flight over?"

'Short," said John as he climbed to the flybridge. "But everything here is in reasonable walking distance. I talked to a couple of cruisers while I was having lunch at the Ponderosa Bar and Grill. They're anchored at the north end of the island."

"Yeah, we came in that way and saw their sailboats. I remember the Ponderosa. We stayed in the hotel upstairs when you flew us in here to go bone fishing."

"Right, they dinghied up that two and a half mile canal and still had a little hike into town. That's where the bone fishing guide picked us up."

"Yeah, I remember now. The food was pretty good at the Ponderosa."

"The Kalik was good and cold, today."

"Any more people living here now?"

"We were here in the 90's. The bartender told me their sea salt business fell off to nothing when the Russians left Cuba. They're down to like 70

190

residents now, mostly old fisherman. The young people have been moving to Nassau and Freeport. A government mail boat comes once a week and it delivers their fish back to a wholesaler in Nassau. The mail boat brings groceries for the grocery store, medicine, propane, gasoline, diesel parts, building supplies, fishing supplies, just about everything."

"So you walked down here from Duncan Town?" asked Gene.

"I started to walk, it's not that far, like a mile and a half. But this guy named Percy stopped and picked me up in his pick-up truck. He owns a pig farm on the island and, in fact, his family owns a big chunk of the island."

"Where's the pig farm?" asked Seth.

"On the other end and he says the pigs go swimming every day."

"Like the ones in the Exumas," said Seth

"Yeah, but the neatest thing is his house. He salvaged a DC-3 a couple of years ago that some drug cowboys crashed at the end of the runway. He set the whole plane on top of his house and opened a bar and a pool room named the Eagle's Nest. He built himself and his wife a new house nearby."

"We'll have to check it out after the operation's over. Why don't you help Gene get the Suzuki hooked up to the gin pole? The Zodiac looks like it is fully inflated."

Five men picked up the inflated Zodiac and slid it in the water. Fred boarded it and tied it up alongside the fishing cockpit with the bow facing aft. Gene and John had the Suzuki in the air within minutes and swung the 230 lb. engine over the Zodiac's transom letting Freddy guide it home. Freddy tightened the clamp bolts with a wrench and he and Scotty started installing the 12 gallon fuel tanks and fuel lines. John wrestled a sealed battery into its box and hooked it up to the ignition system. Freddy pumped the fuel line ball, John turned the key, and the Suzuki started on the first turn. Scotty threw in the lifejacket bag and first aid kit — then jumped in.

"Take us for a ride, John," chortled Scotty.

"Wait for me," said Gene, Doug, and Norm in unison.

They took off south, whooping and hollering, and ran down the length of Little Ragged Island at 20 knots according to Freddy's phone GPS. They hit 30 on the way back.

Bill Pearce climbed up into the flybridge smiling and said to Seth, "Sometimes they still act like little boys."

"I don't know that we ever really get over that, Bill," said Seth.

"I know," laughed Charley. "I've been waiting patiently for, 'Old enough to know better' to kick in."

When the crew was finished blowing off steam, Seth had them test start the Honda scooters, take their Florida license plates off, then load them in the Zodiac. First, one from the Hatteras's cockpit using the gin pole, then the other one from the Huckins fantail using Charley's electric davit. Seth loaded aboard his Remington 700 hog rifle with a night scope, four 9mm Glocks, one of the Beretta AR70 grenade launchers, and two tactical 12 gauge 870 shotguns. All were protected from the salt spray by black 55gallon contractor's plastic cleanup bags. Two long pry bars were lashed fore and aft under the seats. They had extra ammo, tactical flashlights, rain ponchos, and mosquito netting face shields. Seth packed his five million candle power Larson® battery-operated spot light. There was a cooler that would be filled with sandwiches, bottled water, and 5-hour Energy® drinks. When he was satisfied everything was in order, he called Bobby Thompson from the privacy of his cabin.

"Hey, Bobby, we're anchored at Ragged Island south of Duncan Town. The Zodiac and scooters have been tested, and the weather looks good for the next few days. So let's plan on us going in tomorrow night, and we'll grab Dave off the train Sunday afternoon."

"Okay, we'll detonate the bomb in Las Tunas at 3:00 Sunday morning. That should keep the Army busy. We'll rig the train with the C-4 coupler bomb about the same time. The cell phone number to detonate it is 5273-3997. Dave will find another note in his work boot Sunday morning."

"That's great Bobby, thanks for all your help."

"I understand that Robert Cornett is snook fishing in Puerto Padre Bay. He's brought in two fish just a few pounds under the world record of 57 pounds-six ounces. Jorge is more than impressed. His buried equipment is in place at the lat/lon numbers he has, *mierda de perro* (dog poop) and all."

"I'll call you to confirm our departure from Duncan Town Saturday at noon," while laughing at Bobby's parting comments.

Seth sent a text to Beau confirming the train action would take place Sunday afternoon and that his weapons were buried near his ambush site, dog poop and all. Next, he called a skull meeting before dinner for the entire crew aboard *TAR BABY* and handed out packets of charts and Google Earth images of Puerto Padre Bay, Puerto Carupano, and the Delicías area.

"Gentlemen, I've been in touch with Bobby Thompson and unless the weather changes radically, our raid to rescue Dave the Wave and possibly his cellmate will begin Saturday afternoon. Follow along on the charts I've provided, and note that some areas have a close up page. We'll leave here Saturday at noon with the Zodiac in tow and chug for 50 miles — arriving at the Old Bahama Channel at dusk. The only land mass we will pass will be the tiny deserted island of Cayo Santo Domingo which is a Bahamian possession. It will be too far to port to see from our course, but it is lit with a red 30 second flasher at night. The Cayo is 35 miles off Cuba. When we get to 15 miles off Cuba, *TAR BABY* and *ABOUT TIME* will go no closer. It is imperative that we stay at least 12 miles off Cuba ... out in international waters — John, Freddy, Scotty and I will crew the Zodiac. We'll go in under the cover of darkness, but we'll keep our running lights on as we pass through Playa La Boca. Bobby reports there's constant small boat traffic in that area until the bars close. Mastelero Lighthouse sits on the west side of the approach to the inlet, and it flashes a white light every eight seconds. The freighter channel is marked with alternating red and green bell buoys 12 feet high, and the red ones are lit at night. When we get south of the beach town we'll go dark and follow a course to some heavy mangrove cover on the east side of the approach to Puerto Carupano. That will hide us during the day. That night we'll take the long pry bars and remove a section of track to derail the locomotive. When the train comes out of the Deliciás Sugar Mill the scooters will shadow it on the adjacent road. When it's a mile or two from the derailment site we'll blow the coupling bomb. That will disconnect the locomotive and office car from the cane cars in back, where the guards ride with the prison laborers. Dave will be notified by Bobby's agent before the train leaves Las Tunas Sunday morning that a rescue attempt will take place that day. He just won't know exactly where."

"What if another train comes along earlier?" asked Norm.

"Bobby's agents report that the cane train is the only train on this route. If any imports arrive at Puerto Carupano, the cane train takes them back to Las Tunas and they are redirected. Any other questions at this point? ... Okay ... Charley, Doug, and Bill Pearce will man *ABOUT TIME* and Gene and Norm will man *TAR BABY*. The idea is to move east and west among the freighter traffic approximating their speed. Have a couple of fishing lines out. You'll be on Cuban radar but outside their jurisdiction. If a Cuban gunboat pressures you, take off north and call the U.S. Coast Guard at Guantanamo on Channel 16. Then call Bobby on a sat-phone and give him your position."

"What's the rest of the drill on Sunday?" asked Gene.

"Once we have Dave, we should be heading out the inlet around dark. Bobby has arranged some cover fire for us, complete with rubber bullets and smoke bombs, on the west side tracks and road. How fast we leave depends on what kind of pursuit develops. We will conference call on the sat-phones and ask for your positions. Whoever is closest will be our destination. Our hand held GPS will bring us right to you. If we have time we'll transfer the scooters. Then we'll chug back to Ragged Island."

"What's with the rubber bullets?" asked John.

"We don't want to kill anyone if possible, we just want to cause confusion and mayhem. Rubber bullets break ribs and worse. We just want to take the fight out of them."

"What will we do if we see a fast boat closing on one of us on the radar in international waters after we're on our way back to Duncan Town?" asked Scotty.

"Basically, the same plan. I outlined earlier. We'll head for Ragged Island at our top speed. We can tow the Zodiac boat at 24 knots. If we need to go faster we will jettison the Zodiac. If we're still threatened we will call the Coast Guard and Bobby."

"Who gets the other grenade launcher while you guys are in Cuba?" asked Norm.

"You do since there's only two of you, *ABOUT TIME* gets my AR-15 … If there are no more questions let's eat dinner. Charley is grilling steaks on the Huckins tonight. Gene cooked up some green beans, Bill made double-baked hash browns, and Norm made a salad with pecans, craisins, crumbled bacon, and vinaigrette dressing. Charley has a cooler full of cold beer, and a couple of bottles of 2006 Louis Martini Napa Cabernet for us wine lovers. **One more thing guys** … thanks to all of you for signing on for our friend, Dave the Wave. We've got a good chance of liberating him from Cuba and righting a terrible wrong. We've got right and surprise on our side. Now jump in one of the two tenders and let's eat!"

First thing in the morning, all the vitals, both electronic and mechanical, on the Hatteras and Huckins were checked, including all the filters and v-belts — and all the way down to the raw water strainers. After a hearty breakfast on each boat, they were ready to rumble. Seth called Bobby with a thumbs-up and Beau got a sat-phone text in Cuba reconfirming that Sunday was game day.

At 2:00 p.m. the two-boat flotilla chugged out south from the Boat Harbour anchorage at 8 knots and left Ragged Island and Duncan Town behind. *TAR BABY* towed the Zodiac and after the first hour, the pastel blue water turned to indigo blue and the depth fell off to 1000 feet. The first boat they saw was an empty tanker ship headed for the Windward Passage at 20 knots.

Seth called Lori in St. Petersburg, "Hey, happy Saturday, Lori."

"I was hoping you'd call … I was wondering where you are?"

"Well, with the weather being so good, we came pretty much straight down to the lower Bahamas. When the trade winds start blowing from the southeast again we can fish back up towards San Salvador, Rum Cay, and Cat Island with the wind at our backs. Right now, we're south of the Exumas and Long Island — down near Cuba."

"Sounds like the middle of nowhere, like when we cruised and fished back from The Turks and Caicos with John and Stacy a couple of years ago."

"Right, but I always wanted to fish here. There's zero fishing pressure, just a few sailboats here and there."

"Have fun, and be careful. I miss you and I love you."

"I love you, too."

Seth switched his mind back to business and rolled the rescue plan around in his mind over and over. He was glad that Beau was backing him up at Puerto Carupano. He sent a text to his son, Jeb, with his sat-phone to give him a heads up on his whereabouts: *Jeb, fishing was terrific in Key West. We had multiple double-digit days on sails. When Charley got to Safe Harbor we decided to use this spell of good weather to fish down island for marlin. We split the crew and Charley brought ABOUT TIME along too. We ran to Nassau and caught a big (600+ lbs.) blue marlin in the tongue of the ocean on our way in. We ran straight down from Nassau past Long Island while it was still fairly calm. I've got a little deal going on with Bobby Thompson. Might slip into Cuban waters under cover of darkness and pick up Dave the Wave, all on the 'tranquillo'. We'll fish back up with the wind at our backs when the trades kick back in. P.S. Charley likes the way you run the Boatworks.*

He got an immediate response: *You are what you are! Good Luck! Say Hey, to DTW. Be safe!!*

By 7:00 p.m. they were on the northern edge of the Old Bahama Channel, some 20 miles from Puerto Padre Inlet. *TAR BABY'S* AIS was lit up with commercial traffic. Freighters, container ships, cruise ships, commercial fishing boats, and sailboats of all sizes were moving northwest or southeast. Seth and Charley would drift until 11:00, and then move in until they were 15 miles off the inlet's entrance and deploy the Zodiac. Seth, John, Freddy, and Scotty would take the inflatable through the inlet just after midnight. Gene and Charley would run the Hatteras and the Huckins east and west with the commercial traffic until Sunday night … playing a waiting game. They would conference their sat-phones so they all had real time information

***

El Cazador directed his agent, Roberto Torrez, to build a large C-4 charge rigged with a cell phone detonator to use at Las Tunas' Revolution Square. It was identical in design to the small cellphone bomb that his other agent, Pedro Lima, would attach to the train car coupling that night in front of the prison camp. But this bomb would be twenty times more powerful. Roberto's target was Major General Vincente Garcia González's larger than life statue at Las Tunas' Revolution Square. The General, who was from Las Tunas, was a true hero of Cuba's fight for independence from Spain. It had always irritated *El Cazador* that Castro used the General's name, (he died in 1886) to help legitimize his tainted Revolution. When the smoke cleared, General Garcia's sculpted likeness would be blown off of the 1959 Revolution's stone relief façade. He would take pleasure in dialing the detonation phone number that would deface this monument to tyranny. Pedro had already given their prison guard contact the note to slip into Dave's work boot during his rounds of the barracks that night. Roberto's second task was to station himself in their safe house on the main road in Vazquez to watch the Cuban military's reaction to the early morning explosion in Las Tunas.

***

Seth, John, Scotty, and Fred shoved off in the Zodiac at midnight. John steered and ran the boat at 15 knots. They picked a lull to move through the constant flow of tankers and freighters that cluttered the radar. Within twenty minutes they were steering for the steady flash every eight seconds from the Mastelero lighthouse signal visible to the southwest. The night air on the water was actually chilly and they all slipped on their foul weather jackets. Their running lights were on and a faint glow emanated from John's handheld Garmin GPS that he used in his Lance airplane as a back-up. As they passed the 49 foot light house tower, John throttled back to 10 knots. They found the flashing red sea buoy and left it to starboard. They could hear the bell as the buoy rocked gently back and forth in the swells. Looking south they could see the loom of Playa La Boca's lights on both sides of the inlet. The red buoys to starboard were lit and the green buoys were not. Seth guessed the channel's fairway at a quarter of a mile wide. As they approached the mouth of the inlet they could smell the land, cooking aromas, and the pungent odor of rotting fish. As they eased through the opening they could see small boats moving across the wide channel in both directions. They passed a large car ferry tied to a concrete wharf with only a few night-lights burning. They could hear Latin music and laughter wafting across the water from a couple of lit up cantinas. To a casual observer the Zodiac's profile, with the two covered scooters forward, wouldn't look much different than the local pangas plying these waters.

A few minutes later the beach town's lights were behind them. Seth flashed his tactical flashlight shoreward for a second and saw only mangroves, palm trees and scrub jungle going by. They turned their running lights off and disappeared into the darkness. John slowed down to an idle and steered through a gradual turn to starboard, helped by three flashing red lights on top of piling-mounted triangular day markers spaced at 600 foot intervals. As they completed the turn they entered Puerto Padre Bay. A mile or so to the southwest was Puerto Carupano — which was lit up like a Christmas tree. John steered south leaving the port's narrow peninsula to starboard. Two large freighters, moored to the wharves, loomed above the port's buildings. The crew could see the loom of Delicias' lights five miles further south as they traveled two miles south of the port. The GPS led them up a mangrove-lined estuary that stopped a hundred yards short of the railroad tracks and paved road between Delicias and the port. They pulled the Zodiac in under the dense mangroves to hide it during the daylight hours.

Scotty and John took the pry bars from under the Zodiac's seats and headed for the tracks with the aid of a tactical flashlight.

"This must be the sandy path that leads up to the road that we saw on Google Earth, John."

"Yeah, it should follow the mangrove shoreline and then head up to the tracks," whispered John, shining his light further up the path.

"There it goes up the hill through that scrub jungle," said Scotty.

As they crested the hill their flashlights found the road and the tracks before them. The lights of distant Puerto Carupano shone to the north and there was only darkness to the south.

"Douse your flashlight and let your eyes adjust to the darkness," said John.

When they were acclimated they moved to the closest rail section and started working in the dark.

"Pry the spikes out and throw them into the scrub," said John. "Then we'll use the pry bars to move the whole rail outboard a few inches."

They worked for close to 30 minutes in that desolate area before returning to the boat.

"Any problems removing the track?" asked Seth as they climbed back aboard.

"It's done, and it won't be noticed from the adjacent road," said John.

"Okay, now we've got to hunker down for the night. There's plenty of food and drink in the cooler. Let's set up a two hour rotating watch schedule. Put your mosquito net face covers on and try to get some sleep," said Seth as he pulled the fine mesh bag over his head. "I'll take the first watch."

***

El Cazador sat staring out a third story window of a CIA safe house in Las Tunas, which faced towards Revolution Square. When his watch clicked over to 3:00 a.m. he dialed 5723-3999 on his cell phone. He saw a bright flash a mile away, followed by the sound of a huge explosion. Soon sirens wailed and *El Cazador* could see smoke and the flashing, flickering reflections of emergency red and blue lights bouncing off the buildings that surrounded the square.

Two hours later Roberto called him and said, "We got our 'Code Red' level alert. A convoy of army trucks and two tanks just rumbled through Vazquez and are headed south for Las Tunas."

El Cazador stretched out on a bed in the safe house. Later that morning he would walk past Revolution Square and admire his handiwork. Roberto would report when the cane train went through Vazquez, and Pedro would reposition himself and report when the cane train left San Manuel for Delicás.

CHAPTER TWENTY

Dave the Wave started to slip on his left work boot and felt the crumbled piece of paper in the toe. His heart raced, and sweat popped out on his forehead. He retrieved the paper and put it in his pocket. He woke Modesto and on their way to the mess hall for some rice and beans he made a *baños* detour to read the note. There was just one word: TODAY. Dave tore the note into little pieces, flushed it away, checked the toilet bowl twice, and joined Modesto in the food line.

Modesto looked at him quizzically and said, "What?"

Dave nodded his head up and down and said emphatically, "**Today!**"

They both just smiled to themselves as they ate their rice and beans in silence.

***

At dawn, Seth made an assessment of the Zodiac's position. There was a small white sand beach 50 yards north of their position that connected to the sandy trail that John and Scotty traversed last night. John moved the Zodiac to the beach and they manhandled the scooters ashore, hiding them in the scrub jungle. The crew moved the black Zodiac quickly back into the mangroves. Seth texted Charley, Gene, Bobby, and then Beau with their exact GPS location. Now their waiting game began.

***

Beau was having breakfast at the Socucho Hotel at Playa La Boca when Seth's latest text arrived. He planned to head out for another morning of fishing but would arrive at the weapons cache shortly after 12:00 noon ready for action. Beau pulled out his handheld Garmin GPS and entered Seth's coordinates. They appeared on his map just east of his weapons cache, right across the railroad tracks and road near a small beach in the mangroves.

Yesterday, Beau scoped-out the area that he would be occupying this afternoon. After cast netting a baitwell full of small shad, he fished along the mangrove laden western shoreline below Puerto Carupano. After releasing several small snook and a three-foot long tarpon in the crystal clear water, he found what he was looking for. A five foot gap in the dense mangroves opened up and meandered southeast for a hundred yards. Beau poled up the winding two-foot deep channel to a hummock covered in scrub jungle. He pushed the boat ashore and tied it to the mangroves. After stumbling around in the bush for a few minutes, he found a trail of sorts and walked a quarter of a mile to a sandy area populated with small undulating sand dunes. His GPS indicated he was 350 feet west of the weapons cache. It was exactly what he was looking for — a water path through the mangroves southwest of the port docks that was close to his weapons cache.

Beau kneeled down and stayed perfectly still on the edge of the scrub jungle for ten minutes. He saw no movement except for two frigate birds, a pelican, and a few seagulls. Finally, he walked east and saw an area of disturbed sand with some scattered dog turds here and there. The local seagulls probably tried to eat them. The weapons cache dune area provided some cover and a little height overlooking the railroad tracks and a two lane road on the other side of them, 400 feet away. He could see south down the tracks about two miles until the tracks curved eastward towards Deliciás. A hasty retreat could be beat through the scrub back to the water. If that had to happen, the smoke bombs would come in handy. Beau left quickly, brushing his foot prints away with a leafy branch.

***

Bobby scoured the position that Seth had sent him Sunday morning on his real-time satellite observation network. Seth must have hidden the black Zodiac well in the dense mangroves because Bobby couldn't find it. He switched the feed to The Old Bahama's Channel and zoomed in. He found *TAR BABY* and

ABOUT TIME twenty miles off Gibara moving west toward Puerto Padre at about 9 knots.

He sent both Seth and Beau a text: *Diversion in Las Tunas went off with a bang, troops and two tanks were sent there from the provincial army base. Cane train left Las Tunas at first light — is loading cane at Vazquez right now. Coupling C-4 charge is in place and active. Good Luck, I'll be watching!*

***

Mid-morning on Sunday, *El Cazador* walked a half of a mile to his favorite Las Tunas café. He had a leisurely cup of coffee and a *rosquillas*. When he was satisfied that he wasn't being followed, he walked the rest of the way to General Vincente García González Revolution Square, which was cordoned off and occupied by infantry troops and two tanks. Not only had the statue of the General been reduced to rubble, but a gaping hole had been opened in the middle of the facility's stone facade.

A large curious crowd had formed in the area. *El Cazador* overheard an older man say to his wizened old friend standing next to him, "They sent two more truckloads of soldiers to guard the José Marti Square statue, too. Do you think there is a stronger resistance movement forming, Javier?"

"Maybe ... same tactics as 1959," smiled Javier.

El Cazador wanted to tell them the real score - but of course - he couldn't. As long as the United States granted Cuban refugees special immigration status (wet foot-dry foot) the real dissidents kept escaping the country any way they could and settled in America. There would never be enough dissidents in Cuba at one time to mount an effective resistance until they had nowhere else to go.

***

The sun rose higher in the sky and the day got hotter — 83° would be the high on Sunday, dropping to 66° that night. At two o'clock Seth was ready to make a move. He gave Scotty and Freddy a final briefing.

"John and I will take the scooters and ride down near Deliciás. We're going to hide back in some trees and foliage that I saw on Google Earth where the railroad starts to parallel the causeway road to the port. The whole trip is like five miles. Our information is that the train runs at 35 miles an hour or less from Deliciás to the port. As soon as the locomotive and passenger car start to make the northeast turn, I'll detonate the cell phone bomb on the coupler. I have the number on my speed dial. That will leave the cane cars back where there's no parallel road, just farmland. We'll ride out of the brush and speed up next to the passenger car where Bobby's agents tell us Dave and Modesto ride. We both have a rifle in a scabbard and a 9mm pistol. When the train stops we'll swoop in and pick up Dave and Modesto. If the engineer panics and speeds up, the locomotive is going to get derailed right here. I want you two to take up a position back in the scrub, on this side of the road, a hundred feet north from where you took out the section of track. Bobby's placed an armed agent in those little dunes a hundred yards or so out on the other side of the tracks. He'll lay down some cover fire if we need it. You guys will have the Beretta AR 70/grenade launcher and a tactical shotgun. Remember … the Beretta is primarily a 30-shot semi-automatic. We don't want to kill anybody if we can help it. When we're leaving, Bobby's agent should have our backs. The only guard we will have to deal with for sure is the one in the locomotive. The other two guards will be back on the cane cars with the prison labor. Wait about an hour after John and I leave, then move the Zodiac over to the little beach. It will make our getaway smoother. Any questions?"

"I think you have it covered, Cappy," said Freddy. "All we need is a little luck."

Seth had done a little research on police uniforms in Cuba. The police wore light blue shirts, navy blue trousers, and a navy blue baseball cap; Seth, John, Scotty, and Fred all wore light blue Columbia fishing shirts (over their bullet-proof Kevlar mesh), dark blue polyester slacks, and generic navy blue ball caps, purchased in Key West. They would be less recognizable on the scooters and in a shooting situation, it might gain them a hesitation or a look-away. Eye contact with a Cuban policemen could bring on a shakedown for a Cuban citizen.

John and Seth wrestled the Honda scooters out of the underbrush and started them up. They rode them up the sandy path onto the paved road and started south-southwest towards Deliciás. In a matter of minutes, they were two miles down the road where the road abruptly turned away from the gradual curve the railroad took. Seth and John pulled into the stand of trees he had seen on Google Earth. Mimosas, Jacarandas, and fir trees grew around an abandoned house. The weeds in the yard were six feet high and afforded good cover. They leaned the scooters up against a fence that abutted a large parcel of tilled farmland. The town of Deliciás was visible in the distance and the sugar mill's large smoke stacks belched soot and smoke from its boilers. John and Seth engaged in nervous small talk while keeping their eyes peeled for the cane train.

About 4:00 p.m. the train cleared the outskirts of town and ran out onto the flat farmland. Seth and John saw it approaching, started up their scooters, and positioned themselves near the bend in the road. As the locomotive started around the bend Seth hit speed dial #10 on his sat-phone.

***

Modesto and Dave stayed alert. After off-loading the laborers and loading cane in Vazquez, Maniabon, and San Manuel, Dave figured that whatever was going to happen would happen near the water. When all the cane was unloaded in Delíciás and the train was taking on a few hundred sacks of finished product — Dave and Modesto retired to the passenger car for a couple bottles of cold water. They figured something would happen out at Puerto Carupano while the sugar sacks were being unloaded. He and Modesto had a cool drink of water and the air blowing through the open car windows started to cool them off. Suddenly, as the train started into the turn leading out to the port, Dave heard a loud explosion behind him that rocked the car and showered him with little pieces of glass. He struggled to his feet as the locomotive lurched forward and stumbled to the rear door in the passenger car. The door's safety glass was shattered, and Dave could see the cane cars melting away in the distance.

Mateo fell beside him and shouted, "*Carajo*! What the fuck was that? The cane cars are loose — **Stop the train!**"

But the train wasn't stopping, it was speeding up. Modesto pulled himself up off the floor, and Dave could see him taking an inventory of his limbs — he looked all right.

Mateo clawed his way forward trying to climb over Rosita's toppled desk toward the locomotive screaming, "Stop the train! Stop the train!"

Rosita lay dazed under her desk chair.

Dave looked out the side window towards the road and saw why the engineer was applying power. There were two black motor scooters closing in on the train. The riders were dressed like Cuban police and they had rifles slung across their handle bars. As they pulled up even with the passenger car one of the drivers took off his hat.

"Fuckin'-A, it's Seth Stone," said Dave under his breath.

He moved over next to Modesto who had sat back down and was trying to get rid of the cobwebs in his brain.

"Did you hit your head?"

"Yeah, but I'm all right, I'm shaking it off."

Just as he got that out of his mouth there was a big bump and the locomotive and passenger car left the tracks. They careened across the road towards the water and the passenger car jackknifed, rolled on its side, and screeched to a halt. Modesto and Dave were thrown across the car and both landed in a heap. Dave had the wind knocked out of him and was cut by more flying glass. Modesto came through the second traumatic maneuver with a few more bruises.

Dave got his breath back and told Modesto, "Those are our guys."

Modesto checked a comatose Mateo who was breathing okay and wasn't bleeding anywhere.

Dave comforted a banged up Rosita who had nothing broken but was crying hysterically.

"Modesto," said Dave quietly, "*Vámonos*."

They climbed out the broken window in the back door of the car and emerged from the wreckage. The front half of the locomotive had entered the water and there was no visible movement — just a lot of steam from the hot diesel engine being swamped.

Seth rode over to Dave and said, "Get on the back, we have to leave now," as a bullet whizzed over their heads.

"Modesto, get on the back of the other scooter," yelled Dave, as John pulled up. Modesto didn't have to be told twice.

Dave could see the two guards from the cane train running towards them. They stopped to shoot from a half a mile away. As they rode quickly away on the scooters, Seth heard some shooting coming from the sand dunes across from them. *Has to be Beau covering us*, thought Seth.

When Seth and Dave turned in on the sandy path, two more bullets whizzed by overhead. John was right behind him with Modesto. Scotty stepped out of the bushes with the Beretta AR/70 and launched a grenade at the locomotive. Apparently, the locomotive guard had recovered enough to shoot his AK-47. Scotty's grenade was a near miss but it exploded on the road in a ball of fire and smoke. The shrapnel tore holes in the diesel cowlings. The guard and engineer exited the locomotive and ran down the road towards Deliciás in a hail of rubber bullets. They could hear occasional gunshots as Freddy helped

Seth and John load the scooters into the Zodiac. Sirens wailed in the distance. Scotty covered the path until the scooters were secured then ran down and jumped in as John backed out.

"Our cover guy just laid down a couple of smoke bombs out there," said Scotty.

Seth smiled and had John angle east across the bay to slip around the back side of uninhabited Cayo Puerto to avoid being seen from the port. As they ran across at 18 knots, Seth sent some texts, first to Beau: *We're out in the Bay, thanks for the cover – we needed it. How was your front row seat for the train wreck? If you haven't left yet … get going. Text me when you're clear.* Next, he texted Gene and Charley: *Mission accomplished, we have Dave — in Puerto Padre Bay now, coming out after sunset — consolidate your positions and text them to me at 7:00.* He didn't text Bobby because he figured he probably saw it all on his real time satellite feed. Also, this wasn't the time for any post mortems. They still had to get through the inlet and out of Cuban territorial waters. Seth was glad he had brought Beau in, and he would thank Norm again for the use of the grenade launcher.

When they got to Cayo Puerto Seth said, "John, let's just idle around back here, this island is about a mile long and its 5:15, sunset's at 6:10. Put the covers back on the scooters. We'll start through the inlet, slowly, at 6:15 — it should be pitch dark by the time we get up in the populated part of Playa La Boca."

"Sounds like a plan," agreed John.

Everybody took a deep breath and started talking. Dave the Wave was blown away by the rescue and was probably in mild shock. While Freddy cleaned up his glass cuts, Dave thanked Seth and everyone else over and over. Modesto was stoic, and Seth suspected he might have a concussion from the train wreck. John checked Modesto's eyes and thought the same thing. Seth heard a helicopter in the distance, as John was idling up the edge of the mangrove laden shore of the little island.

"Run the Zodiac up under those mangroves, John, and everybody stay still," said Seth.

The armed military helicopter went over and back a couple of times, saw nothing, and finally headed for Playa La Boca.

Seth knew when Dave got over the shock in a few days his emotions would flow like a dam breaking. Seth and Dave's other friends would be there to talk him through it. Each crew member had a bottle of cold water and a sandwich as they yawned their adrenaline rushes away. It would be therapeutic for everyone later tonight and tomorrow to recount this experience with the whole crew in small groups. Everyone would then understand how important each and every member of an operation like this was. Seth needed every one of them to make it successful. Seth's musings were abruptly interrupted by a text from Beau.

***

Earlier, at high noon, Beau kneeled behind the sand dune with the dog turds on it. He'd brought along a 5 gallon bucket, a pair of binoculars, and a filet knife from the hidden flats boat. He dug a hole in the soft sand with the bucket, then scooped up the dog turds and buried them. Beau systematically probed the area with the filet knife until he struck something hard. He used the bucket to uncover the weapons. The weapons were packaged in 6 mil poly film sealed with duct tape. Beau used the filet knife to reveal a late model AK-47, three 30 round magazines with rubber bullets and two 30 round magazines of standard 7.62 cartridges. There was also a 9mm Glock pistol with two extra clips and two Micro Ace canister smoke bombs. He picked the highest dune about 300 feet from the tracks and set up just behind it. With the binoculars, he could see the entire two miles to the bend in the tracks and road that led to Delicias.

He saw Seth and John Harvey pop out of the bushes across the road about 2:15 p.m. on two small black motor scooters. They raced down the road and disappeared around the bend. Beau kept his eye on the bend for the next two hours and only three delivery type trucks drove up and back from the port. Shortly after 4:00 p.m., he heard a faint explosion. Moments later, Beau saw the locomotive come around the bend with only one car behind it. Seth and John raced back up the road on their scooters paralleling the train. The locomotive was gaining speed as it drew near to Beau's position. All at once the train veered and careened off the track. It slid, screeching across the road, and crashed into the mangroves and water, stopping abruptly. The passenger car jackknifed and was flung on its side breaking most of its windows. The water killed the diesels and the hot locomotive put off clouds of steam. Seth and John pulled up outside of the passenger car near the back door. Within minutes Dave the Wave came out dragging a dazed Cuban, also in prison garb, along with him. Beau heard some far off shots being fired. Two uniformed guards ran up the road shooting automatic AK-47's. Beau returned fire with the rubber bullets and both guards dove for cover across the tracks. They ran up another hundred yards, crossed the tracks, and shot at the scooters again as they were leaving. Beau laid down some more fire, which pinned them down. If they didn't stay put he might use real bullets on them. He heard sirens in the distance and more shots close by. The locomotive guard was shooting out of the engineer's window in the direction Seth had gone. Before he could get his gun up, a grenade went off next to the disabled locomotive peppering the side of the train with shrapnel. The engineer and guard jumped down and hauled ass down the road. Beau shot both of them in the butt a couple of times with the rubber bullets to hasten their departure. An unarmed Cuban couple appeared through the steam on the road next to the passenger car. The sirens were getting closer so Beau threw one smoke bomb towards the locomotive and the other straight at the pinned down guards. The afternoon northerly sea breeze took care of the rest as the heavy smoke rendered the road and dunes impassable. Beau beat a hasty retreat to the flats boat. Once in the bay, he threw the AK-47 overboard, but he kept the 9mm handy. He wouldn't deep-six it until he was on his way to the airport.

He heard his sat-phone chime and checked his text messages. Seth was on his way to the inlet.

Beau texted back when he was clear of the Port Carupano: *Light resistance - no one on the train killed, left in a cloud of smoke as first responders were arriving - almost back at Pescar Robalo.*

***

When the sun fell below the horizon, John turned the Zodiac north and throttled her up to 9 knots. They turned on their running lights and gave hats and life jackets to Dave and Modesto. They knew there would be more traffic in the inlet than when they came in and the car ferry would probably still be running. The lights of Playa La Boca loomed ahead as they eased up the inlet. The crew held their breath as each approaching boats passed them by with hardly a second look. The ferry did go across a hundred yards in front of them. They smelled the food cooking ashore and heard the laughter and music from the waterfront bars. Finally, they were clear of the inlet and it was pitch dark around them. Seth turned their running lights off and the Zodiac disappeared. John stayed in the freighter channel using his darkened hand-held GPS, and the lighted red bell buoys for navigation. They passed the Mastelero lighthouse eight second beacon on the west side of the inlet. Only the red sea buoy - a mile away - remained.

Seth said, "Gentlemen it looks like ……." Suddenly — a large spot light flicked on behind them and illuminated the Zodiac and everyone in it. Seth quickly flipped on his 5 million candle power handheld spotlight — pointing it right at the offending spot light. A fifty-foot Cuban gunboat was bearing down on them. As it got closer they could hear the twin diesels growling. The Cuban boat turned on a piercing siren.

Seth yelled to John, **"Full speed towards the sea buoy and zig-zag!"**

John complied with the order and everybody hung on. Seth handed the spotlight to Dave who was sitting next to him.

"Turn the spotlight off until I tell you to turn it back on, then point it right at them."

Seth grabbed the Beretta AR/70 … he groped in the ammo bag until he found a grenade. Seth heard a large caliber machine gun shooting. The bullets whizzed by overhead on the starboard side. **"Keep zig-zagging, John!"**

"The sea buoy is getting close, Seth" yelled John.

"Zig out, then Zag behind it," said Seth, as he chambered the grenade. **"When John zags back, Dave — aim the light at their bow and turn it on."**

Dave turned the light on as John started for the sea buoy and said, **"Oh My God! It's Consuelo."**

And there she was, behind the machine gun mounted on the foredeck, wearing black tights, knee-high black boots, a bolero jacket, with her black hair flowing in the wind. Her red lipstick was smeared on a face contorted with hate. She let go with another volley that narrowly missed as the gunboat drew nearer. Seth aimed and launched a grenade that hit the gunboat's front windshield. The foredeck exploded in a ball of fire, blinding the helmsman. The gunboat ran smack into the sea buoy — and completely exploded — showering the area with flaming debris. John slowed down, turned back, and steered a wide circle around the sea buoy. Dave shone the light on the mangled buoy and the water around it. The gunboat was gone and there were no survivors. There wasn't a piece of wreckage big enough to pick up. Seth took the light from Dave and turned it off. Dave hung his head and couldn't speak.

"So you knew her, Dave?" asked Seth.

All Dave could say was, "Hell hath no fury - like a woman scorned."

"John, leave the lights out and run at full speed on a course of 360 degrees. We need to get out of here, now!" commanded Seth.

As the loom of Playa La Boca faded into the darkness of night, Seth picked up his sat-phone to call Gene and Charley ... he shook his head and said to John, "There's no way you could make this shit up."

CHAPTER TWENTY- ONE

THE RENDEVOUS took place 15 miles off Cuba's coast. Because of the gunboat incident, Seth decided to tow the scooters in the Zodiac until they were at least another 20 miles outside of Cuban waters. They put Modesto and Dave the Wave on Charley's boat with John Harvey who wanted to keep an eye on Modesto's condition. Norm Hogan stayed with Gene along with Seth, Freddy, and Scotty.

"I noticed that the weather has changed some while we've been motoring back and forth for the last twenty-some hours. By this time of night the northerly sea breeze has usually shifted to the east as it clocks southeast after midnight. I checked PassageWeather and we're going to get a little weather from a front that's moving down from the Florida Straits," said Gene.

"What's the prognosis?" asked Seth.

"Around 15 - 20 knots from the north tonight, clocking into the southeast at 15 knots tomorrow."

"Why don't we just head for Cayo Santo Domingo and anchor on its south side tonight. We can transfer the scooters tomorrow morning, along with some diesel, then we'll chug back to Duncan Town at 10 knots. That should put us there around lunchtime and everybody will be rested."

"Yeah, everybody's tired, but we'll still pull watch at the anchorage."

"After what happened on the way out of Puerto Padre, anything might happen. We'll keep both boats' radars on all night at their 24 mile range, and the weapons handy. I'm sure glad we had those grenade launchers, they made the difference."

"I'm anxious to talk to Dave the Wave tomorrow," said Gene.

"Me, too. With all the action and trauma, I didn't get to say much to him. I got an especially weird vibe from him during the gunboat attack," said Seth.

"We should have plenty of time to talk tomorrow."

Seth texted Bobby: *Both boats and all personnel okay. Dave and Modesto on board. Headed to Cayo Santo Domingo to anchor, everyone is exhausted. We fought off a gunboat attack at the sea buoy. You probably couldn't see that on your satellite feed in the dark. Maybe only the explosion. We left a mess behind in Puerto Carupano, but no causalities there that we know of. No survivors on the gunboat, we had a grenade launcher. Thanks for your help, Amigo. P.S. If your buddy, Woodie, has a Coast Guard Boat patrolling in the Old Bahamas Channel tonight, see if he will send it past Cayo Santo Domingo a couple of times.*

The Cay was easy to find because of the 30 second flashing red light on the highest point of the tiny island. Seth pulled *TAR BABY* as close to shore as possible. The north wind whistled over the top of the 40 foot high limestone cliffs on its south side. The crews deployed two anchors from each vessel to compensate for the tide and the expected clockwise shifting of the wind in the early morning.

"I feel safe anchoring at this island because of something that happened here on May 10th of 1980."

"What are you talking about, Seth?" asked Gene.

"A 103 foot Bahamas patrol vessel, captained by Commander Amos Rolle, patrolled these waters around that time to discourage Cuban fishing boats from poaching in Bahamian waters. They caught two Cuban Government-owned fishing trawlers with 3,000 pounds of freshly caught fish, lobsters, and conch at Cayo Santo Domingo. They arrested eight Cuban fisherman and took both boats in tow. The fisherman radioed Puerto Carupano for help. As the *HMBS FLAMINGO* pulled out of this anchorage, two Cuban MIG jets appeared in the sky and began strafing the *FLAMINGO*, which was soon rocked with explosions. They continued to strafe even as the *FLAMINGO* was going down. All, except four, of the 19 crew members aboard made it to one of the Cuban fishing boats. Those four were never found. Commander Rolle, his remaining crew, and the eight Cuban fisherman arrived in Duncan Town, on Ragged Island, about five hours later on the fishing boats. Soon Cuban MIGS and a helicopter full of troops arrived at Duncan Town and buzzed the fishing boats. The Bahamian Government protested and the Cubans withdrew. The U.S. Coast Guard and a Navy destroyer searched for the four lost Bahamian marines. The Cuban Government called it a "regrettable confusion" and started backpedaling. After releasing several implausible stories, Cuba finally accepted full responsibility and compensated The Bahamian Government $5,000,000 for the ship and $100,000 for each of the families of the four lost

211

marines. The Cuban Government also paid the $90,000 fines for each of the eight Cuban poachers aboard the government-owned fishing boats. The *FLAMINGO* affair had unraveled what Castro had taken decades to achieve – 'third world leadership and respectability'. The newly formed country of The Bahamas quickly created its own defense force."

"I never heard that one before," said Gene.

"Probably because May 9th, 1980, was the day the *SUMMIT VENTURE* hit the Skyway Bridge and the southbound span collapsed into Tampa Bay. There was hardly anything else in the news in St. Petersburg for the next month. Anyhow, I don't think the Cubans will follow us into Bahamian waters and chance dredging *FLAMINGO* affair up again."

The crews were up with the sun the next morning. After a well-deserved celebratory breakfast, they reloaded the scooters, reshuffled the crews, and headed for Duncan Town at 10 knots. The Zodiac towed easily with the engine tilted half-way up. Seth wanted Dave the Wave and Modesto on *TAR BABY* with John, Gene, Freddy, and Doug. Norm Hogan, Scotty, and Bill Pearce would crew for Charley Blevins. Seth wanted Dave's friends to help debrief him and he also wanted to spend some time with Modesto and keep John near him. The breeze had already clocked into the northeast and Seth hoped it would soon be off their beam. The ride was lumpy, but not uncomfortable at 10 knots.

Doug steered with John and Modesto up in the flybridge. Doug spoke fluent Spanish, but it wasn't needed because of Modesto's excellent English. Modesto was open and honest about his checkered past in Cuba. His number one goal was to leave Cuba with his family and establish a life in Canada or the United States. He thought his Russian wife would acclimate better in Canada. He could take a year or so of Aeronautical Engineering in the States or Canada and then take the licensing test and earn $150,000 a year as a jet fuel engineer. He had been paid $50 a month in Cuba before he quit to become a driver for a Canadian travel agency where he averaged $750 a month, which was huge money in Cuba. He explained his black market dealings were necessary to finance his family's defection from Cuba.

Down below Dave was giving Seth, Gene, and Freddy a month by month synopsis of his prison experiences.

"When I came out of solitary, where they beat the confession out of me, they sent me to Havana and Morro Castle Prison for my trial and threw me in a holding tank. Two college professors shielded me from the real criminals."

"That was lucky," said Freddy.

"The trial was a farce, the ballplayer lied, and they sent me to a prison work camp. Modesto took me under his wing and helped me learn the ropes. I'd probably be dead if it wasn't for him. Luckily he spoke perfect English. I mean my Spanish was getting better, but they talk too fast."

"I knew where you were — my CIA friend found you," said Seth. "But until you got the tobacco pick-up and delivery job, we couldn't figure a way out for you. Actually, it would have been way easier to get you out of Pinar Del Rio than Las Tunas. We probably could have done it without firing a shot. But then you were gone to Las Tunas, so we called it off."

"It freaked me out when the guy slipped me your note in the Havana cigar factory. But it gave me hope."

"So they were moving lots of prisoners east to help with the sugar cane harvest. How did you and Modesto end up on the cane train as foremen?" asked Gene.

"This is hard for me to talk about, but I wouldn't be here, on my way back home, if it wasn't for you guys. I'm not proud of this, but when I tell you — put yourself in my shoes."

"Are you going to tell us about Consuelo?" asked Seth.

"Yeah, Consuelo was the commandant of the women's prisons in Pinar Del Rio. She was a formidable presence. Modesto and I delivered tobacco, but we also moved furniture, filing cabinets, and different things for the officers and bureaucrats. Word got back to Modesto that she wanted us to teach an English class. Modesto said he'd heard rumors about her being bi-sexual, BDSM, and attracted to blond, blue-eyed men. She was trim, always dressed in black, wore black leather boots and carried a riding crop. Consuelo was attractive in a Latin middle-aged way. You guys know me, I like them young. She invited Modesto and me to join her English class, which met every Thursday night. We taught some of her inmates to speak better English … Spanish was not allowed. Consuelo was trying to give them a skill that could help them get a real job when their sentence was served. I found out from Modesto later it was all a scam, Consuelo kept the supposed BDSM private in her office, her sex with me was under the guise of grading test papers, also alone in her office. It turned out that there was no bondage, Consuelo and the girls, who were all convicted prostitutes, just played cards. The whole thing was concocted to help Modesto find out from me who the big money men were in the Miami baseball syndicate. Modesto was offered commutation of half his remaining prison sentence to find out if I had that information. It was soon obvious to him I didn't know anything about it and we became fast friends. He finally came clean when I asked him if he wanted to join this escape operation. I understood the difficult positon the Cuban Government had placed him in, and I forgave him because I know he is my friend. He readily joined us.

But, the English class provided a real dinner; lobster, green beans, and oysters, not just the monotonous rice and beans for every meal - and all the beer we could drink. It was like dying and going to heaven in that hell hole. Consuelo started out just using me with no emotion ... like a man on a one night stand. I think I know now how a corporate woman whose boss is a sexual predator feels. You're trapped. Then slowly, she fell for me and I played her along. But I have to admit ... I enjoyed the sex with the young girls more. Then I started to take control and I dominated her. I made her do things that pleased only me."

"And that was her behind the machine gun last night?" asked Seth.

"Yes, she realized I had played her — I robbed her of her pride. When Consuelo was transferred to Las Tunas. She asked me if I wanted to come along, and if I wanted to bring Modesto. Her boss arranged our cushy jobs on the cane train. I think she knew I didn't know anything, But she wanted to keep the English class together to be with me."

"I can tell you, in that situation, I'd have done the same thing," said Freddy.

"I think it would have gotten around to the guards and other prisoners that you were connected. It might have saved your life," said Seth.

"Yeah, I was thinking along those lines, too," said Gene.

"Now ... we've got to get Dave back into the states without a passport," said Seth.

"Yeah, they confiscated my passport and all my other I.D."

"You know the last place your passport was stamped was in Cancun. But we don't check out of the United States when we go abroad, we just check back in," said Seth. "If you fly in with John, you'll have to go through customs and you'll both have trouble. What if I put you ashore ... and you just go home. You haven't been gone even six months yet. Apply for a replacement passport ... and say you lost it. I'll drop you at the Riviera Beach Greyhound Bus Station on my cab ride to check through customs at the Palm Beach Airport in West Palm ... or maybe you can get Sonja to drive down and take you back to St. Pete."

"That'll work, but what about Modesto?" asked Dave.

214

"He's got a free pass at Customs and Immigration. I'm planning on stopping at Sailfish Marina on Singer Island. We'll get him to a Catholic Church — they'll take him to customs and help him through the whole process."

"Are we going back through the Okeechobee Waterway?" asked Gene.

"That's the plan right now. It should save time and fuel."

"I haven't been through it for a while, it's a nice trip," said Gene.

"Looks like Ragged Island dead ahead, mates. The anchorage is going to be a little rock n' rolly until the wind goes more south," said Seth. "Let's walk up to the Ponderosa for lunch and then have a beer at Percy's Eagles Nest DC-3 bar on the way back. The wind should be cooperating by then and we'll deflate and pack the Zodiac and load the Suzuki outboard."

"What about the scooters?" asked Freddy.

"I'm going to let Charley use the scooters for spring break in Nassau. His daughters and their friends will have a ball running around on them."

Doug, Norm, and Deputy Pearce opted out of lunch. They wanted to dive along the protected shore of Little Ragged Island just south of them while the sun was high. Charley put his dinghy in for them. The rest of the crew climbed into the black Zodiac and motored over to the beach. When they got back to the anchorage three hours later, Bill Pearce was cleaning conch on *ABOUT TIME'*s swim platform. Norm was fileting some strawberry grouper, and Doug opened the cooler and held up two huge lobsters.

"Look what we caught for dinner, we've got a cooler full," shouted Doug. The whole crew piled aboard Charley's boat and an impromptu beer party started.

"How was downtown?" asked Norm.

"We might have seen ten other people," said John. "We did score some lettuce, tomatoes, and cucumbers at Percy's though. He seems to have a lot going on here."

"He told me he wants to start a nudist resort up past his pig farm," laughed Dave.

"Don't you find that somewhat ironic, Dave?" asked Doug.

"Uh... h, yeah, actually I do."

Seth said, "I don't want to break up this lovefest, but why don't we transfer the other scooter over here and then decommission the Zodiac — by the time we're finished it will really be cocktail hour."

They got everything all packed up and had a couple more brewski's while munching on Bill's cracked conch appetizer.

"It would take a 'Conch' to make cracked conch this good," laughed Dave the Wave at his own funny.

Norm and Doug boiled the lobsters. Modesto whipped up a spicy Cuban salad and Charley grilled the grouper filets over his gas grill.

The dinner was superb and Seth shared a couple of bottles of Adelsheim Pinot Noir from Oregon with Charley, John, and Scotty. Seth was happy to see that Dave and Modesto had thrown off their defensive postures and were relaxing and enjoying the camaraderie.

Both boats would leave for Clarence Town the next morning. John flew out of Duncan Town with a fuel stop planned in Stella Maris with Norm, Freddy, and Doug. His U.S. Port of Entry would be Kendall-Tamiami Executive airport outside of Miami. The flight would take about 2 hours and 45 minutes, not counting ground time at Stella Maris. They should be home in plenty of time for dinner.

ABOUT TIME and *TAR BABY* fueled up in Clarence Town and ran up to Davis Harbor in south Eleuthera and docked overnight. The next day they arrived in Nassau. Seth docked at Hurricane Hole and fueled up that afternoon. The dock master at Hurricane Hole knew *TAR BABY* already had a cruising permit. Seth kept Modesto and Dave below and out of sight the whole time they were in Nassau. Charley docked at Atlantis and took Deputy Pearce to the airport where he flew thru Miami back to Key West. It had been Bill's kind of vacation, he loved the sea time, the adventure and camaraderie.

Seth left Nassau early the next morning for Lake Worth Inlet and docked at Sailfish Marina on Singer Island just before 7:00 p.m. Customs was closed so Seth, Scotty, and John planned to take a cab to the customs facility at West Palm Airport the following morning. Per plan, Seth and Dave took Modesto to St. Francis of Assisi Catholic Church on Riviera Beach in a cab. Modesto had Dave the Wave's surf shop telephone number and Seth's cell phone if he needed help. Seth staked him with $500 from the ship's safe. He and Dave shook hands and hugged. Modesto rang the bell on the rectory door, it opened, and they took him in.

"I'd have never made it if it wasn't for him, Seth. I hope I can keep in touch with him."

"You've got a friend for life there, Dave. I can tell he's a right kind of guy."

"We want to go to the Hampton Inn near the West Palm Airport," said Seth to the cab driver.

"The meter's running, sir, I'll take you anywhere you want to go," answered the driver.

"It's been five hours since I put you on my sat-phone with Sonja, Dave. She should be at the Hampton by now."

"I told her to check in and then wait in the lobby. Thanks for lending me these clothes to get home. I was lucky to find these flip-flops in the gift shop at the marina … I'll give you your clothes back when you get home."

"You can keep them, Dave. Maybe I'll come out to the surf shop and pick out a new pair of board shorts and a Hurley performance t-shirt for myself."

"Whatever you want, buddy? How can I ever repay you?"

"You'd do the same for me, that's what old friends are for. Ah, here's the Hampton," said Seth.

Dave gave Seth a hug and said, "Are you coming in to say hello to Sonja?"

"No, I'm going to leave that to you …Take her to dinner, get a good night's sleep, and drive carefully across Alligator Alley. I'll see you on the flip-flop."

'I wish I could say the right thing to you, but … there are just no words, Seth … Thank You."

"You're welcome, Dave, and thank-you is enough."

As Dave got out, Seth said to the driver, "Round trip, my man, back to the Marina, please."

During the ride back to Sailfish Marina, Seth started thinking about the last phase of this operation … reparations from Hugo Lugo. He hadn't discussed this at all with Dave the Wave … on purpose. It was something he wanted to handle all by himself.

The trip to Stuart and across the waterway was uneventful. The trip home to Saint Petersburg gave Seth, Gene, and Scotty time to unwind from their adventure, and Seth had an idea to make re-entry even easier. They called their significant others and invited them aboard.

Lori, Gene's wife, Helen, and Scotty's girlfriend, Pam were waiting for them at Fort Myers City Marina on the Caloosahatchee River after they exited the Franklin Lock. They had a great reunion and dinner that night at The Veranda.

"How was the ride down, Lori?" asked Gene while they waited in the bar for their table.

"A lot of traffic on I-75 with all the tourists this time of year, especially around Sarasota."

"Any trouble renting a car on such short notice?" asked Scotty.

"Not really. Enterprise in St. Pete Beach seemed happy to be sending a one-way down here."

"You guys are really out-doing yourselves with good ideas this year," said Helen. "I'm looking forward to the boat ride home."

"We're planning on stopping in Captiva at South Seas Plantation tomorrow afternoon and night, and at the Sarasota Yacht Club the following night. We'll get there early enough so you girls can walk to St. Armand's Circle and shop," said Seth. "Later we can have cocktails at the Yacht Club, then take a cab downtown to the Bijou Café for dinner."

***

Spring break was in full swing in Florida when Seth got the expense list for the "The Dave the Wave Operation" compiled. He didn't include round trip fuel to and from the Keys for the Hatteras or Huckins or fuel and crew expenses while fishing in Key West. The fuel to power each boat for 1600 miles at predominately high cruising speeds cost $22,500. Airplane fuel cost and the charter fees were $2600. Next would be charter fees to cover boat wear and tear – and the crews' per diem: the total for both boats, $40,000. The Zodiac and motor, plus accessories, totaled $34,600. The Honda scooters cost $3400. Crew provisions, and outside dinner expense ran $7500. Marina berths at Hurricane Hole, Davis Harbor, and Flying Fish, including electric and water for both boats, came to $1950. Sat-phone rentals and minutes added up to $1600. *TAR BABY'S* Bahamas cruising permit cost $350. Miscellaneous airfare, crew accommodations, targets, and ammunition, amounted to $1800. The grand total added up to $116,300.

He also asked Bobby for one last Dave the Wave favor: would his agents check around and see if Hugo Lugo had committed any felonies in Cuba. Hugo's lack of character dictated Seth's request. A week later Bobby texted: *No felonies, but El Cazador unearthed another bombshell for you. A year before he accused Dave - Hugo fingered Hector Suarez, a Miami born Cuban-American electrician visiting his grandmother in Havana - for the same offense. Hugo met him at the LUNA MEDIA Bar in the Vedado neighborhood, in Havana. Hector was arrested the next morning at his grandmother's house, two blocks away. He was murdered in prison four months ago. I'm sending you an email with all the details. I ran a background check on him here – Hector Suarez was an honest family man. I'll send you his trial transcript along with Dave Perozzi's.*

***

Seth made an appointment with Barry Schwartz, a high profile Tampa lawyer, who had the reputation of being a tough litigator. Barry had won many high dollar civil cases in circumstances where the defendant had not been convicted under criminal law. Seth explained Dave the Wave's situation and outlined his plan to force Hugo Lugo-Ramirez to pay reparations for his willful perjury against Dave in a Cuban Court of Law. He also gave Barry the transcripts of Dave's and Hector Suarez's Havana trials.

"Barry, my question is, if Hugo's agent decides to blow me off, can we file a civil suit in the United States against Hugo Lugo for damages?"

"I would say unequivocally, yes. A United States citizen in a foreign country can be tried and convicted criminally under the foreign law if their law doesn't violate, for example, our first amendment free speech guarantee. It's something called personal jurisdiction. But if he is unfairly treated by one of their citizens, the offender can be tried in our federal civil court system because of 'complete diversity'. Since Hugo Lugo now resides here, has qualified for a green card, and has assets earned in the United States — he would be in jeopardy of owing a settlement decided by a jury, and could possibly lose his green card status."

"Just the publicity of a high profile trial of this nature would be devastating to his Major League Baseball career and to any endorsements his agent may have negotiated for him. He has already made a major impact in the Padre's line-up and promises to be a rising new star in the National League," said Seth.

"I'll take the case on a percentage basis if you need me, Mr. Stone, and I'll call Mrs. Suarez to work on a deal for her."

"Do that, and I'll present both of them to Alex Espinosa. I can only hope that Hugo and his agent will want to do the right thing."

***

"Seth Stone here," said Seth as he answered his cell phone.

"Mr. Stone, this is Alex Espinosa, Hugo Lugo's agent. Sheriff Billy Ray Stodgins called me this morning and said you have some important news for me about Hugo Lugo. He also told me that he holds you in very high esteem."

"Well, I hold Billy Ray in the highest esteem, too."

"He helped a couple of my high profile clients out of a scrape down in Key West. He's the right kind of guy."

"Well, I'll get right to it, Alex."

Seth spent the next 30 minutes explaining how Dave was framed by Hugo, arrested, convicted, and sent to jail to make Hugo look loyal to the Cuban Government after his third unsuccessful defection attempt.

"Dave was the second innocent man that Hugo turned in. A year earlier, he accused a Miami Lakes union electrician named Hector Suarez, whose parents came to Miami during the Mariel boatlift in 1980, of the same crime. Hector was visiting his grandmother in Havana during a vacation from work. He was sentenced to six years of hard labor. Subsequently, he was killed in a prison knife fight four months ago, leaving a wife and two children in Miami. My investigator could not find that he had any ties to Major League Baseball agents, teams, or cartels. My sources in Cuba report that three weeks after Dave Perozzi's conviction, Hugo was reinstated to the Cuban All-Star traveling team. A week after that he defected to Mexico and entered the United States."

"If all this is true, I agree it could be a problem. But where's the proof, Mr. Stone?"

"The full Cuban court proceedings are all on record officially with Amnesty International and the U.N.'s Human Right Watch organizations. We also have copies of those court records. We have three witnesses from the Jaimanitas pig roast who will testify that Dave had a two sentence conversation when they met. Number one was just a cordial introduction. Number two was an expression of admiration for his playing skills. Dave Perozzi escaped from prison a few weeks ago in Cuba and is back in St. Petersburg and ready to tell his story. In light of the lucrative five year contract Mr. Lugo-Ramirez has signed, we ask that Mr. Lugo to step up and compensate Mr. Perozzi with $1,000,000 for the pain, suffering, and the financial hardship he has caused him. Also, his escape from prison was an expensive operation costing $120,000. Beyond that, we ask that Hugo Lugo-Ramirez set up a trust fund for Hector's Suarez's widow, Mrs. Hector Suarez and their two children; contributing $1,000,000 per year over the life of Mr. Lugo-Ramirez's five year Padre's contract to a total of $5,000,000 to cover living expenses and the education of the two children. Had it not been for Mr. Lugo-Ramirez's dishonesty, Mr. Hector Suarez might still be alive."

"I will certainly question and counsel my client to the best of my ability. I would also be remiss if I didn't consult my attorneys. Let me get back to you, Mr. Stone. This is all a bit of a shock."

"I understand completely, Mr. Espinosa. I will give you 48 hours and if we don't get a positive answer in that time frame, our lawyer, Barry Schwartz, will file a defamation of character, wrongful imprisonment, and perjury civil suit against Hugo Lugo in U.S. Federal Court in Tampa for $2,500,000 in damages, plus attorney's fees. Also, we will assist Mrs. Hector Suarez in filing a Federal wrongful death civil suit in the amount of $10,000,000 in Miami."

"I'll be back to you, promptly, Mr. Stone."

Seth was taking an afternoon walk around the Bayshore Drive parks area in downtown St. Petersburg when his phone vibrated in his pocket. It was Alex Espinosa.

"Good afternoon, Alex," said Seth as he stopped and sat down on a bench in Flora Wylie Park overlooking Tampa Bay.

"Hugo and I have met with our lawyers and after considerable discussion and fact checking … Hugo has agreed to settle both claims for $300,000 each, with no admission of any wrongdoing."

"If we're talking settlement, Mr. Espinosa, Mr. Perozzi will settle for no less than $1,000,000, a private verbal apology, and $120,000 for the escape/rescue expenses incurred by me. Mrs. Suarez will settle for the $5,000,000 trust, funded over five years. We'll both sign a non-disclosure agreement. No more negotiations … take it or leave it."

"I'll call you back in a few minutes."

Seth stayed put on the bench and watched three pelicans in the distance dive bomb a school of pilchards out on the Snell Island flats.

His phone vibrated and Seth answered, "What'll it be Alex."

"We'll pay your figures, and Hugo will apologize personally between June 22nd and 24th when the Padres play the Rays in St Petersburg. We will wire the $1,000,000 to Mr. Perozzi's account and the $120,000 in rescue expenses to your account, Mr. Stone. "The Hector Suarez $5,000,000 trust, Mr. Stone, will be funded as specified."

Hugo is truly sorry and is appreciative that you gave him a chance to stay out of court."

"Billy Ray was right about you, Alex. You are a man of principal … Thank you. All three banks will send you the wire routing numbers. All the parties involved will sign the non-disclosure at Barry Schwartz's Tampa office whenever your lawyers send it over."

***

Dave the Wave got his $1,000,000 and very little changed in his life, except he started proceedings to legally get Clarita and her parents out of Cuba. The afternoon of June 23rd, before a Rays - Padres night game at Tropicana Field, Dave met with Hugo Lugo-Ramirez. Alex Espinosa rented a private room at the Vinoy Hotel in downtown St. Petersburg for the one on one meeting. Seth and Alex waited outside. Neither Hugo nor Dave ever revealed the content of their meeting beyond the apology, but 20 minutes later they both left the room smiling. Dave's only comment to Seth was a pragmatic, "We were both in a bad place, and we both got out!"

***

Hugo Lugo went on to be the National League rookie of the year, stole 52 bases (second in the league), and batted .325 (third in the league). His first year endorsements equaled half his baseball salary. Hugo married Monserrat on December 31, 2010.

***

Charley received $12,500 for fuel, plus a $12,000 charter fee, provisions totaling $2200, and miscellaneous expenses of $1650. John Harvey received $1700 for airplane fuel and ground expenses. Scotty received $72 for grenade targets. Each Geezer crew member received a $2200 participation bonus, plus itemized expenses. Beau received airfare, rental car, hotel, and flats boat charter expenses adding up to $3200, plus a participation bonus.

***

Seth spent the hottest part of the summer with Lori at Torch Lake, in Michigan, where it was cool. He sat in a rocking chair on Lori's back porch overlooking the lake and wondered where he should go fishing next spring.

Epilogue

FIVE YEARS later Hugo Lugo's Agent, Alex Espinosa, was in San Diego renegotiating Hugo's new contract. Meanwhile, Hugo was finishing another record breaking season playing against the Marlins at Marlins Park in Miami. The Padres' were poised to win their division in the National League, and Hugo was in the running for his second MVP award. His wife, Monserrat, was expecting their second child in three months.

Tonight he had a date with a new groupie who had been tracking him for the last two days. As was his custom, he met these groupies at B-grade motels and was never seen in public with an escort. He wore a floppy hat to obscure his countenance on any surveillance cameras. The groupie had to rent the room. Her name was Gabriela and she was fantastically tall, blonde, and beautiful in an exotic Cuban way. She was the most exciting looking groupie he had seen in his career so far. Hugo had gone one for four at the plate that afternoon and had been thrown out at second trying to steal because he couldn't concentrate on anything except the picture of Gabriela in his mind. He arranged to meet her at the Ramona Motel on West Flagler in the Overtown section of Miami at 9:00 p.m. Hugo took a cab and paid the driver in cash. He walked through the poorly-lit parking area and knocked on the door of room 14. Gabriela opened the door wearing a black negligee. She had a bottle of Havana Club Rum and a large bottle of Coca-Light on the dresser. Gabriela mixed two "skinny libres", Hugo's favorite drink. She opened the top of her negligee, exposing her perfectly formed breasts and handed Hugo his drink. They clinked their glasses together and said, "Salud." Gabriela set her drink on the nightstand and struck a seductive pose on the bed. Hugo quickly shrugged out of his Bod® jeans and Y-3®t-shirt and joined her. They kissed hungrily and she grasped his throbbing member. Suddenly, the hanging closet louvered doors burst open and four large men wearing ski masks and gloves rushed the

223

bed. Gabriela held on tight as the foursome subdued Hugo and cuffed his hands behind his back and his ankles together.

"Greetings from Hector Suarez, Hugo Lugo," said one of the men in English through a thick Hispanic accent. "We know you have paid compensation to the widow of our compatriot and to the brave gringos who rescued your second victim, the surfer, from the Cuban prison. But the money you gave them meant nothing to you … it was a drop in the bucket. Our *amigo* was a hard working family man who was in Cuba to visit his grandmother. You put him in prison and he was murdered. His blood is on your hands."

Hugo started to protest, and one of the assailants quickly duct-taped his mouth shut. Another drew a Glock 9mm pistol fitted with a silencer and shot him once through each kneecap. Hugo writhed in pain and screamed in vain. As they exited the room the largest Cuban said, "Think of Hector each time you try to walk, *pendejo*."

As the black Escalade pulled out of the motel parking lot, Paco took off his long blonde wig and black negligee and stuffed them in his carryall bag with the rum and coke bottles. He pulled out a brunette Pixie cut wig, a t-shirt, and a pair of short-shorts and wiggled into them. As Paco adjusted the wig in the rear-view mirror, Raphael asked, "Did you get all of your prints?"

"I wiped them clean. Just drop me off at *TWIST* in Miami Beach, *amigos*. I'm scheduled to dance on stage at 10:30."

"Thanks for helping us out, Paco … fucking Hugo certainly fell for 'Gabriela'," chuckled Raphael as he dialed 911 on a prepaid snap phone.

Made in the USA
Columbia, SC
17 October 2020